On the Eve of the Uprising

On the Eve of the Uprising

and other stories from colonial Korea

edited and translated by

Sunyoung Park

in collaboration with

Jefferson J.A. Gatrall

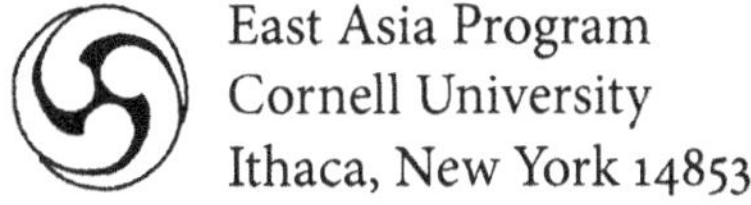

East Asia Program
Cornell University
Ithaca, New York 14853

The Cornell East Asia Series is published by the Cornell University East Asia Program (distinct from Cornell University Press). We publish books on a variety of scholarly topics relating to East Asia as a service to the academic community and the general public. Standing Orders, which provide for automatic notification and invoicing of each title in the series upon publication are accepted.

If after review by internal and external readers a manuscript is accepted for publication, it is published on the basis of camera-ready copy provided by the author who is responsible for any copyediting and manuscript formatting. Alternative arrangements should be made with approval of the Series. Address submission inquiries to CEAS Editorial Board, East Asia Program, Cornell University, Ithaca, New York 14853-7601.

Number 149 in the Cornell East Asia Series

ISSN: 1050-2955
ISBN: 978-1-933947-19-8 hc
ISBN: 978-1-933947-49-5 pb
Library of Congress Control Number: 2009936457

The paper in this book meets the requirements for permanence of ISO 9706:1994.

Contents

Acknowledgments vii

Introduction xi

1 Yŏm Sangsŏp ~ *Mansejŏn, 1924* 1
On the Eve of the Uprising

2 Ch'oe Sŏhae ~ *T'alch'ulgi, 1924* 113
"Escape"

3 Na Tohyang ~ *Pŏngŏri Samnyongi, 1925* 125
"Samnyong the Mute"

4 Pak T'aewŏn ~ *Sosŏlga Kubo Ssi ŭi iril, 1934* 141
A Day in the Life of Kubo the Novelist

5 Kim Namch'ŏn ~ *Maek, 1941* 195
"Barley"

6 Yi T'aejun ~ *Haebang chŏnhu, 1946* 235
"Before and After Liberation"

Glossary 275

Acknowledgments

The original idea behind this collection goes back to my years as a graduate student in comparative literature at Columbia University, a time when I was researching my dissertation on the realist literature of colonial Korea. In developing the project, I had the good fortune of finding an exceptional collaborator in my friend and colleague Jefferson J. A. Gatrall. Throughout the preparation of the manuscript, Jeff was the most attentive, patient, and dedicated editor that one could wish for. He deserves credit for much of what elegance the reader may find in these translations, but more than that, he gave constant encouragement to me and much writerly passion to the project.

This volume would not have been possible without the support I have received over the years from numerous institutions and individuals. The Korean Literature Translation Institute in Seoul provided a generous translation grant as well as a special publication subsidy. Fellowships from the Daesan Foundation and the Department of English and Comparative Literature at Columbia University have supported my research both in Korea and at Columbia. I would also like to thank the staffs of the many libraries I have worked in over the past years, especially the C. V. Starr East Asian Library at Columbia University, the Korean Heritage Library at the University of Southern California, and the National Library of Korea in Seoul. A particular mention is owed to Starr Library's Korean-field librarians, Hyokyung Yi and Hee-sook Shin, who provided very careful and expert assistance at the initial stages of the project.

In addition, I would like to thank Yŏm Huiyŏng and Pak Chaeyŏng for generously releasing the copyrights of respectively *On the*

Eve of the Uprising and *A Day in the Life of Kubo the Novelist*. I am also grateful to Pae Hyunsu at the Leeum, Samsung Museum of Art in Seoul for providing a digital image of the cover picture by painter Yi Insung.

Many scholars at various institutions have sustained my efforts with their research, ideas, and encouragement. I am particularly grateful to Professors Paul Anderer and Charles Armstrong, who were among the first readers and whose enthusiastic support throughout was crucial for my endeavor. In addition, Professors Rebecca Copeland, Henry Em, Theodore Hughes, Kyung Moon Hwang, and Janet Poole all gave of their time, knowledge, and assistance. Janet should be especially thanked for suggesting the title of Yŏm Sangsŏp's novella, which is now also the title of the whole collection. I would also like to acknowledge the contribution of classmates, friends, and family who, over the years, have carefully read and commented on all or parts of the manuscript. These are: Massimo Grassia, Vidhya Guruswamy, Jessica Ko, Jeehyoung Kim, Nancy Lin, and Jenny Wang Medina. Finally, I would like to thank my students in Korean literature classes at Columbia University, the University of Michigan at Ann Arbor, Washington University in St. Louis, and the University of Southern California. Their engaged and appreciative responses to the stories were the biggest reward for the efforts I have put in their translation.

I am particularly glad to see these stories appear in the Cornell East Asia Series, whose standards of excellence are well appreciated both in the field and beyond. Special thanks are due to Professor Michael Shin as well as to two anonymous readers: their probing and thoughtful critiques have made this a much better product than it would have otherwise been. I am also grateful to Mai Shaikhanuar-Cota for all the consideration and professionalism she has shown throughout the process of preparing the manuscript for publication.

Finally, my greatest and barely expressible debt is to my families, both native and marital, for their affection and unwavering support throughout the years. Among my most eager collaborators was my late father, Jungsup Park, who was in his teens during the colonial period and was always willing to relate to me various aspects of life in those times. That he passed away without seeing the publication of this volume is my sole regret. The book is dedicated to his memory.

Introduction

The present collection aims to introduce the English reader to some of the stories from the colonial era that over the years have gained the broadest popularity as well as critical recognition among Korean readers and scholars. The project is a timely one, since literary works from the colonial period (1910–1945) have for long been scarce in English translation. Fortunately, this has been rapidly changing since 1998, with the publication of *A Ready-Made Life: Early Masters of Modern Korean Fiction* by Kim Chong-un and Bruce Fulton. In its pioneering contribution, that volume necessarily had to leave out many works indispensable for our understanding of the intellectual complexity and artistic richness of colonial Korean literature. Other important translations have followed since—in particular those of full-length novels such as Yi Kwangsu's *The Heartless* (Mujŏng, 2005), Yŏm Sangsŏp's *Three Generations* (Samdae, 2006), and Kang Kyŏngae's *From Wŏnso Pond* (In'gan munje, 2009). Meanwhile, the demand for colonial stories in translation has been steadily on the rise, following the growth of Korean studies and also the increasing comparatist tendency within East Asian studies. In making available for the English reader some of the key stories of colonial Korean literature, it is hoped that this volume would contribute to meeting that demand.

Of the six literary works presented in this volume, five were written during the colonial period and the sixth, Yi T'aejun's "Before and After Liberation" (Haebang chŏnhu, 1946), is a rare literary record of the turbulent time immediately following Korea's independence from Japan. Together, the stories present the wide-ranging thematic and stylistic scope of colonial Korean literature, each marking a significant moment in its development.

Despite unresolved debates over its origins, we may positively say that modern Korean literature was shaped primarily under Western and, more immediately, Japanese influences. Although Chosŏn Korea (1392–1910) had developed a thriving literary culture, the rupture of Western modernity was such that, at least initially, the writers that we today characterize as "modern" were inclined to renounce local literary traditions, trying instead to create a new literature based on foreign examples. As the majority of the period's Korean writers received their higher education in Japan, they found the most readily available aesthetic models in the works of contemporary Japanese writers. Accordingly, the confessional narrative style—the main formal feature of the Japanese I-novel—enjoyed wide popularity among the Korean writers of the 1920s and 1930s.

If writers in Korea adopted new literary ideas and forms from Japan, however, their condition as colonial subjects also differentiated their literary experience from that of their Japanese counterparts. All Korean intellectuals wrote under the supervision of the imperial censors, and many of them were at some point imprisoned for their political as well as literary activities. We may understand the literature of colonial Korea, from this perspective, as essentially a constrained literature. Not uncommonly what is written alerts us to what could not be written. And more than is usually the case, perhaps, the pages in this collection are sustained by an absence more than they are by a presence.

Yŏm Sangsŏp's *On the Eve of the Uprising* (Mansejŏn, 1924) is perhaps the best example of how the Japanese confessional came to be adapted to the thematic interests of a colonial writer. In the beginning of the novella, Yŏm's semi-autobiographical protagonist, Inhwa, appears as a self-absorbed liberal iconoclast; he firmly believes that the primary requisite for one's freedom is to liberate one's mind from all conventional binds, especially in matters of romantic concern. As he leaves college in Tokyo to return home to Seoul, however, Inhwa finds himself constantly subject to racial discrimination and police surveillance. Through the experience of fear and humiliation, he awakens to the limits of spiritual enlightenment as a way of emancipating the self. In the remainder of the novella, the confession of Inhwa's interiority gives way to his critical observation of the social ills and injustices of colonial Korea. Yŏm's novella is thus formally close to the Japanese confessional tradition, yet it thematically departs from the works of Japanese I-novelists such as Shiga Naoya and Arishima Takeo, both of whom Yŏm much admired in his early years.

Ch'oe Sŏhae's "Escape" (T'alch'ulgi, 1924) is one of the earliest stories of Korean diaspora in Manchuria, still appreciated in Korea today for its raw emotional appeal. The story is written in epistolatory form, as a letter sent by the main character Pak to his friend Kim in Korea. In the letter Pak relates his own life in Manchuria as a poor Korean emigrant. Despite his initially high hopes for a better life, Pak has been suffering from continuing hardship in the new land. After a long spell of starvation, he eventually decided to join a Korean guerilla troop in the region in order to change a world that is starkly divided into haves and have-nots. As Pak emphatically accuses the evils of social inequalities in the finale, his confessional turns into a rebel's manifesto. Indeed, as primitive as "Escape" may now read, the story is noteworthy for having instigated a thematic revolution in the mid-1920s Korean literature, shifting the previous focus on the modern bourgeois intellectual to the life experiences of lower-class people. In 1984 this proletarian story was made into a popular movie in North Korea.

The influence of socialism is present also in Na Tohyang's "Samnyong the Mute" (Pŏngŏri Samnyongi, 1925), whose plot centers on a house servant's gradual awakening to the injustice of his master's tyranny. Yet, unlike a typical proletarian tale, "Samnyong the Mute" has the look and feel of a folktale, a once-upon-a-time story with a set of stock characters and the conclusion of a poetic justice. Romantic passion trumps class consciousness, as Samnyong develops a forbidden affection for his master's abused young wife. This unique tale of ill-starred love has long enjoyed widespread popularity among Koreans. Since Na Un'gyu first adapted it to the screen in 1929, the story has been made into a movie at least four times.

The 1920s was an era of intense cultural activism in Korea. During this period many young writers joined the proletarian literary movement of the KAPF (Korea Artista Proleta Federatio; 1925–1935), and many others published works of a socialist inclination outside the organization. Even the critics of the socialists would no longer endorse the once popular motto of "art for art's sake," favoring instead a more socially engaged view of literature. As the Korean writers became more politicized, however, the aesthetic quality of their works suffered, and their overall productivity also declined due to the writers' more frequent conflicts with censorship. By the late 1920s, a sense of crisis was felt within literary circles, and writers would often lament the withering of modern Korean literature.

This situation began to change in the early 1930s. Following Japan's invasion of China in 1931, Korea came to occupy a newly important place within the empire as its main military and industrial base outside the mainland. The economic development that ensued created a fertile soil for the new prospering of Korean literary culture. The growth of an educated middle class in the urban centers of Korea, especially in Seoul, led to a proliferation of popular literary magazines. Gradually, a cultural renaissance bloomed upon the ruins of past activist movements, all of which dissolved under Japan's intensified oppression. In sum, the 1930s was a time of drastic social changes characterized by expanding economic opportunities, dwindling political freedom, unprecedented cultural prosperity, and equally unprecedented moral uncertainties.

Against this background flourished a vein of modernist experimental literature, which is perhaps best represented in the works of writers such as Yi Sang and Pak T'aewŏn. In particular, Pak's *A Day in the Life of Kubo the Novelist* (Sosŏlga Kubo Ssi ŭi iril, 1934) gave a most effective literary expression to the excitement and listlessness of the new decade. Pak's characteristic self-effacing, equivocal writing style keenly conveys the increased fluidity and insecurity of modern life experiences. With no definite destination to reach but many places to explore, Kubo spends his day strolling through city streets, recording his fragmentary impressions in a notebook. Through his stream-of-consciousness storytelling, Pak takes the reader to various places of 1930s Seoul, such as a luxurious department store patronized by new middle-class urbanites, a train station crowded with gold mine hunters, a café teeming with jobless intellectuals, and a night street awash in prostitutes. With Kubo's appearance, the self-absorbed dandy of the early 1920s made a return to Korean literature but only as a parody of the sincere, convinced individualists of earlier years. For Pak's sense of ironic humor and his refined literary craftsmanship, the novella has been an enduring favorite among Korean readers, inspiring many rewritings of the original work. The novella is reproduced in this volume along with Yi Sang's original illustrations, which graced its first appearance in newspaper installments.

A leisurely urban stroller, however, was not the only literary figure to haunt Seoul in the 1930s. In the shadows of contemporary modernity stood the so-called thought criminals, the former activists who were now more than ever alienated from the public. These intellectuals were the major target of Japan's policy of *chŏnhyang*, i.e., forced ideological conversion, and Kim Namch'ŏn, himself a former member of the KAPF, was no exception. In "Barley" (Maek, 1941), Kim takes an unusually nuanced look at the anxieties of dissident Korean intellectuals during the rise of Japanese fascism. The novella centers around the conversion of a former socialist to Japan's wartime ideology of pan-Asianism. It is a striking document of Korean intellectuals' ambivalent attitude toward the promise of the Greater East Asian Co-Prosperity Sphere. On the one hand, the story suggests, the new vision seemed to offer an opportunity for a whole new life, in which a colonial intellectual, no longer isolated, would participate in the historical march toward a utopian new world. But on the other hand, Kim's characters are aware of the limits of the pan-Asianist promise, and in their voices one hears a quiet resignation to a private life as the only refuge in an age of totalitarianism. As one of Kim's more experimental writings, "Barley" frequently displays modernist narrative techniques such as flashback and stream of consciousness. The use of these techniques serves to underline the incommunicability and alienation that may be part of universal modern experience but are unavoidably amplified for those under a repressive colonial regime.

Upon the end of the Pacific War in August 1945, many Korean writers were left with a sense of urgency, eager as they were to contribute toward building a new Korea. Nationalists and socialists competed for the cultural hegemony of the newly liberated nation. In the fervor of the period, even the liberal advocates of aestheticism joined the political debate. Yi T'aejun, once the most dedicated patron of pure literature, assumed a prominent position within a leftist writers' organization. In "Before and After Liberation," Yi speaks through an alter ego, Hyŏn, as he remembers the suffocation and helplessness he felt during the war. Hyŏn is now determined not to remain passive. He cannot stand, in his own words, "to just get by in the world without doing some actual work." Soon, however, he discovers that the fate of the new Korean republic is not up to the Koreans alone, and he is faced with conflicting visions for the future of the country. With its scenes of turmoil on the streets of Seoul, this fictionalized memoir offers a vivid portrayal of Korean society just entering the cold-war world order. Yesterday's friends have become today's enemies, each deeming their opponents' aspirations unacceptable. And yet none of them thinks of national division as a desirable solution.

The new Korea that Hyŏn and others dreamed of, in fact, never came to be. In 1948 the country was divided along the 38th parallel, and eventually a civil war broke out. The Korean War, which lasted from 1950 until 1953, consolidated the divided system by internecine bloodshed. The colonial period and the ensuing events had a harsh impact on Korean writers. Among the writers included in this volume Na Tohyang had died young of tuberculosis in 1927, and Ch'oe Sŏhae had passed away in near starvation in 1932. Of those who survived the colonial period, Pak T'aewŏn, Kim Namch'ŏn, and Yi T'aejun went to the North upon national division. They all suffered from post-war political purges; Kim and Yi soon disappeared from the literary scene, whereas Pak was later reinstated. Yŏm Sangsŏp stayed in the South, living under successive dictatorial regimes that suppressed people's freedom of expression.

It is hoped that the six works collected here will further our understanding of the founding period of modern Korean literature. Beyond their academic relevance, these stories also make an interesting read for a general readership on the strength of their aesthetic quality and emotional intensity. A choir of voices arises from these pages—of intellectuals, peasants, servants, housewives, working women, and more. Historically specific as they are, these voices sound vivid and human, and they still resonate powerfully with us today.

1

YŎM SANGSŎP

A native of Seoul, Yŏm Sangsŏp (1897–1963) was one of the foremost literary intellectuals of colonial Korea. Partly through the support of his elder brother, who was a lieutenant in the imperial Japanese army, Yŏm received his higher education at elite schools in Japan, including a brief attendance at Keio University. There he became attracted to socialism, which was increasingly popular in the wake of the Russian Revolution. In 1919 he tried to organize a protest of Korean laborers and students in Osaka in support of recent anti-imperialist uprisings in Korea. For his failed attempt he was imprisoned for four months.

Upon returning to Korea, Yŏm co-founded the literary magazine *P'yehŏ* (Ruins, 1920–1921) and quickly distinguished himself as a leading exponent of the New Literature movement. He joined his activity as a writer and critic with a longtime occupation as a newspaper editor. Indeed, a journalistic impulse marked his fictional works, which often dealt with current political events on the national scene. In 1936, Yŏm moved to Manchuria to work as the editor-in-chief of the *Mansŏn Ilbo*, a newspaper for local Korean residents. He returned to Seoul after the 1945 liberation, and in 1948 he was briefly imprisoned for opposing the division of Korea. He stayed in the South and continued to write until his death in 1963. Today, his lifelike bronze statue greets pedestrians at the Chongmyo Shrine Park in downtown Seoul.

In his fictional as well as critical writings, Yŏm tried to maintain a delicate balance between a nationalist and a socialist ideological commitment. He had a conflicted relationship with the proletarian writers of the KAPF (Korea Artista Proleta Federatio), whom he regarded as dogmatic and who in turn looked upon him as an unreliable middle-of-the-roader. What to some could have appeared as Yŏm's ideological ambivalence, however, may equally be seen as an artist's aesthetic quest for a rendering of reality that shuns generalization and schematism. Yŏm thus devoted serious critical attention to the development of an aesthetic ideal of *realism* in literature. Reflective of this ideal, his most celebrated novel *Samdae* (1931, trans. 2005, *Three generations*) presents itself as a broad literary canvas crowded with a colorful assortment of characters—including corrupt intellectuals, conscientious bourgeois, working-class men and women, and revolutionaries—who together portray the changing everyday life of Korea under Japanese colonial rule.

On the Eve of the Uprising (Mansejŏn, 1924) is at once a refined narrative in the style of the Japanese confessional and an early document of Yŏm's nationalism inflected with socialism. Composed as the travelogue of Inhwa, a partly autobiographical character, the novella traces the nationalist awakening of a colonial intellectual educated in the imperial metropole of Tokyo. Mediating Inhwa's discovery of a national self is a collective portrait of colonial Koreans suffering from racial discrimination and economic exploitation. The nationalist theme here is as intriguing for Yŏm's refreshingly reflective approach to it, a rare instance in Korean literature, as for its surprisingly explicit representation under colonial censorship.

* * *

Translator's Note: There exist two versions of this novella: the colonial-era original and the post-liberation revision. The novella was first serialized in the magazine *Sinsaenghwal* (New life; 1922) in 1922 under the title "Myoji" (Grave) but was discontinued after its third part was expurgated by censorship. Yŏm resumed the novella's publication in the newspaper *Sidae Ilbo* in 1924. After the novella was completed in serial form, it was published as a book in the same year under its current title, *Mansejŏn*. Following liberation, in 1948, the writer published a revised version. Although this later version is the one currently circulating in Korea, I have chosen to translate the earlier one. In his revision, Yŏm made three major changes: he polished his earlier writing by modernizing some expressions, most noticeably replacing Japanese terms with Korean ones; he significantly curtailed those sections of the novella involving the narrator's relationship with his ex-girlfriend Ŭla; and he reinforced the nationalistic tone of the work. The orientation guiding Yŏm's revisions accords with his literary development after 1924 and reflects the changing times. From a historical point of view, however, the earlier version, with its colonial mixture of Japanese and Korean elements, is the more interesting one.

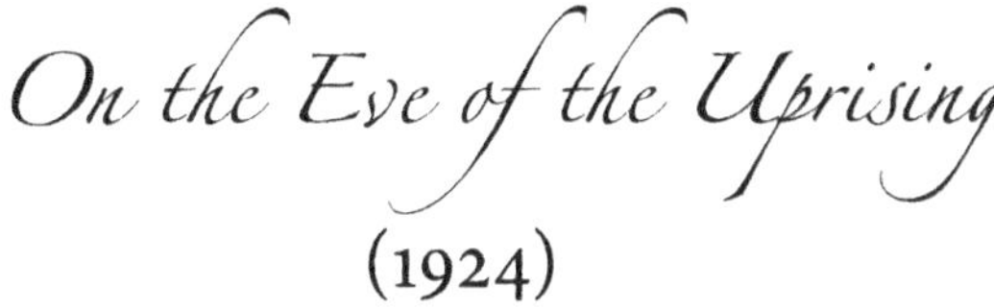

On the Eve of the Uprising

(1924)

1

It was the winter before the March Uprising in Korea, and I suddenly had to leave for Korea in the middle of final exams. I'd received a wire notifying me of the critical condition of my wife, bedridden since having given birth the previous fall.

My memory of those days is still very vivid—the day of my departure from Tokyo coincided with the second day of exams. After a long, four-hour exam, I hurried back to the boarding house just past one in the afternoon. As I arrived, I came across Cold Rice (my nickname for the maid who brought me cold rice at mealtimes) at the corner of the sidewalk. She'd been running, her face blue from the cold and her hands tucked under her arms.

"Ah, Mr. Yi! Right on time! A telegram just arrived. You owe me a treat!" Then she ran past me.

My heart skipped a beat at her words. Ever since I'd received a letter several days ago from my brother in Kimch'ŏn, I'd been waiting for a telegram with a mixed feeling of anticipation and fear. Now that it was here, I felt some sense of relief at the prospect of a resolution, for better or worse.

"Well, what good news could possibly come from Cold Rice? I'll probably have to go back!" I hurried inside. Before I was even through the front door, the landlady looked out from the adjacent room, a smile on her face.

"This arrived a few minutes ago," she said, as she handed me a postal money order and a slip of white paper.

My elder brother had earlier sent me a detailed letter from Seoul, informing me that he'd arrived there with a reputed doctor from Kimch'ŏn after learning of my wife's critical condition. He said he'd telegraph me should her illness take a turn for the worse over the next few days. "Telegraph me for what?" I thought at the time. But now, without even untying my shoes, I rushed to read his second telegram, afraid she might already be dead. Unlike the previous letter, the telegram did not refer to the danger she was in but simply ordered my immediate return and informed me of the enclosed money. Though I had never been overly concerned about my wife, I felt relieved. "So she isn't dead yet . . . " At the same time, I wondered, "If she isn't in danger, are they making this fuss just to get me to see her?" I considered this possibility as I took off my shoes, and momentarily I felt repulsed.

The money order was for one hundred wŏn, which included this month's tuition. Whether the patient was dead or alive, such a large sum was at any rate welcome. I felt as if I had been saved. I had various financial needs, what with exams and the coming New Year, but I didn't have the nerve to ask my overburdened family for more money. I briefly entertained the option of not heeding the order to return on the pretext of the exams. But even apart from my father's scolding and the foreseeable conflicts within my own household, I had no choice but to go back, if only to justify spending part of the money for my own use.

"It seems there's no chance she'll recover," said the landlady with a smile. "You must be upset about losing her." She knew about my wife's illness, but I couldn't tell from her tone of voice whether she was mocking me or offering consolation.

"Of course I'm upset," I retorted. "I hardly have any appetite these days!" Then I went to my room to put down my school bag. I took out my seal from its case and was about to set off again.

Seeing me at the door, the landlady spoke again, half-jokingly and half-sincerely. "But you didn't even have lunch! Why are you in such a hurry? She's not dead yet! Are you grieving so much already that you can't even eat?" She studied my face with her eyes, as if searching for something.

"Yes, of course. I'm just not shedding any tears," I added with a laugh.

"Why should you? That'd be unmanly. Haven't you ever heard the saying that *tatami* and women are only good when they're new? Hmm—, you must be plotting to marry again already. How sly of you," she giggled.

Is she being flirtatious because of the money I received? I looked for a moment at the landlady's heavily powdered, wrinkled face. "Well, we'll see what happens."

With this curt reply, I left her and set out for the post office, where I filled my pocket with ten ten-wŏn bills. I then hurried to W University.

Luckily, I found Professor H, the chair of my department, lingering in the faculty room—he had his hand on his briefcase and was about to leave. I waited for him to put his hat on. When he came out, I drew him aside in the corridor and explained to him in a low voice the reason for my visit.

Professor H listened to me, intermittently adding, "hmm," "aha," or "right!" After deliberating for a while, he finally said, "If that's the situation, it can't be helped. But taking the exams later won't be very convenient for you. Are you sure you can't put off your departure for three or four days?"

"I would, but the situation is bad, and I doubt I'll be able to concentrate . . . "

"Ah, yes, that's true! Well, then, officially . . . " After granting his permission, Professor H offered me a few parting words.

Obtaining permission to leave turned out to be easier than I'd expected, and he even gave me a discount coupon for a train ticket. Still, I was worried that I'd behaved awkwardly, as I'd been nervous that he would mistake my explanation for an excuse to skip out on the exams. In my flustered state, I'd actually told him it was "my mother's illness." I couldn't get over the bad aftertaste of that lie, even after boarding a K street-bound streetcar.

"Why on earth did I say my mother's illness? Why mention my mother when nothing's wrong with saying that I'm leaving because my wife is dying?" My second thoughts weren't helpful.

It was already past three. Although I hadn't really planned on making the four o'clock train, I had no choice now but to take the night train at eleven. With this decision made for me, I got off the streetcar at K street and entered the Tsukatani Shop.

After browsing around for over half an hour, I bought a vest, which I badly needed, and immediately put it on under my suit jacket. I bought a few travel items as well. Aside from the shop, there was nowhere to go in particular. I considered going to a café for lunch, but now that I had quite a bit of time and money to spare, I felt like getting a haircut, so I stopped at the nearby barbershop.

"Would you like full service?" asked the barber, holding the scissors in one hand and combing the back of my head with the other.

"Your hair looks fine. Why don't you just have a shave?"

"Then I'll just have a shave." I suddenly realized the vanity of my whim to have my hair trimmed. Staring at the mirror in front of me, I sneered at myself. As I lay back with my eyes shut, I inwardly questioned my conspicuously relaxed state of mind.

Whether I ever loved her or not, we lived together as husband and wife for six or seven years. Is it because I'm a bad person that nothing affects me, not even a telegram that she's dying? Am I simply in shock? . . . Or do I love someone else? And if so, whom?

I posed these questions to myself in silence, amid the quiet sliding of the razor blade along my skin and the even fainter sound of the barber's pulse. But I did not dare to name whom. I didn't have the courage. Somewhere deep inside me a voice seemed to shout Shizuko! Shizuko! With all resolve I could muster, I echoed in response, "It's Shizuko." Yet, as soon as I did so, I disavowed the thought. In truth, Shizuko was not the answer, though she was as much an answer as any other. In any case, the person for whom I wanted to have my hair cut was clear, and I made no attempt to deny it.

I certainly don't act toward Shizuko with the same indifference that I do toward my wife. But as much as I'm not in love with my wife, I can't love Shizuko either, though for a different reason. In the end, I'm a man incapable of falling in love with anybody. I suddenly felt lonely—it was as if there were no purpose to my life.

And why am I in such a hurry to get away now? Whether I go or not, she won't recover, and if she's already dead, surely someone else can look after the funeral arrangements. Have I actually become attached to her after years of living together? But are we really attached to each other? That's just what people usually say at times like this. Do I feel a sense of loyalty to her, or is it simple common courtesy? Or maybe I'm going in order not to lose face before my relatives, to fulfill the obligations of a husband. Bah! Such thoughts weren't there before, so why be so hypocritical now? Well, then, what on earth am I going for?

I didn't have the courage to think further. Had I continued questioning myself, I might have arrived at a clear answer. Since the last thought irritated me, though, I dropped the whole matter, leaving intact a thin veil over my heart.

After washing my face and freshening up, I left the barber's, but without deciding where to go next.

"Should I just return to the boarding house?" I continued to procrastinate on the street, my mind preoccupied with a certain haunting thought. I decided to go to the Tokyo House to take a look at some new magazines. After thumbing through books for a while, I grabbed one and paid for it. I left the bookstore, stood still for a while looking at the cross-streets, and then finally began to walk downtown. Soon I was at the three-corner junction in X town, my feet coming to a stop before the door of the M Pavilion.

The hall inside—drearier and gloomier than on the street—was not yet bustling with customers. The fire in the stove in the middle of the hall seemed to be dying out.

Next to the kitchen door, which I could see only in its dim outline, a woman stopped wiping the table and turned to greet me. "I'd almost forgotten your face! Where've you been hiding?" It was P.

I pulled up a chair near the stove and sat down. "So you think I should be drinking instead of taking exams? By the way, where is Shizuko? Is she not in today?"

"You always have Shizuko on your mind, day and night. You even see her in exam questions on the blackboard, don't you?" She laughed.

"And behind her face, I see those flashing eyes of yours . . . " I pretended to squint.

"Don't bother trying to fool me. If you two eloped or committed suicide together, it wouldn't affect me one bit." As she called Shizuko, P was smiling but looked a little downcast.

Shizuko silently came down to the hall, tying a freshly ironed apron around her waist. Her hair, cut in a bob like an actress's, was tied back loosely. She first looked at P. "What's all the fuss about?" Then she noticed me and bowed politely. I nodded in reply but said nothing.

"Shizuko! If Mr. Yi doesn't get a good grade, you'll be to blame." P watched the two of us together for a moment and then turned to arrange the tables.

Shizuko made no attempt to reply to her. Instead, she asked me, "So you have exams this week?"

"Well, didn't P just make fun of my touching sincerity in visiting you, despite my exams? But unless one can read my mind, who can tell whether I came for P or you or just for a drink? Miss P! When you're done, please join us upstairs." Leaving behind this invitation for P, I followed Shizuko to the second floor.

Shizuko guided me to a chair near the stove and then crossed over to the other side of the room. For a while, she just gazed at my face with her round nervous eyes, as if searching for something. A smile flickered on her lips. Shizuko was always so alert to everything around her—it was as if all her being were concentrated in her bright eyes. At times, they looked so ice-cold that I inadvertently turned away. But her lips, always smiling, betrayed the passions of a young woman. Her calm, lonely smile, tinged with melancholy, seemed to reveal a heart in turmoil, a turmoil resulting, perhaps, from her desire for the opposite sex, her humane inability to give up on men entirely, no matter how low her opinion of them.

"Why do you look so down?" said Shizuko, attempting to break the awkward silence. She turned to the mirror for a moment to fix her hair. "Tired of studying?" There was a certain resolute quality to her tone, which made me think that a deeper voice would have suited her even better. This was a girl who always wanted to remain reserved, to exercise self-restraint, even in her voice.

"What, who's tired? Why don't you fetch me a drink? It's almost six already." I looked at my pocket watch in order to hasten her.

"Why?" asked Shizuko, turning around on her way out, "Are you going somewhere?"

"Where can I go?"

"Well, now that you're finishing exams, you might want to travel some place where it's quiet. We'll soon find out!" Her eyes were fixed on me, as her fingers toyed with a bag I'd brought and placed on the armoire. Inside the bag were travel necessities I'd bought at the Tsukatani Shop, including a gift box that held a silk scarf for my wife.

After poking around a bit inside the bag, Shizuko exclaimed, "See, I knew it, it's an air pillow! And what's this? Shall I open it? Is it okay to open it?" She started to empty the contents from the bag. I smiled and let her do as she pleased.

She placed an air pillow, a travel cup, a pipe, and a bar of soap, among other things, on the table, and as she reached the bottom of the bag, her lips formed a playful smile. She approached the fireplace, holding out the gift box to me. "Where are you going, and who's this for?" She forced a smile as she attempted to hide her seeming jealousy.

"What do you want to know that for?" I snatched the box away and threw it onto the armoire.

"I'm sorry. No one's stopping you from giving it to whomever you want." She laughed awkwardly.

I regretted my harshness, but I sensed an opportunity here as well. I jumped up, pulled a dark gray scarf with white lining out of the box, rolled it in the wrapping paper, seized Shizuko, and, tightly embracing her, thrust the scarf into her waistband. And then . . .

A few moments later, Shizuko shook off my arms and dashed out, blushing. I was still standing, quietly staring at her back. Then

I moved forward and called to her gently, "Don't be angry. And come back soon with the drink!"

What I'd done was indecent. But I had to do things that way, since I didn't want rumors spreading about me giving her presents.

I stood absentmindedly for a while. Then I collected the scattered things back into the box and returned to my seat.

Shizuko returned with a bottle of whisky and poured me a glass. She sat sullenly for a while. She got up to fix her hair in front of the mirror, turned around again, but then didn't sit down right away. I was rather glad to find her agitated like this. At the same time, since I took her sullenness as a sign of wounded pride, I felt sorry and wanted to comfort her.

"What's wrong? I brought you a small souvenir, because I felt bad about having to go away tonight. You're not offended, are you? I gave it to you like that because if anyone had seen us, it wouldn't have done either one of us any good."

"Of course not! It's me who owe you an apology. So, where are you going? Are you leaving now?" Shizuko spoke with feigned indifference, but it was clear she was suppressing her feelings.

I assumed a serious tone. "Well, I've got some business at home. I might leave tonight, but since exams are still going on . . . "

"What kind of business would make you leave during exams?" She looked up at me. At that moment, our meals arrived. As Shizuko stood up, I told her to call P in.

"Oh—?" Shizuko turned to look at me a moment, then called P and carried in the dishes. P followed.

"I apologize for interrupting," said P, "especially when you're having so much fun!" P plopped down on the chair I put out for her. She picked up a magazine from the table and began to thumb through it.

It was always a pleasure to see P's genial face. Compared to contemplative, nervous, and inexperienced Shizuko, P had tired of this kind of life and become coarse and vulgar, for all her absurd pretense of sophistication. Still, I found her attractive in her own way.

"Why did you obstinately stay downstairs when I told you to come up? Do we have to carry you?" I took the magazine away from P and gave it to Shizuko. Then I began to tease P, patting her hand.

"Who's being stubborn? I stayed away because I wouldn't dare join this exclusive *literati* party." P pulled her hand away, cast a quick glance at Shizuko, then smiled back at me.

Shizuko had always been a thorn in P's side. All the customers, even those friendly with P (myself included), seemed in the end to fall for Shizuko. But Shizuko's educational background—she had attended an all-girl high school for three years and still loved to read novels and magazines—had earned P's respect and won out over her sense of rivalry. In any case, I always enjoyed talking to both at the same time. If either P or Shizuko were engaged in serving another customer, I would even wait till late at night to meet them together. I especially waited when it was P who was not available. Shizuko had noticed this and seemed to wonder about it.

"By the way, when are you leaving?" Shizuko put the magazine down on the table and looked up at me.

"Well . . . " I started, returning her glance.

"Why, are you going somewhere?" asked P. She got up and walked around behind Shizuko's chair.

"Are you leaving tonight?" Shizuko asked again.

The lamp had just been turned on. Gazing into the light, I finally responded, "To tell you the truth, it looks like my wife is sick, and my family is making a fuss about my returning. But I'm still not sure if I should go or not."

"You should go right away! What if she died before you got there?" P cast me a look of reproach.

"If she's dead, she's dead. What can I do?" I grinned at Shizuko, who was sitting quietly on the opposite side of the table.

"Men are all alike! How could you ever depend on a husband like that, trust him with your life?" exclaimed P, ostensibly shocked. She held onto the back of Shizuko's chair, searching her eyes for a sign of agreement.

"Who says a couple needs to depend on each other? In the case of marriage, mutual dependence means loving each other, but loving is ultimately a selfish act, which you do regardless of whether the other person loves you back or not. Even if the other person doesn't play along, a person will go on loving to his heart's content, simply from his own desire to love. We could mock such love for being lonesome and one-sided, but we shouldn't. On the other hand, not loving is also a freedom. An absolutely free choice. Man has the right both to love and to reject love. What law is there that says a husband and wife must love each other?"

Shizuko and P listened with their eyes fixed on me. Shizuko nodded at times, as if reflecting on something.

I emptied my glass and spoke again. "But the problem lies in sitting on the fence, neither good nor evil. It's hypocritical to drop my studies in order to go to see a person, when I couldn't care less whether that person lives or dies. First of all, is it not absurd that I hesitated before coming here for a drink, as if I were committing some sort of crime? Dying is one thing, drinking is another. And yet, drinking while 'my wife' is dying?—so-called morality raises its head. But it's not my conscience speaking. It's only a devil called 'Ideal,' who pulls me by a leash around my neck. Man is a slave to false ideals. True living lies in liberating oneself from false moral ideals. If you don't ever love, you won't know such true life, but when you're in love, you're free to do what your heart desires. "

Suddenly, I sprang from my seat, seized P, and tried to give her a kiss. P—who was leaning over Shizuko, her hands resting on the girl's shoulders—was caught off guard. P screamed aloud, "My God, you'll kill me!"

She ran back to her seat, giggling. In the confusion I collided with Shizuko, who picked herself up with a smile on her face . . .

When I walked to the door, quite drunk, Shizuko followed me and whispered, with her lips almost brushing against my ear, "Are you really leaving by train tonight?"

"Why? I'll do as I like."

"Well . . . " Shizuko was about to say something, but seeing P approach, stepped back instead.

"If I must go, I'd better get going. I'll be back in about a month, so see you then." With this terse farewell, I took my leave.

It was early in the evening but already quite chilly on the streets. The first cold of the season. The sky, which had been dreary since the afternoon, threatened snow as night fell. The shadows of passers-by were growing more and more scarce, while the sound of clogs tapping on the streets seemed louder. The shop lanterns were casting an opaque light, as if they were dozing off or glazed with ice, and looking lonelier than ever.

I wanted to catch a streetcar right away but, tipsy as I was, didn't feel like squeezing in among the crowded passengers. I turned around and walked toward the O bridge.

I felt invigorated as the cold evening wind caressed my feverish cheeks. Yet my heart was restless, tortured by some nameless anxiety. A blind rage rose from deep within my heart, and I experienced an unaccountable urge to do something, anything, though I couldn't make out whether this meant a rebellion against myself or something else. Like a wild man, I pulled my hands out of my pockets and waved them all around; I even imagined taking off my coat and vest and dumping them over the bridge. Meanwhile, my feet continued their mechanical movement forward, as I passed by the streetcar stop at the O bridge. I turned in the direction of the S bridge and wandered down the dark riverside.

As I continued to daydream, I was suddenly overwhelmed by an irrepressible surge of melancholy that brought tears to my eyes. Feeling unbearably lonely and empty inside, I longed to cry and cry, until my eyes ran out of tears. Yet I quickly checked myself. "What am I crying for? Does the taste of salty tears cure emptiness and loneliness? True freedom lies in feeling empty and lonely!"

I was like a man who scowls in the back corner of his house over a blow he received downtown, alternately blaming and excusing his own weakness. This fit of melancholy worsened as my desire to be free from the binds of convention grew more fierce inside me. A discontent with my feeble self—which was mired in self-pity and defensiveness—had brought all this on. I knew I was going to suffocate, unless I relieved myself of all tangible and intangible binds, all restrictions and absurdities. Yet I remained incapable of enacting my own salvation.

I jumped impatiently onto a streetcar bound for the artillery factory, hoping that one look at a beautiful woman on board might have the effect of a camphor injection. At the same time, I ridiculed myself for such a pathetic attempt to gain comfort.

I found nothing on board but contorted faces with skin shriveled up from hard work, starvation, and the cold. All these withered faces were gazing vacantly at each other or stealing glances here and there. I, too, glanced at this person and the next. I imagined what would happen if I suddenly exclaimed, "You're all so wonderful and decent!" and then burst into laughter. I grinned at such a ridiculous thought.

The Japanese and Koreans aren't the only ones who sit upright, assume airs, and survey those around them. All humans have this habit, which demonstrates what a weakling man is. Man aims for cheap victories and a little painless pride. He likes to exaggerate his own power and is apt to build a fortress around himself, ever wary of others. In closely examining and assessing the appearances, clothes, actions, and words of others, man likely fulfills an instinctive desire to gratify his base curiosity. But such meticulous observation also serves other, more essential purposes. First of all, in self-defense, a man needs to size up others' strengths and weaknesses, their wealth, their class status; for an urban man, in particular, there's so much pain and humiliation that go along with failing to keep up with the latest clothes or clichés. If he belongs to the rather narrow social sphere of business groups, the so-called gentry or merchants, this habit is even worse. The members of these groups are compelled to monitor other people's appearance and moods, as they have their own worries to contend with: a need to exchange flattery, a desire to feel superior by cheating without being cheated, a lack of trust in others, and a compulsion to be up-to-date. This type of habit is exacerbated among people of relatively high class and attains its most extreme expression in women, for women desire yet one more thing, their life source: love.

In this regard, what seem most innocent and beautiful are the glances of passionate youths, who constantly seek out objects of adoration, whether on trains, at meetings, or on the streets, yet without ever analyzing what they see—this is the artless ethos of the lower classes. No tainted greed weighs on the minds of youths admiring the opposite sex. They have no need for flattery, no reason to be watchful, no aspiration to compete or cheat, and no impetus to defend and oppose. They admire, seek, and are stirred by beauty alone. Moreover, when their desires fade away, they leave no ugly residues, for such desires are only momentary sparks, like the thousand silvery reflections of the moon across an endless stream. This makes their desires that much more pure and to be savored. But it's the fate of today's men to be unable to live without hypocrisy. Even the young, those green buds of life, never look directly at the face of a beauty—only stolen glances. A habit nastier than all others.

Still lower in the social strata, workers have nothing to hide, show off, or be ashamed of; instead, they share a compassion for the naked souls of their own kind and a defense mechanism against common enemies. Hence, when they meet, they never stare at, assess, or inspect each other. They live the truest and most beautiful of lifestyles. But workers have their own plague: ignorance.

Come to think of it, in the end, those who are more savvy and more civilized are also more hypocritical (though individual cases may differ in degree). Such men are selfish animals who don't act for anything other than themselves, unless they're offered some incentive or contractual agreement. To somersault between two cliffs, your own material interests on the left and everyone else's on the right, therein lies the life of so-called modern man. This clownish figure is indeed the brute called man. If you were to plant both feet together on one side or the other, you'd be judged as either good or bad by the given standard of the day. But if you were to go farther, bravely diving in and submerging your whole being in the pure streams of authentic life flowing between the two cliffs, you had better be prepared to live as a dropout in the eyes of the world.

While contemplating these things, I looked at this man and that. Then I thought of Shizuko. She is a rebel. But does she have the power to take control of her own life? Does she have the courage to take the plunge in search of the wellspring of her life? She has some self-awareness and seems intelligent, but her vanity makes her untrustworthy, both materially and spiritually.

The streetcar, as if exhausted after a full day's work, was dragging its feet. It crawled out of the darkness on road E and then let loose a shrill "yip, yip," intruding on the serenity of the houses where families had gone to bed. Finally, it came to a halt with a sigh in front of a garage lit by lamps, bright as daylight. Inside the car—which had been somnolent—everything was suddenly astir, and people stepped off in groups.

I got off, too, and followed a few factory workers, who were wearing black suit pants and blue shirts and carrying lunch boxes. The wind was chilly.

"Are you still on the night shift? It's so cold today."

"Yes, it's really winter now."

"Why don't you come over here and warm up a bit?"

The conductor, who was standing at the door of the garage, invited the workers in. My envious eyes watched their backs as they disappeared into the warmth of the conductors' resting room. Then I entered the alley next to the garage.

I thought about visiting my neighbor X on my way to the boarding house. After some hesitation before his door, I entered. X looked more surprised than I had been at the news of my departure that night. He seemed to really pity me. I laughed a bit at his compassionate nature and returned with him to the boarding house.

I packed my things with X and left some of them with the landlady. We avoided a long good-bye scene with her and hurried to the streetcar stop with my bags. It was a little past ten o'clock.

"If I'm late," I said in response to X's haste, "I'll just have to leave tomorrow!" But deep down I was in a hurry to get to Tokyo station, too. When I arrived, possibly because my watch was fast, there turned out to be about ten minutes to spare.

I left my bags with X and lined up in front of the ticket booth to buy a train ticket. Someone gently touched my arm from behind, calling my name in a familiar voice.

Caught by surprise, I turned around. It was Shizuko. She was holding some square objects in a purple kerchief. She kept glancing sideways, wary of X's stare.

I was surprised at her unexpected appearance and tried to put her at her ease by starting up a conversation.

"What brought you here on such a cold night?"

"I thought you weren't going to come!"

"Have you been waiting long?"

"No, I thought I'd be late and rushed over."

"I'm sorry, let's get in quickly, then."

Without replying, Shizuko hastened to the opposite ticket gate. . . .

After X left to secure my seat on board, Shizuko bought an admission ticket and walked side by side with me to the end of the platform.

"Will it be a long time before you come back?"

"Well, about two weeks at the most."

"Please write if it's longer. I don't know what might happen to me in the meantime."

"Why, are you planning to go somewhere?"

"Well, I can't always live like this . . . " Her voice trailed off. She stood still a while, looking away, and then came close to gently lean on me, almost clutching. "If you weren't in such a hurry, I could have come with you at least as far as Kyoto . . . " She smiled. I was about to ask her something, but X was hastening me with a wave of his hand. So I just exchanged a quick good-bye with her and got on the train, taking the seat X had reserved.

Shizuko passed me a wrapped package through the window and said there was no need to open it now. I took it, though I usually considered such formalities somewhat of an imposition. I rarely allowed my friends to see me off or to give me farewell presents. Before I could put the package on the shelf, the train began to move.

From about a meter away, I could see the flash of Shizuko's wide open eyes. She was standing with her back straight, but I soon lost sight of her among the waves of people.

2

I dozed off amid the packed crowd of passengers and their strewn-about luggage. When I opened my eyes again, it was still a couple of hours before sunrise. The air inside the car, though fresh from the cold night, smelled of foul breath and cigarette smoke. I closed my eyes, but it was unlikely I'd fall asleep again. I felt a chill and got up to light a cigarette. Then I remembered Shizuko's package. When she gave it to me, I noticed it bulge with what looked like a liquor bottle placed on top of a cookie box. I took down the gift from the shelf and lifted the folded corners of the purple silk kerchief. Underneath was a medium-sized whisky bottle. As I pulled the bottle from its box and took a sip, hoping to chase away the cold, a slender violet envelope fell out.

"Why did she write a letter? Hmm, so that's why she told me not to open it there . . . " I picked up the letter, but after deciding to have a drink first, stuck it under the hat beside me.

A bright girl. I felt sorry for her. She was too intelligent to squander her life as a café waitress, but I'd honestly never had any particular desire to make her my own. Given my rational, calculating nature, I thought about what would happen were I to make a pass to her. I'd end up caught in a mess from which I could neither retreat nor cast her away. Though I wasn't hindered by any ethnic animosity, I was not without the vague idea of eventually finding someone more suitable, even if it turned out I was destined to spend my life with a foreign woman. Receiving a letter in return for a simple scarf, though pleasant, went beyond my expectations. I did have some affection for Shizuko, but not the kind of love that takes complete hold of one's life. Even if I were to become entangled in love, I had no desire to let it disturb my life by creating unnecessary suffering and inducing cheap tears of disillusionment.

I gave her the scarf, for which I had dipped into my tight budget for school and travel expenses, because I wanted to repay her for whatever trouble I'd caused her, as well as to see her smile. Had I wanted love, I would not have resorted to such crass material appeals.

I drank a couple more glasses as I thought through these feelings, then took out the letter. Her lively handwriting on the envelope matched her spirited facial expressions. Although the person in front of me was sleeping, I was afraid others might be watching. I was about to hide the letter in my pocket, but then curiosity finally got the better of me. I tore open the envelope.

Now may not be the best time for this letter. I resent and am ashamed that you would think of me as a common girl susceptible to material temptations. But that is all the more the reason . . .

After opening with this critique of my hypocritical attitude, she wrote of her frustrations as well as her hopes for the future, adding that she might go to Kyoto at the end of the year to stay with her aunt.

I smiled to myself as I read the letter over. My smile, however, signified neither mockery of her nor self-satisfaction at her trust in me. If pressed for a reason, I would say I took a certain pleasure in her clear reasoning and her rational, sensitive mind.

I thought of writing an immediate reply but dropped the idea to avoid drawing the attention of other passengers. I began to drink again.

. . . Why do you mock me? Why do you trifle with me? You find it amusing to flirt with me and P at the same time. This is too cruel. Of course, you, too, must know that love is not something to be trifled with.

No one has ever said that you care at all for me, but my suffering is unbearable. At times, I feel downright insulted. If you can't change your attitude, we'd better stop seeing each other . . .

My flirting with P was Shizuko's most serious complaint. I wrapped the bottle back up and lay down to rest and ponder her letter.

While reflecting on Shizuko's bitter past, as well as on her self-conscious struggle to overcome her circumstances and lead a life of integrity, I grew sentimental and wanted to cry for her. I imagined holding her in the seat next to me, sharing the salty taste of our flowing tears. But this thought was fleeting.

"Love just isn't meant for the kind of man who would analyze the taste of saliva as he kissed a girl."

I recalled the recent scene upstairs at the M Pavilion. What was she thinking at that moment? Was the sense of being insulted the first thing that came to her mind? But if, as she implied in her letter, she had never known the lips of any man, yet was now attracted to me, she must have been entranced. If this were true, Shizuko was still quite a happy girl. I wondered whether integrity isn't after all a condition for happiness, or at least for a passionate heart.

But why was it that even though I had yet to experience true love, I found passion—the privilege and color of youth—all dried up inside me? It was true that I had an abnormal personality. This was the primary cause for my exhausted supply of passion. This deficiency was also indicative of the general degeneration of humanity. On the other hand, since passion needed to be restrained in some cases, so as to keep one's integrity intact, its lack could not always be seen as the sign of an abnormal personality, nor even of the decline of humanity.

Still, one should not try to gratify one's desire in a cowardly way under the pretext of preserving one's own integrity, and trifling with another person remains a sin. Lack of passion is no excuse for toying with someone. Strictly speaking, toying with someone else—and hence toying with life itself—means deceiving and debasing one's own soul.

What good reason did I have to play around with the unfortunate girl, while I myself wanted to live strong and tall? To be honest, my behavior toward Shizuko did warrant her accusations. I had pretended to adore P in front of her, and didn't I try to pander to Shizuko right after I'd caressed P's hand? Was my sordid mind any better than that of a prostitute? A prostitute in spirit! If that wasn't depravity, what else could be. I was too depraved to love a woman. And spiritual depravation is worse than physical depravity. If depravity is not quite the word for it, would it be better to say that I had lost the scent of a human being? Love or what not, it gives me a headache.

I was pondering all this while lying down. I got up, feeling suffocated, and went out to the deck.

The lamps in the car were on, but the fading stars and the sight of passing rural houses, though they still showed no signs of life and their doors remained closed, hinted at the coming sunrise. The morning gusts of wind were so strong that I raised my coat lapels. I stood outside a couple more minutes before I couldn't stand it any more and returned to my seat.

After a couple more hours of sleep, I was awakened by the bustling crowd of people. Looking out the window, I could tell that the train was just now sluggishly pulling out of a station. Since I did not want to bother getting up, I asked the person opposite me, who had just come in, where we were.

"We're in Nagoya."

"Ah, only Nagoya?" I feigned surprise. Then, mulling over where I should spend a night along the route, I fell back to sleep again.

After a long nap, I found the train somewhere around Kinai. I checked the schedule: still three hours to Kyoto and about five hours to Kobe, if I wanted to stay overnight at Kobe.

"Should I visit Ŭlla?" I remembered that I hadn't replied for over a month to Ŭlla's request to send her a brochure for the Tokyo School of Music—she wanted to transfer to the music school for the new academic year starting in the spring. Although my indolence was chiefly to blame, it also felt awkward to suddenly send her a letter after not having written for more than a year. I thought it would be troublesome for both of us to resume our discontinued correspondence.

"If I meet her now, how should I behave?" I sat leaning on the window sill, gazing at the smoke from my cigarette as it curled up into one ring after another, and pictured Ŭlla's neat white face as it affected the most chaste and timid of expressions.

Has she recovered from her case of hysteria? Is she still on intimate terms with Pyŏnghwa? But the fact that she had sent me a letter on the pretext of requesting a school brochure suggested that there might be more trouble brewing.

As I was thinking along these lines, I was seized by a sudden fit of curiosity, which made me want to visit Ŭlla at Kobe. I lay down and began to survey the schedule again.

When I got off at Kobe Station, the silvery evening sun was hovering just above the peak of Mount Rokō. I stretched a bit, since I was finally freed from the prisonlike third-class compartment after almost four hours' worth of motion sickness. I checked in my big suitcase at the crowded station and then stepped outside. A deep breath of fresh air enlivened me.

I considered taking a streetcar right away to Ŭlla's but decided to wait till after dinner. I headed instead for Monomachi street. I entered the basement of Café A, which I had frequented last summer, and took a seat in the corner, avoiding the crowd. I finished a few dishes, but the girl I'd met there last year, who used to strut around with a coquettish air, was nowhere to be seen. I inquired about the girl to the waitress who brought the tea.

With a knowing smile, she replied, "Why do you ask?"

"Why, did she go somewhere? She still works here, right?"

"So when did you meet her? Do you know her?"

"Well, does it matter?"

"She's already gone to Heaven!"

"What? Was she ill?"

"Died right out of the blue. She and her lover committed suicide together with a grenade." She laughed caustically and then ran out to meet newly arriving customers.

Stunned by the news of a double suicide, I waited for the waitress to come back, but she completely ignored me and went about her business. Tired of waiting, I called for the check and asked, "Who'd she do it with?"

The girl just stared at me. "Who knows? Come by next time and I'll tell you." Then she ran away again, her shoes clicking in haste.

"Why should I bother!" Yet as I was leaving, I kept wondering, how did she do it? with whom?

I turned at Fourth Street in Sakecho toward Yamanote and then tried to weave my way through to the C Music School, getting lost along that long untraveled path.

It wasn't late yet, but night was falling. I stood in front of the dorm gate, listening to the soft, sumptuous piano sounds rising from the back corner downstairs. Perhaps an evening practice. Ŭlla came tapping down the stairs, followed by the maid who had taken my message.

"What a surprise! It's been such a long time! Please, come on up." Ŭlla stood casually with her back resting against a pillar. It was as if she had prepared her greeting beforehand. She cast a sideways glance at me, a smile in her distinctive eyes, but then she lowered them with assumed timidity. I untied my shoelaces, looking at her small white feet in red-stringed straw thongs, and followed her in.

"It's cold in the living room, so let's go to my room." Ŭlla led me down the corridor past the staircase she had just run down. On our way, she dropped by somebody else's room, telling me to wait a moment. Through the crack of the slightly open door, I could see her sitting on her knees, chatting about something with whomever was inside the room. After a while she came out, smiling affably, and then took me to her room on the second floor.

"Is it okay," I asked, "to invite a man up without permission?" I glanced at the folded blankets in the corner of the room.

"No problem. If the headmaster comes in later, just pretend to be my brother from Seoul."

"It's not easy playing the role of a rented brother," I said with a straight face and then sat down where she indicated in front of a low table.

"I see—in order to be your brother, I have to sit in the proper chair." Half-joking and half-mocking, I looked at Ŭlla, who was busy clearing away her books, socks, and clothes.

After putting everything aside, Ŭlla sat on her knees, sideways, at the corner of the desk. Casting a reproachful look at me, she said, "What's wrong with you? You've changed so much since last year." She then hung her head as if she were shy.

"Have I changed that much? But it's your face that's really changed! Though your shiny eyes are always the same." I spoke without reserve. Strangely, despite my hesitation and awkwardness in coming to see her—it seemed as if something were stuck in my throat—and despite my worries beforehand about how to approach her, I was preoccupied with a desire to make fun of her to my heart's content, now that I was here and sitting face to face with her. There was no room left in my mind for other reflections.

"That's because I'm growing old. Has my face really changed that much?" Ŭlla, more relaxed now due to my unexpectedly casual flirting, picked up a large stone mirror from the desk and continued talking as she peered into it. "So, are you already on vacation? I'm going home for a visit, too. Shall we go together?"

"My pleasure. But can you get ready tonight?"

"Tonight?"

"I'm leaving tomorrow on the morning train."

"Surely you can wait a couple more days. Besides, tomorrow's Saturday. Stay at least till tomorrow."

"I don't have anything to do here. It turns out the person I took such pains to come here to see made a pact with her lover to commit suicide with a grenade! . . . I might stay if I had someone to commit suicide with . . . "

"It's said that everyone changes, but there's no one who's changed so much as you, Mr. Yi. Ah, really . . . " Ŭlla sighed softly and dropped her head, as if suddenly moved by something. Instantly realizing what she implied, I bristled, irritated at her presumption.

"Then what do you think is the cause of my change?" I blurted out. "Perhaps it's you, Ŭlla? If so, don't you have to take some responsibility?" At the end of my speech, the word "Impudent!" lay poised on the tip of my tongue, but I held it back. Ŭlla, who did not notice the changing expressions on my face, seemed puzzled, unable to tell whether the words I did manage to utter were sincere or meant as a joke. Although acting ignorant was one of her usual habits, Ŭlla momentarily blushed under my reproach this time.

"What good is it to say such things," she said, furrowing her eyebrows. "Really, let's leave together the day after tomorrow. If that doesn't work, I'll be free tomorrow in the afternoon. There are some things I want to tell you, and I can show you around . . . You don't have any urgent business, do you?" Since she was feeling bored and lonesome and yearned for the company of the opposite sex, my visit was not just unexpected but genuinely welcome.

"Hmm, that sounds okay. But, really, I've seen Kobe so many times that I'm sick and tired of it. Is there anything new to see?"

"Well, I was planning to go to a concert at the Osaka Concert Hall. How about going there together? On weekends, the students around here all go home and stay with their parents . . . "

How tactful she is, I thought. I remembered the rumor that she had had an affair with a Japanese man—the owner of a boarding house or maybe a monk—before she entered the dorm last fall. I looked again at Ŭlla's fair oval face.

"Let's take things as they come," I said. "So where's Pyŏnghwa nowadays?"

"Why are you asking me?" Ŭlla suddenly blushed. "If anyone knows, it'd be you."

I'm thick-skinned, but so are you, I thought. "No," I replied aloud, unperturbed, "I asked because I wondered if he'd been in Seoul lately. But why are you acting so surprised?"

Ŭlla lowered her voice, as if she regretted the sharpness of her reply. "Well, you're always under the misunderstanding that I have some sort of intimate relationship with Pyŏnghwa . . . "

"Who's misunderstanding whom? All men are free to love whoever they choose, and without love, there'd be only death. Whether one misunder*stands*, or stands on top of everything, or even lies on top of someone else, what does all that matter?" I laughed aloud. "I'm afraid it's getting late. I should probably be going shortly . . . " I picked up my hat and fidgeted with it for a while. Then, as if spitting the words out to myself alone, I muttered, "How tedious this damn life is." Then I sprang to my feet.

"What's the matter? Why did you come if you were going to leave like that . . . and what's so tedious?" Ŭlla remained sitting, trying to detain me. It seemed the word "tedious" had livened her up.

"You think I stopped here to see you? I came all this distance because I had someone to meet, but she turned herself into a fireball with some scoundrel she didn't even give a damn about. The world is unfair, isn't it? What on earth can be done!"

"Is that true? Who's the girl? Japanese? Korean?" Ŭlla looked up at me with a coaxing smile. Her face did not look twenty-five years old.

"What do you want to know for? Really, I should be going. See you next time." I held out my hand to see how she would respond. For all her nerve, she didn't seem to have the courage to shake my hand. She just stared at my face.

"Where will you go if you leave now? Can't you leave tomorrow?"

"I'll see what happens. I'll go to a hotel and decide from there."

"Tomorrow's concert promises to be really good. They're all first-rate musicians from Tokyo . . . "

"First-rate or second-rate, what's a concert when I have a stiff corpse to deal with? Damn it, I'm leaving. Why should I stay? So I can call you my 'big' sister in front of the headmaster?"

"Why can't you call me your little sister? And what do you mean by 'corpse'? Why are you acting so strange? Stop talking in riddles. It's like you're possessed."

As we walked down the steps together, I explained the reason for my trip. Ŭlla looked surprised. "That's awful! Why did you ever stop here? A man can be so heartless, even when his wife is about to pass away . . . " Ŭlla, perhaps because she found my excuse plausible, seemed to feel half ashamed and half contrite for her vain attempt to delay my departure. A subdued sullenness replaced the reproachful expression on her face. But she still seemed to harbor some expectations from the significance implied by my sudden visit.

"Right, so don't even exchange words with men. Especially with a scoundrel like me. Well, then . . . "

Tossing these words of farewell, I dashed out into the darkness before she'd even finished her good-bye.

During my parting with Ŭlla, I could barely suppress a chuckle, so amused was I by a perverse sense of pleasure. I spent that night quietly in the back room of a small inn next to Kobe station. It wasn't until evening that I would be able to board a ferryboat.

Moving along with a flood of people that gushed forth like water from a broken dam, I reached the waiting room for the ferry.

I thought of boarding immediately so as to avoid the usual tiresome wrangling at the customs office, but since boarding seemed not to have started yet, I had no choice but to remain in the waiting room. As I stood in front of a kiosk, trying to decide whether to buy something for supper, a strange man in a raincoat approached me. He tipped his hat and inquired about my citizenship (which he had somehow managed to sniff out). I stared at him in silence for some time, handed him my business card, and quickly returned to the kiosk. The man in the raincoat took the card. He waited until I was through with my purchase but then began pestering me again.

"And your hometown?" Without uttering a word, I took the card and gave it back with my Korean address written on it. Then I picked up the snack I had bought and returned to my seat, where I'd left my luggage. Yet the man continued to hound me.

"Your age? School? On what business? Destination? . . . " He kept harassing me. Helpless and irritated, I wanted to ask out loud why on earth he needed to know. Instead, I replied curtly, in one-word answers, then picked up my bags and walked out of the waiting room.

"My apologies," he said, a hint of scorn in his voice. I saw a glint of rage in his eyes. But then I was just as incensed as he was.

A crowd of passengers lined up in front of the ladder to the boat, and I squeezed into line.

As I worked my way through the bustling crowd, I was assaulted by the nauseating stench of rotten fish in phenol water. Everyone was racing to get a place in the third-class cabin. I placed my luggage on the upper tier of a bunk bed (one too dirty and nondescript to inspire any poetic fantasy), changed my clothes, and then hurried to the bathing area.

Though I thought I'd be the first to arrive, a few men were already chattering away in the bathtub.

"It seems that the ship's going to rock quite a bit today!" said a man who looked like a peasant fresh from the countryside. He turned his dark, rugged face to look around at the others, constantly shifting his large innocent eyes back and forth.

"Well, it rocks now because we're still on shore. The wind isn't that strong," replied one of his companions, who seemed to be a merchant.

"It must be pretty cold now in Korea?"

"But with an *ondol*, you don't have to worry, so long as you stay indoors," explained the merchant-like man, who seemed familiar with the local customs of Korea.

"Yes, I heard about the *ondol*."

As the peasant spoke, the man sitting opposite me was gazing at him with predatory eyes. He finally addressed the peasant, "Is this your first time, friend?" His condescending, imposing manner of speaking, coupled with his thin lips, suggested that he must be a pawnbroker's middleman or something along those lines.

"Why are you setting out in this cold? Where're you headed for?"

"I have an older brother in Taegu, and my mother's not feeling well . . . "

"What a coincidence! I'm going to Taegu, too. What's your brother do?"

"He's in the army."

"Eh? In the Taegu squad?" At the peasant's mention of the army, the man suddenly lit up and changed his tone. I couldn't help but take another look at his face, hard as the pit of a date. "Ah . . . then, excuse my asking, but who's your brother? What's his rank?"

"Well, X is his name. He's still just a sergeant. Do you know him? Have you been in Korea a long time?"

"Of course, I know him," the man replied, after eyeing the peasant for a while. Though the gentleman might not know me . . . Oh, me? I managed to survive several years among the *yobos.*"

"Oh, then you must've amassed quite a fortune." This time, it was the merchantlike man who spoke.

"Not really. Now that Korea has gotten so expensive, making a fortune is very—"

"How do you find the Koreans?"

"The *yobos*? The young ones are pretty good, but in the countryside, they're maybe only slightly better than Taiwanese beasts. You'll find out soon enough."

Everyone in the tub, except me, chuckled at the phrase "Taiwanese beasts." I had been sitting quietly till that point, but now I looked up involuntarily, biting my lip. Thanks to the hot steam, they didn't seem to notice.

To be honest, I was hardly a noble-minded patriot. At times, I could see clearly, with a pang at the recognition, that I belonged to a people who had lost their nation. But till now, seven years after having become one of the nationless, I remained for the most part oblivious to the general state of affairs. Circumstances, it's true, had been kind enough to leave me alone. Back when I was in public school, I'd been a rather impassioned patriot, full of naïveté, and after an altercation with a Japanese teacher I'd even talked about transferring to a private school run by Koreans. But ever since I reached the age of discretion, I had been living in Tokyo. Aside from times when I was treated unfairly, or subjected to a customs inquiry in Pusan and Seoul on yearly visits to my family, I rarely experienced anything that provoked my enmity or resistance. Enmity and resistance, as the only viable means of survival, increase in proportion to oppression and abuse. But during my seven years in Tokyo, with the exception of the police, no one had especially provoked me toward a sense of national consciousness. And given my usual lack of interest in politics, it would be fair to say that I had never thought at length about such problems. But as time passed, one year after another, I couldn't prevent my nerves from becoming increasingly frayed. This revealed to me that enmity and resistance are not the results of some voluntary rational development under ordinary conditions but the manifestations of a passive emotional response. Such incidents as the casual remarks and everyday habits of the Japanese were bringing the animosity of all Koreans to a boiling point. All these stimuli were fueling Koreans' determination to save themselves from the fate of racial degradation.

So while the conversation I overheard in the bathing area was offensive, there was a part of me that wished such conversations could be heard by as many Koreans as possible, so that they could serve, like a poison bitter to the tongue but salubrious for the body, as a means for awakening Koreans from their long slumber.

The men continued their talk.

"So isn't it dangerous in the countryside?" asked the peasant.

"Not at all. Wherever you go, you don't need to worry. They're bestial, but those *yobos* are quite docile, and with the police and gendarmes everywhere, they can't lift a finger. That tells you what a tight grip Mr. Uchimura has. And what a man he is!" The man seemed genuinely moved.

"What can you do in the countryside?"

"There're lots to do. No matter what, you won't have any worries about going on an empty stomach. Lately, there's been one trade that's really been raking in the money. It requires no capital and little sweat."

"What kind of work is that?" The peasant's eyes opened wider as he stared at the man with a kind of eager curiosity.

"Why? Do you want to give it a try?" The con man watched the peasant closely, luring him in with a cunning smile on his malicious face.

"It's better than dropping dead after digging dirt all your life in the countryside. Besides, you can make as much money as you want . . . " He kept smiling, coaxing the peasant, who seemed so simple in his artless sincerity.

"If it's that easy, of course I'd try it." The peasant was being lured in.

"You do need some capital for starters. First off, you need to pay a small sum as a security deposit. You also have to buy a suit. But for you, since you have a brother in the army, you might be able to get by without the deposit . . . "

He said all this as if in passing, shrugging his shoulders in a nonchalant manner. He was insinuating that everyone must pay a security deposit to get the job, but that he would make a special exception in this case. He was not being forthright about what kind of a job it was, though. I was enticed myself, overhearing their conversation, but the peasant's eyes seemed to be literally glowing with curiosity. The con man's reserve about giving away details was apparently the result of either his reluctance to let me and the others overhear or a ploy to get the hick so worked up he'd swear an oath to be the man's lackey.

"Sounds like a great job," said the peasant's companion, "How do you apply?" This second peasant had been quietly listening in on their conversation. As he hoisted his red, glowing body up out of the water, the con man also got up and went through the motions of scrubbing his back with a towel. He then quickly looked around to check that everyone else, aside from the three of them, was sitting and minding their own business in the corner. Seemingly reassured, the con man finally began to speak in a low voice.

"In fact, it's pretty easy. I'm doing it for the third time now. The job is to contact companies on the mainland and deliver *yobos* to them—I mean Korean coolies, laborers. In general, recruiting is easy in Kyŏngsang or Hamgyŏng, or in Kangwŏn as well, even in Pyŏngan. But the Kyŏngsang province is the easiest of all." The man let out a sly chuckle.

What he said shocked me. At the thought of all those poor Korean laborers being sold to hellish factories across Japan, after having fallen into the hands of this damn swindler, I couldn't help but take another look at his insolent face. "I see, he plans to exploit the other guy, since his brother is a sergeant!" I sat motionless, all ears.

The man looked at the stupefied faces of the other two men and, smiling, continued talking. "The new recruits are mostly concentrated in the southern region and decrease toward the north. The Japanese have infiltrated the south more and really seized power there, so the natives have no choice but to either be driven north to Manchuria or south to Japan. Since everybody prefers the sunny side of things, they beg to be taken. They reckon, 'Hell, if I have to farm twelve months a year and still starve, eating nothing but corn and grass half the time, and then croak from a bloated belly, I'd rather go to a rich city like Osaka or Tokyo and live it up a bit.' But in the northern region of Korea, because it's sparsely populated and the Japanese haven't reached there yet, the wretches live in peace, though eventually they'll come begging, too."

As if impressed by his own speech, the man laughed coarsely again, content with his audience's positive response and proud of his own knowledge.

"So if you do the recruitment, how much do you make?" the peasant asked. He was so tantalized that he was almost drooling.

"What do you mean how much? Your travel expenses are paid, you get a daily wage and one or two wŏn per head—though, that varies depending on the company and the kind of work. Something like a girl at a textile factory is cheap labor and so the recruiter's take is low, whereas a miner, say, brings in anything between one wŏn fifty or two wŏn. So, suppose you take a thousand men. Without counting the leftover change from the travel expenses and the wage for two to three months, that makes one thousand and a few hundred wŏn, nearly two thousand, if you're lucky. When I went to Cheju island for my first recruitment, I gathered five hundred men and netted eight, nine hundred, no, almost a thousand wŏn in profit, and the second time, which was this fall, I sent eight hundred men to the Hokkaido mine and earned nearly two thousand wŏn."

The recruiter stood up out of the water in excitement, making quotes of thousands of wŏn until his mouth ran dry.

"Wow!" The peasant had been listening wide-eyed to the sound of one thousand, two thousand wŏn, a sum he had never seen in his whole life. He finished scrubbing and plunged his huge bronze body back into the water. Satisfied, he began to ask more questions.

"Are those Korean peasants good at factory work?"

"Whether they're good or bad, that's not really my concern. But *yobos* are obedient, good at difficult jobs, and cheap. Just perfect for the factory. Of course, when you meet them, you have to sweet-talk them at first with promises of high wages and easy work. But what kind of idiot would refuse when you advance him a little money for the trip, give him permission for his wife and kids to tag along, and even pay off all his debts? Once he signs on, he's like a rat in a cage because of his debt to you. Even if he kicks the bucket from starvation, not to mention the hard work and low wages, he can't do a thing . . . "

As if it were now all arranged that the peasant would work for him, the con man was pompously letting out the secret of his recruiting tactic, with a proud grin on his face.

I was deliberately lingering to hear more, but the boarding seemed to have finished. All of a sudden the bathing area became crowded, so I began to dry myself off, while mulling over the strange, horrific story I had just heard.

Since I had been only a bookish student, I could not help but be amazed at such a story. Needless to say, all my ideas on life, humanity, and society were no more than empty theories in a classroom. I could prattle on about life, nature, poetry, and the novel, having done a little bit of reading and study thanks to my father and our ancestors, but I had not even once had to face the truth of actual facts, real life, or real society. In the end, all my criticisms were nothing but the complaints of a satiated belly; they had no relevance. They were completely out of touch with the facts hidden behind the curtain. At that moment in the bathing area, I was helplessly seized by grave doubt about what I had been doing and what I would do in the future. When I heard the words—"There's nothing I can do but get by on vegetables for half a year, no matter how hard I sweat day in and day out all year long . . . "—I was so stunned that I doubted whether this could indeed be true. I had grown up in a rural Ch'ungch'ŏng village, my parents' hometown, till the age of eight or nine, and I visited the countryside once or twice a year after that, but I had never imagined such misery in a peasant's life.

They say, plow the land instead of composing a poem. But isn't plowing the land already a poem in itself? Man comes from the earth and returns to the earth. How happy are those who are drunk from the scent of soil! The fragrant vitality of the earth, that is the eternal source of the new life awaiting thee, the human . . .

I felt so ashamed of this idle, shallow thought, which I had entertained last spring while writing a prose poem. It was not that the scent of soil was not fragrant. A man who could drink the scent of the earth to his heart's content might, after all, be truly happy. If one could work in the field only in the mornings and evenings, armed with a straw hat and a pair of sunglasses, lest he should be infected by the current epidemic among high-class drones (namely, a sore stomach after their morning nap), he might well be happy or even feel poetic. But was there really a poem to be found in suffering from a miserable diet of thin vegetable gruel and the resultant swelling of one's face, after working as hard as a horse full twelve months a year? When those men strike the earth with their hoes, their hands burnt raw under the scorching midsummer sun, can they really be happy? They are slaves of the land. Slaves of their lot. All they have is sweat and blood. Starvation. The only thing foredestined as they slipped out of their mothers' wombs was that they were to fertilize the land with their sweat and blood until their pores became clogged and their veins dried up. And so, with ten drops of sweat and a hundred drops of blood, they grow a grain of rice. But to whose mouth does it go? What do they receive in return? More than anything else, starvation is their wage. . . .

I finished drying myself off and went to the changing area.

I was hurrying to put on my suit trousers amid the bustle of people coming and going, when a strange man opened the door halfway and thrust his head in. A fedora hat was perched on his head. He looked around the room, apparently embarrassed, and asked, "Excuse me, is there a Yi Inhwa here?"

"Yes—, that's me. What's the matter?" I took a few steps in his direction.

Now grinning and seemingly pleased to have found me after a long search, the man opened the door wide and loudly ordered me to step out. The build under his student uniform and the studied fluency of his Japanese convinced me that he was Korean. Still, he insisted on speaking Japanese and appeared uneasy, seemingly afraid that his real identity would be disclosed, all of which made him suspicious and irritating to me. The Japanese bathers, who guessed from my name and his accent that we were Koreans, moved their eyes back and forth between the two of us. We were like parrots staging a comical show in front of the Japanese.

"I don't know what you want, but why don't you talk to me here?" I replied in Japanese as well.

"Why don't you just step outside for a second?"

"Wait for me outside, then." I answered in a vexed voice, since I knew from his tone what kind of man he was, and his bluntness was rubbing me the wrong way.

I returned to my spot and began to put on my clothes, one item after the other. I could feel the many contemptuous eyes still stuck on my face like a spider web. Also, I was sure that the three men who had been talking earlier were now casting sidelong glances at me. I avoided meeting their eyes. My throat was almost choking with anger, but my shoulders slouched, as my strength was sapped.

I finished dressing and came out to find the man waiting for me, leaning on the other side of the wall, his shoulders hunched.

He walked behind me and spoke in a supplicating tone, his attitude much more relenting than before.

"I'm sorry, but let's collect your bags and go over there."

"Who are you? Where do you want me to go?"

"Ah, well, I came from the XX police station. Please, let's just stop by the station for a moment."

He grew polite and even sheepish in his speech and manners, perhaps because he felt that he had been wrong to order me to follow him before identifying himself. Or maybe he was ashamed for having pretended to be Japanese and was now afraid of my exposing him by asking, "Aren't you Korean?" Seeing him now so humbled, I pitied him somewhat. While walking down the staircase beside him I took a look at his face. His blank smile failed to hide his obvious discomfort.

I went to my cabin, passed him two bags, and added simply, "I don't have time to get off board, and these are the only bags I have. Take them yourself and come back with them after investigating whatever you want."

"No, that won't work. I can open them only in your presence. Please, just come for a moment. I'll carry your bags."

Hundreds of eyes in the cabin all turned toward me; whispers were heard here and there. My face was burning with anger, and I could no longer remain calm.

I started shouting at him. "Do you have any reason to believe that I stole something? What more do you want? I told you to take my bags and do what you want with them. If necessary, tell them to come here and do their investigation. You should know better than to ask a man to get off a ship that's about to leave port."

"Please, don't be so angry. Let's go just for a minute. I'll make sure that you leave today on this ship. You're only wasting time now. We're trying to avoid embarrassing you here."

"Embarrassing? What do you mean embarrassing? How can I be more embarrassed than I already am? Don't worry about me. Do as you please."

Although I had shouted all this in genuine anger, I decided to follow him, partly because I found his supplicating tone—though hateful—to be pitiful, and partly because dragging out the affair would, as he said, lead to no good. Besides, time was quickly slipping away. I put on my jacket, and since it was impossible to tell what might happen, I also grabbed the lunch I had bought earlier. I went out with the detective, who walked ahead of me, carrying my bags.

The man now looked triumphant, as if he had accomplished some heroic task. "You could have complied earlier." My fists clenched of their own accord at his derisive grin.

Still on board, I insisted on having the investigator come to the hatchway, but my request was denied. In the end, I walked down to the dock, holding my anger in check, as if suppressing the pain of torture.

In front of the waiting room, the Raincoat Man who had taken my business card earlier was keeping a strict watch with another man in a Western suit and overcoat. Having seen us, they silently led us behind the mountains of ship cargo in the dockyard. The Korean detective followed them without a word, carrying my bags. I felt my heart grow cold. With no means of resistance, I had no choice but to follow like a cow hauled to slaughter. As if practicing something we'd rehearsed beforehand, the four of us walked in step with one another, nimbly and silently, which reminded me of a band of robbers in a motion picture, or of the detectives stalking after them. The four of us stopped at a place blocked by cargo from the sight of passers-by. The electric light from the window of the waiting room silently flickered on the glasses of the man dressed in Western style.

"Can't you stay here one more night?" Western Suit had my bags handed over to him. His low voice, deep and rough, sounded otherworldly in the narrow alley between the piles of cargo. I stood absent-mindedly, looking like an idiot, and gazed blankly at his chubby face, which was dappled with white reflections from his glasses. He, too, was glaring at me menacingly, with his lips tightly closed, as if to show his determination not to miss a single change in my facial expression.

"Why don't you leave after tomorrow?" he asked again, his voice softening suddenly. Now he sounded as if he were trying to detain an important, welcome visitor. Despite my innocence, the mixture of menace and persuasion in the shadowy alley filled me with anxiety. Had I been a millionaire, I would have been afraid of being mugged at that moment.

I wanted to think clearly and make a sharp reply, but I was completely at a loss for words. "Where am I supposed to stay? Do you mean jail? I agreed to come along because he promised me that I could leave by tonight's ship, so let's keep that promise."

Despite my resolute words, I had lost all composure and was extremely nervous. Although a man like me was too ordinary to have any need to fear the police, missing the ship would certainly mean a night in jail. At all costs, I must not miss the ship. I shored up my resolve, but my heart was pounding hard.

"Then should we conduct the inquiry here?" Western Suit looked at me and Raincoat both, and a discussion between the three of us ensued. For the moment, I felt relieved.

"Yes, let's do that." At Raincoat's agreement, Western Suit turned around and asked me, "Do you mind if I open this bag?" He asked for the key. I quickly gave my consent. The bag easily opened at his touch.

He ransacked the suitcase—which was the size of a child's coffin—on a spot next to a tower of cargo lit from the window above. Meanwhile, Raincoat examined the briefcase. I stood alongside Student Uniform and watched their four hands at work. Western Suit stirred the contents of my suitcase for a moment, then pulled out my Western and Japanese clothes lying on top, tossed them to the detective next to me, and started to browse busily through the papers and books that were packed underneath. Raincoat, having found nothing, closed the briefcase, put it aside, and watched the other man; following an order by Western Suit, he proceeded to write down the titles of my books in his notebook, picking them up one by one. The four hands rummaging through my suitcase moved quicker and quicker by the minute. Anxious about what other absurd requests they might make, I fixed my eyes on Western Suit's cheek, which glowed in the electric light.

Eight eyes and four hands were all focused on the suitcase; four pairs of lips remained clamped shut, nobody breathing a word to break the tension. An absolute silence descended on the dark narrow alley, like a mysterious fog. The only sound I heard was the noise of crumpling paper each time the icy, fish-smelling sea winds blew past my ears. All louder sounds—such as the sound of dockyard workers busy loading ships or of waves breaking under the dock—seemed lost on the four of us. Against the dim light and the sullen silence, our moving silhouettes, whether sitting or standing, presented a grave, desolate scene. It was as if we were examining a drowned corpse. As the time passed, one minute, two minutes, three, four, five, ten minutes . . . the thumping in my head grew louder in proportion to the stillness in my ears. The three men were not being deliberately slow, but all the same I became so restless that I wanted to snatch the bags from them and finish the inspection myself.

Having run out of patience, I took out my watch and said, to hasten them, "Now there's only two minutes left. I'm leaving."

It was only then that Western Suit stopped the swift motions of his hands, lifting up a bundle of papers.

"You wouldn't mind my keeping these for a closer look? I can mail them to your address later."

I gave my instant approval. In fact, the bundle contained nothing but a few letters from home, a draft for my novel, and some other manuscripts. As for the list they painstakingly made of my books, I had never had anything to do with the "S" of socialism or the "L" of Lenin, not to mention the "I" of independence, all of which should have been obvious by the subject I had chosen as my major. And even if I had studied socialism or owned hundreds of books on Bolshevism, I should, of course, have been allowed my academic freedom. Suppose they were to detect an idea of independence in my brain by using an X-ray or by photographing my mind; what could they do so long as I had not realized this idea in action? This stream of thoughts, however, came to me only later. At that very moment, I was just happy to be safe and free to go. I left the place with the other men after quickly gathering my things.

Carrying my lightened bags in both hands, I was hurried on by sailors and barely made it to the ship on time. Soon, a symphony of loud yet forlorn sounds—a shrieking horn, a neighing whistle, and a sonorous gong—sent ripples through the dark, deserted harbor. The ship silently glided away and was soon four or five meters from the dock. The scattered shadows of hotel workers and servants, who had come to see off their guests, gradually disappeared from sight; the flame of a swinging lamp, which someone was carrying across the dock, flared up occasionally, blown by lonely winds.

I stood on the murky deck instead of retiring to the cabin, my shoulders hunched in the cold winds. The harbor, now asleep, lay serenely in the dark, exhausted after hard work in the cold, and the lights that guarded the resting city at nightfall were already dozing off as well, going out one by one.

Like a wanderer leaving the human world, I thought of how each of those lights must be guarding a door with a peaceful family behind it, and I found the dim, receding lights warmer than frigid stars. My mind was all in a jumble. I felt a burning sensation in my eyes.

I simply stood there, my hands pressed into my coat pockets. Hot tears, without my noticing them, rolled down my flushed cheeks. As I stood there, not bothering to wipe the tears away, the wind dried them with its chilling touch.

3

A man becomes most conscious of his station in life when faced with someone above or below him. Men of equal status, since they share the same circumstances, can communicate and sympathize with each other, feeling no need to swagger or bow. But when there is a big difference, the consciousness of one's own status precludes any communication or compassion. Hence, one swaggers, and the other bows. When patted on the back, a weakling feels grateful and feigns sincerity, while a proud man feels humiliated and resentful; when one adopts an imposing attitude toward someone, that person either cowers and assumes a subordinate position or turns rebellious. Such is man's lot. It doesn't matter whether the origin of inequality lies within the social system, education, or man's innate nature, be it benevolent or malignant.

The happiness and elation that results from a proud, joyful recognition of one's superiority, however, is far exceeded by the unhappiness, pain, and dejection that arises from the humiliating awareness of one's inferiority. For an unusually self-respecting man, the impact of this awareness is compounded ten, twenty, a hundred times. When the sense of superiority and inferiority derives from one's background, apart from simple individual relationships, the effects penetrate even deeper into a person's mind, at times turning openly destructive, at others maturing into a kind of strength.

Fortunately, a proud, strong-willed man can channel the negative emotions caused by his humiliation into a drive for self-improvement. Yet, the question remains, how strong can a man be. Given my general belief that a man boasts or hates, laughs or cries, under no compulsion, but simply because he's weak, I can't trust my own strength, either.

As ridiculously sentimental as I was, I continued to stand on the deck, suppressing my tears. The winds blew with increasing harshness, until finally I could no longer bear the frigid, numbing cold on my freshly bathed body. I picked up my bags and went down to the cabin. The bed I had reserved earlier was, needless to say, occupied by someone else, and there remained nowhere for me to squeeze into. In my fruitless anger, I grabbed a sailor and somehow managed to wedge myself in with his help, but the condescending, curious stares of the Japanese passengers sitting next to me made me self-conscious. I considered opening my lunch box, but for fear that such an act would only belittle me further and add to my bitterness, I simply lay down, pulling my coat over my head.

From Tokyo to the customs office, I could generally travel in peace, not because I deliberately pretended to be Japanese but because I was not so glaringly visible; once on board the ferry, though, the air would always seem dangerous for some reason, and a certain premonition would pinch the back of my neck. Now, after the inspection, this unpleasant feeling could not help but be worse than usual. Even when lying down with my eyes closed, I felt a rage surging through my body; I bit my lips unconsciously. No matter where I looked, there was no one I could turn to. Even if I happened to come across a compatriot in the same situation, I would not have been able to communicate my frustration to him. For we were on a ship, a ship that carried those superior masters who looked down on us.

The morning arrived. As soon as the sun was up, people slowly got up one by one and began clambering up and down the staircase. I, too, was awakened by their noise and got up to wash myself. The cabin, which looked like a communal bedroom of monks in a Buddhist temple, was littered all over with garbage in the aftermath of hundreds of passengers having spent the night there, squeezed together like a can of sardines. Since the stench gave me a headache, I went up to the deck right after washing myself. With the sun not yet very high, the water looked black, and the sky, too, was still relatively dark, only the obscure outlines of clouds showing through. The air was cold but refreshing. Down in the cabin, breakfast seemed to have begun. Barrels of rice were being carried in, and the people on the deck hurried after them.

As a group, these third-class passengers, from wherever they happened to hail, were competitive about everything. They competed to enter first, competed to exit first, competed to sleep, and, most fiercely of all, competed to eat. If I could have afforded it, I would have bought a second-class ticket for the ferry, but with the usual slimming down of my wallet after end-of-semester expenditures (and partly as a result of my general habit of setting aside enough money for drink), I always ended up spending the night in that horrible place, which was not much better than a homeless shelter. In any case, judging from the group's overall appearance and language, it seemed that a pack of hungry ghosts from the lower classes, aside from a few odd petty bureaucrats, formed the majority here. When I encountered them, I always behaved extremely courteously and tried to keep my distance. There was more reason for this than their racial superiority as Japanese. Even if I thought of them simply as laborers or proletarians, I still did not want to mingle with them. Although ethics and books had taught me to believe that no one could share a more solid bond of partnership or camaraderie with us than the so-called proletariat, in truth, once I met a proletarian face to face, I could not help it if my nose flared up a little. Perhaps I should have resisted my strong repulsion and instead revived my resolution to work harder for the downtrodden. As I reasoned, the fault, after all, did not lie with them. Yet it was a simple truth that my sentiments did not mesh well with theirs.

Since I had skipped last night's dinner, I was feeling hungry and withdrew to the cabin. A big crowd was standing in front of the table, where the first round of breakfast had already been served. A ruckus had started.

A short man with a black mustache and an angular, hysterical face was yelling savagely. "So why the hell can't I take a seat before the table is set?" His face, which did not appear too vulgar, suggested that he might be an official.

"Because there's no point," replied a ship's hand in a black student uniform. "The food goes in order, so even if you take a seat now, you're still not getting served." His tone was cynical, placid, as if he were mocking the man.

"Aren't we guests on this ship? How can you treat guests like that? What do you take us for, *yobos*?" He invoked *yobo* apparently for no good reason.

"Who's treating you badly? How so? What's wrong with asking you to come and eat when the table is set?"

"What's wrong with demanding quick service when I'm in a rush? This kind of nonsense happens only in Korea. Who do you think you are, acting so high and mighty?"

As the mustached man quieted down, other spectators grew louder, as if they wanted to add fuel to a dying fire.

"Give him a good beating. To behave like an official, how insolent . . ."

"What an arrogant prig."

"Bastard, a low-life sailor who acts like an official, how disgusting . . ."

The place became filled with such shouts. The passengers seemed to imply that had the sailor been an actual official, he could have casually given such an order without provoking their disobedience.

"It's because the railways in Korea are still run by the government. That's why a measly employee can put on airs like an official. If they were privatized, he wouldn't dare talk back." An indignant gentleman was even reasoning in as far-fetched a manner as this.

At the uproar of the passengers, the sailor shut up and quietly sneaked away. The clamor gradually subsided. Those who had been standing around were busy taking their seats at the table. As I watched the thoroughly disagreeable commotion, I wanted to go out again, but hunger prevented me. At no one's invitation, I hesitantly sat down in a corner and reluctantly began to eat.

"All my complaining about these squalid, ignoble, hungry ghosts comes to nothing in the face of a growling stomach." At this thought, I smirked to myself. I put down my chopsticks and drank some water. Inside the cabin a hubbub once again arose; some of those lucky enough to have had something to eat now began to pack up their luggage, but others were retching up their hard-won breakfasts. I also felt seasick after the meal and lay down where I was sitting.

The ship was not moving very fast, a sign that the shore was nearby, and half of the passengers were already out on the deck. I also packed my bags and went up. The shore appeared closer than I had expected. The sailors were busily running around, up and down, back and forth, in preparation for the landing. The sonorous yet desolate sound of a horn bellowed in the morning wind. In yet another pandemonium of competitiveness, people thronged to get ahead in line behind a rope that had been set up to separate them from the first- and second-class passengers. They would not be let off until all the higher-class passengers disembarked.

The ship reached the harbor.

"Heave-ho! Heave-ho!"

Among the workers who were reeling in the anchor cable were Koreans in their dirty, yellowing white clothes. The sight of them filled my heart with a deep sense of relief.

Scarcely had the ladder been lowered overboard when three men climbed up onto the ship: an assistant policeman wearing a white-brimmed hat and a coat; a Japanese policeman with the black strap of a revolver slung over his shoulder; and a gendarme in a khaki uniform, also carrying a revolver. As soon as they got on board, they planted themselves on either side of the exit, blocking the passengers' way out. Only after they took their positions as guards were the first- and second-class passengers allowed to disembark. We, the third-class passengers, were pushed to the side to make room for the traffic. We watched the scene with envious eyes, like boat people barred from landing.

"Three wŏn! If only I'd paid three more wŏn, I'd be living in style!" Such grumblings came from the crowd.

Finally, it was our turn. I slowly walked in the middle of the crowd. One step down the ladder, it felt as if someone were pulling the hem of my coat from behind. Before I'd taken ten steps down, I saw four eyes looking up from below. The eyes belonged to an assistant policeman and an assistant gendarme, neither of whom carried their own revolvers; needless to say, these two were Koreans.

Taking as little notice of them as possible, I reached the last step with a steady gait and tried to feign indifference, all the while hoping and praying that they would take me for Japanese. My conspicuous nonchalance displayed about as much composure as that of a cow entering a slaughterhouse.

"*Yobo, yobo.*" The voice I heard, of course, had a Japanese accent.

I distrusted my ears. Since I had counted on running into trouble only once this trip, as was the usual case, I thought the call might simply be my imagination. I ignored it and walked on, but a man who wore Japanese clothes and a raincoat stepped out of the crowd and blocked my way; his eyes, strangely glistening under his crumpled winter cap, were menacing. I felt cold sweat trickling down my back.

"Let's go over there," the man said in a threatening tone. He led me toward the police station. I followed in silence. Baggage carriers, unaware of what was going on, eagerly ran after us, calling, "Sir, sir." Their voices were trembling from the cold and had the sad, faltering tone of beggars. I just kept shaking my head until I entered the police station.

At the police station, I was again at a loss for words, overcome by anxiety and a fear of something vague, unlike what I usually felt during a customs inspection. I also knew that I could not be as churlish as I normally was with these types in Japan. Despite inward jeers at my own cowardice, my voice grew docile, and I let my head hang low.

The inquiry was simpler than I'd anticipated; standard questions only. When they asked what was in my bags, I told them that the customs officials had taken whatever might be of interest, but that if they were suspicious, they were welcome to open them. I held out the key. Men must laugh, even if they are detectives. Grinning, the men told me to keep the key for myself and, as if doing me a favor, dismissed me without further ado. They seemed to have been in communication with the detectives at the customs office. I breathed in great relief. I had a carrier take my bags to the train station, rushed to check them in, and began my solitary stroll.

4

When a poor man drowns, the first thing to float up, without fail, is his purse. Even in good times, a poor man's purse swells only on the last day of the month, after having thinned out over the preceding twenty-nine days, just as the belly of a man who has been starving for three generations gets a bit bloated after he wolfs down a meal. Even a stolen purse lasts but a few hours. After that, all that remains is the lament that money has wings.

"Alas, money is bewitched! Coins are so combustible—one after another they end up in smoke. Whether I put in my purse one wŏn or ten wŏn's worth of change, the money just flies away. How on earth do I keep letting this happen!"

That's all he says, looking up at the sky, holding out his flat penniless purse. "I'm going to starve to death in this world," he concludes.

There's a reason for this all too common lot of the destitute man. When he earns some money, he gets overly excited, as if it were a sum his family had not laid eyes on for generations. Not knowing how to manage the money that falls into his hands every once in a long while, he blows it all on random spending sprees, without considering the consequences—as if holding any of it back might somehow make him ill. Whether this indiscretion arises from his poverty or his habit keeps him poor, the fate of a poor man is to regret the squandering of his money without ever keeping track of how it's squandered. Whether such a lot is rather preferable or not is of secondary importance. In any case, the general lot of Koreans is no better than that of such a poor man.

A month of elementary school education would be enough for anyone to learn that Pusan is the finest harbor in Korea, the most important gateway to the Peninsula. The harbor city represents the country in miniature; it's a symbol of Korea. If a foreign tourist wants to see Korea, taking him to Pusan and showing him around the city would satisfy his purpose. Sacred Pusan! The city that bears the destiny of Korea on its shoulders! The fortune of Pusan is the fate of Korea, and the future of Korea is the fate of Pusan.

I had a couple hours to spare, and since I was still a bit hungry after having eaten on the ship, I decided first to look for a Korean restaurant. Also, I had yet to explore the downtown area of this city, which I'd always simply traveled through.

As I left the harbor behind and headed west along the streetcar line on the main road, I did not spot a single Korean house among the two-story residences lining either side. The streetcar line turned to the north after two or three blocks, but all I could see after that were colorful pictures and flags that suggested theaters for drama or motion pictures. At an intersection of three streets, I looked around in every direction, finally having to ask a baggage carrier where the Koreans lived. After thinking a while, he pointed to an avenue leading south to the seaside, saying that some lived over there. I turned to walk in that direction. I followed a winding path past scattered seafood storehouses, which smelled fishy and rancid. At last I came upon a dirty, narrow alley that opened onto the seaside. On each side stood several shabby, poorly constructed, two-story Japanese houses. It didn't seem that they could possibly belong to Koreans, yet the people who went in and out of them were indeed Korean. As I walked along, I peeped into the houses and saw a *changgo* in the upstairs window of one of them. But the doorplate of the house said "Inn." I could tell at a glance that it housed the usual kind of business around a harbor. Still, there was no sign of women.

"Maybe after drinking and making merry all night long, they've got their clock backward and are still in bed."

As I turned around, I was tempted by curiosity to enter, but I hastened to walk away out of concern for being late for the train. Back on the main road, I walked toward the station, checking every side street in the hope of finding a Korean restaurant. The food would not suit my taste, nor would it be any match for the fare in Seoul, yet I wanted to eat *kimchi* and dine with a spoon. But there was not a single Korean-style building to be found. Occasionally, I found a flat Korean house, but all these houses had Japanese window frames mounted on their walls. Strangely, though, Koreans seemed to count for over half of the passers-by in the modest downtown area, both on the major roads and on the side streets.

"Where do all these people go at night?" I wondered, thinking about the destiny of the pitiable, white-clad Koreans.

Whether Koreans are being driven to the outskirts of cities—leaving behind the land that their ancestors had tamed inch by inch through patient efforts over hundreds, thousands of years—or whether they are retreating deeper into the countryside, they each must feel as if they alone are coming or going. Even when a man sells off his land and is evicted from the very house he built, its ownership passing from one hand to another as the interest on his debts spirals out of control, he leaves his family's hometown without much protest beyond a simple saying: a man's bound to go through all kinds of troubles in this life. He moves somewhere beyond the city gates or to some mountain village, attributing his loss to fate in a gesture of self-resignation or cheap optimism. He never suspects that some power might be behind his misfortune, or that his own lack of integrity, self-restraint, and perseverance might have brought about his downfall. If a household disappears from a town of a thousand houses, people might say a word or two about it around the dinner table: "That family is moving away to that town." Yet no one questions why the neighbor has to leave. After all, the disappearance of one house in a thousand has little impact on the remaining nine hundred ninety-nine houses. The majority of the town's population is often not even aware of the setback. Thus one house disappears, two houses, ten, a hundred of them; meanwhile, yet another run-down house is demolished, soon to be replaced with a new one. A one-story house is converted into a two-story one, an *ondol* into a *tatami*, and an oil lamp into electric light bulbs.

"That family's house stands in the way of a new road." The men gossip as they puff on leaf tobacco from their long pipes before heading off to bed. By the time they get up, the air is already astir with the sounds of digging and shoveling, which will last for days on end. Soon the rails are laid out, automobiles honk their way through and splash mud all around, and the clapping sound of clogs grows louder and louder. A new post office opens up, and a gendarme's residence is installed where an old county office had once stood. The traditional inns and bars serve fewer and fewer customers, while a new geisha house springs up around the corner, from which soon float the twangs of a *shamisen*, before anyone in the village even notices. If the men in the village, greeted with such novelty items as syphilis and gonorrhea, complain of the inconvenience of having no hospital nearby, some quack is always on standby ready to serve them, apologizing for his lateness in his characteristically courteous manner. The world has truly become a rather convenient place.

"They installed electric lamps in town, and railway service has started up, too. You should come and see. A few nice restaurants have opened as well. Have you seen a Japanese prostitute? I'll take you to one next time."

Things unheard of in the family, not even once in its history of hundreds and thousands of years, have come to pass. The time has come for unrestrained prodigality. When one man sells a hectare of rice field to enjoy the new comforts, luxuries, and entertainments, another plays fast with two hectares, saying, "My town now has quite a number of two-story houses and even a few Western-style ones. In the summer a *tatami* is indeed more convenient. Good for hygiene, too."

But to whom do the two-story houses belong, and for whom does the hygiene matter?

The tailor keeps visiting a man to claim his debts; the restaurant's owner threatens him with a law suit; there's pressure for payment on the electricity bill; the newspaper bills go unpaid for months. As he worries, "How can I visit friends without cigarettes? How can I go out without the streetcar fare?" the man's house changes hands and ends up in the possession of the Development Bank, soon to be occupied by a new owner. In such a manner, one after another, a hundred more houses are lost, and a few hundred more households disappear entirely.

"There's just no way to survive. Country life is better, tilling the earth is the surest thing!" As new people replace the old in a downtown that is prospering more and more everyday, the last of the thousand houses is swept away. By the time the thousandth household is driven out, the man who had been the first to leave town has already crossed the Yalu River, carrying a wooden cup with a carved paulownia leaf as his last cherished possession. He's getting tipsy on a cup of sorghum liquor, which he's just knocked back to relieve his fatigue from the long journey.

A wasteful people. Even as they were throwing away everything, the shirt off their back included, they could not have guessed that they're going to be kicked out on the street. In the same way a poor man doesn't consider how he will live without food and shelter, even as he's spending the last coin in his pocket. Still, no one dreamed during the gradual disappearance of the natives that their kind would completely vanish, and now alien newcomers have come to monopolize the streets. The old ones have vanished like the coins of a poor man.

I could almost see "the vanquished," each family carrying their paltry belongings on their backs, receding in a line farther and farther to the north. I didn't feel like wandering any longer in the windy, abandoned streets, and so even though it was still early I began to quicken my pace. The sight of a young girl doing the morning cleaning in front of a Japanese noodle shop brought me to a halt. I suddenly wanted to go in. All my indignation and invective evaporated in the blink of an eye, as my attention was drawn to the red underwear hanging out from under her skirt and her frozen yet shapely white calves.

"Come on in." She welcomed me and lifted her rather dark face, which was so distinct from her pale, powdered neck.

"Come in, come in." Two or three girls came out to greet me. The fact that such a small shop kept several young girls made it obvious what the main business of the place was. Despite a foreboding that I would become trapped, I succumbed to a base curiosity as they rushed me to the second floor and sat me down in the corner of a room. I first told them to heat some liquor and then ordered a simple meal. While I was waiting, another server came in to change the coals in the stove. The girl poured burning coals into the stove and began to scrape the embers with tongs.

As she paused to take a short break, she turned to me and asked, "Where are you headed?" Her wide-set eyebrows made her face look gloomy, and her little too broad forehead somewhat marred her appearance. Still, she was quite pretty.

"Seoul. Where are you from?"

She ignored my question. "Seoul. Ah, I wish I could go see Seoul . . . it must be better than here."

"I don't know if it's much better, but it is a bit better."

The food was brought in. I drank several glasses like a man who'd been dying for a sip and urged the girls to drink as well. Without much protest, they took turns pouring drinks for each other. Soon, another girl brought in a new bottle. This girl, too, took a seat in front of the stove and joined the drinking. Whether or not they were pretty, drinking with three girls could not be called unpleasant. Yet their open disregard for decorum was unpleasant and bordered on offensive. The girls' real priority was to sell as many bottles as possible—not to enjoy free drink—so as to keep up their credit with the owner and earn his approving smile. Their behavior was excusable according to the moral standard of their world. But I felt that they were taking too many liberties with me, coming in as a group as they had and indulging themselves in eating and drinking—all because I was Korean. I decided to take a derisive, condescending attitude toward them. I treated them like children: when did babies like them learn how to drink; it must be only a matter of days since they were weaned from their mothers' milk. The girl who brought in the coals was the least noisy, but she looked more crestfallen than calm and merely watched the prattling nonsense of the others with a quiet smile.

"*Tambagu, tambagu, tambagu* of Tongnae and Mount Uru . . . "

I was listening to one of them sing the Song of Tobacco in a comical imitation of the original Korean pronunciation. "You sing well. So how many years have you been here?"

I always asked this question upon first greeting any Japanese person staying in Korea, whether man or woman. From their answers, I could judge how arrogant and impudent they would be in dealing with Koreans. Even a mean-looking *nogada* (this is what we Koreans call Japanese laborers) would be obliging at first and, being unfamiliar with the foreign customs of the country, would even experience a certain fear. But a change would start to take place in him after half a year, and again a year later. It goes without saying that those who pass five, ten, twenty years in Korea become snakes. One should reflect on precisely what it is that increases their contempt as the years go by, what makes them ten times, a hundred times more arrogant and rude than they were originally.

There are many possible reasons for this. But one thing is certain—Koreans do not reveal much of themselves to foreigners, aside from a few basic characteristics, such as that they smoke in bed as soon as the sun is up, that their bars are crowded from the morning onward, that they kill time joking about other people's parents or saying such nonsense as "Call me dad" or "I think of you as my grandson," that the first phrase a Korean child learns to speak is "Just kidding," that Koreans spend whole nights on useless arguments only to get up at noon the next day . . . but that when it comes to scientific knowledge, they don't even realize that if their pot had a heavier lid, it would cook rice better. Koreans teach these lessons to foreigners by demonstrating them in their lives. So, the longer a foreigner stays, the more reason he has to disdain us.

"*Tanbagu, tanbagu* . . . Without you, where can I go . . . "

The girl sang on, beating out a rhythm on the stove with chopsticks, her lips moving in a strange way, now pouting and now opening wide. Suddenly, she stopped singing and pointed at the girl who had brought the coals and had been sitting quietly.

"She sings best. We've only been here three or four years."

"Really? How long have you been here?"

It surprised me that the quiet girl, who had not talked much and who appeared naïve and inexperienced, could speak the best Korean.

"She grew up here. Her mother is Korean." The girl who had been singing quickly replied for the other girl, as if she could not wait to explain this. "Aren't I right?" she said, studying the other girl's expression.

The loudness of her voice made her question sound mocking. The girl who had a Japanese father and a Korean mother blushed and twitched her eyes. For some reason, she seemed to feel ashamed of her Korean mother.

Out of curiosity, I asked, "Is that true? Where's your mother, then?"

She looked up at me. " . . . She's in Taegu."

"Then why did you come here? Do you still hear from her?" Although my question could have been taken as a joke, my tone was sincere.

"Well," she smiled at me, "I'd like to ask someone going to Taegu to contact her, but I haven't had the chance . . . I don't know how to write in Korean." She laughed aloud as if she saw something absurd in this. She was apparently laughing at herself.

"Then, your father, you're not living with him?"

"I've been separated from him for a long time. Since I was about ten years old. He left for Nagasaki when I was nine."

"And have you heard from him since?"

"I did for a while, but now I don't know his whereabouts . . . but after New Year's, I'm going to go and look for him."

She laughed awkwardly once again, as if close to tears. Her laughter seemed to reflect at once self-mockery and resignation at her mixed lot in life; hers was like the helpless laughter of someone who has just unwittingly committed some grave error and remains at a loss how to explain it.

"Even if she is Korean," I said, "you can't choose your mother, the person who brought you up, now can you? Whoever your father might be, he wouldn't welcome you with open arms, even if you could find him!" I could not help but pity the mother more than the girl. The girl's preference for Japanese language and clothes and her intention to live with her Japanese father rather than her Korean mother—despite having been raised by the latter—all this revealed that her desire to find her father derived from something other than a child's natural love for her parent.

"I feel sorry for my mother, but my father, since he's not a bad person, he wouldn't disown me." Her gaze became blank, as if she were picturing the reunion.

"But you don't want your mother because she's Korean and you want to leave here because it's Korea. If Korea were as good as Japan, you wouldn't find it shameful to have been born to a Korean. And you wouldn't think of trying to locate your father, either, would you?"

I continued to ask such needless questions simply from spite. She just smiled without a word. I was very tempted to carry on the conversation, but since I could not stay there forever, I started to eat the rice.

The girl who had sung the Song of Tobacco began to talk frivolously, half teasing, half admonishing. "Hey, ask this gentleman to take you! You're such an ungrateful daughter. What kind of slut abandons her own mother and runs away?"

"Right, you'd better," added a second girl by her side, also in a mocking tone. "You don't think you'll stumble onto some kind of miracle here, do you? If I still had a mother, I'd have gone to her a long time ago." This latest speaker had thick, drooping lips and a flat nose. They all seemed to look down on the half-Korean girl and yet were envious of her beauty.

I stopped eating and replied to the speaker in an attempt to give some support to the mocked girl, "So why are *you* living it up in a place like this, so far from home?"

"Well, I haven't got a parent or anyone else I can count on," the girl retorted, a bit angrily. "Let's drink more and talk less. Should I bring more?"

Before I could stop her, she was out of the room.

"But even if you find your father," I teased the mocked girl, "since you have such a pretty face, who knows what he'll do with you? Wouldn't it be better to marry a well-off Korean man and live comfortably? Korea is full of men who'd love to have a girl like you."

She stiffened at the suggestion. "Well, I don't like Korean men. Even if one had money or even gold." She seemed to be sick and tired of Korea in general, as if it were a spell that had cast a dark shadow on her destiny.

Then, thinking of Shizuko, I laughed. "Then I'm out of the game, too."

She also smiled and gave me a friendly look. The ugly girl with the drooping lips returned, holding a new bottle. I reluctantly accepted a glass.

"Look here, I was trying to flatter this beauty in order to whisk her away, but despite all my efforts, she says no Korean! How can I help but weep? You wouldn't be that heartless, would you?"

"You seem to want something badly, now that you're far away from home. Well, if you promise a huge treat . . . hee, hee, hee." The girl had made her own interpretation of my words and made an indecorous reply.

"You're even cheaper than I thought!" I told them to call a rickshaw and got up to leave.

I barely managed to prevail against their attempts to detain me before I got away from the place.

"So this is why peasants fall into their traps!" On the rickshaw, I thought about what had just happened and felt a bit irritated.

I almost missed the train. The men who had watched me so closely as I checked in my luggage seemed to have been looking for me. Raincoat Man from the previous encounter saw my rickshaw rushing in and grinned at me. But I paid little attention to him and, after claiming my baggage, jumped onto the train. The detective approached the window and said something with a nod, so I opened the window.

"You're going straight to Seoul, right?" For some reason, he shouted louder than necessary. Smiling back, I told him that since I'd even skipped my exams to go see my dying wife, I would of course be going straight there. My reply was overly detailed (I later laughed at this to myself). He seemed to say something more, but the train began to move, and I could not hear him well over the wind. But there was something suspicious about how he kept looking to his left while talking to me. When the train was already moving, I happened to catch sight of a man in a Western suit entering through a door on the other side of the traincar.

5

When the train arrived at Kimch'ŏn Station, my elder brother, who I thought would be in Seoul, came to meet me, wearing a frockcoat and his officer's hat with a gold braid. I was looking out the window, searching for a familiar face, and was surprised to see him in the crowd. As I was trying to open the window to greet him, he drew nearer and gestured for me to get off. After hesitating a moment, I reasoned that his very absence from Seoul and the smile on his face meant that the situation with my wife was not quite an emergency. I gathered my bags in a hurry, passed him my suitcase through the window, and got off the train. Western Suit also got off in a hurry, following me.

My brother had brought a servant along with him to carry my luggage. We gave the bags to the boy, who was waiting by the exit. We were about to leave, when the assistant gendarme, who was standing on guard, stopped whispering to Western Suit and turned to my brother.

"Is your younger brother visiting you? Is he leaving this evening?"

"Yes, yes!" replied my brother with a smile. His hand almost mechanically touched the brim of his hat. I found his gesture amusing and pathetic. But thanks to my brother, I escaped safely without much hassle.

As he walked, my brother wrapped his left hand tightly around his black gilded sword, which was visible below his frockcoat, and gingerly tiptoed to prevent it from brushing against his leg. He slowly told me about the latest developments.

"The morning I wired you the money, it looked like just a matter of hours, but then that afternoon she began to recover. By the time

I left, the day before yesterday, she was out of danger. Still, we can't relax, not for at least a while longer. Things have been going on like this for a few months. By the way, why didn't you leave right away? I thought you'd arrive yesterday and waited here two days in a row."

I thought of making up a lie but answered as the words came to me. "I did leave that night but stayed at Kobe for one night."

"What urgent business made you stay over, paying for lodging?" He asked in a reproachful tone.

"I didn't have any special business, but I was sick, and it was such a long, exhausting trip."

"You should've come straight away unless it couldn't be helped. You're always late," he frowned.

This brother of mine was a country gentleman whose education consisted of the Chinese classics. He was not ignorant of the new teachings, though, and was an indispensable person in my family. If it weren't for my brother, I would have been reduced to starvation long ago, let alone studying overseas as I was now. My father had made lavish use of the family fortune around the time of the Annexation, when he was running back and forth between Seoul and Tokyo in hot pursuit of political fame. Thanks to my brother's tightfisted management of the family fortune, we were living comfortably at present. The simple fact that my brother had saved over two thousand wŏn working as the mere schoolmaster of an elementary school demonstrated how frugal he was. Although I respected him, we had our disagreements. Come to think of it, the three of us—my father, my brother, and myself—couldn't be more different from each other in terms of lifestyle. It was a mystery how my sentimental, profligate character and the conservative, conventional character of my brother could have descended from the same father, who was a political fanatic.

"So what happened to your exams?" my brother asked, after a few moments of silence.

I hesitated, fearing how he would respond. "I had to drop them." Again, I told the truth.

"If I'd known that, I would have telegraphed you again to come later!"

He seemed to regret that I had walked out on the exams, whereas I thought it rather fortunate that he had not sent another telegram.

"Then, you'll have to take a make-up exam? Didn't you return early once before, saying that you'd take a make-up exam? You spent all that money on education and still failed to get good grades. . . . Anyway, literature is good-for-nothing. What can you do with it in today's world?"

I always heard this argument twice whenever I returned to Korea: once from my brother and once from my father. Sometimes my father could be insufferable. I used to argue heatedly with him. In self-defense, I would argue that since the purpose of education was to make "a human being," not a machine, an education could not be immediately converted into a monthly income or into "brimshit" (I always said "brimshit" when referring to the gold braid on the brims of officials' hats). I also said that individuality was precious and that everyone should be educated according to one's individual inclination. But in the end I learned that I just had to give up. I discovered that there was no common ground between their world and mine, that these two worlds were as disparate as death and life. I made up my mind not to waste time speaking with them, except for the kinds of pleasantries routine between father and son, or between brothers, and for unavoidable discussions about school expenses. I figured that if I behaved toward them as I did toward my mother, my wife, and my sister, then the house would rest in peace. As I saw it, our family conflicts usually resulted from my vain insistence on being understood, on expressing my opinion. Once I reached this conclusion, however, I felt isolated, and my house came to resemble an inn where I was given no more than bed and board—and the most disagreeable of inns at that.

Now, I was upset again, subjected as I was to the scolding of my brother, whom I was seeing for the first time in a year. But I held my silence, remembering last summer, when after a long argument with my father and brother about my schooling, I had decided, "I'd rather go to an inn, if they're only going to harass me when I'm at home." Afterward, I would leave the house at times just to wander around, staying over at a friend's place for a couple of days. I felt sad and lonely now, just as I did then.

We reached the entrance to my brother's neighborhood without exchanging further words. On the street I discovered a new Japanese store, and along the alley there were two houses bearing Japanese nameplates. I pointed them out to my brother.

"There's been quite a change!"

My brother, seemingly lost in thought, just smiled and nodded in reply. Following him into his house, I noticed that the gate was more run-down than it had been last year.

"It's falling apart," I said, as if to myself. "Why don't you have the gate repaired?"

"To last how much longer! This neighborhood will soon turn into a Japanese community, too. I'm only holding onto the place so I can sell it for a good price next year. This area doesn't look like much, but prices are higher here than anywhere else now."

My brother seemed pleased that the price had almost tripled since he had bought the place seven years ago. I recalled the scenes I had seen in Pusan that morning.

"But haven't the prices of other things also shot up? Some things cost three or four times as much now."

We went inside. My sister-in-law and their seven-year-old girl, who began to jump around at the sight of her uncle, came from the inner room to greet me. They had a new maid, who, unlike the previous one, didn't look especially vulgar. I entered the room, exchanged a ceremonial bow with my sister-in-law, and also received my niece's bow. Only then did I regret not having brought at least a box of cookies.

When all the necessary bows had been made, my brother, who had been sitting quietly, turned to his wife and said, "Tell her to come out, too!"

She stood still for a moment and then said to her daughter, "Go to the side room and ask your second mother to come here."

"What second mother?" I looked at my sister-in-law in confusion.

Then something dawned on me. She stood silently with a forced smile on her face.

"I meant to tell you," said my brother, smiling, "but because of the bad news, I didn't get a chance. You've got a second sister-in-law." Although it did not make sense to have a second sister-in-law when I had only one brother, the picture was already quite clear to me.

Still, I asked again, "What do you mean by a second sister-in-law?"

"I died in the meantime," replied my sister-in-law, affecting a smile. It did look as if she had aged considerably since the last time I'd seen her. The skin around her eyes had turned somewhat bluish, and wrinkles were clearly visible on her forehead and at the sides of her eyes. My brother was about to say something to her but kept quiet upon the arrival of my second sister-in-law. A young country girl, adorned as a new bride, stepped gingerly through the door, which the first wife held open. She had a white powdered face, a pink blouse, and a dark blue skirt. She looked neat and elegant—nineteen years old at most. Her broad forehead and wide nose seemed to augur a son, something sorely lacking in the household. Maybe because of this thought I noticed the slight swelling under her bulky skirt and a telltale luster in her shining face. Next to my "first" sister-in-law, she looked like a daughter-in-law. As my brother wished, I went through the motions of a ceremonious introduction with her. After we finished bowing to each other, my sister-in-law quickly left the room. My new sister-in-law followed. My first sister-in-law sat down on the veranda and instructed the servant who had carried my luggage to go and buy something. My new sister-in-law and the new maid were apparently preparing lunch for me. From the window I watched the small, aging body of my sister-in-law as she walked back and forth along the edge of the veranda.

Her hair was unkempt. I compared her to a withering chrysanthemum and felt sorry for her.

"It's quite strange that these three are living peacefully together," I thought.

As I sat bewildered, my brother seemed to want to say something but hesitated.

"It's been a year since your last visit?"

"I wasn't here last summer."

He lowered his voice. "Yes . . . you might have guessed, but you remember Mr. Ch'oe who lived in Ch'ŏngju?"

"Yes."

"His family is now in bad shape. He gambled away his considerable fortune. None of it remained when he passed away. The woman you just met is his second daughter. You must have seen her as a child?"

"I see—," I laughed inadvertently. Mr. Ch'oe, who had lived next door when I was young, had been one of the richest men not just in the town of Ch'ŏngju but in the whole province of Ch'ungch'ŏng. He was infamous for drinking and womanizing but no less famous for his bravado. When I entered elementary school, my so-called second sister-in-law was about as young as my brother's daughter, now playing around outside the room. I realized then why the old woman who was preparing my lunch in the kitchen had looked somewhat familiar.

"Then, isn't that Mrs. Ch'oe?" I asked, smiling, glad to recognize her.

My brother's face brightened up. "Right, um, didn't you used to go to their house to play?"

Then he looked at me. I felt a sharp sense of embarrassment. Mrs. Ch'oe had only daughters. When I would go over to her house as a child, she would fuss over me, saying things like "Oh, my son's here!" or "My son-in-law has come!"

"Kŭmsun, Kŭmsun! Who will you marry? Why don't you marry Inhwa?" My present sister-in-law would stare at me with her round eyes. At times she would say "Yes!" but at other times she became angry at the very suggestion of marriage. Since she was a year older than my sister, who was then still in school, she must have been two years younger than I was. I vaguely recalled her hanging around with me and my sister fourteen or fifteen years ago. My face reddened at the recollection. Since it was a childhood memory, she must have forgotten it, and my sister wouldn't remember, either. But when I thought that the old woman would recognize me and recall how she used to call me, in vain, her son or her son-in-law, I realized that I wouldn't have the nerve to face her. What strange ties we had. Since *yangban* still insisted on their distinction at the time, the adults in the two families did not visit each other much, and the Ch'oes might have talked nonsense with me but would not have dared to ask my parents to take their daughter. Yet Kŭmsun's mother, now my brother's mother-in-law, must then have been nurturing the idea of marrying off her second daughter to me. Thus I found it odd that she should have chosen my brother for her daughter, instead.

"I knew that Mr. Ch'oe had gone bankrupt after our move to Seoul," my brother began again, after a brief pause, "and last year he died of despair. But I didn't know just how miserable his family had become. This summer, when I went to Ch'ŏngju to try to settle the dispute over our ancestral land, I met Ch'oe's first son-in-law. He told me that his mother-in-law and sister-in-law were living with him. Since he had also failed in his business and was even about to give up his car, he had no idea how he would finance his sister-in-law's dowry. She was by then already well past marrying age. He insinuated that he wished me to lend him money. Later, when I visited father in Seoul, I happened to mention what he'd said . . . "

"You mean, Ch'oe's first son-in-law," I cut in, "Kim Hyŏnmuk, who married while we were still living there?" I pictured a youngster with a straw hat on.

"That's right! He was only twelve years old then, but now he's a sturdy grown man. And because he's very reliable, he has good credit in Choch'iwŏn. Father said lending him some money would be fine but suggested I also bring his sister-in-law home with me. At the time I let that suggestion pass. But later on, father went to meet Kim Hyŏnmuk and asked him to offer her to me, since I don't have a son yet. He asked him to sound out the girl's opinion on the match. Once father had broached the issue, Hyŏnmuk was, of course, completely willing, for all he really wanted was to create a bond between us. The girl's family didn't want to marry her to a man who already had a wife. But perhaps because they were in such dire straits at the time, and knew our family well, in the end, they gave their approval."

"What did mother and your wife think about it?"

"Father never really liked your first sister-in-law anyway. Mother at first objected, but eventually conceded, saying that it was better than receiving a grandson from a concubine. My wife herself, since she couldn't hope to bear any more children, just said that she'd obey my will. So I let things take their course."

I listened without replying. I had my doubts that having a son was such an exceedingly important matter. I'd never understood the old saying that having no heir was a sin to your ancestors and a disobedience to your parents. If a child is born, either by design or by chance, one should bring it up well, as others do their children. But why go to such lengths to bring a life into being? It seemed men were greater trouble-seekers than I'd realized. Even if you took the pains of having and nourishing a child, what benefit would you receive? Unless you happened to live longer than your own child, you'd have a son to follow your funeral procession. But who can tell what happens afterward? If the child turned out to be responsible, he would spend his life tilling the land inherited from his parents and eventually turn right back into dust; if he were not, he would squander the family fortune and ruin not only his own life but also those of his wife and children. And should he be at all gifted, he would suffer in solitude until he perished, without leaving so much as a footprint behind. He might even curse his fate and resent his parents for bringing him into this world. Perpetuating the species might be regarded as the natural instinct of any living being. But is preservation of the species any kind of reason for a man to marry?

Isn't there something in the human heart that speaks out more urgently than that? If my father, let alone my brother, had cherished his daughter-in-law like his own daughter, regardless of her failure to bear a son, he would not have needed to pressure his son to acquire a second wife! What did it mean to bear a son? What use was having offspring?

After following this train of thought, I said, "Why don't you bring my son from Seoul and let him live with you here? His mother is dying, and I'd prefer to be without the worry." I waited for my brother's reaction.

In handing over my son, I wanted to be relieved of the burden of raising a child. My brother seemed to interpret my words as a reproach, however, taking them to mean that he could have adopted an heir instead of committing the callous act of taking a second wife.

"Well, that remains an option, but when you think of the future, we'd better not do that. Besides, the Ch'oes' situation was so dire that I considered it as a way of saving a life. And so I decided to bring her home." My brother was trying to excuse his action. I knew that there was no need for further discussion, but the phrase "saving a life" rubbed me the wrong way. I spoke in Japanese so that those outside would not be able to overhear us.

"I'm afraid you're mistaken there, brother. If you decided to marry her in order to save her, then you overestimate yourself. And even if you did save her through marriage, you shouldn't take credit for it. As a matter of fact, such a consideration should only be of secondary importance. Whoever believes himself the sole means of salvation for a woman might harbor good intentions. Still, he overrates himself as something more than the imperfect mortal he truly is." As my brother made no attempt to reply, I spoke again. "True love lies in one's desire for a woman's happiness, not in one's intervention in her life or control of her destiny. Saying that a man can save another's life is conceited. Such an idea might sound beautiful at first, but it's really empty and meaningless."

My brother listened attentively, seemingly reflecting in silence on what I had said. Then he replied, looking at me with a smile, "If there's no such thing as saving someone in this world, you'd be the first to starve to death! And if you saw my child crawling into the well, wouldn't you rush to stop her?"

"I'd do it out of duty, not for praise." Irked by his gentle mockery of me, I raised my voice as I continued. "We observe what must and must not be done from a sense of duty. Educating one's child or holding a child back from the edge of a well is an act of carrying out one's obligations, not of charity. If someone prevents a man from committing suicide, the act of prevention is done neither from charity nor for that man's happiness. Rather, the act of preventing a suicide is an effort to assimilate those who deny life to one's own positive view on the universal matter of living. In the end, isn't it all just selfish? In any case, people only consider the notion of charity or saving someone in beautiful and rosy terms; in fact, such things are only evidence of a social illness. Strictly speaking, there is no word more arrogant than 'to save' and no act more hypocritical than charity. If one were to save anyone, saving oneself would be a more proper and pressing place to start."

My brother seemed to have something to say in response, but he just smiled, perhaps so as to mollify his younger brother, who had traveled a long way. Then he said in a mild tone, "How can anyone live in this world with such extreme views? Even if it were possible, there'd be no ideals left in this world, no purpose in life." He fell silent. His attitude had changed since our earlier conversation, when he had frowned at my studying literature.

"I've never thought about there being an ideal for human life. If there is any, it would be to live for oneself. But I don't mean this in a narrow sense."

At this reply, my brother looked at me for a moment and then lowered his head, as if thinking something over. I also grew quiet.

After we had eaten the lunch that had been so busily prepared for us, I rested a bit on the warmer side of the room. Soon I dozed off. When I awoke from a long nap, the room was darker; the sun appeared to be setting in the overcast sky. My brother left for the school after lunch, but he was back already and could be heard in the side room. As I asked for some water to brush my teeth, my brother came over to my room to see me.

"It might snow. How about having a drink before you leave?" He told the women outside to bring in a drink.

It was very unusual of my brother to ask me to have a drink with him. On his way back from school today he'd even bought a bottle of Japanese rice wine, which he himself did not usually drink. 'Is this supposed to be a substitute for the wedding banquet?' I smiled to myself at such a ridiculous notion. I filled my glass and enjoyed the wine. My brother forced himself to drink a few glasses in order to keep me company.

"When you go to Seoul this time," he said, after emptying his second glass, "stay at the house and oversee the drug prescriptions. Have things arranged so that you're in charge of everything."

I made no reply. In all honesty, I knew nothing about medications. He changed the topic again.

"I'll come as well in a few days, as soon as I can, but tell father that it'll be several days before I receive final approval for the burial site. It seems there's no way to get around the public cemetery law."

This struck me as strange. Even if my wife's death were a *fait accompli*, worrying about a hole to bury her in before she was actually dead seemed even more insensitive than marrying just to have a son. Nothing but the vanity of an idle mind.

"Why, are you afraid of not having a place to bury her? What difference does it make if she's cremated or buried at sea, or even buried in a public cemetery? Father worries about such insignificant things sometimes. In this hectic world," I said with a frown, "whether we should even bother with all this is something to consider."

"What's so insignificant?" My brother glared at me, then continued, "If you have any discretion at all, think about the situation we're in. Though we have to obey the Governor-General's new public cemetery law, what if one day our ancestral burial grounds should fall into someone else's hands, especially now when our parents don't have much time left to live? Can you imagine burying mother and father in a public cemetery? Even beyond the question of filial duty, think how shameful that would be. Your wife, too, should the unfortunate occur, will be buried up on the small hill. What a sight that would be to have the family buried all over the place!"

My brother looked furious. But I could not understand him in the least.

"So what will you do?" I laughed to myself.

"Whatever happens, since the governor of Ch'ungch'ŏng is an acquaintance of father's, and I'm no stranger to him either, I'll get permission first for mother and father on the small hill; and since nobody can tell what might happen with your wife, we'd better secure a spot for her now as well. What's more urgent, though, is to get the logging ban lifted for the large and middle hills, so that we can replant the trees before the next memorial ceremony for our ancestors. It's so messy over there, the graves all but naked. . . . "

I laughed inwardly at his description of the graves being *naked*.

"So that problem hasn't been settled yet?" I drank another glass.

"Far from being settled, the problem's getting more and more complicated, and I'm exhausted from trying to have it resolved. What should I do . . . " he frowned. "It's too late to track him down now and throw him in jail."

"That problem" referred to the fraudulent sale of the family burial grounds by our cousin, our third uncle's son, who had forged the deed. Although we were not the head family, we were the rightful owners—that is to say, the estate belonged to us. I had no idea how extensive the land was, but in any event, our cousin sold it all in order to pay back his gambling debt—all three hills, including a thick pine forest. Everything except for a few gravesites. The person who bought it had paid such a low price that he wasn't willing to rescind the contract no matter what was offered in return. If my brother wanted to fertilize the grounds and plant rice and barley, I couldn't care less, but I agreed that the contract should be repealed, if only to rectify the strained relationship between the two families.

"But we can revoke the contract, can't we?" I took another sip from my glass.

"If uncle were to agree to take the witness stand, we would likely recover the land for the original sum. But he insists on his ignorance, despite the fact that he himself was involved and knows about everything in detail. What should have been easily resolved has now gotten out of control."

"Then uncle knew about it?"

"That's why I say he's getting old. What's more, he even complains to me of all people, protesting that his son simply turned out bad, so it's out of his hands. Isn't that just preposterous?"

"Can't we solve things by taking him to court?"

"He packed up long ago, but nowadays it looks like he's back at home. The other day I visited his mother. She began whimpering, saying that he's a lost cause, that I should take him to prison or wring his neck if I felt like it, but that there's no use in visiting her house any more. It upsets me to think that his disappearance was nothing but a lie, and everyone has been plotting together to give me a hard time."

Our third uncle was my father's stepbrother. He and his sons had squandered his share of the family fortune and had been causing nothing but trouble ever since. Once our flippant uncle said to me, "What a sorry sight your brother is! What does he think will be solved by getting his cousin thrown in jail? Wouldn't it be simpler if he just paid up and bought the land back? Even if my son squanders the pittance he got for it, how much better-off will he be?" Since this kind of topic usually gave me a headache, I simply avoided talking about the matter. "What do I know? Talk to my brother."

I remembered that scene now. "Whatever happens, deal with things peacefully." I kept my silence after that.

After a dinner, I headed back to the station with my brother and his servant, who again carried my bags. It was already dark. On the main streets, which were speckled here and there with beaming electric lights, pedestrians had already grown scarce. The strong wind sprinkled my face with light clusters of snowflakes.

"There'll be quite a lot of snow on the ground tonight!" exclaimed my brother, who was walking ahead of me. Inside the station, the assistant policeman exchanged greetings with my brother, and although he looked me over with his eyes, did not allude to any investigation. After checking in my luggage, a Japanese office clerk, who happened to know my brother, invited us to his office. We went in and huddled around the stove. Two other clerks there turned to greet us.

"It's really cold, isn't it?" said the clerk who had called us in. "I see you're visiting for the winter vacation." He stood next to me and warmed himself. At times like this, I came to think that the Japanese were more polite than the Koreans. Even in the case of a policeman or gendarme, the Japanese are often more mild-mannered than their Korean counterparts. Where a Japanese policeman would just glare, a Korean policeman would often growl and get rough. The latter's psychology is similar to that of a child growing up with a stepmother. When two men in the same miserable condition meet, they sometimes sympathize with each other; yet the more one of them is embittered by his fate, and the more he hates himself, the more he takes out his hatred on the other without provocation. I wondered whether the attitude of Korean bureaucrats toward their own people was the result of a similar psychology.

While we were pleasantly conversing with the clerk, a young Korean station employee, thoroughly bundled up in a hooded raincoat, hurried in with a round glass lamp in his hand. He looked disconcerted.

"The signal light wouldn't turn on," he said in Japanese. The white snow on his raincoat slowly melted in the warmth of the room, turning into small beads of water.

The clerk, who had been amiably talking with me so far, glowered at the man. "Idiot! What do you mean it won't turn on? Time is almost up!" Then he shouted an order, half in Korean and half in Japanese, to another employee sitting in a far corner. "Mr. Yi, Mr. Yi, go and turn it on, hurry!"

I was surprised to see the sudden ferocity in the clerk's chubby face. The two Korean men lit another lamp and hurried out with it. After they left, the clerk calmed down again and looked at me with a broad grin.

"What an idiot!"

I smiled back, but in my head I was picturing the shadows of the two young men in the snowstorm outside as they scrambled up a signal pole. A short while later, the bell clanged a few times and the station employees returned. The clerk left us and set out to look through the luggage. We went out to the platform.

The traincar, unevenly lit by oil lamps, was dark and reeked of oil. At the thought of spending the night there, I regretted not having remained with my brother and catching an express tomorrow. But I soon abandoned this idea and took a seat in front of the stove. The traincar did not have many passengers. Around the stove sat several men from the country, who were shabbily dressed and wore oilpaper hat-covers, as well as a few men in Western suits. I was glad to spot a young girl who wore a purple Korean overcoat made of two-toned Japanese silk. She looked like a *kisaeng*. She sat on the other side some distance away but with her face turned in my direction. Most likely she had boarded at Taegu. I took out a magazine to pass the time but managed to read no more than a few pages in the dim light. On the other side, in the middle of the traincar, sat a gentleman about forty years old. His back was turned to the *kisaeng*. He reminded me of Counselor Kim, who at one time often came to my house. I could not tell whether the *kisaeng* was with him, but he looked well-off enough with his fine otter-fur coat and gold-rimmed glasses. He moved his cunning eyes from side to side behind his glasses, examining the faces of the other men in the traincar.

When the train reached Ch'up'ungnyŏng, a group of Japanese hunters boarded with two dogs. After putting down their rifles and untying their bullet belts, they gathered around the stove. I moved to the seat behind the *kisaeng* to avoid them. The other Koreans also got up one by one and moved away from the group.

"Sir! What are you doing here?" shouted someone out loud. I turned my head to look around. It was one of the men standing with his back to the stove. He had a pockmarked face, and a winter cap covered his head. He was holding a half-burnt cigar between his fingers. With his tattered safari jacket, heavy padded socks, and Korean straw shoes, he appeared to be one of the hunters. Indeed, he seemed to enjoy the highest rank among them, judging from how his companions made room for him in front of the stove. "Just what are *you* doing here?" responded Gold Rim, without getting up.

"I was out with the folks from the county office," Pockmark laughed, "but now it's snowing."

"At such a busy time? A hunting trip sounds a bit too genteel, ha ha ha. What if they cut your salary for neglect of duty?" Gold Rim assumed a condescending attitude.

"The season might be busy for someone like you, who's actually in the business of making money. But ever since I settled down in the countryside, things have been slow and easygoing. So where are you coming from now?"

"I went to Taegu and was detained by the governor . . . "

"Really? So how did it go?"

"What do you mean?" Gold Rim affected ignorance.

"Well, I mean that real estate case," said Pockmark. He blushed, his drunken face turning even more red.

"In fact, I went there to take care of the matter. The contract is sealed, but my business is still in trouble. . . . He wouldn't let me go for two days. Everyday he's with *kisaeng*, I really got fed up. He drinks like a fish. . . . "

"Really! Really!" replied Pockmark, with seeming admiration, even envy. "So are you heading now for Inch'ŏn?"

Gold Rim suddenly furrowed his eyebrows.

"That wasn't my intention originally. My man takes care of everything. By the way, is there any way you can work out that matter he talked to you about?" He lowered his voice and smiled in a friendly manner. "Why don't you give it a try? It won't be too difficult for you, and he'll see to it that it doesn't hurt your reputation."

"Well, I'll let you know how it all goes later, but the approval is half taken care of. That's all I can say for now."

Pockmark quickly glanced around. Their conversation was cut short, and Pockmark sat down on an empty seat nearby. It had sounded like an exchange of encoded messages, but I was able to follow it by and large. I was pleased to confirm my insight in having earlier compared Gold Rim with Counselor Kim.

Counselor Kim—I will never forget the time that I followed him to the army command headquarters in Chin'gogae. My family was still living in the countryside at the time. After graduating from elementary school, I went to Seoul, where I commuted between Counselor Kim's house and my junior high school. He had just moved back with his wife after living at his concubine's place for some time. His room and mine faced each other across the yard. The incident in question took place during a rainy afternoon in late August, when the air began to smell like autumn. As I was about to enter the house on my way back from school, the Counselor's wife rushed out with a troubled expression on her face. She immediately took my books from me.

"Kyŏngsik's father was just arrested! They took him in that direction. Please go and run after them!" She looked confused. Surprised myself, I dashed out in the indicated direction and soon found Counselor Kim in a ramie Korean overcoat being dragged away by two men in Western suits. My heart was pounding, but I continued to follow them from a distance.

This was his second arrest. A few months before, soon after I enrolled at the new school (and just a few days after Counselor Kim had left his concubine and returned home), a policeman dropped in to collect a public hygiene tax, or maybe a garbage collecting tax.

"How can I pay money I don't have? If you really want to, take me instead!" Counselor Kim cursed and yelled at the policeman, and when the policeman did actually try to escort him out, he planted his feet firmly on the threshold of his house in resistance.

"You bastard, you're killing me! Ow, he's killing me!" He was cursing louder and worse than the policeman. When he was later dragged away, I trailed behind to find out where they were taking him. That day, I believed Counselor Kim was the most honorable man on earth. In my rural hometown, I had been taught to fear officers as the most terrifying of men; they were men who carried sabers, beat people up, and arrested whomever they pleased. But Counselor Kim had just hurled names at such one dreaded officer. He said all he wanted to say, and even gave him orders as if to his own servant.

"Wait right there! We'll see who's wrong!" He went back inside and undertook a lengthy process of preparation; he changed his clothes, applied litharge mixed with oil to his shin, which had been scraped during the struggle at the gate. He left with an elated spirit, leading the way. As a young boy, I was thrilled at the sight. I scorned the policeman, who had at first seemed such an imposing figure, and revered a man whom I had previously spurned. Moreover, after following them to the police station, I watched in amazement as Counselor Kim exchanged a few words with somebody inside and then walked out with a grin on his face. I marveled at the influence he had.

But this time, as he was dragged off by the two men in Western suits, he hung his head in silence, like a dog on a leash. They vanished behind a big blue door guarded by soldiers on either side. Too terrified to go closer, I hurried back to make a full report to his family. From that day forward, Kyŏngsik and the family's head servant busied themselves with delivering him three meals a day. About two weeks later, Counselor Kim returned home. At that moment, the look in his pale face did not appear at all honorable. Even I could guess what had happened to him. Strangely, after his release, he behaved as if he had suddenly become rich: he bought some new Western suits, invited his estranged concubine to live together with him and his wife, and returned home drunk every night, sometimes with rips in his new clothes. After about a month, he said he'd bought a house and land in the countryside and moved away from the city with his wife and concubine. Only then did it become clear why Counselor Kim, who had more than held his own against the first dreaded officer, had been as docile as a dog on a leash two months later.

Before I left for Japan, I heard that he had founded a village school and become a principal; later, that he had moved to a nearby town and was running a rice-cleaning mill. When I came home for a vacation, I learned that he had lost his entire fortune in Inchŏn and moved in with another concubine. At the mention of a trip to Inchŏn and a real estate contract, I could picture to myself the possibility that the gentleman wearing a fine coat and gold-rimmed glasses might also have once been arrested, returned to his native village, run a rice mill, and now become involved in rice speculation in Inchŏn.

"And will he soon, too, be taking care of funeral arrangements?"

I laughed to myself and looked back at Gold Rim one last time.

When the train pulled into Yŏngdong Station, the hunters got off and a group of new passengers swarmed in. A few peddlers also got on and clambered around to find seats, talking loudly with one another.

"Will the market be open tomorrow with all this snow? I don't know how much I lost today alone. . . . "

"Stop whining! No one's going to steal your junk. Ha, ha, ha."

Every time the train stopped, a policeman and an assistant gendarme stepped on, one after the other, to make a quick inspection. Then the train began to move again.

In front of me sat a rural man, who looked about thirty years old. He was wearing an oilpaper hat-cover over a Korean top hat and carried an umbrella with a towel tied around its handle. He crushed some tobacco leaves and stuffed his pipe with them. He then put his hand into his Korean overcoat and searched through all his pockets, until he finally spotted a matchbox lying in front of me.

"May I, for a second . . . " he asked, looking up at me. The hesitant manner with which he nodded toward the matchbox was incongruous with the dignity of his hat. He must have taken me for Japanese. I passed the matchbox over to him with a smile.

After lighting his pipe, he nodded once again and gave the matchbox back to me. As if relieved, he looked at my face for a while and then smiled.

"Why don't we introduce ourselves?" said he in Korean.

A rather reckless fellow, I thought. Yet I complied with his suggestion.

After the introduction, he blew a few intense, toxic puffs of smoke.

"Where are you coming from?" he asked.

"From Kimch'ŏn," I answered, looking at his sun-burnt face, his protruding cheekbones, and his thick, widely parted lips.

"Is that your hometown?"

"Yes—"

"But you don't have the accent?"

". . ."

He also fell quiet, as if wearied. Then he addressed me again.

"What school do you go to? You're coming from Japan, aren't you?"

"How did you guess?" I smiled.

"Ah, those who wear suits like yours come from Japan," he smiled knowingly, glancing at the golden badge, visible above my collar, on the lapel of my school uniform.

I changed the topic. "What do you do for a living?"

"Well—, I sell Korean hats."

"Traditional Korean hats? Do they sell well nowadays?"

"So-so. People still wear them in the countryside."

That was news to me. The conversation tailed off for a while.

"Why don't you get a haircut?" I asked. "It's not just that the times have changed. Isn't it a bit of a hassle? Costly, too."

"No, actually. In the countryside, it's getting a haircut that's more troublesome. And more expensive. If you want to cut your hair, you must first know how to speak Japanese and have some knowledge of current affairs. If a person has short hair but can't speak Japanese, he's likely to be harassed even worse by officials and policemen. But if his hair is worn up in a traditional topknot, they let minor offenses pass, because he's just a *yobo*. So doesn't it make more sense not to get a haircut?"

He uttered a hoarse laugh. I found his reasoning sensible and sympathized with him, but I continued arguing to see how he would respond.

"But Koreans in Western clothes are treated differently among Koreans. You'd get more respect from them if you cut your hair. And how much longer do you want to bow under their sneers and be called a '*yobo*,' anyway?"

"When they sneer or call me '*yobo*,' the bad feeling lasts for just a moment. But if I have my hair cut, wear a fedora hat, and carry around a walking stick, I'd be harassed everywhere I go. I'd get roughed up if anything goes wrong, and I'd be staring at the prison walls at least once a month! People like you are at least fluent in Japanese. But people like me, if we get beaten, there's nothing we can do. Ha ha ha."

No respect is worth a beating! No wonder, then. To win the favor of the Japanese, it's better to pretend to be a lunatic. Or to act like a child or a sycophant. If you can make them laugh, that removes the immediate pressure at least. Though they might call you names behind your back, if they have smiles on their faces, you're safe from trouble for the time being. Carelessness, hypocrisy, subservience, cowardice . . . to be well versed in these arts is the most salutary way of living for Koreans and the smartest way to get on in this world. If Koreans have an insidious character, it's not their fault. It's the fault of conventional politics. The Japanese say that swindling is the most prevalent crime among Koreans, but it, too, can be ascribed to the same cause. . . .

As I was immersed in such thoughts, the man glanced around cautiously and then began to speak again. "At any rate, as long as they treat us as their equals, we'll go on living, no matter what might happen later." The man looked around again and lowered his voice further. "Take the example of the public cemetery law. If Japan had the same law, we would observe it regardless of our own preference. You would know, probably, is there a law like that in Japan?"

The man had unexpectedly referred to the new public cemeteries. I found it odd that this issue had come up again, after my brother had already given me a long lecture on it. When the law had passed and how it was to be enforced were none of my concern, and I couldn't have cared less about its consequences. Yet it seemed to be a hot topic everywhere. I checked my impulse to laugh his words away.

"The Japanese do have public cemeteries."

Also afraid of being overheard, I glanced at a suspicious-looking Japanese man who was lying down in a dark corner behind us, his coat pulled up so as to reveal nothing but a hat with a gold braid on its brim. I also looked at the man in a Western suit who had been following me since Kimch'ŏn. I was by no means denouncing the Governor-General's policy, but the possibility of a misunderstanding made me nervous.

"Are there public cemeteries in Japan? Then the rich must still go and do things differently."

"There is a difference, but in Japan cremation is rather popular, and so it's only the leftover bones from the fire that get buried. They usually choose one bone to bury, such as the Adam's apple, and use a piece of wood or a slab for the gravestone. Land is very scarce there already, even for the living, and so every inch is as precious as gold. If the dead were given spacious lots, this world would soon turn into one huge graveyard." I laughed but became thoughtful as I spoke—who was getting all the land freed up by the tight control over graveyards?

The man nodded, seemingly agreeing with what I said, but he had an objection.

"But how can someone burn his parents, wife, or children right away, even if they are dead? Besides, for an ancestral ground that has been inherited generation after generation. . . . "

"What's wrong with cremation? In ancient times, in a country called Egypt, the corpses of kings and ministers were embalmed and put into wooden coffins, which were then put into solid stone cases that were themselves stored in huge caves called 'pyramids.' But now they're nothing but mummies. So what good was it to have a corpse adorned in fine damask and brocade and buried over hundreds of acres? What's the use of setting up a bronze statue or a monument?"

Some of the details I'd mentioned were apparently lost on the peddler, who looked puzzled.

"What did you say? What's a mummy?"

"A mummy is the corpse of a man that's been petrified after hundreds of years of preservation. I don't know if the Korean Museum has a mummy, but the Imperial Museum in Japan has one."

"Wow! Is there really such a thing?"

"Come to think of it, how vain a man's life is. If I'm buried in the earth, my flesh will disintegrate into various elements. Some will wander though the atmosphere. Others will be inhaled through the mouths and nostrils of my children, grandchildren, and great grandchildren, turn into their bones and blood, and swim out again in their excrement. Meanwhile, my bones, all broken in pieces after hundreds of years, might end up in a museum and roll around in the hands of geologists, physiognomists, and anthropologists. Isn't it foolish and idle, then, to be concerned about where to be buried, when you ought to be worrying about how to keep your belly full?"

I made a litany to the stranger of all the complaints that I had wanted to communicate to my brother. Afterward I felt a bit embarrassed. My talk seemed to have attracted the attention of others. The *kisaeng* behind me, for instance, turned around and seemed to be listening attentively to what must have been incomprehensible to her.

"I don't know," said the peddler, unconvinced. "You, too, must have parents. What will you do with them?"

"I'll take things as they come," I smiled and then grew silent.

"Isn't the custom of caring for our parents and ancestors a good thing?"

I had meant to remain silent, as there was no use wasting more breath on the matter, but I decided to make one more reply so as to prevent any misunderstanding.

"Who said it's bad? Of course, we should care for our parents and ancestors. But you can't say that organizing a grand funeral and building a luxurious tomb reflects filial piety. Looking after an ancestor's grave is a good thing, but it isn't necessary to add frills on top of that. If you were to decorate your grandparents' graves for the sake of your parents, and your great grandparents' for your grandparents' sake, why not also do the same with the graves of ancestors ten generations back for the sake of the five generations up the line? And then why not also take care of graves a hundred generations back for those ten generations in turn? Do you even know where your first ancestor's grave is? In the end, we care more for those who are close to us and visit their graves more often than other ones. All we need is to find some way of expressing our innermost feelings, isn't it? It would even be alright if you choose not to express them but to hold onto them in your heart."

"I don't know," the peddler grinned. I finished my speech but felt somewhat ungratified. Perhaps it was indiscreet to have started such a dispute with a hat peddler. I felt ashamed to think how others might have laughed at me had they overheard our conversation.

We were silent as the train arrived at Simch'ŏn Station. A police inspector strutted through the quiet traincar and inspected its few passengers. Then a Korean assistant gendarme, a short man in baggy khaki pants, came on board. He was wearing a long saber that extended almost down to his boots. All eyes focused on this small man in a khaki jacket. The man's slit eyes were opened wide as he slowly walked by, checking every face along his path. He was apparently looking for someone. My heart went cold for no particular reason, but soon I felt more at ease, reminded of the fact that there was already a detective trailing me. The traincar was silent except for the shuffling of the gendarme's ungainly boots. But people were trembling inwardly, like the flares of a lamp flickering in the darkness. As the gendarme passed by one passenger after another, the face of each lit up in a sign of relief. Some passengers even let out a deep sigh. The sound of the gendarme's footsteps approached nearer and nearer. I sat still with my back turned, while the hat peddler opposite me, holding his pipe in one hand, was staring straight at the gendarme's face. The sound of footsteps came to a halt at my seat. My heart missed a beat. I inadvertently looked up at him. But he ignored me and looked down at the peddler for a moment. Then he unfolded a piece of paper. I felt as if my throat was finally cleared of whatever had been blocking it.

"You, what's your name?"

"Me? I'm Kim—," the peddler answered, scrambling to his feet.

"Did you mail Korean hats from Yŏngdong?"

"Yes."

"Then let's get off for a moment."

The deathly silence in the traincar was at last broken. Whispers were heard here and there. My conversation partner hurried off the train, followed by the gendarme.

After he stepped out, I noticed his old umbrella standing perched against the edge of his chair. I pushed open the window and shouted after him into the darkness outside, but he had already vanished. . . . I gave the umbrella to a station worker, who had gotten on to put more coals in the stoves. He asked in broken Japanese whose it was. Sensing that he was a fellow countryman, I replied in Korean. But he asked again in Japanese, "What?" pretending not to have understood me—I was speechless.

The train arrived at Taejŏn past noon. The gentleman who resembled Kim got off, followed by the man who had been sitting in front of him carrying a large leather suitcase with a blanket tied to it. The *kisaeng* remained seated.

I asked a janitor how long the stop would be. He yelled "Thirty minutes" and then rushed away. I was so bored that I put on my hat and listlessly made my way down to the platform. The snow on the ground had increased by more than several inches. In response to the light but chilling wind, I hugged my shoulders close, like a turtle pulling in its head. In the last car, two young men with milky smooth faces, who were wearing winter hats and narrow-sleeved turquoise Korean overcoats, were talking and laughing with a gendarme in a khaki uniform. Judging from the resemblance in their facial features, the two men seemed to be brothers, and the gendarme was obviously Japanese, as a black gun strap was hanging across his chest. I walked up to the window out of curiosity. The three whispered something, all of them smiling. But the awkwardness of the young men's smiles—their lips twisted up as if frozen in place—painted a portrait of fear. I turned around, went to the wooden ticket gate, and, without hesitating, pushed it open with my hands. Beyond the gate stood a group of people around a stove in the middle of an open-air waiting area. Snow swirled freely about them. "If they have to wait outside like this, wouldn't it be much better simply to let them board right away?" I glanced around the stove and saw several criminals sitting on wooden chairs and bound to each other by ropes. There were a few policemen standing guard at their sides. I was surprised to find among them a young woman with disheveled hair. Her filthy Korean clothes were tousled loose. Unabashed, she looked at me enviously for a moment, then dropped her head. On her back slept a baby. I felt as if my heart had been pierced. My legs were giving way underneath me. The whole sight seemed to evoke the faint memory of a scene I had once seen, perhaps in a book. I wondered whether I was dreaming.

I left the station and walked down a broad street, snow crunching under my feet. I could not even make out the way to the diner where I had bought lunch seven years ago, on the very day of my first journey to Japan. The houses lining both sides of the street apparently belonged to the Japanese, though I couldn't see them well in the dark. I stood a while, watching the cart of a Japanese noodle vendor, whose loud bells, with their melancholy sounds, disturbed the serenity of the night air.

As I returned to the station's waiting area, I wondered about the whereabouts of the thirty-odd-year-old woman who had owned the old diner. The passengers, who had been sitting quietly and motionless, as if frozen solid, looked up at my face as I approached, my shoulders hunched. The bound woman looked at me again. Even the policeman next to her was a pitiful sight. As I passed back through the wooden gate, I saw that the two young men and the gendarme were still talking. Suddenly, my heart swelled with sadness, sending a quiver through my body. All my memories seemed like a dream, and everything I laid eyes on looked forlorn. I was on the verge of tears. As I climbed up the stairs to the traincar, anger surged within me.

"What kind of life is this?" I cried out loud. "Let them all drop dead!"

I bit my lips upon entering the traincar.

"This is a grave. A grave full of maggots!" I threw my hat onto the seat and warmed myself in front of the stove. The stove had heated up considerably. A red flame, flickering like a snake's tongue, shone through the slit of the stove door. It was still chilly in the traincar, though hazy with smoke and ash. The dim lamps kept vigil over the people curled up asleep underneath them. The light seemed to be silently pressing down on the passengers with its ponderous weight.

"This is a public cemetery!" I thought, quickly looking around. "A cemetery overrun by maggots!"

This train might as well be a public cemetery. They don't want to be buried in a cemetery, because they are already living in one. It's a grave swarming with maggots. Everyone is a maggot. You and I are all maggots. Even inside the grave, the evolutionary process continues, not losing one minute! There will be natural selection and the struggle for survival, while we snarl in competition against one another. Each of these maggots will soon disintegrate into elements, turn into earth, seep into my mouth and your nose, and when you and I die, soon enough we too will become maggots, we too will turn into elements, into earth. Let's all go to hell! Be wiped out, leave no roots behind! Be ruined, utterly! If we could only be over and done with, maybe then something better might grow. . . .

I went back to my seat and lay down before the train set off again. I lay with my eyes closed, every now and then breathing in the scent of the *kisaeng*'s hair and the fragrance of her oil and powder, which wafted over the seat and enticed my nose.

"This, too, is the smell of rotting maggots."

Despite this thought, I did not attempt to cover my nose. The train started to move. Soon, I was asleep.

After a restless sleep, I opened my eyes and found that it was broad daylight outside. The night had ended. I drew up close to the stove to warm my chilled body. I asked the person beside me where we were and was told that the train had just departed from Sihŭng.

I'm almost in Seoul! I could not help feeling glad. When the train crossed the iron bridge over the Han river, past Yŏngdŭngp'o, I stretched my muscles and looked out at an icy, abandoned field, on which there seemed to lie a lattice of cracked marble. At Yongsan Station, the *kisaeng* stood and tidied herself up, as if preparing to get off, but then hesitated and cast a meaningful glance at me. She sat down again, as the train whistled its departure. I suspected that she remained on board not because she was going to Seoul, but because she felt uneasy at there being no familiar faces in sight. As I retrieved my luggage from the shelf and returned to my seat, she followed my movements with her eyes. She seemed on the verge of saying something but did not open her lips. I wanted to speak first, since she seemed to have something she needed to ask, perhaps directions to somewhere in Seoul. Out of respect for my college cap and uniform I kept quiet.

The train arrived at Namdaemun. My eldest uncle's son, whom my family had dispatched to meet me, was waiting with a rickshaw and helped me with my bags. I could still see the *kisaeng* standing in the distance, alone and confused in front of the wooden gate at the exit. But then my rickshaw changed direction from south to north.

6

The snow had continued through the night and was now over ten inches deep. The rickshaw man was pulling with all his might, but the wheels turned with difficulty. The winds sweeping down from Mount Pugak needled my toes and the end of my nose. My eyes were teary and my glasses fogged up. The streets were empty except for occasional passers-by, most likely servants from various taverns. With their hands tucked under their arms and their overcoats as black as a chimney sweeper's shirt, they hurried toward the Namdaemun market, each carrying a large round wicker basket. Lanterns shone from eavesdrops with a tired, misty light. The rickshaw man continued to breathe heavily, the rickshaw rattling on the well-trodden snow.

Glad to be back after a year's absence, I stayed on the lookout for various places in the city. Then a pale, haggard face appeared in my mind.

"She must be waiting for me, her undeserving husband."

All of a sudden, I remembered the face of the Taegu *kisaeng*, her oval, dark-skinned face, her pleading eyes full of insecurity.

"Where is she wandering now? I should have spoken to her!" I recalled with regret how lost she had looked at the station, searching for a familiar face. "But what good would it have done to talk to her? Those who must leave should leave right away, and those who are to perish should perish sooner than later."

As I was sitting absent-mindedly, oblivious to the cold, the rickshaw rode right past the gateway to my neighborhood. I had the rickshaw man turn back, despite his protests, and got off.

My family was already up and waiting for me.

"Your studies may be important, but you should have come back by now."

My mother's voice was already choking up.

"Still, it's fortunate that you'll get to see her before she passes away," she said, bursting into tears. My elder sister, who had been living in the house since her husband died, was also crying. So was my younger sister. My cousin's wife, who had been watching from the yard, turned away and appeared to pull her apron up to her nose. My father, though, came over to greet me and received my bow without losing his composure.

"Is there a funeral going on? Why are you all crying?" I used to be annoyed at my mother's annual tears upon my return. My wife would hide in her room and also weep quietly. I had never understood the reason for their tears. Sometimes, in solitary moments, tears would well up in my own eyes, but when I saw others crying, I felt like laughing or had nothing to say.

"How is she?" I asked my mother.

"So-so, come and see her." My mother led me from her room to my wife's.

"My dearest . . . your husband is here. Look, your husband's back from Japan. . . . "

The patient woke up from a deep sleep. She looked at her mother-in-law's face, then stared at me by her side. She seemed to force herself to form a smile on her dark, parched lips. But she quickly turned away, as tears clouded over her eyes. Her chest was heaving under a thick blanket, and she sobbed bitterly.

"Stop crying, come now, you'll get better."

Even as she tried to comfort the patient, my mother also started to sniffle and had to leave the room. The room, which had long been turned into a patient's ward, was protected with a windscreen. The place reeked of feces and urine. I felt nauseous at the foul smell, mixed with the odor of medications, my stomach already upset from the overnight train ride. But I could not simply leave, so I sat down next to her.

"Don't cry. It's bad for your health."

I managed to say this much but then just sat by idly. I didn't know how to console her any more.

"Chunggi, did you see Chunggi?" she asked in a feeble voice. She wiped away her tears and looked at me. When I saw her hand receive a towel from the servant girl at her bedside, I finally felt some pity for her. Her wasted, bony hand was trembling slightly.

Is that the plump hand I used to adore, the same hand that used to touch my body? The thought made me frown.

" . . . I'm, I'm dying . . . But, but, Chunggi . . . "

Her frail voice broke off. She seemed to want to speak out loud but couldn't. Having little strength left, she simply shed tears instead.

"Don't talk like that. Who says you're dying? If you just stay calm, you'll soon feel better."

"I don't want to live any longer . . . Please, look after our boy," she said, sobbing again. "It's for his sake alone that I'm trying to live one, one more day . . . " She managed to utter this much aloud, but her voice kept choking up until it trailed off entirely.

I was at a loss for a reply. I found her concern for our child in her last hours poignant, and yet at the same time melodramatic. It was getting hot. To be honest, since I did not want to stay any longer, I told her again not to cry and then went over to my mother's room, where I changed out of my Japanese clothes and into Korean ones. The clothes were warm since my mother had spread them out on the heated floor. On his way back to his room my cousin told me, "Your father wants to see you." This cousin, the firstborn son of my eldest uncle, had lived in this house for forty years without lifting a finger, thanks to his status as the head family's heir. That he still didn't have a child was a matter of great concern in the family.

I went over to the guestroom to see my father and was surprised to find Counselor Kim sitting there as well. He reminded me of Gold Rim in the train yesterday. Since when has he been staying here again?

I went in and greeted him.

"How have you been? How worried you must be!" Counselor Kim, with a long pipe in his mouth, had taken to putting on genteel airs even more than before.

"Have a seat there," said my father. Soon as I sat down, he began to tell me in detail about my wife's illness: what kinds of medicine had led to what changes, how effective a certain syrup had been, what had gone wrong, how her condition had taken a turn for the worse, and so on. I did not grasp all of the details. I listened to him in silence.

"It would have been better," I ventured after waiting for him to finish, "had she had the tumor removed early on at the Government-General Hospital."

My reply angered my father. "What do those Western doctors know? Your brother said the same thing, so I told him if I'm going to lose her, I'd rather have her die under my own care . . . " I said nothing further.

Back in my mother's room, I sat down for breakfast, which had just been prepared.

"Why is Counselor Kim here again?" I asked my mother.

"He's been here quite a while, ever since he lost his house and had to give up his concubine."

"What about his wife's house?"

"When did he ever care about his family? Besides, she now lives in a rented room at someone else's place. He drinks everyday and is quite a nuisance." My mother frowned.

"Then why did you let him in?" After my initial admiration for him had passed, I had really begun to dislike the sight of him.

"What do you mean why did I let him in? Your father thinks there's not a better man alive. If anyone says anything, your father yells like the devil and insists on dining alone with him . . . "

It turned out that Counselor Kim had moved into a house that belonged to a certain Viscount Sŏ, who had played a considerable role in the Annexation as a member of the cabinet. After Sŏ's death last summer, though, Counselor Kim was apparently driven out of the house. He did take over Sŏ's affairs, but that meant little more than supervising funerals.

"Not only that, but he was just in prison," said my sister, who had been busy at her desk preparing for exams that were only a few days away. "He was released only the day before yesterday . . . wearing a *morning coat*." She burst into laughter.

"Really? What for?" I asked, laughing.

"Who knows? Two weeks ago, he was caught at a restaurant in the middle of the night by the vagabond patrol. He just got back." She continued to giggle.

While laughing with her, I remembered the incident of my following him to army headquarters. I wondered who had followed him this time.

"You, too, don't you go out at night," warned my mother. "The vagabond patrol has become quite strict lately."

"Why? I'm not a vagabond." I turned to my sister, "So, what did he say when he got back?"

"Father says he was arrested because someone informed on him, but cousin says they were rounding up everyone at all the restaurants. He said Kim boasted about how he defied the Minister of State Affairs," she giggled. "What a crazy man!"

"How can you call someone else's husband crazy? It's you who's crazy!"

After chiding my sister, my mother left the room. But then she saw the maid coming out of another room carrying Chunggi, who had just awakened. My mother returned with the baby.

"Now, look at daddy. Daddy's come home. How long has it been?"

My mother gently rocked the baby in her arms and then held him out to me. The little lump of flesh still seemed to smell of blood. Shivering, his arms curled up, the tiny baby was cold despite his quilt. He turned his pale, emaciated face toward me and soon after started crying.

"Why does he look so ugly?" I frowned and looked away.

"What's the matter? Isn't he cute? Babies look like that at three months . . . But then he also drank very little of his mother's breast milk. His nanny left after only a month, so he's being fed now only on cow's milk."

The baby, once he had started crying, showed no sign of stopping. His crying even began to get worse. He threw the room into a commotion by flailing, kicking, and hoisting his belly up and down. His pale face turned ashen.

"Oh, what a racket!" My sister closed the book she had been reading and, frowning, left the room. I, too, pushed the table aside and went to the outer quarters. I was lying in a side room, smoking, when a strange young man came looking for me. He said that he had just been transferred from his previous assignment to the Honmachi station and that he would be in charge of keeping track of me.

"You won't be staying long, will you? I won't be following you all the time. I'll just drop in occasionally. But if you do go past the city gates, or travel to the countryside somewhere, please notify the local police office." He repeated his request, as if doing me a favor, and then took his leave. I told him to do as he wished.

7

I passed a few idle days at home. My father was always busy with something. Everyday he went out with Kim after breakfast and came back drunk at dusk, sometimes accompanied by a group of friends. My cousin claimed that the reason for all this was the upcoming annual general assembly of the Tonguhoe.

"Why does he insist on going to the meeting? Especially after I begged him not to get involved? Those people are all half crazy, always quarrelling or hatching some new plot. Why can't father see that Kim is only dragging him along so that he can get the better of him and eat up all his money?"

"How do I know? He goes because he wants to get a title. Maybe he thinks he'll become the Vice Counselor of the Chunggu district."

"That post was abolished long ago. And even if it were still available, why would he want it? It's so frivolous."

"But Kim promised to campaign for your father's election to some position."

"Idiot! How can Kim get someone a position he can't obtain for himself? Unless he wants to go back to jail."

"But Kim says that he's on the closest terms with the Governor-General and the Minister of State Affairs."

"What's closest to his heart is his scheme to flatter father enough that he'll buy him a house to replace Sŏ's."

"I see . . . "

The Tonguhoe was an ostentatious fraternity between Japanese and Koreans, in which some aristocrats and their entourage of swindlers gathered to waste time on chess and late-night drinking parties. The fraternity's only real business was to sponsor *kisaeng* concerts and supervise the funerals of so-called personages.

"I'm too busy to look after the medicine right now," said my father, on the morning of the day of my arrival. "You stay home during the day and take care of everything."

As I did not have any particular place I wanted to visit (not that I had nowhere to go), I found myself always lying around at home with my cousin, drinking in the evening and passing the time in the outer quarters during the day. My father was entirely preoccupied with that spurious organization. I visited my sick wife once or twice a day, but she seemed to get neither better nor worse. When the doctor came, he would examine her pulse and write a prescription, which my cousin took right away to have filled. My wife apparently took whatever concoction was given to her. Only my mother still seemed to care. The other family members were exhausted and wearied by the protracted illness; their daily routine consisted merely of serving my wife medicine. I was not in any position to control the situation, since I had no clue about the mysteries of medicine.

"Wouldn't it be good," my mother once complained, "if your father would quit that blasted organization and do something to get better medicine."

On some days, my mother would catch my father on the way back from his daily visit to his daughter-in-law's room and ask him in a reproachful tone, "Are you going out again? Something seems to be wrong with her since last night . . . "

"I might be a bit late today! She didn't seem any different," he would make such a curt reply and take his leave. Whether my wife actually got better or worse, her outward appearance remained, in fact, more or less the same. A few more dreary days passed by.

I wish it would be over soon! Whenever this thought entered my head, it was always followed by an image of Shizuko.

"What's she doing now? Has she really gone to Kyoto?" A week after my return, I decided to send her a postcard.

On the day I mailed the postcard, I visited Pyŏnghwa, partly to see if Ŭlla had arrived in the meantime. During our school days in Tokyo, Pyŏnghwa used to act as my supervisor. For a while he had remained on fairly close terms with me, but ever since Ŭlla had come between us, we drifted apart. If we happened to come across one another, it was like scratching an old wound, and we both felt awkward. He was my cousin's stepbrother, but since the two weren't on good terms with each other, he visited my parent's house only once or twice a year.

I got off the streetcar at Tongdaemun. Stumbling down the street, which was muddy from the melted snow, I took pleasure in seeing the old, familiar places. I used to visit this neighborhood everyday last summer. I hardly let a day pass without taking Ŭlla and Pyŏnghwa's wife out on the streets of Seoul, whether in the daytime or at night. It was then that I visited a Buddhist nunnery in T'apkol with Ŭlla, Pyŏnghwa, and his wife. More than once they detained me at their place, making excuses for the late hour, and sometimes I would be persuaded to stay for a few days.

What a fool I was then!

I walked in the footprints of others, taking care to step only on dry ground. Layers of snow covered the fallow vegetable field, the thickets that served as a living fence were leafless and dry, and the straw ropes between them were black and rotted. In those days, this fence was a tangle of zucchini and cucumber bines and dangling yellow flowers.

After passing a brickwork pavilion, which probably belonged to a newly titled aristocrat, I walked about a hundred meters along a narrow alley till I came upon a cliff on the right.

"Ah, that's where I used to bathe myself, where Ŭlla and I would frolic on moonlit nights, splashing water at each other." I looked below the rocks. It was as if the brook had run dry, and the surface was covered with a white, glazed-over snow.

"When did you get here? I heard you'd returned and wanted to come over, but work kept me busy . . . " Pyŏnghwa rushed out to welcome me. He was wearing a Western suit and seemed to have returned home himself just a few moments ago. I followed him into the room and sat down on the warm side of the floor.

Pyŏnghwa's wife, who held a newborn baby in her arms, also warmly greeted me. She sat down opposite me. "How's your wife?"

"She'll live if she doesn't die. She gave birth. Something lost, something gained," I laughed.

"Heavens, you say such horrible things sometimes."

"Well, has she gotten any better? It would have been better had she received an operation from a Western doctor first and then been treated with Oriental medicine. . . . I suggested this once, but your father seemed affronted at the mere thought, so I gave up. I don't want to poke my nose in where I'm not wanted . . . "

"I'm also letting him have his way. It's useless to argue with him now. I leave things as they are so that he won't be able to say I caused troubles over my wife. But she won't last long."

"Are you inviting evil?" Pyŏnghwa's wife furrowed her eyebrows, though without altering her quiet smile. After briefly discussing my wife's condition, I looked at her for a moment.

"By the way, Ŭlla hasn't come by here yet, has she?"

"No. Why? Is she back?" She smiled, studying my face. Pyŏnghwa pretended not to have heard my question and got up to change his clothes.

"No, I was just wondering if she'd come back."

"No," she said, still smiling affably. She turned her eyes to the baby in her arms. It seemed to me that she was lying.

"When I visited her at Kobe on my way back," I said, also smiling, "she insisted that we leave together, but I turned down her proposal. She told me then that she planned to leave within a few days."

"I see—," she looked at me for a while. "Why did you drop by her place when you were in such a hurry?"

"I was bored, and I also wanted to report the local news to Pyŏnghwa." I grinned nonchalantly. She laughed at my absurdity.

"You're funny," Pyŏnghwa added, also smiling. Having changed his clothes, he returned to his seat. He tried to change the subject.

"Why don't you have someone go and buy something delicious?"

"Oh, but I'm leaving soon . . . By the way, do you remember last year?" Out of spite I started to talk again about Ŭlla with Pyŏnghwa's wife. He blushed and forced a smile. I, too, felt my face turning red.

Pyŏnghwa looked at me and smiled, "You've changed a lot."

He seemed to find it strange and somewhat disconcerting that I, who used to blush whenever someone mentioned anything even remotely related to Ŭlla, should so tactlessly, and in such a casual manner, continue to dwell on her now.

Pyŏnghwa's wife seemed to be lost in thought for a while, perhaps picturing a scene from last year, when she had been anxious for the two of us.

"So, are her studies going well?" she asked.

"She's still the same." I picked up my hat and got up.

"Wait a bit longer. Let's have a drink. I've got a good bottle of liquor. Or should we go out somewhere for a drink?"

"Where did you get the liquor? Ah yes, you added a new name to the family registry this fall. Isn't it the proper thing for you to treat me to a drink?" I laughed, and Pyŏnghwa happily joined in my laughter as well.

"Anyhow, please stay and sit down. Someone gave me a bottle of Western liquor . . . " Pyŏnghwa said, without my asking. In fact, the baby's birth seemed to have brought with it new things for the house. A Western coat rack stood at one corner of the room, and a new watch hung on a gold chain over Pyŏnghwa's vest. He seemed far better off than he had been formerly, when he used to lie alone on his bed in a tiny boarding room and secretly snack on baked potatoes, which he bought with the inadequate allowance his father gave him. I wanted to stay longer and listen to his story, but I was afraid of the possible troubles involved in returning home late. I cited my wife's sickness and excused myself.

When I reached home at about sunset, the old men had already taken over the guestroom and were having a drinking party. "If only I'd known, I'd have stayed out later," I thought. Dinner and drinks were being served at the same time, as a result of which the room was a mess, with things scattered everywhere. Such disarray ill-suited a house with a dying patient.

"Who's in the guestroom?" I asked my sister. She was fanning the stove, on which sat a small pot for extracting medicine.

"Who knows? *Ch'aji*'s here again," she cackled.

"What? What do you mean?"

"You don't know '*ch'aji*'? If you don't, you studied Japanese in vain."

My cousin laughed at me. He was standing, somewhat drunk, on the stone foundation of the wall. The women giggled.

"Is *Ch'aji* someone's nickname?"

"No, so you don't understand the meaning of '*ch'aji*'?" my cousin laughed again.

I joined him in his laughter but didn't know why he was laughing. "So what is *Ch'aji*?"

"'Ch'a' means 'difference' and 'Ji' means 'sustenance.' Read the Chinese characters in the Japanese way," my sister instructed me, still laughing.

"*Sasisukae*?"

"That's right!"

Still perplexed, I inquired further. I learned that the guest inside was Kim's "dupe." When my father had invited this man into the guestroom on his first visit, he pretended to know Japanese and asked, "Is there no *ch'aji*?" My cousin heard him and later asked Kim what this meant. Kim explained that the phrase was a literal Korean translation of "Excuse me" in Japanese. My cousin made a joke of it afterward, and the nickname stuck. My family, who had never seen the man previously and still didn't know his name, called him Ch'aji.

"What an idiot! What does he do?" I asked my cousin.

"What do you mean what does he do? He's being duped by Kim. . . . By the way, why don't we have a drink?" My cousin came inside and wanted to drink some more, using my company as a pretext.

"Another drink? Have one by yourself."

"Are you already drunk? I've had a few myself."

I was tempted, but I worried about how my drinking habit always became aggravated whenever I came back to Korea. This problem was partly due to the fact that I had nothing to do in Korea but drink and while away my time. But then, come to think of it, what drunks Koreans are! They drink a glass in the morning, a glass in the afternoon, and a glass in the evening; the rich drink because they are rich and the poor because they are poor. Transcending immediate reality is one of the highest goals in life, and there is no better way to go about it than drinking. Koreans don't live; they're dragged along by their stomachs. It's not "to live," but "to be compelled to live." Not active but passive. Since they have never really had an ideal, some vision of life, they don't bother with one now. They consider their lives as a form of meaningless excess. Take drinking away from Koreans?—that would mean suicide for them all.

"Drink! Drink and forget!" This alone is their view of life.

"Okay, let's drink." I invited my cousin into the inner room.

As I sat down at the dinner table, my mother came in. "A doctor came for a visit today from the countryside, on the recommendation of Kim's friend. But should we really change medications again?" She looked at me with a doubtful expression.

"Which friend of Kim's?"

"She means Ch'aji," replied my cousin, who had been waiting for me to finish my glass.

"What does a man like that know . . . " I frowned.

"That's what I mean. Can anything Kim or Ch'aji recommends be worthwhile?"

"I don't know. Let father decide."

Mother looked upset at my reply. "If you don't know, who does? Your father is always out or wasting his time drinking. . . . "

"Well, what do I know? So are they entertaining the doctor in there, too?"

"No," replied my cousin. "You know Kim was sent to prison the other day, right?"

"Yes, I heard about that."

"That very day Ch'aji paid for Kim to have a good time. And then on the day of his release, Ch'aji treated him again to cheer him up after the whole ordeal. So today, after a long preparation—and who knows where he got the money—Kim brought one wŏn and five hundred *chŏn* to return the favor. The doctor or whoever he is, simply speaking, counts as a little extra, something on the side."

"Treating Kim to dinner and drink not once, but twice—what is Ch'aji after?"

"It's all a fraud. I don't know the details, but judging from what I've heard, Ch'aji seems to be going around right now squandering money in the hopes of winning the title of a magistrate or even guardian of a royal mausoleum. . . . If I had someone to dupe like him, I would suck him dry to my heart's content and then dump him." My cousin burst into laughter.

My mother, sitting next to him, also smiled. "It takes talent, too. You think just anybody can be a swindler?"

"So, that's why he's going around pretending to speak Japanese, 'Is there *ch'aji* or no *ch'aji*.' He's really quite a nuisance." I found the whole thing foolish. After pouring myself one more glass, I asked, "So is father in on it?"

"No, of course not," my cousin answered. "Kim wouldn't talk to him about something like that."

Deceive and be deceived, take and be taken, eat, drink, and be merry . . . and they call this life. Why do they live? Why don't they die! But they can't die in peace for fear that they might end up buried in a public cemetery. Oh well . . . I held out my glass for another drink.

The more I drank, the more the strong liquor stimulated my appetite for drink, and so I ignored my mother's plea to stop and have dinner. I had a new bottle of whiskey brought in, one which I'd opened the day before.

"You seem to be here to drink, not to look after your sick wife. With a dying woman in the house, there are drinking parties in every room . . . My heavens!" My mother sighed and began to eat. Although she was right, it couldn't be helped.

"Oh, by the way, I went to Pyŏnghwa's." I remembered his having urged me to stay for some Western liquor.

"Yes? How are they doing? He got a promotion but then didn't even mention anything about giving me an allowance." My cousin, now tipsy, was about to start complaining again about his younger brother.

"What?" I cut him off. "Does he owe you anything? Whether he does or doesn't, you don't have a right to any say in the matter. Why should you complain? He has to make his own living."

"Which is more right, to be supported by your own brother or to beg from an uncle or a cousin?"

". . ."

"Is it right that he should be keeping two women," he kept shouting, "and yet ignore his own brother?"

"What do you mean he keeps two women?"

"Well, isn't he paying tuition for that bitch, Ŭlla? When I visited him the day before yesterday, she was there!"

"What? She's there? Then why didn't you tell me earlier?" My tone was reproachful, as I remembered how Pyŏnghwa's wife had smiled without giving a definite answer.

"Pyŏnghwa's wife told me not to tell you for some reason."

"I see!" I laughed. I was not upset but regretted that she had kept Ŭlla's arrival hidden.

"So Pyŏnghwa is really paying Ŭlla's tuition?"

"It's true. He's been paying for the past year. About thirty wŏn a month." He explained how he had happened to see a letter about this on one of his visits there.

Why, when another man is also paying for her? What a shameless slut . . . I laughed inwardly.

The next morning Pyŏnghwa's wife came for a visit with Ŭlla.

"I heard you came over yesterday. I arrived this morning by train. I left my luggage at a friend's place, and as soon as I'd visited with her a bit, she dragged me here." Ŭlla was making up excuses even before I said anything.

"So did you meet Pyŏnghwa?" I asked, smiling.

"I arrived after he'd left for work." She gave this vague response, avoiding my eyes. Noticing a small golden watch around her wrist, I frowned.

8

The patient—for whose quick recovery everyone had been praying, yet whose lingering life proved so taxing to all—finally drew her last breath. Whether the doctor whom Counselor Kim and Ch'aji recommended had made an error in his treatment or had simply had the bad luck of intervening during the final stage of an illness, my wife died two days after he changed her medication. My mother was beyond herself with grief, weeping more than anyone else. I wondered whether, after two people became attached to each other, something really could hurt that much. As my mother noted with regret, my wife had lived with me for only a few years of our marriage. Since we had tied the knot when she was fifteen and I was thirteen, it could be said that she had been my wife for ten long years. Yet I fled to Japan when I turned fifteen, and from then on she remained my wife in name only. This was like saying on New Year's Day that a bride you married the night before had been your wife for a whole year, simply because the calendar changed.

"It couldn't be helped. You die early because you're destined to."

Every time my mother cried from pity for her, I made this stolid reply. Later she began to resent Counselor Kim. "When that scoundrel said he'd recommend a doctor, I had a bad feeling. . . . " Nothing, however, could be changed now. Death remained an indisputable fact.

On the night of my wife's death, I had fallen fast asleep from exhaustion, when someone shook me. I opened my eyes and saw my cousin, wide-eyed and pale. "Get up, hurry!" he kept saying. Putting on my clothes, I thought, "Things must have taken a turn for the worse!" My father, who had been in bed in the next room, also got up quickly. We rushed to my wife's room. The small room was packed with people. My mother was muttering something, rubbing rosary beads. She stepped aside and gestured at me to move closer to my wife's bedside. No one spoke. Everyone was standing in anticipation, holding their breath as if waiting to see a spectacle or some sort of a show. I drew close to the patient, as I had been told to do, and held my hand out over her nose. A warm, faint breath touched my hand.

My father's drowsy, husky voice could be heard from behind. "When did it begin?" The throbbing pulse in the patient's neck grew more rapid. She opened her eyes slightly. Catching sight of me sitting at her side, she suddenly opened them wide and stared at me for a while. Then they closed again. I felt a shiver run through me. My heart almost stopped, but a faint smile on her lips afforded me some relief.

A bowl of watery gruel was brought in. Following my mother's instructions, I took a spoonful of it and let it trickle through the patient's parched lips. She opened her eyes feebly one last time but soon shut them. I fed her another spoonful. As the gruel trickled into her mouth, she exerted herself twice in apparent attempts to swallow, opening her mouth slightly, lowering her emaciated jaw, and tilting her head back a little. A soft rattling sound came from her throat, as if phlegm was obstructing it.

All who were present watched wide-eyed and leaned forward to see better. My mother, still reciting a Buddhist chant, lay the patient's head back gently onto the pillow. When my mother drew her hands away from the pillow, a faint gasp filled the room, which was now bright in the morning light, serene, emptied of all other sounds, with no one else breathing, so that it seemed as if the gasp resounded in every corner before at last passing through the open door. . . . That was all. There was nothing more to it. It felt strange. So this is death. I stared down at her white face and her tightly shut eyes. Nothing stirred within me, neither pity nor sorrow. But how she had stared at me! Her staring eyes and her peaceful smiling lips haunted my mind. At the same time, I felt pleased to have spoon-fed her the gruel, as if I had actually done something for her. My mother gently pressed down on her daughter-in-law's upper lip till the mouth closed. She looked closely at her face for a while. The rosary dropped from her hand, and large teardrops fell from her eyes.

I rose from my seat and quickly left the room. As I was sitting at my desk, smoking a cigarette, my cousin at last returned with the Western doctor he'd been sent for. I recognized the doctor and invited him to stay and warm himself up, but at the word "death," he left immediately. I scoffed at his timidity.

The next day, after dark, my brother arrived from Kimch'ŏn with his wife and daughter to make the appropriate funeral arrangements. I left everything to him and spent my time just smoking in bed. I firmly objected, however, to the idea of transferring the body to Ch'ŏngju. I was also adamantly against letting the funeral process drag on for five days. Instead, I made sure she was buried in a public cemetery within three. My in-laws looked upset and seemed to resent me for this, suspecting that I thought nothing more about her death than being rid of something troublesome. Regardless, I held fast to my opinion on the matter.

During the funeral I had trouble wailing aloud while having no tears. This, too, was talked about among the relatives, both on my side and on my wife's; yet I could not shed a single tear until the funeral was over.

One time, while drinking alone in the inner room, I overheard my widowed sister speaking in the living room: "If you're a girl, you're born unlucky. How could he not show any tears. . . . "

"Husbands are all like that," whispered my sister-in-law. "Just wait and see. He'll bring in a schoolgirl before a month passes." I laughed to myself.

Two days after the funeral my brother and I were sharing a quiet breakfast. "Isn't your graduation next spring?" my brother asked suddenly. "What do you plan to do? Are you going to come back and get a job? Or do you want to study longer?"

"I'll take things as they come. But whatever happens, it'd be best if you let me decide things on my own."

I then provided a brief outline of my plans. If my son grew up without any mishaps, my brother would be free to adopt him; and in case my brother happened to have a son of his own in the meantime, my cousin could adopt him. I agreed with my brother that half of whatever inheritance I received should be used to cover the expenses of the child's rearing and schooling. Any money leftover should be transferred to my son when he came of age. Although the negotiation had been simple, I felt much relieved and liberated when it was finished.

The clear winter weather continued for a week. Then one morning the sky threatened a downpour, looking as foreboding as the grimace of a jealous woman. Ashen clouds hovered low over the white frozen earth. The outer quarters of the house were quiet and weary, heavy with silence and slumber. Kim had not made an appearance since the day of the funeral, perhaps because he felt somewhat guilty and was afraid of being reproached.

Lying alone in my gloomy room all day long, I felt as if lead or a heavy stone were pressing down on my chest. From the inner quarters a shaman could be heard scratching at a wicker basket. She was singing a strange song to "purge" the house. Mingled with this noise was the occasional sound of women crying. Then a certain mur-

muring continued for a long while, which was regularly followed by a low voice responding, "That's right!"

"What the hell is right?" I lay still and continued to listen attentively. Before long, someone was heard rushing into the outer quarters. After a few loud stomping sounds, something was thrown onto the floor. I jumped up in surprise and quickly pushed open the door to find a portly woman in her forties standing in front of the veranda with a bowl of white salt in her hand. Her bloodshot eyes darting around, she was throwing handfuls of white powder all over the veranda. Whether she noticed me or not, she threw the salt into the window of my room, too.

"Does she think I'm dead, or is she paying a courtesy call now for my death later on?" I was outraged, but I simply closed the window and lay down again. My spirits were flagging, and yet in my heart something irrepressible was boiling up.

"Why on earth did I come back?" When I had left Japan, I was happy to be getting away, but now I could not help but regret my rash decision. "Damn it all! I'm going back. There's nothing more comforting than being left alone in peace!"

Having made up my mind, I got up and started arranging things in my suitcase. I was folding the clothes I wanted to take with me when Pyŏnghwa's wife dropped in with Ŭlla. They stopped in front of my room.

"Is anyone there?"

Since I didn't want them to notice that I was packing, I pushed the suitcase into the corner and looked out, blocking the entrance to my room with my body.

"How awful you must feel," greeted Ŭlla, whom I met now for the first time after my wife's death.

I stared at her face for a while. "If you consider birth and death to be natural parts of life, there's nothing much to complain of."

"You must still be sorry." Ŭlla looked up at me, apparently studying my face. In her eyes there flickered the obvious sign of a smile.

"I must *still* be sorry?"—I repeated her words to myself, thinking that they were rather unusual for a condolence.

"No matter how hard I try, I can't think of her as dead. But then neither can I think she's alive." Such an inane reply had slipped out of my mouth before I could reflect on it.

After the two left my room, I finished packing and picked up a letter from Shizuko. After reading it one last time, I shredded it to pieces and threw them into the stove. I had quickly looked the letter over sometime before the funeral, when it had arrived. Upon rereading it now, I definitely caught her hints about my paying her tuition and even about our moving in together. In any case, I thought that it was far better for her to go to her aunt's in Kyoto than to stay at the café.

"If she asks for one hundred wŏn as a one-time gift, I might be able to help her."

As I waited for my brother to come home, I pondered over what attitude I should take toward Shizuko.

"No matter what happens, I can't possibly live with her!" I closed the desk drawer and was thinking over how to communicate my present thoughts to her, without causing any misunderstanding, when the gate creaked open. Surprised, I peered through the window and saw my brother. Pyŏnghwa followed him in. I stepped out and greeted Pyŏnghwa, but I ushered only my brother into the guestroom, "Brother, just a moment . . . " Pyŏnghwa went on to the inner quarters.

"Brother! I'm leaving today," I began abruptly.

My brother looked a bit surprised. "Why so early?"

"I have to find some peace and quiet alone to do my own thinking. And besides, I need time to prepare for the make-up exam."

As I was looking at my brother, I remembered how I had lied to Professor H, claiming that my mother was ill as a clumsy excuse for my departure.

"Still, why can't you stay a couple days longer? You'll upset mother if you leave now."

Although I understood his concern, my desire to leave was too urgent for me to take my family's feelings into consideration.

"In any case, I need three hundred wŏn. Though I'll probably come back before too long. . . . "

"Where are you going with three hundred wŏn?"

Normally, he would have been surprised at such a request and would have started to lecture me. This time, however, he gave in immediately, since he did not want to contradict me in the aftermath of the funeral. He had also saved some money on the funeral expenses, which cost only half of what had been initially budgeted for them.

After my brother went to the inner quarters, I returned to my room. I was about to start writing a letter to Shizuko when Pyŏnghwa stepped in.

As soon as he sat down, he asked, "Are you leaving today?" He seemed surprised.

"Yes, I'm considering it." I put down my pen and answered in an affable tone of voice, although I found his presence irritating.

"School doesn't start for a while?"

"Yes. There's still a couple of weeks before school begins, but I had to miss an exam and must make it up. Since graduation is not that far off, I should go back as soon as possible."

"That makes sense." He sat quietly for a while. "Do you have some time now?"

"Why do you ask?"

"Ah, well, this time round, during your stay, we didn't have much time to talk together. . . . "

"I'm a bit busy now," I replied, with a hint of refusal. "I'll be back again in a few months." I had divined what his intentions were.

"Still, let's go for a drink. Just a quick one."

"If you want to have a drink, let's drink here. Just wait a moment in the other room while I finish this letter." I touched my pen.

"Well—," Pyŏnghwa remained in his seat, quietly gauging my mood. "Drinking is okay, too. But since you said you're leaving today, and Ŭlla is over here anyways, now would be a good time for us to get together. Ŭlla has been suggesting for a long time that we should all spend an evening together, since it seems there's also some misunderstanding that needs clearing up."

"What misunderstanding?" I pretended not to understand. "I can't remember having misunderstood anything in particular."

"Oh, I mean, there might have been some sort of misunderstanding, as we've grown apart since last year, for no particular reason." He stopped short my attempt to reply. "Also, this time, because of your misfortune, you must be grieving, and she also means that we should all meet together to help console you."

Judging from his peculiar choice of words, Pyŏnghwa seemed to think that I was still in the dark about everything.

"Whether there's some reason or other, I don't know, but in any case, since I don't harbor any misunderstanding on my side, you'd better say so to Ŭlla. And whether I'm grieving or not, Ŭlla must have been joking when she talked about some sort of special consolation."

". . ."

"But thank you for your offer. And please, tell Ŭlla that I thank her, too."

"You must have misunderstood something. Your hypersensitivity always makes you over-analyze everything. That's your problem."

What Pyŏnghwa was saying sounded rather strange to me. It seemed as if he thought I was exaggerating everything in my suspicion that he had had a relationship with Ŭlla. Yet it was beyond any doubt that he had felt affection for Ŭlla at some point, and that Ŭlla had responded to his courting—no matter what might have happened later—by opening up her heart to him to a certain extent. That was why he was still paying her tuition. Moreover, Ŭlla was now in a position where she had a foot in both camps. She was trying to be on close terms with me by using Pyŏnghwa as a go-between. I found her scheming despicable and found his acting as her agent so shameless that I had to take a second look at his face. I made no reply and grabbed the pen.

"I don't know what you're thinking that makes you so angry, but Ŭlla considers you a lifelong friend and sympathizes with you a lot."

I couldn't believe he could utter something like that and still be sober. I slammed down my pen and looked him straight in the eyes.

"What are you talking about?" I kept my voice calm as possible.

"You, of course, don't think something's happening now between Ŭlla and me."

I stared hard at his lowered face. "You don't mean to leave her to my care now, do you?"

"Just what do you mean by that? Now or before even, what do you suppose I'm doing? I'm just saying that she has a deep sympathy for you. Yet you always seem to get the wrong idea, but I . . . "

I became so irritated that I lashed out without holding anything back. "Can't you lay off that tired story? I don't have time now to listen to fairy tales. In other words, I'm not the kind of man who wants someone's sympathy, nor do I know how to sympathize with someone else. Bear that in mind. And Ŭlla's talk of sympathy and whatever . . . I'm sorry to be so blunt, but that's a joke. Doesn't she know that sympathizing with someone means ignoring the man's selfhood, depriving him of his self-esteem? Sympathy is not a word that she should use freely about anyone."

"It's not like that. Maybe I said it wrong, but you're being unfair to her." He seemed defenseless against my unexpected attack.

"Maybe I'm overreacting, but we all need to try to think rationally now and each go our own separate way. It's time to calm down and do some self-reflection before babbling on about sympathizing with other people. You, Ŭlla, and I, we've all led outgoing lives. Now we should start focusing inwardly on ourselves. In any case, we should first try to keep our hearts clear and think a bit harder. To take control of our lives, we need to change their direction first."

Pyŏnghwa looked a bit ashamed. After staying about ten more minutes, he got up. "I must have somehow said something wrong, but, anyhow, don't take it the wrong way."

I laughed gleefully to myself and began writing.

Thank you for your letter from Kyoto. When I think of you, I always remember fondly our night together at Tokyo Station. But circumstances, which do not permit me my freedom and leisure, forbid me to indulge in pleasant memories. All around me, it's like a public cemetery. How can I dream of "Beautiful Seoul," buried as I am in this grave swarming with ghosts—all so many lifeless Koreans. Nothing I see or hear soothes or delights me. In such a situation, I'll suffocate before long, not like a bee intoxicated by the pungent odor of rose blossoms, but like a maggot fossilized in an airless grave.

Dear Shizuko!

I realize that I have a responsibility to save myself. I realize that I owe it to myself to find my own way and plow ahead. My wife has taken her last breath. But it would be a big mistake to consider her dead. For she left me, her husband, an important, invaluable lesson—"Save yourself! Improve your lot!" Yes, it's true. She passed away, leaving this lesson to me, who should have been the most affectionate presence in her life but who turned out to be the most heartless of husbands. I cannot think her dead. Her body has returned to the earth, but her spirit is forever wedded to mine. She left me a son. He is my only child and will always remain so. I have an obligation to see that this offspring of mine grows up better than others'. I have proposed that the child be adopted by my elder cousin, the heir of our head family, offering half of my future inheritance as my son's share. Yet this is only a formal arrangement, and I am clearly aware that the duty of ensuring his happiness lies with me.

Dear Shizuko!

I've just now been wondering why I ever decided to return, and scoffed at my foolishness. I've also decided to leave tonight. All things considered, my trip was not in vain. First and foremost, I lost my wife—and yet I cannot help but think that I rather gained her. We should find our own paths in life. Whether death means annihilation or eternal life, and whatever else it might signify, we do not have any right to meddle with it. We should realize that the stern fact of our being alive, with our consciousness still intact, obliges us to confront reality and to be steadfast in treading our own path.

Dear Shizuko!

You know that the horrific carnage in Europe has now ended with the signing of an armistice. Not just Europe but the whole world is brimming over with hope for a new and better life. If one person epitomizes the whole, then this glorious rebirth must start and end with each individual. And so let us guide our lives toward the right, toward the light, until we feel the first joyous heartbeats of a new life. You once wept, lamenting how the bitterness of a lost love cost you all your pride, all your hope, all the vigor of your youth. But the new world emerging now will have no room for idle sighs. . . . Expand your chest and inhale, deep into your lungs, all the vitality of life.

Dear Shizuko!

You asked me to visit you on my way back to Tokyo. Please, don't be upset. I could not wish any more than I already do that we should meet. But circumstances do not permit me this. I am completely tied up. As you know, I had to leave before completing my exams, and I also haven't touched my thesis. Can you forgive me?

You must certainly know that love is not intrusive or possessive. It goes without saying that interfering with each other's lives in the hope of securing a more intimate union cannot bring the highest form of love. In the same way, the culmination of love is not the satisfaction one gains by completely possessing another. Even if it were, this would not be ideal love. I've always said that the only real love is the wholehearted blessing of another person's happiness. How comforting and blissful it is to enjoy even the mere knowledge that someone in this world cares for me, that I am beloved. This alone is pure, divine love.

Excuse me for writing such a long-winded letter. The rest of my words I will keep folded up safe until the day I see you again. I pray for your well-being.

Enclosed is my humble contribution to your tuition. I hope you will accept it without thinking any less of me.

Humbly yours,

Yi Inhwa

After writing "To Miss Shizuko Nishimura" on the envelope, I looked at my watch and set off for the post office, carrying in my hand the letter. Enclosed was the three hundred wŏn my brother had given me.

* * *

At the station, five people came to see me off—my brother, my cousin, Pyŏnghwa, his wife, and Ŭlla. Ŭlla, for good reason, stood by in silence. Pyŏnghwa and his wife could barely suppress yawns as they watched the clock on the roof of the platform. Perhaps I was just being self-conscious, but I seemed to see a sort of relieved look in Pyŏnghwa's face.

When the train was about to depart, my brother approached the car entrance, where I was standing.

"Shouldn't you marry again when you come back next spring?" he asked, unexpectedly. "Do you have any plans yet?"

I laughed. "Brother, I'm just escaping from a grave now. Maybe when the warm springtime comes and I become rich enough to boast of owning a summer house. . . . "

2

CH'OE SŎHAE

An iconic figure of Korean proletarian literature, Ch'oe Haksong (1901–1932), whose pen name is Sŏhae, was born in the Hamgyŏng province. Known to have received only an elementary school education, Ch'oe was only fifteen when three of his poems appeared in *Hakchigwang* (Light of Learning), a literary periodical run by Korean students in Tokyo. In 1918 Ch'oe emigrated to Chientao, Manchuria, along with his recently widowed mother. For the next five years he struggled with extreme poverty and worked on a variety of menial jobs, at one point joining a Korean guerilla troop operating in the region.

Upon his return to Korea in 1923, Ch'oe established himself as a rising figure within the proletarian literature movement, achieving fame with the publication of "T'alch'ulgi" (1925, trans. here "Escape") as well as "Hongyŏm" (1927, Scarlet flame). During this period Ch'oe made his living as an editor of the literary magazine *Chosŏn Mundan* (Korean literary world). When the magazine's publication was discontinued in 1927, however, Ch'oe was again left in a condition of extreme poverty. In 1929 he was expelled from the KAPF (Korea Artista Proleta Federatio) for accepting a position in a pro-Japanese newspaper. He died prematurely in 1932 while being operated for an esophageal stricture, a condition caused by his poverty.

"Escape" is an autobiographical story closely based on Ch'oe own experiences in Chientao. As is the case with "Hongyŏm," "Escape" too features a peasant character who, strangled by poverty in a hostile environment, transforms himself into a rebel prone to committing acts of crime and violence. The story's setting in Manchuria, where most ethnic Koreans lived as peasants under Chinese landlords, naturally lent itself to the converging themes of national resistance and class struggle, setting a standard for much of proletarian literature during the 1920s and 1930s.

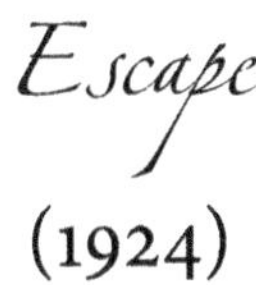

(1924)

1

Kim! I was glad to receive your letters, though I had not been able to reply to any of them. I'm grateful for your loyalty, of course, but I cannot accept your advice.

Pak! I cannot approve of your leaving home. I cannot approve of your deserting your aging mother, your young wife, and your child in a hostile foreign land. Pak! Go back! Make haste! I can just see your family wandering the streets of a foreign land. Only in your arms will they find rest. You have a responsibility to save them. You are the pillar of your household. Can a house stand without a pillar? Abandoning home for the sake of avoiding a little pain—this is too cowardly for such a resolute man as yourself. I heard from Hwang that you've joined the XX regiment and gone off to the X frontier, but I still can't believe it. How can someone save society when he can't save his own family?

Pak, I hope with all my heart that you'll go back. When you think of your family being trampled under the feet of others, you must surely find it difficult to set your conscience at ease.

You wrote the same thing every letter, Kim. I appreciate your good intentions. How can I not be grateful for your sympathy toward my beloved family? A close friend's rebuke always brings tears to my eyes. But I cannot follow your advice. Will you be hurt and offended? All I can say is that my wayward path may still lead to happiness.

Kim, I'm human, too. I have a heart. How can I not be upset about the degradation of my family, who is as precious to me as my own life? No one could fathom even a thousandth of my pain.

I'll tell you my reason for leaving my family. Whether you sympathize or not, that's your choice. I'm simply telling you everything as it is. For I have an irrepressible urge to explain myself, if not to you, then to anyone who will listen.

But I swear to you—human as you are, you won't be able to deny what I say.

2

It was five years ago that I left my native village. This you know well, Kim. At that time, I set off with my wife and mother. You know that I went to Chientao, full of fresh hope and longing for a new world—a world where I could replenish my body and soul, which had long been withering away in my all too impoverished existence.

They say Chientao is a promised land. Wherever you go, there's always fertile land to plow. Farming yields abundant rice, and rich forests allay all worries about firewood. And so I'll sow seeds in the fields, keep my belly full, and my house warm. I'll build a small cabin, read books, teach illiterate peasants, and found a utopian community. In this way, I'll cultivate the great expanse of Chientao.

Thus I envisioned my new life as I set off for Chientao. How elated I felt then! Crossing the Tumen River along the Barbarian Ridge, I looked across a boundless plain and saw mountains and streams in the distance, and my heart was afire with idealism. My stirring tales and high spirits enchanted my wife and mother as well.

As we climbed to the top of the ridge, a spring gust from the northwest lashed our cheeks.

"Goodness gracious! It's still winter here," said my mother, sitting in the cart. She pulled her quilt over her head.

"Why, we should breathe in the wind for success," I said with enthusiasm. I was so excited and lively, then.

3

But my ideal came to naught, Kim. Before the first month had passed in Chientao, tumultuous waves were crashing down relentlessly upon our three souls.

I searched for land to till. There was no free land. Unless you paid for it, not even an acre was to be had. You could become a tenant on Chinese land, paying rent either through a predetermined amount of rice or a certain percentage of the harvest. Still, as a tenant, by the end of the first year, you wouldn't even be in a position to pay back the debt on the provisions borrowed from the Chinese landlord. Not that this mattered, as no one was willing to rent land to a novice like me anyway.

Since the place was new to me and the people were strangers, there was nobody to whom I could turn for advice on where to go or what to do. While I procrastinated in a rented room in a town called H, two weeks passed, then a month. Meanwhile, I wasn't able to secure so much as a job, let alone land, and what small amount of my fortune remained was frittered away. Finally, I rolled up my sleeves and set off to look for something to do. Wandering from house to house, I fixed *ondol* floors and installed stoves. In this way, I scraped together a living. Soon I was known as "the *ondol* fixer" in the town. I couldn't even change out of my sooty clothes, for we had no clothes to spare.

H was a small town. There weren't always *ondol* to fix. I could not survive on this job alone. I also cut hay for sale and picked weeds on scorching summer days. To help make ends meet, my wife and mother worked as hired hands at a mill and went down to the riverside to gather tinder.

From that period on, Kim, I began to experience the terrible affliction that can befall a human being. I became ever more amazed at how painful life can be. I have never shed tears over my own hardships, but when my mother collected tinder or my young wife worked as a day laborer, my eyes clouded over and my blood boiled.

"Good God," my mother once exclaimed in tears, as I lay groaning in bed, "I would rather be ill myself than watching you suffer like this." I didn't take any particular notice of her words right then, but now I understand the truth in them.

Time and again, I would strike my chest, "I can take my own scabs and battered bones, but I can't bear to see my wife and mother starving and despised." Day and night, through wind and rain, I toiled at all kinds of sundry jobs—weeding, chopping wood, running other people's errands.

"You must be hungry again today. You ate so little for breakfast," my mother would say in a tearful voice, as I returned home late after a day's work. "If only I could live to see you getting by without starving, I'd be able to rest in peace in the next world."

"Who says I'm hungry?" I replied, blithely.

My wife was a woman of few words. She was gentle and quietly obeyed me, no matter what I told her to do. I pitied her all the more for this. I felt more ashamed before my wife than before my mother.

"Why did I ever marry when I had no means to support even myself?" I sometimes regretted my marriage, which had been arranged by my parents. And the more I felt this way, the more I was sorry for my wife and felt grateful to her.

"What must I do to survive? . . . " The thought tormented me. The proverb "Blessed are the meek" seemed an outright lie. Until then, I had believed firmly in the supreme truth of this maxim, but I gradually came to doubt it and eventually dismissed it altogether.

As for diligence, how could anyone be more diligent than we were? And as for honesty, could there be any family more honest than my own? Yet our poverty grew worse with each passing day. At times, we would go without a morsel of food for two or three days straight. Once, returning home hungry after two futile days of searching for work, I saw my wife—her pregnant belly as big as a mountain—nibbling at something in front of the kitchen. Surprised, she quickly threw into the stove whatever it was that she had in her hand. A feeling of bitterness rose in my heart.

What was she eating? Where did she get it? What food has she been hiding from us? So! That's a wife for you! But could she really . . . yet she was eating something. . . . I was suspicious and resentful and even hated my wife at that moment. She stood there silently for a while, taking deep breaths, her head hanging awkwardly. At last she went out. She looked flustered.

After she left, I rummaged through the stove to find out what she had been eating. Poking at the cold ash with a stick, I spotted something reddish. I picked it up. It was a tangerine peel. It had teeth-marks in it. My hand, holding the tangerine peel, trembled, and my eyes, looking at the teeth-marks, filled with tears.

Kim! How can I adequately express what I felt then? How hungry must she have been, my pregnant wife, to chew on an orange peel that had been thrown away on the street! Oh, I'm such a bastard! How could I suspect my wife? What kind of an animal would bear a grudge against a wife like her? Can any man be more callous than that? How can I face her now with a clean conscience? At these thoughts, I shed tears and choked back a sob.

"Why are you crying? Pull yourself together. We'll live to see better times. It won't always be like this."

Someone was tapping on my shoulder. I knew that it was my mother.

Oh, mother, I'm such an awful son—I wanted to cry on and on, clutching my mother's arm. But instead I hardened my heart and left her without a word.

"Why am I crying? What good is it to cry? Let's live! Live! Live no matter what it takes! My wife and mother, they must live, too. So long as I'm alive, let's work!"

I ground my teeth and clenched my fists. But the tears kept flowing. My wife approached while I was crying silently and, fingering the string tie of her skirt, began to cry herself. My wife, who had been raised on a farm, was so shy that she could do no more than join me in tears, not knowing any words to console me.

4

The summer did not last long, Kim.

A wind blew in from the west, and with it the first frost. The cold cruelly menaced our poorly clad bodies. In the fall, I began to peddle codfish. I would buy ten codfish for three wŏn and carry them to the surrounding villages, looking to exchange them for soybeans. I could carry ten fish on the trip out, but not fifty gallons of beans back. So for three days, I had to go back and forth over a distance of ten miles carrying ten gallons at a time. With the beans in hand, we started to make tofu to sell. My wife and I turned the millstone all day long, our arms aching so much that they seemed ready to fall off.

While I suffered a great deal, how much more painful it must have been for my wife, who had given birth to a child just a short time before. Her face was always swollen. Still, whenever I felt a need to complain, I cursed her. I'd regret doing so immediately afterward. In our tiny kitchen, in addition to the wood pile and hanging clothes, we'd installed a stove and brought in a millstone. Thus there was little room for anyone to sit. The rising steam caused tears in the paper windows and dampened the walls. Everything was soggy, so that it felt as if we were sitting in lukewarm water fully clothed. Sometimes, the bean-curd dregs, which we took such pains to grind, turned sour from the steam. As the soymilk boiled over in the pot, we were relieved if a butter-colored, yellowish grease started to curdle on the surface. But if the liquid turned whitish, with no grease, my wife's face, her eyes fixed on the pot, would lose all its color. If after a sprinkle of vinegar, we still failed to produce any curd, we'd be devastated.

"It went sour again!" said my mother in a tearful voice. "What are we going to do?" She was staring at the boiling liquid, a crying, hungry baby in her arms. When something like this happened, the atmosphere in the whole house turned bitter, and we were engulfed in grief, desolation, and inexpressible sorrow.

"After all your hard work! Grinding till your arm aches . . . I was really hoping to buy food with the money from the tofu . . . " My mother burst into tears and struck her breast.

My wife's head hung low; she seemed to be crying as well. A tofu sale never brought in any great amount. At best, twenty to thirty chŏn. We survived on that money. My mother was weeping over that twenty to thirty chŏn, and my wife's spirit was broken. I, too, was apprehensive.

On such days, we dined on sour soymilk. The child screamed all night long for breast milk. In our household, having a child was only a burden.

5

Whether we liked it or not, we had no choice but to try once more to make tofu. This time, though, we ran out of firewood. I left the house with a sickle. On such occasions, my wife, still weak from childbirth, would follow me out, a sickle in her hand. My mother and I would try to stop her, but she wouldn't listen. I had to cut my own wood in secret. If the owner of the forest caught me, I'd be severely punished. So we went to the forest at sunset and returned with wood late at night. My wife carried her bundle on her head, while I kept mine on my back. We descended the mountainside together in the dark. Each time my foot slipped or I stumbled on a stone, I fell backward onto my bundle of wood. As I struggled under the weight of the wood, my wife quietly put down her load and helped pull me to my feet. But after I managed to stand up with my load, my wife wasn't able to set hers back on her head. And when I put down my bundle to help her, I couldn't lift mine again. With no one else to help, I set down my load on a large rock and helped her.

After we managed to climb down the mountain slope, we saw my mother, shivering with our child on her back. Who knows how long she'd been waiting at the foot of the mountain.

"At last! I was so worried that you'd been caught again."

My heart ached whenever she said such things. I'd been taken to the police station and beaten up several times already.

Whenever this happened, our neighbors would mock us, and the Chinese police would treat us as criminals.

"Scum! Don't they have anything better to do? What an ugly sight—no job, peddling tofu, and look at those jaundiced eyes! You'd have to have no guts to live like that."

Thus the neighbors sneered at us. And when any forest owner reported missing wood, the police searched my house first, before any inquiry, and beat me during the interrogation. I had no one to whom I could appeal.

6

The winter was fast approaching, Kim, and with it cold and hunger. Still no job. . . . But I couldn't just sit by and do nothing. I couldn't just watch my whole family starve, their skin turning blue from the cold. I was in such a desperate situation that there seemed to be nothing left to do but grab a sharp knife and stab my whole family to death, if only to spare us one more day of misery; or commit a robbery, so as to ease the cold and hunger.

The less work I had and the more hardship was anticipated, the more anxiety overcame me. Some days, I would close my eyes and remain deep in thought, as if in a trance. It was during those days that an idea began to take shape in my mind. In hindsight, it was this idea that determined the future course of my destiny.

This idea did not come from anyone else's teachings, nor did it arise through a deliberate act of my will. Like sprouts in spring, it grew ever larger in my mind.

I have been faithful to the world thus far. I have always tried to remain true. Tried to live by my own earnest efforts, even if that meant my wife and mother had to suffer broken bones and torn flesh. But the world betrayed us. It has not respected our good faith. We have been insulted, scorned, and abused. We have been living an illusion up till now. I hadn't realized that the world not only permits but condones the tyrannical, the deceitful, and the wicked. It's not only us, but everyone in the world, who seems blind to this. I have been in a drunken stupor till now. We have been living not as ourselves, but as the victims of a brutal system.

Kim, I don't blame people. But I can't ignore those who are drunken of an evil potion and remain unaware of what is really going on, even as they eke out a blood offering through their own toil. And so I cannot let a system like this continue, one which condones and protects the deceitful, the wicked, the depraved, and the idle.

In this environment, no matter how hard we work, we will never taste the joys of life. Even were we to manage to survive somehow, all that we would pass on to our children would be the spirit of a life spent waiting for death. Even now, I can't hold back my sorrow and indignation when I think of the future awaiting my young child, now crying in his mother's arms. If I remain in this condition (which is all but inevitable), he will end up abandoned under a bridge or at somebody else's door, and never see the inside of a schoolhouse. Is it not heartrending to let a worthy life perish through no fault of its own? Am I not then to be held accountable for this crime?

Kim, I can't stand it any more. I must save my own life first. Up till now, I have been under hypnosis, a living corpse. Can someone who is himself already dead save others? For the salvation of my family, I must destroy those who would hypnotize me, those responsible for this brutal state of affairs.

I consider this fight to be an inherent human longing, the fulfillment of a man's life. I will take great satisfaction in it. I already feel a sense of elation. This idea has enabled me to escape from home, to join the XX troop, and to stand, day and night, wind or rain, on a frontier more dangerous than the edge of a precipice.

Kim, I repeat—I, too, am a man. I have a conscience. I knew that my family would fall deeper into misery from the day of my departure. I know well that they may end up starving to death in the snow or in a ditch somewhere, without even being fully aware that they're dying. For that reason, I can't look indifferently at the servants, male and female, from local households, nor at beggars wandering the streets.

Ah! When I imagine how my family might now be at this very moment, tears flow of their own accord, and I clutch my aching heart.

Yet I grind my teeth and clench my fists. I try not to shed tears or let grief weigh me down. It is already too late for tears, and to remain grief-stricken merely betrays our frailty. I am determined to endure any pain and battle onward.

This is the main reason for my leaving home, Kim. I do not intend to write even my family until I've accomplished my goal. Even if they die, even if I die. . . .

I won't ever feel regret, even though I may well die without success. For I will have fulfilled my duty to our age and to our people.

Ah, Kim! I've said it all, yet my heart still bursts with emotion!

3

NA TOHYANG

Born to a medical family in Seoul, Na Kyŏngson (1902–1926), better known by his pen name Tohyang, entered the Kyŏngsŏng Medical College in 1919, but he dropped out after only a year. He wanted to study literature at Waseda University but could not fulfill this aspiration due to the opposition of his family. Na made his literary debut as a founding member of *Paekcho* (White tides, 1922–1923), a magazine known for its members' inclination for romanticism. Among his contributions to the magazine were works, such as "Chŏlmŭni ŭi sijŏl" (A young man's life, 1922), characterized by a sentimentalist style and the theme of a star-crossed love. When Na died of tuberculosis in 1926, his tragically premature death was mourned by his contemporaries as the symbolic end of the brief era of Korean romanticism.

An urgent aspiration for social justice pervades Na's mature stories such as "Mullebanga" (1925, The Watermill) and "Pŏngŏri Samnyongi" (1925, trans. here "Samnyong the Mute"). In "Samnyong the

Mute," the title character is a servant who develops a passionate romantic affection for his master's abused young bride. As his feelings keep growing, however, they arouse in Samnyong an overwhelming sense of moral indignation over the tyranny of the feudal hierarchy. This tragic tale of unusual emotional intensity is today a familiar classic for Korean readers, well known both in Na's own version and through the numerous popular films that were subsequently based on it.

Samnyong the Mute

(1925)

1

It all happened fourteen or fifteen years ago. I must have been almost ten. The place has since been renamed Green Leaf Village, but it was known as Lotus Flower Peak back then. Lotus Flower Peak was the name of a mountain visible from the South Gate, where a cannon used to go off at noontime. The village—also called Lotus Flower Peak—lay between the mountain and the city gates. Now the village is nothing but a slum where laborers live in filthy quarters. But at the time, its residents held their heads high.

There were only about a dozen households in the village then, and the villagers generally made their living by either keeping an orchard, planting vegetables, or growing bean sprouts.

In the village there lived a man who owned the largest orchard and enjoyed the most comfortable lifestyle. His name I've forgotten, but the villagers called him Sir Oh.

His face was round and handsome, and the sound of his voice rang out as loud as a cicada crying in full summer throttle from a willow tree.

Being a very industrious old man, he would wake up at dawn and supervise the household chores, his hands clasped behind his back. Since he was like a clock, the villagers rose when they heard him up. If he wasn't heard chiding servants during his morning rounds, people found it so strange they would visit his house to see what was the matter. He was bound to be in bed, not feeling well.

But such a thing happened no more than once a year, hardly once in two or three years even.

Since he always wore an official's skullcap, the villagers called him *yangban,* even though he was just a newcomer. In return, he tried not to lose the goodwill of the villagers. He distributed strings of dried pollack and bundles of laver in December and stocked up on spare farming equipment, which he lent to his neighbors for free upon request. As a result, his family came to be respected as among the most generous as well as the most influential in the village.

In his household there lived a deaf-mute servant named Samnyong. He was short and stocky and had hardly any neck, so that it looked as if his head were glued to his shoulders. In addition, he had a pockmarked face and a huge mouth. His master had had him cut off his wispy ponytail, after which his hair always stuck up like a chestnut burr. When he walked, he looked out of breath and sluggish, like an ugly toad standing on its hind legs. The villagers never referred to him by his name but always called him "Mute, Mute" or "Parrot, Parrot." But Samnyong couldn't hear any of these things anyway.

His master had brought him along when the entire household first moved in. Samnyong was honest, loyal, hard-working, and strong. Although he was a mute who got by through reading people's faces, in certain circumstances he could be more sensible than those who could speak and hear. Besides, he was always cautious and never made a mistake.

As soon as he got up in the morning, he swept the yard and fed the cows and pigs. During the summer, he weeded the fields and carried in firewood to be chopped; during the winter, he shoveled the snow and ran all kinds of errands. The master took good care of the mute and appreciated him above all for his diligence. If the mute looked sick, he was allowed to rest. He was given what he wanted to eat, was clothed however he needed to be, and was allowed to sleep regular hours.

The master had one son, the sole heir for the third straight generation. He was seventeen years old but looked more like fourteen.

Since he had been greatly pampered during his upbringing, the boy ended up being ill-mannered toward everyone, behaving like a spoiled child and reacting with cruelty to people and animals alike.

The villagers often cursed the boy. "Bastard! A son like that—he won't ever be anything but a burden to his father. Better not to have a son at all!"

Whenever the son did something wrong, the master's wife said to her husband, "Why don't you give him a good beating? How can you be so lenient?" At times, she looked ready to whip the boy herself.

"Well, he hasn't come of age yet," the master would say. "He won't be like that when he grows up a bit more."

"How old does he have to be?" shrieked his wife like a heron. "He'll be twenty in no time. He'll soon be marrying and having children. If he acts like that, what on earth will he be fit for?" She continued to lash out at her husband. "You're the one who spoiled him. All you ever do is pamper him, you'll never teach him manners. . . . "

When she started in on him like this, the master would quietly walk away.

The son did not regard the mute as a human being. Counting on the poor servant's inability to speak, the boy, on his way in or out, would punch the mute in the side or kick him from behind.

But at such times the mute simply considered the youth rather endearing; he was even amused at the small helpless limbs poking at his iron body. So he would just turn away, move to a different place, and forget the matter.

Once the son put dung into the mute's mouth while the latter was taking a nap. Another time the boy stealthily tied up the mute's arms and legs, lit matches between all his fingers and toes, and watched in glee as the mute, taken by surprise, leapt up and writhed in pain, as if about to perish.

On such occasions, the mute's heart was filled with indignation. But he resented his own deformity rather than his master's son. He'd curse the world but not the boy.

The mute never shed a tear. He didn't have any tears. His eyes were like a dried-out fountain—ready to flow but never flowing. Like a dog that never abandons its master, the mute believed that he could not live anywhere but in his old master's house and that he could trust no one except the people who resided there. He figured that it was simply his fate to live and die in that house. All the abuse he received from his master's son—the pinching, punching, and kicking—he regarded as merely inherent to his place in the world. The pain he suffered was what fate held in store for him, the bitterness of pain no more than what he deserved. He never thought of avoiding his due.

Although he never considered leaving the house or breaking free from his circumstances, he did think of his powerful fists whenever his master's son pestered and mistreated him. He knew that he was strong enough to restrain the son.

At times, when he was immersed in pain and bitterness, the mute could feel his fists start to tremble. He would be tempted to strike his young master. But he suppressed this impulse along with his terrible pain. "No, he is the son of my master," he repeated to himself, "he is my young master."

He would forget soon enough. When the boy came home later in tears after playing with other children in the village, the mute would go fight for him like a bull on a wild rampage. No troublemaker in the village dared challenge the master's son for fear of the mute. And the boy, in turn, always sought out the mute whenever he was in trouble. Like a faithful dog that crawls back after a beating, the mute did all he could, without reservation, for the sake of his master's son.

2

Needless to say, the mute, despite his twenty-three years, had never had any opportunity to become acquainted with the fairer sex. He would experience a languid pleasure, mingled with anger and irritation, when the village girls mocked him, shouting "Mute, Mute," and making strange gestures with their hands and bodies. But he had never felt love for a woman.

Since the mute was a man and therefore experienced desire, his blood did not simply run cold. In fact, his blood may well have been hotter than others', but simply hardened, like toffee that curdled at high heat. With added heat or sunshine, his blood might just have boiled over. It was not that he did not let the odd sigh escape late into the night, as he wove straw shoes under a flickering oil lamp; rather, he'd given up any hope of satisfying his bodily desire so long ago that he could readily suppress it now.

Hidden deep in his heart there lay simmering passion, like a dormant volcano, the eruption of which none could foretell. The time for that had yet to come. Although the mute himself could feel his desire smolder within, threatening to explode, no occasion for release had presented itself. Indeed, external circumstances had suppressed his desire for so long that it seemed unlikely to manifest itself of its own accord. For in his repressed condition, he had developed a fortified self-control and an ever vigilant resignation.

"I'm a mute." He felt deep resentment at this thought, but at the same time he believed that he wasn't entitled to the same rights and freedoms as others. When he followed this line of reasoning, his self-resignation—the growth of which he could not have prevented, even had he wanted—continued to deepen, so that by now, like a machine, he took his slavery in his master's house as the hand of fate, believing that there was no other life for him.

3

It all happened in the autumn of that year. The master's son had just been married. The bride was nineteen, two years older than the bridegroom. The master had always been resentful of his family's low status and had coveted, more than anything else, a daughter-in-law with a noble lineage. But noble families do not let go of their daughters so easily. As a result, he had all but bought the daughter of certain fallen aristocrat from a southern village. He cajoled the aristocrat's widow into giving up her only daughter, then hurried to get the wedding ceremony over with lest the widow should change her mind.

He spent 30,000 *nyang*—a lot of money in those days—on the wedding and arranged to send his son's mother-in-law a monthly allowance of 2,500 *nyang*, supposedly in exchange for her continuing to do all her daughter's sewing and laundry.

The bride's family had been moderately well-off till her father's death, and since she had been brought up with great care, she was well-educated, having been taught all that could be learned in an old-fashioned household and having read all that was proper for a bride. There was no hint of any dark shadow to be seen in her person or manners.

As soon as the bride moved in, people began to find fault with the bridegroom.

"Compared with his bride, he's a crow next to a peacock."

"Still has no self-control."

"He'll play second fiddle to his wife."

"She deserves better than a bridegroom like him."

These were the kinds of things that gossip-mongering wives said when they gathered together. One woman who liked to poke her nose into other people's business even stopped the son once and said, as if reprimanding him, "Well, you should know better now that you're an adult. How can you keep a wife and still behave like you do? Aren't you ashamed of entering her room?"

On such occasions, the son's heart would become filled with animosity toward the speaker. Thinking that they were deliberately trying to humiliate him, he'd decline to greet or even address them the next time their paths crossed.

"You're an adult now. You're old enough to know better by now. Aren't you ashamed in front of your wife?" His aunt scolded him like this whenever she dropped in.

But instead of feeling ashamed at such reproaches, the nephew grew more resentful of his wife for having placed him in such an awkward position.

"What's a wife good for? All this trouble started after that wench came."

A few days after the wedding, he stopped visiting his wife's room. The household was turned upside-down as a result. The family even tried to push him into the bridal chamber, as if they were breeding a pig or a horse, but to no avail.

Every time such a circus occurred, the newlywed husband picked up whatever he could lay his hands on and swung it around indiscriminately. Once he hit his maternal cousin in the forehead, cutting her badly.

The family, at a loss about what to do, handed the matter over to the father. But that was no use, either, and caused only more turmoil. Upon being dismissed after a long sermon from his father, the son went to his wife's room and, without warning, grabbed her hair and threw her out into the corridor. "You bitch! Go back to your home!" he yelled, "I don't even want to look at you. Don't ever show up here again."

If a meal was served, the table would end up somersaulting in the middle of the yard, and if new clothes were brought in, they'd be dumped into a trash bin.

And so from the time of the wedding onward the bride cried day and night over her misfortune.

She was beaten for the wickedness of her weeping and struck for the dim-wittedness of her silence. Not a day of peace passed in the house.

Among those who witnessed her daily misery, one person in particular was filled with dark forebodings, namely, Samnyong the mute.

He could not understand for all the world how anyone could beat such an angelic woman, someone so beautiful, so affectionate, and so modest that he himself would never have dared lay a finger on.

It made no sense to abuse a lady so pleasing to the eye and too sacred to ever be touched. As for himself, he deserved nothing more than to be thrashed like a dog or a pig by the young master. Yet it appalled him to no end to watch his mistress—who was as far above him as an angel over a beast—receive the same blows. The mute even worried that his young master would incur divine retribution.

On one moonlit night, when all was silent and forlorn, stars flickering here and there, the half moon hanging lucid in the air, and the world as crystal-clear as if purified with mercury, Samnyong lay stretched out on a straw mattress, lost in thought, his hand stroking the back of Blackie the dog, and his eyes gazing up at the sky.

When he thought of his new mistress, images of the moon and stars came to mind. Yet she seemed more graceful than the moon and purer than the stars. She had a heart more beautiful and tender than the silvery moonlight, which washed everything clean. It was as if she were the moon or a star come down to earth, or as if she could metamorphose into the moon or a star by merely reaching up to the sky.

Samnyong recalled how her eyes glistened with pity whenever the young master beat him, though she did not dare speak out. Petting Blackie's soft fur with his hand, Samnyong felt a warmth fill his heart. The dog licked his hand and wagged its tail, innocently believing that the mute's gentle caresses were meant for it alone.

Samnyong's heart was filled with compassion for his mistress and with the resolve that he would gladly give his life for her. These sentiments arose as instinctively within him as water fills the mouth of a hungry man at the scent of food.

4

Since the arrival of the new mistress, the inner quarters of the house had become off-limits to the servants, but the mute could come and go freely, untroubled by the suspicions of others, just as a dog goes in and out of the house as it pleases.

One day, Samnyong found his young master prostrate on the street, utterly drunk—a new habit with him. He'd been badly beaten by some brute. Samnyong carried his young master home on his back. When he brought him inside, he found his mistress sewing alone in her room. She felt grateful to the mute. A little while later she presented him with a silken pouch to store his flint as a token of her gratitude.

When the young master noticed the pouch one night, he dragged his wife from her bed and threw her out into the inner yard, her hair completely disheveled. Then he beat her black and blue.

On seeing this, the mute became inflamed with indignation. He rushed in like a wild boar, pulled the young master away, and flung his mistress over his shoulder. Then he ran, like a deer, to his aging master, and lay her down before him. The mute explained his case with repeated hand signs and other gestures.

The next morning, the young master struck the mute hard in the face with an ash-tree whip. One side of his face bled, his eye and cheek swelling up as large as a fist.

"Damn mute, how dare you touch my wife!" cursed the young master, as he whipped the mute. Then he grabbed the mute's pouch, tore it off, and threw away its pieces into the privy hole.

"Bastard! Now he even hits his own master. That bastard deserves to die!" He lashed the whip at the nape of the mute's neck, causing him to fall to the ground.

The mute joined his hands, pleading for forgiveness. Instead of apologizing with words, he made one deep bow after another, his nose almost touching the ground. But in his heart a desire for justice was beginning to stir. In his pain, he suppressed a seething anger.

From then on, the mute was forbidden to enter the inner quarters. The prohibition aroused his curiosity, which imperceptibly transformed more and more into a longing to see his mistress. The longer he went without seeing her, the stronger the flame in his heart burned. He ached with sorrow. Yet the desire to see her, even just once, also awakened a new sensibility in his soul. This nameless sensation, despite all his grief, brought him such joy that it made him feel alive; he would have gladly exchanged his life for this sensation. At times, he wanted to break through the wall of the house with his head, just to see his mistress. But he kept such impulses in check.

Since this awakening, he ceased to eat well. Nor could he concentrate on his work. During breaks he dreamed of entering the inner quarters.

The old master now took better care of him, giving him more food, and tried to make his life a little more comfortable. But the mute was not content. At night, sleepless, he would wander around the walls of the house.

5

One day, after the young master came home drunk again, the house was thrown into a commotion. A servant girl ran for medicine. The mute seized her on her way back in the hope of finding out what was going on inside.

The girl touched the back of her head with a closed fist, gently let her hand slide down her face, and then held out an index finger. According to the conventions worked out between the servants and the mute, a thumb meant the old master, an index finger the young master, a fist on the back of the head the wife, and rubbing the face—caressing.

Then the servant girl stuck out her tongue, rolled back her eyes, spread her arms wide, and fell backward. This gesture meant that a person was dying or seriously ill.

The mute watched the girl wide-eyed, took a few steps closer to her, then stood still, stunned.

His heart beat rapidly. Did this mean that his beloved mistress was dead? He clapped his hands together and let out a deep sigh. Then he went to his room and sat there for hours, motionless, as if deep in thought.

He became restless as the night grew dark. He would alternately stand up and sit down, and at about two o'clock he finally went out, heading toward the back of the house.

Like a thief, he stole up to the wall beneath the back window of his mistress's room. After hesitating a moment, he jumped over the wall. He peered into the room through a gap between its two windows. Then, with a shudder, he stepped back.

In the dark, his hands and feet trembled like the leaves of the persimmon tree close behind him. Suddenly, he rushed into the room, kicking the door open. The next moment, the mistress was struggling in his arms, clutching a long silken towel in one hand and shoving his chest with the other. The mute, wide-eyed, uttered, "Uh-uh-uh," all the while trying to pull the towel away.

By now, the house was in an uproar.

"The family's done for!"

"Of all men, why the mute!"

"Things like that, they're hard to fathom."

Such whispers could be heard from one corner of the house to the other.

6

The next morning, the mute lay groaning in the yard, his prostrate body aching all over, blood dripping from his mouth. The young master, interrogating him, stood with an iron-chained club in his hand.

"Bastard!"

The young master pointed at his wife's room, making all kinds of obscene gestures. But the mute only waved his hands. Before long, the club was covered with pieces of flesh. And blood flowed.

The mute, his throat burning, was unable to utter a sound and just shook his head. He fell and vomited blood but continued to bow his head, scraping his forehead against the ground. The soil was soaked with his blood. The young master tied a piece of lead to the end of a whip, swung it at the mute's chest, and pulled it back with all his might. The mute fell in silence.

The young master was still not content. He ran for a sickle, the blade of which the mute himself had recently sharpened. He raised the sickle high. When the blade was about to strike, the mute grabbed the handle with one hand. Others rushed from inside the house to stop the young master. The mute wrenched the sickle from his young master's hand and threw it away.

The old master took to his bed, mourning the fall of his house. He kept the door of his room closed and pretended not to see or hear anything. The family debated whether or not to cast the mistress out. That evening the mute was dragged out again. The young master gave him his clothes and shoes.

"Go!" he barked. "You're not welcome in my house any more." He glared at the mute and pointed into the distance with his finger.

The mute was incredulous. There was nowhere else for him to go. No place to live. He had always believed that he would live and die in this house. He clasped his young master's legs and begged. Using gestures and facial expressions, he articulated a sincere and voiceless plea. But the young master kicked him aside and gave an order.

"Throw the bastard out."

The mute was hauled out like a dead dog and thrown headfirst into a ditch. After struggling a while to get back onto his feet, he returned to the house, only to find that the gate had already been bolted shut. He pounded on the gate. In his heart, he was calling out to his old master, but his voice remained silent. The gate, which he used to open and close each day, now banished him. It would not open for him no matter how much he pleaded. All that he had managed and cared for was now turning against him. The reward for years of faithful service from his childhood till now, during which he had exerted all his body and soul, was eviction.

In the end, he concluded that everyone he had trusted and relied on was his enemy. He had better get rid of them all, including himself.

In the night air, the only sounds that could be heard were the crows of a rooster and the dog's barking. A flame suddenly flared up around Sir Oh's house, once the mute's home. The fire, as if by design, spread along the grass and encircled the walls. Seen from above, the bright flame would have cast an arabesque of the house.

The fire, like a demon's tongue as it savors a morsel of raw flesh, engulfed the entire house in no time. Into this fire a man braved his way. The man was none other than Samnyong, who had been driven from the same house earlier that day. He first went to his old master's room, broke open the door, carried the master out on his back, and laid him on the grass outside. Then he went back again, not heeding the burnt, charring flesh on his face, back, and legs.

The mute rushed into his mistress's room, but she wasn't there. He ran to the inner room, but she wasn't there, either. Instead, he met his young master, who clutched at his arm and begged for his life. But the mute shoved him aside. Parts of the rafter, now in flames, fell upon the mute's head, but he barely noticed. He went to the kitchen; on his way out, a doorpost fell and broke his arm. But he didn't pay attention to that, either. He headed for the storage room. Even there he couldn't find her. He returned to her room. Only then did he see her. He found her lying under a quilt, wishing for death. He gathered her up in his arms and looked for a way out. But there wasn't any to be found. Left with no other option, he climbed out onto the roof. He realized that he could no longer move his body freely. Yet he also felt a sense of delight in his heart unlike anything he had ever known. As he clutched his mistress to his chest, he felt fully alive for the first time. When he sensed that his end was drawing near, he embraced his mistress tightly and then bore his way out through the fire. He put her down outside, his own life already slipping away. The whole house had burned down, and the mute lay in his mistress's lap.

Had his indignation died out with the fire? A happy, peaceful smile formed faintly on his lips.

4

PAK T'AEWŎN

Along with his best friend Yi Sang, Pak T'aewŏn (1910–1986) was the most successful and accomplished modernist writer of colonial Korea. He was born in Seoul to a traditional medical family, but he chose to study English literature at Hōsei University in Japan. Among his defining intellectual experiences was the reading of Itō Sei's Japanese translation of James Joyce's *Ulysses*. In 1933 Pak was invited by Yi T'aejun to join the *Kuinhoe* (Group of nine), an influential circle of intellectuals promoting modernist literature, poetry, and arts. Pak's experimental works soon established him as one of the most exciting and controversial writers of his time.

Initially a writer of a private, individualist inspiration, over the years Pak shifted to more socially involved narratives that addressed the experiences of Seoulians living under a colonial regime. He depicted a variety of lower-class urban characters in the omnibus novel *Ch'ŏnbyŏn p'unggyŏng* (1936–1937, Streamside sketches), a work beloved today for its heartwarming snapshots of ordinary lives in the city. Facing the strictures of increased censorship, however, he gradually retreated to the translation of Chinese classics for the rest of the colonial period. Upon national division, having joined the North in 1950, Pak resumed there his literary activity, whose highlights include the publication of the epic trilogy *Kabo nongmin chŏnjaeng* (The 1894 peasant war) between 1977 and 1986.

A Day in the Life of Kubo the Novelist (Sosŏlga Kubo Ssi ŭi iril) is Pak's most famous work. It is rendered here along with Yi Sang's original illustrations, as they appeared when the novella was first serialized in the newspaper *Chungang Ilbo* in 1934. The novella is written in Pak's signature experimentalist style, featuring stream-of-consciousness narration, peculiar shifts of tense, impossibly long-winded sentences, and the surrealistic incorporation of extraliterary material. Kubo, Pak's endearing autobiographical character, is a young aspiring writer strolling the streets of Seoul. Half lonely intellectual and half spirited observer of the dazzling scenes of the metropolis, he captures through his reflections the sense of alienation and ennui that characterized an intellectual life during the increasingly repressive decade of the 1930s. The novella was a sensation upon its first appearance, and it became a frequent inspiration for writers in subsequent decades. Ch'oe Inhun published a same-titled parody of Pak's *Kubo* in 1972; Chu Insŏk followed with his postmodernist Kubo stories in the 1990s; and Kubo appeared in hypertext form in *Digital Kubo 2001*, by Ch'oe Hyesil and others. The popularity of Pak's character is such that today "Kubo" has become a generic term in Korean for an urban stroller leisurely pondering the scenes of the metropolis.

* * *

Translator's note: I have made two major adjustments in translating Pak T'ae-wŏn's experimental novella into English. First, the writer uses a peculiar mixture of verb tenses: he habitually starts a paragraph in the past tense and then, as if staging a scene, narrates the rest in the present. Also, he tends to assign the past tense to external actions, while everything that is filtered through Kubo's perception is described in the present tense. However, Pak is not consistent on these points. To avoid confusion in English, I have simplified the tense in some parts. Second, the writer makes a unique use of commas in Korean, often splitting the subject from the predicate. In translation, these commas do not produce the same effects as in the original. I have omitted most of the commas between subject and predicate and, in other places, have replaced them with other forms of punctuation, such as the dash.

A Day in the Life of Kubo the Novelist

(1934)

The Mother

heard the son leave his room and put on his shoes at the edge of the veranda. He's taking his walking stick off the nail on the rack and walking toward the middle gate.

"Are you going out?"

No answer.

The son, now at the door, might not have heard what she said. Or his reply might not have reached her ear. The mother, figuring it must be one or the other, raises her voice this time so as to be heard from the other side of the gate.

"Come back early!"

Again, there is no response.

The door creaks open and then shuts again. The mother tries to console herself, as she is feeling a bit frustrated. If only the door had not creaked so loud, she might have heard the son's "Yes!" . . .

She resumes her sewing, wondering, just where, does he go, everyday, like that.

The jobless, wifeless twenty-six-year-old son brought his aging mother all kinds of worries, troubles. For instance, if he went out in the afternoon, he returned only very late at night.

The frail, old mother lies down on the bare floor, her head resting on her arm. Waiting for her son, she soon falls asleep. Such uncomfortable sleep doesn't last more than two or three hours at a stretch. Each time she wakes up, after having briefly dozed off, she takes a look at the son's room and then at the clock on the wall.

Midnight—not too late. Now the son will be back. Praying that he comes back soon, she nods off again.

It's half past one or two when she wakes up for the second time. The light is on in the son's room.

The son always turns off the light when he goes to bed. Can it be that he has already come back without her knowing and is now reading in bed? That would be just like him.

The mother tiptoes to the son's room and cautiously listens in. Finally, she opens the door. What is keeping him out this late? Her face forlorn, she is about to close the door behind her, but instead stops and enters the room.

Her grown-up son's room, lacking any hint of perfume or fragrant oil, makes the mother sad. She fixes his bedding and pillow, which remain as they had been arranged earlier in the evening, and sits next to them. She has raised him all these twenty-six years, but you never feel at ease when it comes to your child. Even if these twenty-six years were multiplied by as many years again, her heart would always be burdened by worries. Still, the mother thinks, if only she could marry him off, she would at least not have this late-night anguish.

"Why doesn't he want to get married?"

Whenever she began to talk about marriage, the son would say,

"How could I support a wife when I'm penniless?"

But . . . there must be a way. Whatever job he ends up taking, he'll surely be able to support a family of two. . . .

The mother feels heavy-hearted and sorry for her son, who has no intention of looking for a regular job, always just reading and writing, and wandering aimlessly in the dead of the night.

"He'll change his mind once he's married."

"He will, naturally, think about making money, if he loves his wife."

Last summer he was introduced to a nice girl. If it could be that girl, he wouldn't turn her down. I'll have a good talk with him when he comes home. . . . Soon the mother pictures a grandson to herself.

The Son

came back, but before the mother could say anything—you're still not in bed, good night now—he changed into pajamas, sat at his desk, and opened his writing pad.

If she were to say anything right now, the son would assume an offended air. That always hurt her. All right, hurry to bed now, it's late, the mother barely managed to say, you can write all that tomorrow. . . . Then she left his room.

"The talk can wait till morning."

But the next day, the son got up at eleven or maybe noon, ate his meal without a word, and was off again.

Sometimes, he earned some money by selling his writings. On one occasion, he asked her, is there anything special you'd like to eat?

The mother was amazed and delighted at the fact that her jobless son could somehow earn a little money and offer her something like that.

"Don't worry about me. Buy some new socks for yourself instead."

Then the son, as usual, grew stubborn. Needless to say, she didn't like his obstinacy. But in a case like this, the more stubbornly he insisted, the more satisfied she grew. A mother's love does not seek reward, and yet when her child shows his love, it gladdens her heart.

Just what will you buy for me? Whatever you wish. Can it be something other than food? Certainly. So the mother ventured what she really desired.

"Could you buy me a skirt?"

Seeing that the son readily approved,

"Aren't you going to buy one for your sister-in-law, too?"

He asked how much two skirts would cost, and his face suddenly grew dark. Maybe the money he had earned, after all those sleepless nights, wasn't so great a sum after all.

"Okay," the mother said, "Then just buy hers."

The son: No, I have enough. Take this and buy them.

And he gave her the money.

The mother hesitated a moment. But, in the end, she accepted the money with pride, Let's go buy fabrics, look, your brother-in-law gave me money for skirts. Your brother-in-law. . . . In this way, she surprised her daughter-in-law at the sewing machine in the next room.

When the skirt was finished, the mother put it on, went out.

In a relative's house, sitting with his wife, the mother, childlike, waited for a chance to show off her skirt. If the woman, unwittingly, said, ah, you've got such a nice skirt, the mother answered right away,

"This is a present from my second son," before even being asked. "He bought one for his sister-in-law and this one. . . . " She took such pride in her son. When boasting of her son, she lost all inhibitions.

However, such scenes do not happen often. The mother thinks having a regular job is much better than writing, and concludes that her gifted son will do well in whatever he does. He talks about how difficult it is to get a job these days. Yet she has seen others doing just fine at companies or in public office, even though they had only an elementary school education and never earned a high school diploma. So she can't for all the world believe that her son, who graduated from high school and has even been to Japan to study, can't find a job.

Kubo,

now out of the house, walks along the riverside road toward the Kwanggyo Bridge and regrets not having said a simple "yes" to his mother. In fact, the word had been on the tip of his tongue at the gate. But the distance between the outer-quarters gate and the inner room required quite a loud voice, and just then three schoolgirls were passing by, laughing and chattering away.

Still, he should have answered. Kubo imagines the lonely look on his mother's face. The girls have drifted out of sight.

At last he reaches the foundation of the bridge. He has been walking, seemingly with a purpose, but now he stops. Where now? He can go anywhere. There is nowhere for him to go.

On the sunlit street, Kubo suddenly feels an acute headache coming on. Though he has a good appetite and sleeps well, he must be having a nervous breakdown.

He looks glum.

KBr 4.0
$NaBr$ 2.0NH_4Br 2.0
MgI_2 4.0
Water 200. 0
3 times a day, before each meal, for 2 days

This medicine—the young nurse at the hospital always calls it 3 *ppisui*—has no effect on him whatsoever.

Kubo abruptly steps aside. At that instant a bicycle rushes past, narrowly missing him. The young man on the bicycle throws back a contemptuous look. He must have been ringing his bell loudly from quite a distance away. Kubo's narrow escape is not necessarily due to the fact that he had been trying to recall the prescription for "3Bsu."†

Kubo is doubtful of his left ear's capacity. The young medical assistant who examined his ear was by no means skillful, yet he dared to declare that nothing was wrong, except that the ear was very dirty inside. Kubo felt a profound sense of humiliation on hearing this diagnosis, for he'd rather have a four-week treatment for an ear infection than a lump of earwax. Still, he carried on nervously cleaning out his ear every day.

But fortunately he did seem to have an infection. On one occasion, he browsed through a medical dictionary and, for no particular reason, decided that he had *otitis media catarrh.* According to the dictionary, *otitis media catarrh* can be acute or chronic, the chronic type having two subtypes, one wet and one dry. Kubo has concluded that his disease must be of the chronic wet type.

But then, besides his left ear, something else seems wrong. Kubo doesn't have much confidence in his right ear, either. He has neglected it for a year now, always thinking that he should see a specialist soon. Someday, in the not so distant future, having overused the comparatively sound right ear to compensate for the dysfunctional left one, he may have to wear a Dunkel ear trumpet or an electronic hearing aid.

Kubo

decides to start walking. For he realizes anew the senselessness of standing idle by the bridge. He walks toward the Chongno intersection. He has no business there. Only that his right foot, randomly put forth, happened to veer leftward.

Out of the blue, a man appears and crosses his path. Kubo imagines their collision and staggers to a halt.

† Translator's note: "B" stands for bromide and "su" is the Korean pronunciation of the Chinese character for water. The nurse's pronunciation reflects a Japanese accent.

The next moment, he curses his eyesight, which cannot be trusted even in broad daylight. The 24° eyeglasses perching on his nose help mitigate his shortsightedness, but have no effect on the numerous scotomata on his retina. His vision test chart, from his days at the Government General Hospital, may well still be lying in his gloomy drawer, entitled,

Ophthalmologist Follow-up Visit. R, 4 L, 3

Kubo now remembers the optical perimeter, which he saw on a small table at the ophthalmologist's during his first visit, when he had gone to complain about his weakened eyesight after two weeks of suffering from fever. The doctor, who himself wore a rather thick pair of glasses, coarsely marked all the scotomata with chalk.

Despite all this, Kubo crosses two railroad tracks, with a confident gait, and then walks to Hwasin. Before he notices it, his foot steps into the department store.

A young married couple with a four- or five-year-old boy waits for an elevator. Now they'll want to enjoy a nice lunch at some restaurant. A desire to show off their happiness to Kubo seems to gleam in the couple's eyes. For a second, he considers cursing them, but instantly changes his mind and instead gives them his blessing. In fact, he may be envying the couple, who are enjoying this day out together, renewing their sense of happiness, despite several years already of married life together. They clearly have a home, where they must be happy.

The elevator descends, the door opens, closes, and the young couple disappears from Kubo's sight with their boy Luckie or Rich.

On his way out, Kubo wonders where he would ever find happiness of his own. He follows his feet to the safety zone at a streetcar station, and now, standing there, looks down at his hands. A walking stick in one hand and a notebook in the other—Kubo, of course, cannot find his happiness in them.

In the safety zone, people are waiting for a streetcar. To them, happiness is unknown. Yet they do have a place to go, at least.

The streetcar arrives. People get off and on. Kubo stands there for a while, absent-minded. But when he sees all those who have just been standing with him step into the streetcar, he feels sad and lonely at the thought of being left behind. He jumps on the moving car.

On the Streetcar

Kubo, at first, couldn't find a seat. The last seat was taken by a young woman who had boarded just before him. Standing at a corner near the conductor's seat, he wonders, where he should go on this Tongdaemun-bound streetcar, at which stop might happiness await.

Now the streetcar is running around Tongdaemun Gate and past the Kyŏngsŏng Stadium . . . Kubo looks at the window, which is lined with blue flannelette. The Train Bureau posts news there. But recently, people don't seem to be playing either soccer or baseball.

To Changch'ungdan, to Ch'ŏngnyangni, or to Songbuktong. . . . Nowadays, Kubo doesn't like the outskirts. Nature and leisure are there for the taking, it's true. And even solitude, all prepared for him. Nowadays, he fears solitude.

He had loved it once. But to say he'd loved solitude might not be an accurate description of his previous state of mind. Perhaps he had never really loved it. Maybe, he'd always dreaded it. No matter how often he wrestled with solitude, he could never conquer it. Kubo might have just let himself become lost in it at times and pretended to be in love with it. . . .

Tickets, please—the conductor is coming near. Kubo rests his walking stick on his left arm, and thrusts his hand into his pant pocket. But after he sorts out five coins, the streetcar stops at Chong-myo, and the conductor returns to his seat.

Kubo lowers his eyes and looks at the five coins in his hand. They had all by chance come out tails. *Taisho* twelfth year, eleventh year, eighteenth year. . . . Kubo tries to discern meaning in the figures. But this proves fruitless, and even if he could make sense of them, this would still not be "happiness."

The conductor again approaches him. Sir, where are you going? Kubo takes note of where the streetcar is headed. How about going to Ch'anggyŏng Park. But he doesn't make any sign to the conductor. Once on a streetcar, a man with no destination has nowhere to get off.

The streetcar stops and then sets off again. Looking out the window, Kubo thinks that he could have dropped by the university hospital at least. A friend studies psychosis in the lab there. Visiting him and seeing a different world may not bring happiness, but it would have counted as business at least. . . .

When Kubo turns around, he sees a woman who seems to have just gotten on the car, and to his surprise, he recognizes her. If he tells his mother back at home, I met *her*, the mother, her face all lit up, would naturally keep pressing him, "and then and then?" If he says that's all, the mother would be disappointed and accuse him of tactlessness. But then if someone else hears about it and talks of the son's timidity, the mother would excuse him, saying, since my son is so shy by nature. . . .

Afraid of meeting her eyes, Kubo looks nowhere in particular, wondering, did she see me standing here?

The Woman

perhaps saw him. There are few passengers in the streetcar, and a man standing in a corner, heedless of the empty seats, is readily visible. She would have certainly seen him. But did she recognize him?

That's uncertain. She couldn't have that easily recognized a man whom she met only once last summer, and has never met since, not even on the street. To reflect that all memory of you is lost to a woman whom you remember is, for any man, a lonely and disconsolate experience. Thinking that his bold, or rather insolent, attitude at the time must have left her with quite an impression, Kubo wants to believe that she, too, sometimes thought of him.

She must have seen me and knows who I am. In which case, what is her feeling now? This piques Kubo's curiosity.

He glances, with timidity, at the profile of the woman, who's sitting diagonally across from him about ten feet away. Instantly, he looks elsewhere, afraid of meeting her eyes, thinking that she may also have glanced at him and noticed him stealing a look at her. She may know him to be the man, and also know that he knows she's the woman. So, what should I do now? Kubo racks his brain. Maybe I should greet her. But then maybe it's more polite to pretend not to have noticed her. I wish I knew which of the two she wants. Then, suddenly, he feels funny and strange that he should be nervous about such a thing. How can I be so worked up over such a trifle? Maybe, in those days, I really had a secret longing for her in my heart. But when he recalls that he has never once seen her in his dreams since their meeting last year, it dawns on him that he was probably never really in love with her.

And if not, then all this mind-reading and flights of fancy would be, to say the least, an emotional violation, a sin of sorts.

But what if she did long for him—.

Just as he turns to look at her, she gets up, picks up her umbrella, and gets off at Tongdaemun. Kubo, his heart troubled once more, feels like getting off himself, as he sees her standing in the safety zone waiting for a Ch'ŏngnyangni-bound streetcar. Still, if she finds him again on the same streetcar and discovers that he got on for no other reason but to try his luck with her, how crass she would find him. While he wavers, the streetcar moves on, and the two grow farther apart. Finally, she is completely out of sight, and only then, all of a sudden, damn, Kubo regrets.

—that happiness for which he so yearns—might have departed forever with her. A bearer of happiness for him, she may have longed for him to open his heart. Why can't I be more daring? Kubo lists all her merits one by one. Will there ever be someone else who could offer me some promise of happiness?

With the destination board changed to the Han River Bridge, the streetcar passes the Training Center. Kubo sits down and sorts out five-chŏn coins from his pocket, wondering whether she might after all be the only woman for him, even if she never had appeared in his dreams.

His belief that he has never thought much of her might be nothing more than a kind of self-deception. When he returned home after first meeting her, he certainly did express an opinion, a "she-might-do" to his anxiously waiting mother. All the same, Kubo forbade his mother to make a proposal to her family. He did so not simply from vanity. He didn't want to cause unsolicited trouble for her, in case she might not be interested in him. Kubo wanted to respect her feelings and opinions.

Of course, no word was heard from her. From time to time, Kubo wondered whether she could be secretly waiting for a word from him. Yet to entertain such an idea was ridiculously self-conceited. Meanwhile, time passed, and he began to lose interest in the issue. Perhaps, if her parents had sent word first—. Then Kubo would have been able to rouse his interest again. At one point, an old lady, who was somehow related to her family, had come and hinted that they were observing the moves on his side; Kubo smiled wryly, and thought that if this were true, then it's not a comedy, but rather a tragedy. Still, he was not willing to take any action to save them both from tragedy.

As the streetcar passes by Yakch'ojŏng, Kubo is distracted from this absorbing line of thought upon seeing a young woman sitting in front of him with an umbrella between her knees. He grins slyly. In a certain magazine, he learned that this suggests a woman is not a virgin. In fact, aside from her done-up hairstyle, a woman of her age would naturally have a husband. *Her*, where did she place her umbrella. Kubo, toying with such a wayward idea, considers whether someone who makes such an observation about a woman isn't bound to make whomever he marries unhappy. Yet a woman—. Will a woman be able to make him happy? He considers all his female acquaintances one after another, and softly sighs.

Once

Kubo had harbored an unrequited love for his friend's sister. On those summer evenings, while visiting his friend, this sister, who came to the door to meet him, may well have been beautiful and pure, sufficiently so for young Kubo to admire. The fifteen-year-old bookish boy thought that he wanted to love her, thought that he would certainly be happy if he could marry her someday; he visited his friend frequently in the hope of meeting her, blushed at chance encounters, and, upon returning home, drafted many late-night love poems. But the knowledge that she was three years older than him made him feel insecure. When he reaches an age at which confessions of love to a woman would no longer be awkward, she will have already embraced another, older man.

Before he could devise any solution to this problem, she, indeed, ended up nestling into an older man's arms. Seventeen-year-old Kubo liked to think that his heart became quite filled with sorrow, and yet he tried to wish for their happiness, especially the man's. A great deal had been written about such sentiments in the books he'd read. Three thousand wŏn to cover the wedding expenses. A honeymoon in Tokyo. A house in Kwansudong, recently renovated for the newlyweds. This seemed to guarantee their happiness.

This spring Kubo and his friend visited the couple. With the wife, who was already a mother of two, Kubo could carry on an ordinary conversation without blushing. When he complimented her clever seven-year-old boy, the young mother complained that the boy was the youngest in the neighborhood, and that the older children behaved so nastily toward the smaller ones. She even proudly told him how she once marked each of her son's cards with a pencil, since she pitied him for always coming home after losing his cards to the other children. When he returned that day with all his cards gone, she summoned the children in the neighborhood and recovered the cards by picking out "my" child's from the ones they had. . . .

Kubo sighs gently. It's no loss that he couldn't marry her after all. With that kind of woman, he would probably never have gained the chance to know what happiness is.

He got off the streetcar at the Chosŏn Bank and headed for Changgokch'ŏnjŏng. Tired of thinking, he'll now stop at a teahouse to enjoy a cup of tea.

What time is it? But he has no watch. If he could, he would choose an elegant pocket watch. A wristwatch—that suits only a young girl's taste. Kubo recalls a girl who wanted a wristwatch. She desired an 18K gold watch at a local pawnshop. It carried a price tag of four wŏn and eighty chŏn. And the girl thought she would reach the pinnacle of happiness if she could also buy a new skirt, aside from the watch.

A voile skirt woven with "Bemberg" strands. Three wŏn and sixty chŏn. In all, eight wŏn and forty chŏn might have completed her happiness. But Kubo has not heard whether her modest wish was ever granted.

Kubo wonders just how much he would need to be happy.

In the Teahouse

about two in the afternoon, jobless types are sitting around on cane chairs, talking, drinking tea, smoking cigarettes, and listening to records. They are mostly young and yet, despite their youth, look already world-wearied. In the dark, partially lit place, their eyes broadcast a litany of trials and tribulations. Occasionally, a buoyant footstep glides into the teahouse, or a bright laugh fills the room. But such luxuries are out of place here. The teahouse regulars disdain them above all else. After ordering coffee and cigarettes from a young waiter, Kubo heads for a cane table in the corner. Just how much would I need. . . . A poster hangs over his head, a certain painter's "**Farewell Exhibition upon Leaving for Europe**." Kubo imagines that if he had money to go abroad, he would be almost completely happy, at least for a time. Even just to Tokyo. Tokyo is just as good. Kubo thinks that he'd like to see how Tokyo has changed since he left. Or even a place closer to home. Somewhere right nearby would also do. Kubo believes that he would certainly feel happy, were he to find himself at Kyŏngsŏng Station with his small suitcase, even if his destination were no farther than twelve miles away. That is a happiness only time and money can offer. He is prepared to go on a trip at any moment. . . .

Sipping his coffee, he counts all the types of happiness a little money can buy. He, too, even with only eight wŏn and forty chŏn, would be able to acquire, for a time, some small happiness, or even more. Kubo doesn't want to mock himself for that thought. A heart that can be consoled for a while with a little money, doesn't it deserve sympathy, love even?

What on earth is my greatest wish? Kubo lit a cigarette. Ishikawa Takuboku once asked, cleaning his pipe at a hearth, what is my real desire? Yet even though it seemed that there should be such a desire, he found there wasn't one. Probably true. But if you try, anything can be put into words. Tzu Lu wanted to go for a carriage ride with a friend, wearing light clothes and enjoying himself to his heart's content, while Kong Jung wished for a room full of guests and a glass of wine that never ran dry. Kubo wishes that he, too, could find pleasure among good friends.

All of a sudden, Kubo yearns for a friend. He wishes he had a friend here to chat with over coffee, to share the same thoughts. . . .

Outside, footsteps on the pavement stop in front of the teahouse, and the door silently opens. But the man is not one of Kubo's friends. Moreover, whenever their eyes meet, the two almost simultaneously turn their heads away, and melancholy settles over Kubo's quiet heart.

With the Man,

Kubo exchanged greetings once. Still, that was on a dark street. A friend introduced them. I've heard a lot about you, the man said. In fact, he must have known Kubo's name and face from before. Yet Kubo, Kubo didn't know him. The meeting in the dark ended without his seeing much of the stranger, and when he came across the man afterward, he failed to recognize him. The man must have felt insulted when Kubo passed by without acknowledging him. If the man thought that Kubo recognized him but pretended not to, it was only natural that he should take offense. But Kubo, Kubo didn't know this, and could appear quite at ease in his ignorance. He just found the man odd, for whenever they encountered each other, the man would avert his eyes, looking embarrassed and upset. As long as Kubo had found the man merely odd, he felt fine. When he finally recollected who the man was, though, a shadow was cast over his heart. Since then, Kubo, when spotting the stranger, would involuntarily turn away, equally embarrassed and confused. Kubo, now trying to block out one corner of the teahouse from view, can't help but feel anew the complexity of human relationships.

Leaving a couple of silver coins on the table, he exits the teahouse with notebook in hand. Where now? He walks toward the Prefecture Hall. In any case, I'd like to see a friend. In his mind Kubo watches the faces of all his friends parade before him according to the order of their streets. But none was likely to be home at this time of day. Where now? In the middle of the street, he looks up beyond the spacious yard at the Taehanmun Gate. Try the swing at the children's park . . . but the shabbiness, the shabbiness of the old palace, this is also something that weighs down on one's heart.

As he throws away his cigarette butt on the street, he notices a boy standing beside him. In his hand he holds the walking stick that Kubo left behind in the teahouse. Thanks. Kubo, chuckling at his own absent-mindedness, gazes a while at the back of the boy running back to the teahouse, and he himself follows the same path back.

In the back alley next to the teahouse. A young painter runs an antique store there. Kubo knows nothing about painting. But at any rate, it suits his taste, and if chance permits, he would like to hear a few stories about that profession. A novelist requires all kinds of knowledge.

But the friend is not in. "Master just went out." Looking at the clock on the wall, the clerk adds, "About ten minutes ago."

Walking along the alley toward the railway line, Kubo wonders, what effect will those ten minutes have on him.

In the street people come and go, in a hurry, at work. Standing on the pavement, Kubo suddenly thinks of going somewhere, maybe even just to the Sŏsomun area, for the sake of his writing. For so long he's been lazy in his *modernology*.

Yet with that thought Kubo feels an acute headache and a general fatigue, and so he can't take a single step further. Kubo stands there a while on the street, in a stupor. . . .

After a While

Kubo decides to walk again. The scorching midsummer sun on his bare head has made him dizzy. He can't stay there standing like that. Neurasthenia. Of course, it's not just his nerves breaking down. With this head of mine, with this body, how much work will I ever accomplish—. Kubo, feeling somewhat threatened by the energetic body and resilient gait of a virile man just then passing by, suddenly regrets his having read *The Tale of Chunhyang* at the age of nine, hidden away from the watchful eyes of the adults in the family. After a visit with his mother to one of their relatives, Kubo thought, he, too, like them, wanted to read storybooks. But this was forbidden in his house. Kubo privately consulted a housemaid. She told him that a certain rental place had all kinds of books and lent them for one wŏn a volume, not more. But you'll get a scolding—. And then, she muttered to herself, for fun nothing beats *The Tale of Chunhyang*. A coin and the lid of a copper bowl. Those objects from seventeen years ago might have been the beginning of everything that followed afterward, as well as all that is yet to come. The storybooks he used to read. The novels he spent his nights with. Kubo's health must have suffered irreparable damage in his boyhood.

Constipation. Irregular urination. Fatigue. Ennui. Headache. Heavy-headedness. Syncope. Dr. Morida Masao's training therapy . . . Whatever his illness is, T'aep'yŏngt'ong Street, humble, no, rather barren, and cluttered, darkens Kubo's mind. While thinking of how to drive those dirty junkmen off the streets, he suddenly remembers how Sŏhae papered over his ceiling to hide its loud patterns from his sight. Another unmistakable case of nervous exhaustion, a nameless grin forms on Kubo's lips. Sŏhae's horselaugh. Come to think of it, that, too, was a hollow, lonely sound.

Kubo remembers how he hasn't even looked at one page of *Scarlet Flame*, a book the late friend had given to him, and feels regret. It's not just Sŏhae's work that he has not read. Already three years behind in his reading. One time Kubo noticed the dearth of his knowledge and was dumbfounded.

Suddenly a young man passed into Kubo's line of sight. He came from the direction toward which Kubo is walking. He seems familiar. Someone Kubo should definitely recognize. Finally, when the distance between the two is reduced to less than six feet, Kubo discerns in the man's face one of his old buddies from childhood. The good old days. A good old friend. They haven't seen each other since their elementary school days. Yet Kubo even manages to extract from his memory the name of this friend.

But the old friend has had a hard lot in life. He looks so shabby in his ramie overcoat, white rubber shoes, and straw hat—this hat is the only new thing about him. Kubo hesitates. Should I pass without taking notice. The old friend seems to have clearly recognized him. And he seems to be afraid of Kubo's noticing him. But, finally, just as the two are passing each other, at the very last moment, Kubo musters his courage.

"Long time no see, Mr. Yu."

Yet the friend, at that instant, even blushes a bit.

"Yeah, it's been a while."

"Have you been in Seoul all this time?"

"Yes."

"Where have you been hiding?"

Having managed to say no more than this, Kubo feels downhearted and wishes he could add something more. But the friend, Excuse me. Saying that, he leaves Kubo, and goes on his way.

Kubo stands a while longer and then resumes his walk, his head low, hopelessly fending off tears.

A Little

joy, this is what Kubo decides to look for by taking a stroll through the Namdaemun market. But all he finds there are a few baggage carriers listlessly squatting on either side of the path, no wind blowing in.

Feeling lonely, Kubo thinks he wants to go where people are, where crowds are lively. He sees Kyŏngsŏng Station ahead of him. There would certainly be life there. The scent and feel of ancient capital city. It's only proper that an urban novelist should be well acquainted with the gates of the city. But of course such professional conscientiousness isn't what's important. It would be enough for Kubo if he could only escape his loneliness amid the crowd in the third-class waiting room.

Yet that is just where loneliness dwells. Although the place is so packed with people that Kubo can't even find a seat to squeeze into, there's no human warmth. Without exchanging a word with those sitting next to them, these people are preoccupied with their own business, and should they happen to say anything to each other, it's only to check the train schedule or something along those lines. Other than their travel companions, they would never ask anyone else to watch their luggage while they run to the restroom. Their distrustful eyes look weary and pathetic.

Setting himself up in a corner, Kubo looks at an old granny in front of him. She may have lived in somebody's house as hired help, and now, dragging her old frail body along, she's on her way to visit her daughter in some impoverished countryside. The palsied muscles of her face will never be smoothed out, not by any stroke of luck, and her cloudy eyes may never move again, not even if her daughter takes the best possible care of her. The middle-aged country gentleman next to her probably runs a small general store in his village. His shop likely carries silk fabrics, everyday goods, and regular medicines. Soon he'll pick up the parcels next to him and proudly get on board. Kubo notices how the man is trying to keep his distance from the old woman, and Kubo despises him. If the man had been given an ounce each of savviness and courage, he would, with all his arrogance, have taken a seat in the first- or second-class waiting room, his third-class ticket safely tucked away in a pocket.

Suddenly Kubo realizes that the man's face is swollen and walks away from him. Nephritis. In addition, the man's face stirs up the unpleasant memory of Kubo's own chronic gastrectasia. But when he walks to a kiosk, he finds himself once again face-to-face with a sick man. A forty-year-old laborer, goiter on his neck, protruding

eyeballs. Plus the trembling hand, evidently Basedow's disease. Doesn't seem very hygienic. Though the seats on either side of him are empty, people are not willing to sit in them. About ten feet away from the man, a young wife with a child on her back drops a peach by mistake while taking it from her basket. She sees it rolling toward the feet of the invalid and gives up chasing after it.

Kubo is drawn to this small incident and opens his notebook. But he detects a man standing by the door, dressed in a linen suit with a turned-up collar, watching him with suspicious eyes, and Kubo hastens to leave, once again gloomy.

In Front of the Ticket Barrier

two men are standing. Kubo confidently judges them to be unemployed from their worn panama hats, ramie overcoats, yellow shoes, and empty hands. Nowadays these jobless types are mostly gold-mine brokers. He looks around the waiting room again. Their kind could be seen here and there. The Age of Gold Mines.

Kubo lets escape a deep sigh. To search for gold, to search for gold . . . this, too, is an honest way of life, clearly. Their lives might, in any case, be more sincere than his own, which he spends aimlessly wandering the streets with a walking stick in one hand and a notebook in the other. Those countless mining offices scattered throughout downtown. The stamp duty, a hundred wŏn. The admission fee, five wŏn. The service fee, ten wŏn. The guidance fee, eighteen wŏn. . . . Applied and registered mining claims, seventy percent of all of Korea. Day after day people are made rich in an instant and then lose everything. The Age of Gold Mines. Among them are men of letters, including critics and poets. Kubo at one time thought that he wanted to visit his friend's mine and take down details for his writing. Speculative minds, the dreadful power of gold—he wanted to see and feel such things. Yet the most severe cases of gold fever were to be found in the Government General Hall, among the highest offices of the Oriental Development Company, and in the library of the Mining Bureau. . . .

Suddenly, one man, with a smile on his round, vulgar face, extends his shapeless hand to Kubo. He, too, could be called a friend. A slow classmate from his junior high school days. Kubo almost smiles and awkwardly reaches out his hand, walking stick still in it. How long has it been. Are you going somewhere. Yes, and *jah-neh*—?

Kubo always feels irritated when addressed as *jah-neh* by a mere acquaintance. An imperative verb is more tolerable than the condescending second-person pronoun. The man takes out a gold watch from his pocket. Then, looking at Kubo's face, why don't we have tea together? The second son of a pawnshop owner. Kubo has no intention of drinking tea with such a man. Yet, he has not enough nerve to turn down the offer by making up an excuse. The man takes the lead. Well—then let's go over there. But he is not just addressing Kubo.

Kubo sees a woman following behind. One glance is enough to reveal that she is his lover. Since when does this kind of man care about love? He notices again the man's vulgar face. But then now is an age when even sentimental poets are becoming gold maniacs.

The man sits down casually on the chair and says to the waitress, Calpis for me. Then, to Kubo, for you, too. But Kubo hurries to shake his head. Tea or coffee for me. Kubo is not fond of Calpis. The milky drink has an obscene color. Also, the taste doesn't agree with him. Sipping on his tea, Kubo suddenly wonders, wouldn't it be possible to figure out a person's character, taste, and education level from the drinks they order at a teahouse? Then again, drinks can also express passing moods.

Casually responding to the coarse stories of the man sitting in front of him, Kubo plans on conducting research on this subject someday.

To Wŏlmi Island,

on a picnic, they appeared to be going. Leaving them, Kubo steps out of the station by himself. Departing at this hour, they'll stay there at least overnight. He imagines the man's face to be now even uglier, with a lewd grin, as he wantonly caresses her naked body. Kubo feels nauseous.

That woman, she certainly was pretty. She may well be more attractive than all the women Kubo has so far found beautiful. And that's not all. She was also sensible enough to turn down the man's recommendation of Calpis, ordering a bowl of ice cream instead.

Kubo wonders why such a woman would want to love that kind of man, or why she allows him to love her. It must be the gold, of course. Women easily find happiness in gold. At once pitying and resenting her, Kubo is suddenly seized with envy for the man's wealth. In fact, money would only be wasted on such a man. He would stuff himself with rich delicacies, enjoy plump whores, and proudly show off his gold watch to everybody.

For a brief moment, Kubo smacks his lips, imagining that the money the man throws about is actually his. But he immediately rebukes himself. Since when have I been so obsessed with money. . . . He knocks the tip of his shoes with his walking stick, quickly crosses the railway tracks, and is soon heading along the pavement.

But that woman, she certainly was pretty, and . . . Kubo suddenly wonders if she gave herself to the man a long time ago. The mere thought upsets him. In the end, she is far from being sensible. On second thought, something in her reeks of indecency. Her figure has no grace. Only somewhat pretty.

But her easy smiles for the man need not cause Kubo to underestimate her. The man enjoys her body, the woman consumes his gold, and both might be happy enough. Happiness is very subjective. . . .

Kubo arrived at the Chosŏn bank. Feeling as he does now, he doesn't want to go home. Then where now—. He is again beset by loneliness and fatigue. Shine your shoes. Bewildered, Kubo gazes at the man, who apparently scrutinizes others' shoes and always finds fault with them, however minor. Kubo walks on. Does the man have any right to criticize someone else's shoes? Cursing all kinds of irritations on the street, Kubo suddenly senses the danger of being out alone at a time like this. Anybody would do. With a friend, if with a friend, Kubo might cheer up a bit. Or pretend to be cheerful.

At last, one friend comes to mind, and Kubo phones him from a tailor's shop. Fortunately, the friend is still at his office. Just about to leave, he says.

Kubo begs him to come to the teahouse; while fumbling a moment for something to say, he grows anxious, lest the other should hang up the phone, and so, faltering, adds,

"Please, come right away—."

Fortunately

the teahouse he returned to is not crowded. Also, when he looks around, self-consciously, remembering his friend who is not a friend, he realizes that the man is already gone. Kubo sits close to the counter and starts to develop a fondness for the teahouse, which is now playing Schipa's *Ahi Ahi Ahi*. If it were allowed, he would change his cane chair for an armchair and enjoy a sweet nap. If he were to see the cobbler he saw a short time ago, he would be able to tolerate him now without being irritated.

In a far corner, a small puppy is licking the tasteless shoe tips of a man, who in turn is munching on his toast. The man withdraws his foot, shoo— shoo—, driving the puppy away. The dog continues to wag its tail for a while, looking at the man's face, then turns around and heads to the next table. The young lady there is obviously afraid of the dog. With her legs all curled up and the color draining from her face, she follows the dog's movement wide-eyed. The dog, still wagging its tail, seems able to recognize those who like him. He does not stay there long, instead moves on to the next table. But from where Kubo is sitting this table is hard to see. He can't tell what kind of treatment the poor pup receives there. Whatever the case, the dog doesn't seem to have achieved a satisfactory result. It leaves there and falls on its side, its legs stretched out about six feet away from Kubo, as if once and for all renouncing its search for man's love.

Loneliness seems to be lurking in its half-closed eyes. And with it, a renunciation of all the world. What poor pup. Kubo wants to let it know that at least one man in this place cares about it. It occurs to him that he has not yet expressed his love for the dog by caressing its head, or by letting it lick his hand, and so he holds out his hand to attract it now. One usually whistles in such cases. Yet Kubo doesn't know how to whistle. After a moment of reflection, he finally whispers *Come here,* just loud enough to be heard by the dog alone.

Maybe it doesn't understand English.

It lifts its head, looks at Kubo, and again drops its head, as if not at all interested. Kubo leans forward once more, this time a bit louder, but in as coaxing a voice as possible, *Come here*, and translates, "Come here." But the puppy does nothing but repeat its previous motions, this time opening its mouth in what appears to be a yawn before closing its eyes.

Kubo becomes anxious, even angry, but suppresses his feelings. This time, he goes so far as to leave his chair to caress the puppy's head. But before he can touch it, the startled puppy jumps up, confronts Kubo in a hostile pose, barks—*ruff ruff*, and, scared of its own barking, dashes off behind the counter.

Kubo blushes despite himself. Cursing the dog's fickleness, he wipes his face with a handkerchief, although he is not sweating. He feels slightly angry at his friend who is not showing up despite his pleading.

At Length

the friend arrived. Though Kubo had earlier contemplated accusing the friend of being late, his face beams with welcome. In fact, he now feels happy to have a friend.

The friend is a poet, yet one with quite a robust body and who works as a journalist in the local news section of a newspaper. There were times when this situation saddened Kubo. Still, still, sitting with him, Kubo feels somewhat lighter at heart.

"For me, soda, please."

The friend likes to order soda. Kubo always finds this funny. But of course there's no offense in his feeling.

While the friend may always order soda at a teahouse, like a schoolgirl, he has a great passion for the development of Korean literature. The fact that a man like him has to visit, twice a day, the Chongno police station, the provincial government, and the post office, is, perhaps, a tragedy of their times. With the same pen that is meant for poetry, he has to write run-of-the-mill articles on murderers, robbers, and pyromaniacs. So when he has free time, he pours out his repressed passion for literature.

Today's talk is mostly about Kubo's last novel. He is one of Kubo's regular readers. Also, one of his supporters, someone who gives enthusiastic reviews of his works. Nevertheless, despite the friend's good will, Kubo does not trust his opinion much. Once, the friend, after reading only a mediocre piece, presumed that he knew everything about Kubo.

Today, however, Kubo has no choice but to listen to him. The friend points out that in his new novel, the writer appears much older than Kubo's own age. But that's not all. The friend, in addition, judges that the writer is not really old, but just pretends to be. That is possible. Kubo might have that slant in him. On second thought, that the friend found the inflated age merely a disguise, and not a sign of the writer's actual senility, is something that should please Kubo.

But it may be that Kubo is unable to be youthful in his fiction. If he had tried to be young, the friend would have said that the writer is assuming an unnatural pretense. And that would certainly hurt Kubo's feelings. . . . Kubo finds the topic boring, and without realizing it, turns to the question of "the five apples" instead. Say we have five apples, what order should we eat them in? Three strategies immediately present themselves. Start with the most delicious one. That would give us the satisfaction of thinking that we are always eating the tastiest of the bunch. But in the end, wouldn't that land us in misery? On the contrary, start with the least delicious one. A gradually improving taste. But in that way, we will be always eating the worst of the bunch. Lastly, pick indiscriminately, without a scheme. That . . .

By bringing up this irrelevant, playful question, Kubo baffles the friend sitting across from him, who's been busy quoting André Gide to back up his ideas on literature. The friend, wondering what kind of connection the five apples could possibly have with literature, says that he has never thought of such a problem before.

"So . . . what about it?"

"Nothing comes to mind."

And Kubo, for the first time today, laughs a lively, or at least apparently lively, laugh.

Suddenly

from the street outside the window, a child is heard crying. It's a child crying alright. But the voice seems rather closer to an animal's than to a child's. Paying no attention to the friend's oration on *Ulysses*, Kubo thinks, someone has given birth to yet another child of sin. . . .

Kubo once had a poor friend. The friend had had many childhood misfortunes, suffered from all kinds of hardships, and these experiences had made him exceptionally generous with others. He was more or less Kubo's friend. Yet he had a most unfortunate human failing. If Kubo were now with him, he would proffer such a proverb as "love much, regret much." But that was nothing but rhetoric, for the friend's uncontrolled sexual urges certainly appeared pathetic to everyone. Kubo, from time to time, even doubted his friend's taste in women. Still, things were alright for a while. Then finally tragedy struck. The friend took to a woman neither beautiful nor intelligent, and the woman thought of him as her one true love in life. And so the seeds of misfortune were sown. One evening, as the woman was sitting beside the man, blushing considerably, she confessed that she now had more than herself to think of. By then, though, he had already lost almost all affection for her. She had wanted to know the joys of motherhood, and foolishly believed that she could secure the man's love through a child. But the man only resented all this, and maybe even hated the woman, already a mother, because now he had to take responsibility for her.

The woman, however, seemed not to have noticed his change of heart. Besides, even if she had by chance taken it into account, she might not have had any choice by that point. Carrying a year-old baby in her arms, she had traveled to Seoul, looking for him. But there was no happy ending there waiting for moth-

er and child. The friend had a wife, to whom he had already been married a long time, and so compared with her, the newcomer turned out to be a distant second in everything. A quick comparison between their children made this especially poignant. The poor bastard had a huge body, quite disproportionate to its age, and an idiotic face, too.

Still, all that alone might have been tolerable. Yet when people heard the baby crying, they couldn't help but feel a strange repulsion. That cry was inhuman. It sounded as if a god, furious with their (particularly the man's) sin, were damning their (particularly his) sin, through the child's uncanny voice, casting an eternal curse. . . .

Kubo, his attention wandering back to his friend's discussion of *Ulysses*, abruptly, one should of course admire this new experiment by James Joyce. Still, novelty alone is not a just cause for praising it. Just as the friend is about to mount a protest, Kubo rises from his chair, touches the friend's shoulder, well—let's go now.

When they step outside, the sun is setting. Kubo, taking in the serenity of the street at this hour, turns to the friend.

"Now where should we go?"

"Home."

The friend answers without a moment's hesitation. Kubo feels at a loss as to whom he should spend the rest of the night with.

By Streetcar

the friend had already set off for home. Not home. An inn. Did he have to leave now to make it back in time for dinner, to an inn where nobody's waiting except his host family? If it's just a matter of not missing dinner. . . .

"What are you going to do at home?"

That, of course, was a silly question. A man with a "life" should naturally dine at home. Compared with Kubo, the friend really did have a life.

After being tied up all day with the affairs of the world, he could now enjoy some quiet hours alone after dinner, reading and writing. Kubo, Kubo can't share in this pleasure.

Shortly thereafter, Kubo stands at the Chongno intersection, gazing at the twilight, as well as at the loose women who usually appear at this time on the streets. Today again, they are out in force, in all their indiscretion. The night is falling fast, and the night belongs to them. Kubo looks down at the pavement and, stealing glances at various splendid and not so splendid legs. How perilously they walk. Not all of them are unused to high heels. And yet, all of them walk in the most clumsy and unnatural of fashions. One is certainly justified in calling them "the precarious."

They, but of course, they themselves aren't aware of this. They're not aware of how unsteady their footsteps are in the world. Not a single one of them has a firm goal in life, but ignorance blinds them to their common instability.

But what resounds on the pavement is not just the rickety heels of their shoes. All the toes, belonging to those who have a life, a life, are heading home. Home, home, they are so happily walking in search of supper, their families' faces, and some rest after the daily grind. Takuboku's *haiku* flows from Kubo's lips.

The sorrow of everyone having a home
Like entering a grave
They return home to sleep

Not that such a sentiment really applies to Kubo on the twilit street. He doesn't have to go home yet. And as small as Seoul is, there are still streets for him to roam till late, places to visit.

But this twilight . . . with whom . . . Kubo starts to walk, almost confident now. There's a friend. A friend with whom to spend the rest of the night together. He passes by the Chongno police station and drops in on a white, small teahouse.

But the owner is out. Kubo turns around, full of regret. Why didn't I make an appointment with him? But just then the young clerk says, as if it has just dawned on him, oh, the master said he'd be back soon, he said a visitor could wait for him. "A visitor," possibly, might refer to a specific person. Maybe this friend won't be able to keep Kubo company. Still, one must have hope, and Kubo, who has no other friend to call on, has no choice but to sit there and wait for his friend's return.

With a Woman

a young man is sitting, close to the music box. He seems to be feeling very proud and happy that he is sipping tea with a girl who's not a prostitute. His body is healthy, his suit elegant, and his woman so readily smiling at him that Kubo can't help but feel slightly jealous, admire him. There's more. The youth seems to be shamelessly proud even of his *ŭndan* pill-box and Roto eyewash. Kubo sincerely envies his superficiality.

Mixed in with all these sentiments might have been a certain twilight melancholy, loneliness. Aware of the expression on his face, which must look far too gloomy, Kubo considers it fortunate that the place has no mirror. A poet once called the state of mind Kubo is now in the "bachelor's blues." Though this seems right at first glance, in fact it's not quite that. For a long time now, Kubo has been unwilling to seek new love and has depended on the good will of friends.

Without his noticing, both the woman and the lucky guy have disappeared, the night air wafting in and out of the teahouse. Now where should I go? Then, Kubo realizes that he has forgotten the friend he's waiting for. He smiles wryly. This slip-up is definitely more pathetic than the time when he felt weary and lonely with his love sitting right in front of him.

A new thought lights up Kubo's eyes. Just whatever became of her? A memory, however good or bad, calms one's heart, inspires joy.

It all took place during a certain autumn in Tokyo. After buying a new nail clipper in a hardware store in Kanda, Kubo visited his favorite teahouse at Jimbocho. But this time he decidedly had not stopped for tea or relaxation. He stopped for the sole purpose of trying out the nail clipper. A table in the farthest corner, a chair in the farthest corner. The setting of all those romances that popular writers write. In this ill-lit place, Kubo stumbled upon a college notebook, on which was written "Ethics" and a family name, "Yim."

Picking it up was probably a sin of sorts. But that degree of curiosity is permissible for young men. One way or another, Kubo, in a place not easily visible from other seats, opened the notebook and forgot all about clipping his nails.

> *Chap I. Introduction. 1. The Definition of Ethics. 2. Normative Science. Chap II. Principal Argument. Object of Ethical Judgment. C Motivism and Consequentialism. Example 1. The Son of a Poor Family Steals to Support His Parents. 2. Charity to Gratify One's Vanity. Second Semester. 3. Elements of Personality Formation. 1. The Will to Believe. . . .*

And in the margins, the following was written in pencil: "But a sense of shame heightens a lover's ability to imagine." "Shame gives life over to love." "The first section of Stendhal's *De L'amour . . .* "—and then, without connection—"*All Quiet on the Western Front.* Yoshiiya Nobuko, Akutagawa Ryunosuke." "Where did you go yesterday?" "Did you see *A Love Parade. . . .* "

The owner of the teahouse returned. Ah, when did you get here? Have you been waiting for long? Any good news? Kubo gets up without answering, picks up his notebook and walking stick, let's go for dinner, and tries to resume his reverie on this little romance from a time long past.

Outside the Teahouse,

walking with his friend toward the Taech'angok restaurant, Kubo remembers the postcard that was lying between the leaves of the notebook. Of course, he hesitated at first. But he could not pass up this opportunity, knowing that he could learn where she lived. First of all, he was young, and the mystery was intriguing. After having immersed himself that night in all kinds of fantasies from novels, Kubo tracked her down the next morning. Ushigomeku Yaraicho. Her boarding house was near the Shincho Publisher, where he worked. After a kind-hearted landlady appeared and then disappeared, the owner of the notebook came to the door, and she was certainly . . . A beauty is approaching from the direction toward which Kubo and his friend are walking. She smiles at them and passes by. A barmaid from the café next door to the friend's teahouse. The friend turns around and asks Kubo's opinion. Isn't she pretty? In fact, the girl has a beauty rather rare in women of her class. But *she* must have been more beautiful than this barmaid.

Come on in. Sŏlŏnt'ang for two—. When Kubo took out the notebook and apologized for having gone searching for her, she, instantly, blushed. There seemed to be something more in that blush than her having just received a courtesy from a strange man. Where did you go yesterday? Yoshiiya Nobuko. Kubo remembered her scribblings, and smiled to himself. Across the table, the friend brings the hand holding his soup-spoon to a stop. He is staring at Kubo. His eyes seem to be asking, what are you thinking about? Kubo replies with a meaningless smile, to guard his secret. Why don't you come in, she said. Her tone was calm, yet her cheeks flush, fitting for a virgin. Kubo, taking up her offer, halted, and then suddenly, would you like to go for a walk with me, if you're free? The day was Sunday, and she had her Sunday dress on, apparently about to go somewhere. A popular novel should have a quick pace. The day before, when he had picked up the ethics notebook, Kubo had already become the hero—as well as the writer—of a popular novel. He even thought that, should she turn out to be Christian, he'd be willing to go listen to a minister's ho hum sermon. She blushed again, but when Kubo said, if you have other business . . . she, in haste—no (then) please just wait a second, and she came out carrying a handbag. Kubo, encouraged by her apparent trust in him, well, have you been to the Musashino Theater this weekend? He worried that, walking around like this with her, he must look like a good-for-nothing jobless type, and that if she were to succumb so easily to his seduction, it wouldn't be credible, not even in a popular novel. Kubo sniggered to himself. But even if she readily followed him, Kubo didn't want to think her frivolous. It can't be frivolousness. Kubo, for all his self-esteem, wanted to believe that she was wise enough to find him trustworthy, even during their first encounter.

So she was. As they were stepping out of the streetcar in front of the theater, Kubo had to pause for a moment. Not so as to wait for her to get off first. Rather, for a foreign lady who was standing in front of him, grinning. His English teacher alternately looked at him and then the girl, smiled knowingly, hope you're having a good day, and went on her way. Insinuated here may have been a thirty-year-old spinster's sarcasm toward a young couple. Kubo becomes aware that he's sweating copiously, just like a schoolboy, both on his forehead and along the bridge of his nose. Kubo pulls out a handkerchief from his pant pocket to wipe himself off. The bowl of Sŏlŏngt'ang is too hot on this summer evening.

Outside

they stand motionless on the street. After all, Seoul is small. If it were Tokyo, Kubo would now head for Ginza. In fact, he had wanted to ask the girl, would you like to go to Ginza for tea? Yet, at that very instant, a scene from a movie he had just seen flashed through his mind. This may have been the reason why Kubo lost his self-confidence. A rogue had tempted a respectable girl to go see an opera, and on their way back late at night, he drives the car to his villa. In this fleeting image, the rogue's profile seemed to bear some resemblance to Kubo's. Kubo smiled grimly, but, dismissing the remembrance, let's have tea around here, it's no Ginza, but. . . . Ah, how forgetful I am! The friend suddenly exclaims that he has someone he must meet at this hour, and makes an apologetic face, knowing that Kubo will feel lonely, left to himself. When the girl glanced at Kubo, hesitating, I should be going home now, she must also have had such an expression on her face. Let's meet at the teahouse around ten o'clock. Ten o'clock? Yes, half past ten at the latest. Then the friend walks away toward the railway stop.

Gazing at the back of the friend, who crosses the tracks and vanishes into the crowd on the other side of the street, for no clear reason, Kubo remembers the sad girl in front of Hibiya Park on a certain drizzly evening.

Ah, Kubo jerks his head up, aimlessly looks around, and then mechanically takes a few steps forward. Ah, I remember. . . . Oh, why did I fumble through memories for the one incident I had hoped to forget, forever? A sad and bitter memory is the last thing to help keep one's heart calm, cheerful.

She had a fiancé, to whom she had already been engaged before meeting Kubo, and she pleaded for his advice. Unfortunately, Kubo knew the man. A classmate from his junior high school days. Though more than five years had elapsed since they had heard from each other, the man's face remained distinct in Kubo's mind. An honest, ordinary face. Moreover, the thought of his gentle eyes stung Kubo to the quick. In the rain-drenched park, deep in thought, in tears, they wandered around, oblivious to the setting sun.

Restless, Kubo starts to walk. In fact, I may have acted like a coward. Maybe I should have felt more elated to have her love all to myself. When she blamed him through her sobs, saying that his sense of loyalty and his fear of reproach, all these derived from a lack of love, passion, she was evidently right . . . right.

Kubo offered to walk her home. No, leave me alone, I'll go by myself. Her back wet in the rain, tears, she walked down the street in the dusk, on and on, without even taking a streetcar. She didn't marry her fiancé. If she were unhappy, this was the result of one man's indecisiveness. Though Kubo at times wanted to believe that she lived happily in some other, more fortunate place, the mere thought rang hollow.

Finding himself at the crossroads of Hwangt'o Maru, Kubo pauses, on an impulse, and lets out a tortured sigh. Ah, I miss her. I want to know where she is. For seven hours, ever since he'd left home that afternoon, this might have been his only real goal. Ah, I miss her. If only I could know how she's doing . . .

Kwanghwamun Avenue

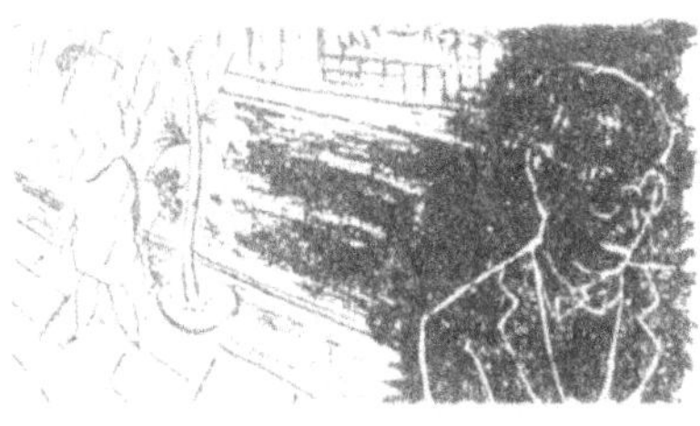

Randomly walking on this deserted and inelegantly broad street, Kubo wonders whether he was not, perhaps, a hypocrite. That would be a consequence of his irresolute personality. Ah, all the evils caused by the frailty of men, all the misfortunes. . . .

Once again he sees the pitiful sight of her receding figure. Rain running down her raincoat, without hat or umbrella, her head soaked and sorrowful. Spiritless, impossible to keep up her spirits, her drooping shoulders. Hands in her pockets, her head hanging low, one step forward, another step, her small, frail feet, not at all sturdy. Should have run after her. Should have rushed and seized her slender shoulders, should have said that all my words till now have been lies, that I can never give up our love, that we must fight for our love against all obstacles, and should then have cried together with her in a heart-wrenching lament on that rainy street in Tokyo.

Kubo, with all his might, kicks a pebble at his foot. Maybe he had wanted to derive some worthless pride from his ability to restrain his ardor, his true desire. Wanted to think that the tragedy was the natural finale to their love. Wanted to believe, again remembering the friend's gentle eyes, that his well-rounded personality and wealth would make her happy. In the end, this misguided sentiment had obscured the true calling of his heart. And that's not as it should be. What right had he to toy with her feelings, or his own. He would never be able to make her happy, despite his true love for her—hadn't that sense of his own imperfection driven everyone, especially her, his poor love, into misery? Scattering the myriad pebbles on the road with his strenuous kicks, Kubo, Oh, I was wrong, so wrong.

Humming a springtime song, a child of about ten passes by. The child has no worries. Two drunkards, their arms around each other's shoulders, slur the Song of Sorrow. They're feeling happy now. Kubo, suddenly, is struck by a bright idea, and stops in his tracks on the dark street. If I were to meet her again now, I would no longer be weak. I wouldn't make the same mistake. We would never be apart again. . . .

But where can I find her? My God, how empty and blind an idea can be. How can a man's heart feel so lonely and wretched, on these broad, open streets of Kwanghwamun.

A student in a college cap passes by, walking shoulder to shoulder with a young woman. Their steps bounce, their voices whisper. Dear lovers, let there always shine a ray of light on your love. Like an old benevolent father, Kubo, with his heart full of generosity and love, bestows on the couple his wholehearted blessing.

Now

seemingly having forgotten where he was going, seemingly no longer needing to go anywhere at all, Kubo stands in one spot absent-mindedly. Poor love. Is the ending to this story good enough as it now stands? Now, and in the future, are they fated always to remain sad and lonely? Without ever meeting one another again, each nurturing their wounds alone? Yet, at the same time, ah . . . let's leave this thought alone. Kubo self-consciously shakes his head, and hastens to retrace the path along which he came. Still, pain lingers in his heart, and as he is walking on the street, his head hanging low, pebbles are rolling around his feet, countless fragments of memory. Again, shaking his head, Kubo, let's . . . let's really forget this thought. . . .

He should go back to the teahouse, rejoin his friend there, and find a way to alleviate the night's anxiety. But before he manages to cross the railway tracks, someone calls out to him, "Uncle Eye—," and, when he stops to look around, his hands, still holding his walking stick and notebook, are seized by the little hands of children. Where have you been? Kubo showers them with smiles. Nephews of a friend. The children call him Uncle Eye because of his glasses. We were at the night fair. Why don't you ever come by anymore, Uncle Eye? Oh, I have been busy. . . . But that's a lie. Kubo, at that very instant, remembers how completely he has forgotten the guileless boys for over a month, and he feels truly sorry.

Poor children. They have hardly known a father's love. Their father started another family in the countryside five years ago, and so they have been brought up almost exclusively by their mother. The mother was not to blame. The father, then. The father, too, was, generally speaking, a good man. Yet he certainly had a streak of libertinism when it came to women. Despite severe hardships, the mother still sends the boys to school. A sixteen-year-old daughter and three younger brothers. The youngest will reach school-age next year.

When the mother talked joyfully about sending the youngest to an elementary school, even as she complained about her difficulties, Kubo felt like bowing to her to show his respect.

Kubo loves children. Likes to be loved by children. Sometimes, he even tries to ingratiate himself with children. If the children he loves should happen not to take a liking to him—, that idea alone makes him sad and lonely. But children are so simple. They are always drawn to those who care for them.

Uncle Eye, have you seen our new place? It's right there in that alley. Come with us, won't you?

He himself half wants to go. Yet, considering the time, and afraid of missing his friend, he cannot help but abandon the idea. What to do. Kubo spots a cart piled high with watermelons on the other side of the road. You're not having stomach problems, are you? No, why? He buys two watermelons, one for each to carry. Here, take them to your mother and ask her to slice them for you. You should each have the same size portion, no fighting. The older boy replies, the last time Uncle P'irun brought bananas, our sister was sick and couldn't eat, so we teased her a lot. . . . Kubo grins at the image of the tomboy's face on the brink of tears. A woman, who just then happens to pass by, throws a sharp glance at him. She is far from being pretty. Plus, for whatever reason, she has dozens of patches all over her face. Naturally, she must have felt insulted by his grin. Without intending to, Kubo bursts into a roar of laughter. Maybe, now, he'll be cheerful.

Still

the children wanted him to visit their house. After sending them away, Kubo heads for the teahouse. At night this area generally has few pedestrians, and the streetcar crawls sluggishly along the middle of the road. A few odd wom-en are standing on this poorly lit street, and a couple others are sitting under a tree. They, most likely, are not *belles de jour*. Still, against this forlorn darkness, their figures cut an alluring, if somber, presence. All of a sudden, a debauched sexual desire takes hold of him.

Right at that moment, a telegraph messenger rides by on a bicycle, as lithe as a swallow. What kinds of lives are compressed into the small bag hung around his waist? Uncertainty, anxiety, expectation. . . . Words on a small piece of paper exercise such a sure and effective sway over one's emotions. When a man receives a telegraph addressed to him, his hand trembles unawares. Kubo has a sudden craving for the experience of holding an unopened telegraph. If not a telegraph, any ordinary mail will do. At this point, even a postcard would impress him.

Hah, Kubo scoffs. That craving must be another manifestation of his sexual desire. But of course he has no intention of simply dismissing this not-so-unnatural, almost physical craving. In fact, he keeps forgetting to write to all his friends who live outside Seoul, and they, too, haven't contacted him for a long time. What are they all doing now? He feels a spontaneous rush of sweet nostalgia, even for a certain friend who sends him only a New Year's card once a year. Soon, with thousands of blank postcards on the table in the corner of the teahouse, Kubo finds himself writing to friends with unchecked abandon. On one postcard after another, without noticing his burnt-out cigarette in the ashtray, he scribbles out the names and addresses of all the friends he can remember. . . . He smiles contentedly. This is not so bad an ending for a short story. But what kind of short story? Kubo, of course, has not thought up its plot yet.

Apart from such literary concerns, he really wants to receive a letter from his friends. Won't somebody permit me this joy? Suddenly, Kubo slackens his pace, maybe there's a letter waiting for me at home, some impassioned words from the least expected of old friends. . . . Though he knows how groundless this fantasy is, Kubo does not want his melancholy reverie to be so mercilessly dispelled. The letter at home need not have been sent by a friend. Possibly, a newspaper company, or a magazine publisher. . . . Then, the mother, hopeful and expectant in front of the printed envelope, as if it carried within it a grand future for her son, holds it up and down, against the light bulb . . . even worrying about the possibility that her son, who does not return, despite all her waiting, might read the letter too late and hence miss an opportunity. But the letter upon which the poor mother piles so much hope, once opened, likely turns out to be just an order for an essay, a piece to fill one issue of a newspaper, or a page in a magazine.

Kubo smiles wryly, then enters the teahouse. There is a large crowd, but no friend. He now has to wait here for his friend.

The Teahouse's

patrons, for whatever reason, favor seats in the corner. Kubo has no choice but to take the one remaining table in the middle of the room. Still, he can enjoy Elman's *Valse Sentimentale*, his mind calm, at ease. But before the melody plays itself out, a rude voice, aren't you Mr. Kupo? Sensing that all eyes in the teahouse are now on him, Kubo looks to where the voice came from. A certain man who finished junior high two or three years earlier than he did. Heard he'd become a salesman at a life insurance company. His red drunken face might account for his pretension of familiarity, for there had been no previous correspondence between them. Kubo gives a slight nod, his face expressionless, and promptly turns away. But when the man again, just as loud, says, won't you join us, Kubo has no choice but to get up, albeit sluggishly, and switch tables. Come and sit right here. Mr. Ch'oe, this is Mr. Kupo, the novelist.

The man for some reason pronounces Kubo's name each time as Kupo. He waves his empty bottle of beer, shouts at the boy for more, and again turns to Kubo. So are you still writing a lot? I must *confess* that I haven't written much. Kubo finds it quite unpalatable that he is compelled to associate with such a man, and has decided to keep his distance by uttering polite trivialities. But this clueless man seems rather flattered by Kubo's honorific tone. Furthermore, by ordering beer, the man might already have felt a sense of superiority over those who are sipping tea (which costs a measly ten chŏn per cup) and thus might now be savoring an even higher level of happiness.

He offers a glass to Kubo, I'm a fan of Mr. Kupo's works. He notices that Kubo shows no sign of being impressed by such a comment and adds,

"In fact, with everyone I meet, I talk about Mr. Kupo."

Then he roars himself hoarse with laughter. Kubo, an ambiguous smile on his face, has a fleeting thought. What if he were to hire this presumptuous ignoramus to sell his books? He might be able to secure tens, even hundreds, of new readers. Kubo chuckles to himself. Mr. Kupo, the man called Mr. Ch'oe intervenes, seeking Kubo's agreement that Tokkyŏn's *The Tragic Melody of a Buddhist Temple* and Yun Paengnam's *The Tale of a Great Robber* are masterpieces. And this man, who may well be a salesman at some fire insurance company, deftly adds,

"Of course, aside from your works. . . . "

As Kubo, with considerable effort, brings himself to say that those are good books, Ch'oe again ventures to ask, how much is the remuneration rate for writing in Korea? Kubo appreciates the fact that he didn't say "renumeration," but feels no obligation to discuss the financial status of Korean writers with this kind of man.

So, Kubo, knowing full well that he will be humiliating the other, explains curtly that he knows nothing about it, since he never receives any. Right then, he sees his friend coming in. Excuse me now. Before the two can say anything, Kubo returns to his seat, picks up his notebook and walking stick, and, to the friend, who is just about to sit down,

"Let's get out of here. Let's go some place else."

Outside, a summer night, a cool, pleasant breeze.

comes up alongside them, as they silently walk down the night-darkened street. Even during the day this street is hardly busy. Any good news these days? Kubo asks casually, looking at the three-story Kyŏngsŏng post office. Good news? The friend's eyes, turning toward him, reveal signs of fatigue. They continue their walk toward Hwanggŭmjŏng. Have you ever had, for example, some small joy, a modest joy, such as receiving a surprise postcard from an unexpected friend . . .

"Sure."

The friend readily replies. The kind of letter which a good-for-nothing like you will never receive in your lifetime, and he sniggers. Yet his laughter rings hollow. Certified mail, most likely. In times like these, even running a small teahouse isn't easy. Three months unpaid rent. The sky has become overcast, the shimmering stars disappearing from sight. The friend suddenly whistles. A poor novelist, and a poor poet. . . . Kubo's thoughts drift toward his country, so poor, and his mind clouds over.

"Don't you want to find someone new to love?"

The friend stops whistling and sends a playful glance to Kubo. Kubo smiles. A lover, good. A girl who's not a lover, still fine. What Kubo wants right now might just be any girl at all. Or maybe a wise, caring wife. . . . A bold idea crosses his mind, I wish I could adopt a daughter, instead of a wife or lover, a seventeen- or eighteen-year-old, if possible. The girl must be pretty, cheerful, also smart. He would be a benevolent, devoted father, and take her on trips—.

Kubo suddenly laughs in spite of himself. Have I grown that old already? Still, he can't dismiss his fantasy so quickly. Keeping in check an urge to share it with his friend, he privately indulges in this line of thought. Three choices. With only one of them he might easily reach happiness. But then maybe even with all three choices fulfilled, he still wouldn't find peace for his wearied heart.

No doubt this is an idea inspired by "loneliness."

Even the Round Moon Does Not Know What I Want

Kubo recited aloud the one-line poem by Satō Haruo. The sky is dark, as if threatening a downpour. Indeed, Kubo likely does not know, let alone the round moon. Soon, they are back in Chongno, and Kubo, suddenly feeling the weight of the walking stick and notebook in his hand, turns to his friend. Can you buy me a drink tonight? The friend nods without thinking twice. Kubo, a new bounce to his step, goes to a bar in the Chonggak area, which they both patronize now and then, but the barmaid who used to serve them is no longer there. Kubo learns from a woman the name of the café in Nagwŏnjŏng where the barmaid has gone, and insists, let's go there, dragging his ostensibly tired friend by the arm. Kubo doesn't even know her name. In other words, she's a girl his friend is interested in. But Kubo perhaps wanted to enjoy the cheap thrill of chasing after a girl, just like a teenage boy.

At First

the friend, though, would not follow Kubo. Maybe the friend was no longer interested in the barmaid. But should he still have any feelings for her, it stands to reason that these feelings would amount to more than just mild interest. They walk at length to Nagwŏnjŏng, in search of the café where she works, but then Kubo discovers that the friend feels neither passionate nor indifferent toward her. Or it might be that he does not care which way he feels. The friend has grown old, too. He is still young age-wise but lacks energy and passion. So what he's constantly seeking is, maybe, any kind of stimulus at all.

Three barmaids, and then two more, come to their table. What attracts so many "belles" to them is, of course, neither their physique nor their wallets. It is only that they are new to the place, and these kinds of girls enjoy making the acquaintance of many men. The friend asks their names one by one. For some reason all their names end with "ko." This suffix indicates a certain lack of taste, and saddens Kubo's heart.

"Why, have you come to conduct a census?"

A new girl comes to their table. It's her. Seeing that both men greet the girl with apparent familiarity, the two girls sitting next to them move awkwardly to give up their seats. The girl declines, no, stay seated as you are, yet she still sits down next to the friend. This girl is no prettier than the other five. Still, there's a kind of grace about her, somehow. While the friend is exchanging a few words with her alone, three of the girls leave for other tables. Barmaids never remain interested in a customer who appears to be intimate with one of their colleagues.

"Come on, have a drink," urges the girl in charge of the table, targeting his friend in particular. While three bottles of beer are empty on the table, the friend seems to have drunk no more than a glass or so. In fact, the friend, glass in hand, only pretends to sip but then places it back on the table. He has alcohol intolerance. But of course the girls have never heard of such a disease. Upon learning from Kubo that it is a kind of mental disorder, their credulous eyes open wide. And again they burst, indiscreetly, into laughter. One girl tells the story of a man, just an occasional drinker, who once nearly fainted after drinking a gallon of Japanese liquor, and she asks Kubo whether that, too, could be a case of mental disorder. That is dipsomania. The twenty-third volume of *The Modern Medi-*

cal Encyclopedia, which he'd read with interest sometime before, apparently proves quite a useful reference.

Kubo feels a strong impulse to regard all kinds of people as mental patients. Indeed, there are all kinds of mental disorder to suffer from. Flights of Ideas. Paraphasia. Megalomania. Coprolalia. Nymphomania. Desultory Thoughts. Jealous Delusion. Satyriasis. Pathological Odd Behaviors. Pathological Pseudology. Pathological Immorality. Pathological Lavishness.

Then, Kubo realizes that he himself, who takes interest in such a topic, must make a psychotic case, if only for that particular interest, and laughs cheerfully.

Then

is everybody in the world a psychopath? A barmaid, who has been quietly listening to Kubo in the next seat, asks naturally enough. Kubo changes his position to face her obliquely, and excuse me, using such a phrase, asks her age. The girl, after a moment's hesitation,

"Twenty."

A woman's age is always an enigma. Yet this girl could not possibly be twenty. Twenty-five, twenty-six. At least twenty-four. Abruptly, and somewhat cruelly, Kubo tells her that she, too, is a patient. Paralogia. The friend, intrigued, asks for details about this disease. Kubo opens his notebook on the table and reads out a dialogue between a doctor and a patient. How many noses do you have? I can't tell whether there're two or more. How many ears do you have? Just one. Three plus two? Seven. How old are you? Twenty-one (in truth, thirty-eight). What about your wife? Eighty-one years old. Closing the notebook, Kubo has a good laugh with his friend. The girls join in as well. Yet, with the exception of the girl sitting next to his friend, they obviously don't know how to understand the anecdote. The girl next to Kubo, in particular, laughs without noticing whatsoever that the story is intended as a slight jab at her transparent pretensions. Every time she laughs or speaks, she affectedly covers her mouth with a handkerchief. She must think her mouth looks ugly. Kubo feels pity and sympathy for her modesty. But these sentiments, of course, should be distinguished from affection. Pity and sympathy are quite similar to affection, and yet never quite mean the same thing. But hatred—, sometimes hatred erupts from true love. . . . In one of his early works, he had thought of using this sentence, which was nothing more than an inference from his narrow experience. It might be true, though. As Kubo mulls over this idle thought, a girl asks. Then you must be the only one in the world who's not crazy. Kubo smiling, why me, too . . . I, my illness,

"It's called Compulsive Talking."

"What is Compulsive Talking?"

"Oh, constantly prattling on in senseless small talk is also a mental disorder."

"So that's what Compulsive Talking is. . . . "

Two other girls also repeat to themselves the name of Kubo's disease. Kubo takes out his fountain pen from his inside pocket and scrawls in his notebook. Any observation is useful to a writer, and one cannot be lax, even at a café, in one's preparations for writing: the barmaid sought to obtain all kinds of knowledge by talking to a wide variety of customers—. Holding his pen up for a moment, Kubo gazes at the table facing him, and again, gently smiling, with satisfaction, sets his pen in motion. Now what vile thing are you writing? The friend, half raising himself, reads aloud as Kubo writes. *As the woman was sitting in front of him, she stretched out her legs from under the table. Not because she was afraid that his worn-out shoes would trample hers, which were more delicate. Rather, she was at last wearing the ivory-colored silk stockings that she had so long desired and of which she was so proud.*

Huh, the friend sneers and says, one shouldn't make friends with a novelist, but whatever you choose to write, please leave out my alcohol intolerance—. And they laugh whole-heartedly.

Kubo and His Friend,

as well as most of their conversation, the girls, of course, cannot comprehend. Still, they pretend to be capable of understanding everything. But, there's no harm in that, and one shouldn't ridicule their ignorance. Kubo grabs his pen. Isn't ignorance, perhaps, a necessity for these girls? Were they more intelligent, they would suffer more from things like pain, sorrow, and resentment . . . and a sudden sense of misery would lay siege to their hearts. The blissful, ephemeral delights that they enjoy, no matter how worthless they may appear, are made possible only by ignorance . . . as truths are. Kubo writes in his notebook, and does not turn down the drinks the girls offer him.

Soon, it's raining outside. A soft rain. A gentle rain. When it rains this gently, so late at night, Kubo often becomes sad. The girls are sad as well. Without umbrellas at hand, each of them worries about her only dress, as well as about her shoes and socks getting wet in the rain.

Miss Yuki—. A drunken voice calls out. Looking at the darkness beyond the window, Kubo, suddenly, remembers a woman. "Yuki"—the Japanese word for snow might have provoked that memory. The woman, who was calling to Kubo in a feeble voice in front of a Kwanggyo café, was clearly wearing snowy white mourning clothes. May I ask you a question, said the woman almost in a whisper, and she turned around as soon as she caught the glimpse of him stopping. She hesitantly stretched her hand out toward the café.

"What does it say the place needs?"

The flier posted by the teahouse window had the two lines

Barmaids Wanted
Barmaids Wanted

written on it. Kubo studied her anew, and felt a pang in his heart. She was destitute, that much was clear. But she apparently had been able to keep off the street, not needing to look for a job. Then an unforeseeable misfortune had struck, and she was left with no alternative but to take to the streets, her grief still raw. She might have a son, all but grown-up. Maybe it was not a son but a daughter, and that was why this poor woman now had to struggle to make ends meet on her own. Before she was married, she might have lived well, been lovingly cared for. Her pale face had grace, even a sort of dignity. When Kubo cautiously explained the advertisement for barmaids, the woman, who must have been over forty, didn't even wait for him to finish, and, with an expression of disgust and despair, bowed to him in silence and calmly left the spot. . . .

Kubo turns to look at the barmaids. Who's more unhappy, that widow or these girls? Whose suffering, whose misery in life is greater? He sighs at the thought. But maybe it's not right to dwell on such a thought in a place like this. He puts a fresh cigarette between his lips. But the two matchboxes on the table are both empty.

A petite barmaid runs to the counter to fetch a match. The girl is almost a child. If she said sixteen or seventeen, he would scarcely doubt her. Her clear eyes, the dimples on her cheeks, are yet to be sullied by the grime of this world. It might not be only on account of his drunkenness that Kubo immediately feels pity and attraction for her. Won't you go somewhere with me tomorrow afternoon? He makes this spontaneous proposal and thinks that if she were to agree, he'd be happy to spend half a day strolling around outdoors. But she just gently smiles. The dimples certainly make her look adorable.

Kubo, suddenly, hands her his pocketbook and fountain pen. Check O if yes, and X if no, and if O, then come to the roof of Hwasin tomorrow at noon, and don't worry, whatever mark you make, I won't open the note until tomorrow morning. Kubo laughs cheerfully at this new diversion.

At Two a.m.

The Chongno intersection—. Though it's raining, a constant stream of people is never lacking there. All these people are perhaps madly in love with the night. Maybe they set out to find some pleasure for the night, maybe they've just as easily found it. And, for a brief moment, each one of them might have felt himself the happiest of men. But signs of weariness are visibly inscribed on their faces, in their gait. As their sorrow and fatigue find no respite, they now have to go back to their homes, to their rooms, which they had forgotten for a while, or tried to forget.

At this late hour his mother would still be awake, waiting for him. The fact that he didn't take an umbrella might have caused her added worry. Kubo thinks of her small, sad, lonely face. And he himself cannot help feeling sad and lonely. Kubo had forced his lonely mother almost entirely out of his thoughts. But his mother must have thought, worried, in anguish, about her son, all day long. Oh, a mother's love, how infinitely deep and infinitely sad. From the parents to the husband, and then on to the son, shifts a woman's love—yet, is it not the stage of motherhood that renders a woman's love so powerful, so sacred?

Though the friend said, see you again tomorrow, Kubo hardly hears him. Now I'll have a life. Have a life. A life for myself, and comfort and rest for my mother—. Good night, the friend says again. Kubo at last turns to him, and silently nods. See you again tomorrow night. But, Kubo, after a slight hesitation, tomorrow, from tomorrow, I will stay at home, will write—.

"Write a good novel."

Says the friend in good faith, and they part. I will write a truly good novel. Finding happiness in that thought, Kubo takes no offense when a patrolling policeman casts a disparaging look at him.

"Kubo—"

Suddenly, the friend calls him back. By the way, see what she checked in your pocketbook. Kubo pulls it out of his inside pocket and sees a big, unequivocal X. With a wry smile, to the friend, I guess I won't be going to Hwasin tomorrow at noon. Yet Kubo hardly feels disappointed. Even if the mark were O, he would feel no joy. Maybe, now, he wants to think more of his mother's happiness than of his own. He is preoccupied, perhaps, with that alone. Kubo walks along the street in the soft drizzling rain, hastening home.

Perhaps, now, if his mother broaches the subject of marriage, Kubo may not flatly reject her wishes.

5

KIM NAMCH'ŎN

Kim Hyosik (1911–1953?), better known by his pen name Namch'ŏn, was born in Sŏngch'ŏn, a rural town near Pyongyang. As a young literary aspirant at Pyongyang high school, Kim was an ardent admirer of Japanese modernist aesthetes, in particular Akutagawa Ryunosuke. While attending Hōsei University in Tokyo, however, he chose to become, in his own words, "a foot soldier in politics rather than a master in art" by joining the socialist writers of the KAPF (Korea Artista Proleta Federatio). In 1931 Kim was expelled from Hōsei University for his involvement in socialist activism, and shortly thereafter he was arrested for his participation in a labor strike in Pyongyang. He served two years in prison before being released on sick bail in 1933. After the 1945 national liberation Kim played a central role in rebuilding the leftist literary camp in Seoul, and he subsequently joined the communist regime in the North. He is believed to have been executed there in 1953, the victim of a political purge.

Beyond writing fiction, Kim was also a critic actively invested in the aesthetic innovation of Korean proletarian literature. His essays drew much inspiration from the works of Marxist thinkers such as Tosaka Jun and Georg Lukács. He criticized what he perceived as the dogmatism and schematism of Korean proletarian writers, calling for the creation of a literature better grounded in the daily lives of Korean workers and peasants. An admirer of contemporary modernist Pak T'aewŏn, Kim saw literary experimentalism primarily as a tool in the execution of this aesthetic project.

Kim's most celebrated fictional writings, clustered in a few very productive years, testify to an extremely refined literary sensibility. The historical novel *Taeha* (1938, Great currents) depicts in an epic canvas panoramic scenes of early twentieth-century Korean society in the process of colonial modernization. Shorter works such as "Noksŏngdang" (1939, The Green Star pharmacy) and the trilogy of "Nangbi" (1940–1941, Waste), "Kyŏngyŏng" (1940, Management), and "Maek" (1941, translated here as "Barley") equally provide sensitive psychological portraits of life in a fast modernizing yet increasingly oppressive colonial society. Kim's characters are often attracted to the new opportunities brought by the wartime economic boom in Korea, but they are also painfully aware of their condition as subjects of a foreign empire.

The experience of *chŏnhyang*, or forced political conversion, profoundly marked Kim's life as well as works of fiction. It was Japan's policy that nationalist and socialist intellectuals, pending torture and imprisonment, should recant their ideological commitment and declare allegiance to the cause of Japanese imperialism. In *Barley*, Kim left us an exceptional document of the emotional as well as existential implications of the practice of conversion. The story features the character of a working woman, Mugyŏng, who is abandoned by her fiancé upon his conversion to the official ideology of pan-Asianism. As Mugyŏng tries to piece together her existence out of fragments she cannot understand, the theme of betrayal reverberates at multiple levels of the narrative. Eventually a rational critique of pan-Asianism is suggested, but even more poignant is the expression of a pervading anxiety through the characters' emotional sufferings as well as their failures to communicate.

Barley

(1941)

1

The young salary man in Apartment 22 was moving out today. He bought a house in Tonamchŏng, where he would finally be joined by his new wife. Until now she had stayed at her parents' place, while he had continued to live in his apartment and looked for a new house. Around six o'clock in the evening, the salary man and his wife came with a truck and a mover to take his belongings. Even with the mover's help, it took them a full hour to carry his stuff from the third-floor apartment into the truck. Ch'oe Mugyŏng oversaw the move from inside the management office. Although it was past the end of her work day, and she was not going to be of much help, she had to wait for the move to be completed, and besides, for a long time she had been the salary man's next-door neighbor. Old man Kang, who also worked at the office, helped where he could. He looked up and down to make sure that nothing was left behind, and he also helped the mover with heavy items such as the wardrobe, a desk, and a table. Having finished loading the truck, the salary man came back to the office with his wife.

"Your rent for this month is twenty-eight wŏn. Here's the difference on your monthly installment, seventy-seven wŏn." Mugyŏng took out the bills from the safe and handed them to the salary man. As he received them, the man lifted up his hands a bit in a gesture of thanks. He then pocketed them without taking another look.

"Please count the bills." At Mugyŏng's urging, the salary man pulled out the roll again, held it up against the light, and began to count the bills one by one. "It's exactly right." When he again looked at her, Mugyŏng was writing out a receipt for him. Putting down her pen, she smiled at his young wife, "Here's your receipt. Please sign here. And the revenue stamp is on the housing office." The young wife smiled back, revealing her regular white teeth, "Thank you."

After depositing the carbon copy of the receipt and the other documents in the safe, Mugyŏng glanced again at the couple. They looked full of happiness. "Full of happiness" sounded cliché, but she could not think of a better alternative.

"Our new house is at Samsŏnp'yŏng in Tonamchŏng. If you keep to the right, you'll find a new residential district there. Follow the broad path and then turn into the third alley. The second door is my house. The building number is four hundred fifty, and our apartment number is seventeen. If you happen to be in the area, please do visit us."

No matter how intelligent, a person could not possibly remember such complex directions. Yet people often give out their address in this way, especially when they come across old acquaintances on the street. As if possessing perfect memory, the listener invariably answers, "Yes, of course. If I'm in the neighborhood, I'll call on you for sure."

"Thank you," said the couple, although they probably didn't care much whether or not Mugyŏng actually intended to come.

After his wife left the office, the salary man lingered at the threshold for a moment to thank Mugyŏng, "Thanks to you, I was able to feel at home here." The couple walked away lightheartedly, whispering something to each other. Mugyŏng stood for a while and watched their backs recede against the darkening sky.

Old man Kang finished cleaning the emptied apartment and came back downstairs with a trash can and a bucket. The bucket was packed with things—coffee cups, glasses, an old hat, and so on. The salary man must have left them behind, having no use for them in his new house. Kang always collected the leftovers of former residents, either selling them to a junk dealer or keeping them for himself.

Mugyŏng closed out the account, and since it was too late to cook, she headed to the cafeteria for dinner. Just as she was finishing her cutlets, Kang called to her and approached her table. She was wanted on the phone.

"The person's asking if we have a vacancy. I said yes . . . "

"Who is it?" Mugyŏng asked, sipping her tea.

"Well, I didn't ask the name. Why don't you answer the phone? It's a woman."

"A woman? Is she a barmaid or someone like that? If she is, it would've been better if you'd said there's no vacancy." Mugyŏng went to the office to answer the phone.

"Hello, I'm sorry to keep you waiting for so long . . . Yes, it's Yamado Apartments. May I ask who this is? . . . The Ch'ŏngŭi Boutique in Myŏngch'ichŏng? Ah, I see. Then is it someone at the boutique who wants to rent an apartment?"

Mugyŏng listened for a while. "A lecturer at the Imperial University? Certainly, please do come and take a look at the apartment. The monthly rent is thirty-five wŏn, fixed-rate. Three months' rent upfront . . . Yes, please come by . . . Yes, yes, thank you very much."

According to the caller, the prospective tenant was a university lecturer looking to rent a studio where he could write for a few months. So what was the woman's connection to the lecturer? Mugyŏng wondered this in passing.

"She said she'll come over right now. Please show her the room and let me know if she wants it. I'll be in my room." She left the office to Kang, who was having a late dinner there.

Mugyŏng returned to her own apartment. Apartment twenty-three on the third floor. Passing by the door next to hers, where the salary man used to live, she thought that it would be nice to have a bookish, scholarly type for a neighbor. She unlocked the door to her apartment and flicked on the light switch.

As usual, she washed her hands before anything else. Then she took off her jacket, changed into a light cardigan, and redid her makeup. Soon it would be March, but she still felt cold at night. She turned on the radiator and sat down on the edge of her bed. She thought of the salary man and his bride. Together, they looked drunk with happiness. They themselves must have felt so. The shadows of the two walking side by side behind the truck. . . .

Suddenly Mugyŏng thought, Can such happiness last a lifetime? Will the young man love his wife forever? Will the couple be able to keep their love and trust strong and enduring, no matter what happens? These were idle thoughts. Who could vouch for undying love? Who on earth could foresee whether the man would always love his bride—now as young and fresh as a new flower blossom—without ever having a change of heart?

Mugyŏng was thus preoccupied with the future of the young couple who had left the apartment with a happy smile on their faces, intoxicated by the sweet dream of a love nest in Tonamchŏng.

There are many couples in the world who live out their lives in peace and comfort. But who can tell what's in the wife's heart? Who can guarantee the husband's love for his wife? Can anyone be certain even of his own heart?

A disquieting thought crept up on her. Mugyŏng shook it off and jumped up from the bed. "I'll live alone. I can live alone."

She looked up at the photo on the wall. It had been taken at her mother's wedding last fall. The two of them were standing side by side, looking awkward and forlorn. Her mother was dressed all in bridal white, while Mugyŏng wore her best clothes, a long, trailing blue skirt and a purple blouse with shiny golden prints on its ribbon. For twenty-two years, until the age of forty-two, her mother had lived alone. Then, last fall, she married Chŏng Ilsu. It occurred to Mugyŏng that she, too, might someday change her mind. But would she ever be able to fall in love again, to plan a life together with someone else? Her wound cut deep, and in fact it was still open. Her relationship had not ended yet. Whenever she became unsure of herself, Mugyŏng renewed her determination "to live alone."

Last summer, after two years of trying everything, she had finally succeeded in having Sihyŏng released on bail. Her mother, a devout Presbyterian, had not liked him in the first place, and after his imprisonment she was even more opposed to their marriage. Meanwhile Sihyŏng's father, a member of the City Council in Pyongyang and a high official of the Chamber of Commerce, was equally unyielding in his objections. It was not only that he disapproved of Mugyŏng, a nondescript girl of his son's choosing. He was also unhappy with Sihyŏng's decision to work as an analyst at a stock company in Seoul after graduating college. The father further objected to his son's views on society, not to mention his general attitude toward life. He wanted Sihyŏng to return to Pyongyang and help run the family business. The father hoped that his son would marry the genteel daughter of a certain local dignitary, a recently retired governor. Such a match, he believed, offered the surest path to his son's success. In the midst of this family quarrel, Sihyŏng was arrested for his involvement in an unlawful incident. His imprisonment deeply shook the father, who had been planning his son's life as if it were an extension of his own. It was a grave blow to a man of his reputation and status. Having lost face, the father became furious, and in the end he all but disowned his only son. Had he been older, he might have taken a softer stance. But he was in his fifties, still robust, and so he could be hard-hearted enough to overlook his son's sufferings.

Two years passed in this situation. In the meantime, Mugyŏng found a job to provide for Sihyŏng in prison, persuaded her mother to accept their relationship, and eventually secured his release through arduous lobbying efforts. It was also for him that she rented her apartment at Yamado.

But after Sihyŏng's release, things had taken a few unexpected turns. Sihyŏng had soon made it known that his ideological orientation had changed. In his own words, he had converted from economics to philosophy, from a universal view of history to a pluralistic one. Thanks to his conversion, he said, he had become academically invested in Oriental Studies. He also grew conscious of his identity as an Asian in response to the rapidly changing international political situation. Yet there was no reason, she thought, that such a change in his academic interests, or even a complete reorientation, should cause any rift between them. Mugyŏng had always thought that she need not concern herself much about Sihyŏng's politics. She felt that she had neither the ability nor the leisure to poke her nose into such issues. So she had no idea what he meant by his conversion, or what bearing it would have on either their relationship or his way of life. As long as he loved her, she was content. She had also become rather complacent, proudly enjoying the thought of her unflagging devotion. But without her noticing, Sihyŏng was undergoing a complex psychological transformation. No outsider could fathom the intricate interiority of a man who had spent two years in prison. Mugyŏng caught a glimpse of Sihyŏng's complex inner self when his father, whom the couple had so far regarded as their archenemy, paid them a visit upon hearing of his son's release. Sihyŏng straightaway reconciled with his father. It was not just that he had been starved of human affection, nor that he was moved by the sudden change of attitude in his father, with whom he had argued constantly in the past. It would likewise have been too easy to say that they could not but be reconciled, that cutting blood ties was like parting water with a sword. Rather, what was most decisive was the change in Sihyŏng's mental outlook; he seemed ready to reconcile with all that he had previously resisted.

Soon after, Sihyŏng followed his father back to Pyongyang.

At about this time, there was another surprise in store for Mugyŏng: her mother married. When Mugyŏng first realized that her mother was dating someone, she felt a deep sense of disappointment. On the one hand, she was repulsed by her mother's late-blooming passion; on the other, she was also jealous.

She had lost her mother as well as the only man she had ever loved. She had gotten a job to provide for Sihyŏng while he was in prison. It was for his sake that she had rented an apartment. She lost the two people she had relied on, believed in, and cared for. With them she had also lost all her hopes for the future. Where could she find again the meaning of life, a purpose for living. . . . For some time, Mugyŏng felt numb and empty, not knowing what to do.

Yet she was born with a strong will to live. Whenever she encountered difficulties, her innate strength showed through in her determination to overcome them. She believed that a person could emerge stronger and greater from one's struggle to confront, resolve, and move beyond any obstacle. Now, in the face of a seemingly insurmountable obstacle, she thought about "active resignation," a path in which one willingly drinks from whatever cup that destiny offers—no matter how poisonous. Mugyŏng was thus determined not to criticize, resent, or envy Sihyŏng and her mother. Instead, she tried to put herself in their shoes.

Sihyŏng must have had ample opportunity for thought and self-reflection during his two years in prison. His ideas must have grown subtler, denser, and richer. In changing his academic and ideological orientation, he was probably searching for a spiritual rebirth. Perhaps, too, he was instinctively avoiding any path that would lead back to a life in confinement, where he rarely saw the light of day. It was very likely that he had made up his mind to put himself on more mature and harmonious terms with his father. In effect, he had every reason to believe that a return to Pyongyang, his hometown, would benefit both his health and his relationship with the authorities. Going back to Pyongyang with his father, then, was essential for his future. If so, Mugyŏng figured, how trivial must a rented apartment in Seoul have appeared? What did it matter if his departure had left her feeling somewhat empty?

It was the same with her mother. Since becoming a widow at the age of twenty, her mother had lived only for Mugyŏng. If her daughter married, who would take care of her? On whom could she rely? It was Mugyŏng who had first betrayed her mother's trust and love. How could she not understand? Her mother must have lost her faith in widowhood as she decided to approve of her daughter's love. Mugyŏng had been an anchor, and mother finally let go. If that was the case, how could she blame her mother for pursuing her own happiness? Wasn't it, after all, only proper that Sihyŏng should plan for his future and her mother for her own? What about Mugyŏng, then, who was left behind?

"I'll have a life of my own!" This was the conclusion that always rescued Mugyŏng from her state of dejection.

She decided to move into the apartment she had rented for Sihyŏng. When her mother went to live with Mr. Chŏng after their marriage, she sold their old house. Thanks to real estate inflation, the sale brought in seven hundred wŏn per four square yards. Altogether, fifteen thousand wŏn were deposited into Mugyŏng's savings account. Mugyŏng packed her things and left most of them with her mother, bringing with her only basic cooking utensils and a few necessities. Mugyŏng had inherited from her father a piece of land that yielded annually about seventy bags of rice. She let Mr. Chŏng manage it in exchange for an allowance of two thousand wŏn per year. The couple invited her to live with them, eager as they were to help her live comfortably. But Mugyŏng insisted on keeping her job as a housing office accountant.

Despite what had happened, Mugyŏng was still unwilling to entirely abandon her trust in Sihyŏng. When she first learned from him of his intention to return to Pyongyang, she instinctively sensed his change of heart. She knew that there was another woman in Pyongyang, an ex-governor's daughter, whom Sihyŏng's father favored as his future daughter-in-law. Mugyŏng thought of the woman as a dark shadow lurking behind Sihyŏng's decision. Still, neither of them wanted to talk openly about the issue of marriage. Was it because she believed in him? Or had she rather given up, realizing that even the most firm promise can change with time?

One day her mother asked, "Have you heard anything more from Sihyŏng about his father's engagement plans for him?" Mugyŏng was caught off guard by the question. "Nothing in particular," she said. But the answer did not satisfy her mother. Hesitantly, her lips opening and closing a few times before making any sound, the mother finally said, "Well, that's good, then. Though they may as well have discussed it, since he came all the way to take his son home. So, I suppose, his father also didn't say anything about your marrying him."

Mugyŏng felt her heart sink, but she quickly gathered herself. "Let him do what he likes. He can marry whomever, a governor's daughter or a princess. . . . "

The mother was taken aback at this reply and didn't know how to press on.

A week after Sihyŏng left Seoul, he sent Mugyŏng a letter. It contained no affectionate words, only a confession of his own anxieties, written in dry phrases.

Now I am focused on thinking of my future, of how I can be spiritually reborn as a stronger, better self. I had known previously the spirit of criticism. But ceaseless criticism can become self-torment. I don't want to be addicted to self-torment. Besides, I don't agree with the mistaken belief among intellectuals that all will go well so long as they continue to criticize society. Those who only criticize create nothing. Thus I cannot but nurture this new green sprout growing in my heart, even if it may lead me to egotism or compromise. Neither can I help it if, in this charged political climate, I have to abuse and sacrifice all that belonged to my past on the road to a new future.

There was no mention of marriage in the letter. Mugyŏng tried to believe that their love for each other would never change. But she also could not help feeling the faint pricking of a little needle in her heart. For a while, she had carefully kept a thin coating over its sharp point. But one slight pull would be enough for it to pierce through to her vulnerable heart. Such a state never lasts long. Nor was Mugyŏng naïve enough to remain in the dark for long. The time soon arrived when she at last deciphered the concrete facts hidden behind Sihyŏng's abstract words.

Although Mugyŏng had sent several letters to Sihyŏng, she never received any reply from him. Then, one day, a brief letter came. It said that he was going to a hot spring for some absolute peace and quiet. He wanted her to excuse him for keeping his address unknown, since he had decided not to reveal it to anyone. Frequent communications would be inconvenient for him for many reasons.

In her letters Mugyŏng had always been cautious not to write anything that would distract Sihyŏng from the task of reorganizing and focusing his thoughts. She thought that he should be left alone to resolve his own problems without anyone's intervention. Let him deal with them on his own! Let him find his salvation in a new ideology! Such was her genuine wish. But what was the real meaning of his letter? Wasn't it actually saying that he now wanted to be liberated from Mugyŏng, to forget both her and all the memories associated with her name?

For some time afterward Mugyŏng had to endure a sharp, piercing pain in her heart. Soon it was fall. Winter came. New Year's Day passed. And then it was spring again. Still no news from Sihyŏng. Meanwhile, Mugyŏng made up her mind to spend the rest of her life alone, and with this new determination came an almost spiteful desire for her own share of spiritual growth. "To have a life of my own! To cultivate intellectual autonomy so that I can articulate my ideas in my own words!" Before, under Sihyŏng's influence, she had studied economics. Now, following his footsteps again, she decided to study philosophy. "I follow you but only to outrun you!" In this motto she sought to bury all her feelings of jealousy, anger, disappointment, sadness, loneliness, and contempt.

Mugyŏng shook off her thoughts and walked away from her mother's photo. For some months now she had been reading Iwanami's *Lectures on Philosophy*. The book had many parts that she could not easily understand, but as she read on, as if studying for an important exam, she could feel her ideas gradually maturing. This feeling made her happy. Every time she closed the book for the night or opened it the next morning, she smiled, saying to herself, "I am growing up."

A while after the clock struck nine o'clock, she heard Kang's footsteps in the corridor along with those from a pair of high heels. The sounds stopped at the next door. Mugyŏng heard whispering. She knew that Kang had come to show the room to the new applicant, but she kept to her seat.

If the tenant wanted to rent a room only for the purpose of writing, this would likely mean no more than a few months. It was a bit odd that Mugyŏng should have so willingly offered the person the vacancy. Given the current housing shortage in the city, she could have easily found another applicant for a long-term lease. . . . Mugyŏng regretted her lack of foresight. Although it was still possible to reconsider, she could not bring herself to turn down such a respectable applicant as a university lecturer. As a matter of fact, since beginning to study philosophy, she'd grown more interested in the university. The more esoteric the passages she read, the more awed she became of scholars. Mugyŏng's business sense was usually as clear-cut as an abacus, but her present state of mind disposed her to offer the lease without making many inquiries.

Someone was approaching. Two heavy knocks—it was Kang. She answered the door.

"She likes the apartment . . . " Kang said in a low voice. As Mugyŏng was putting on her shoes and stepping out into the corridor, a woman in Western clothes could be seen already heading down the staircase. They followed her downstairs.

"Please come in," Mugyŏng ushered the woman into the office. The woman, most likely in her thirties, was wearing colorful makeup and looked quite beautiful. As was fitting for a boutique owner, she wore a dress that elegantly outlined her body. Because of her rather bold makeup, though, Mugyŏng would not have been able to tell her apart from a woman of the lower professions, such as an actress or barmaid.

"I'm Ch'oe Mugyŏng. I work at the housing office."

"I'm Mun Ranju. I'm sorry to disturb you so late." Despite her words, Ranju glanced at the clock on the wall as if to point out that it was not even ten o'clock yet. "I like the apartment. Is it okay to move in tonight?"

"Sure. Actually, we have a rule against short-term leases. . . ." Although it felt awkward, Mugyŏng could not help but raise the issue.

"He says he needs it only for his writing, but who knows? He may stay for longer. They say that in Tokyo all novelists keep an extra apartment in addition to their house." Ranju replied with a casual but measured smile. "Then I'll have him move right away. Is it okay if he pays his security deposit tomorrow morning?"

"As you like. Early in the morning is good. Then I'll see you in the morning." Mugyŏng turned to Kang and said, "Please look after his moving in, though it may get a bit late for you. And please don't forget to lock the door behind him. By the way," she continued, turning back to Ranju, "we don't have any particular rules, but we put this together to help our residents enjoy their communal life better. Please take a look at it at your convenience. And could you write here the name of the professor?"

Mugyŏng gave Ranju a pamphlet and a piece of paper. Ranju wrote "Yi Kwanhyŏng" on the paper, accepted the pamphlet, and then took her leave.

"I'll see you again soon."

"Good night."

One woman went outside; the other went upstairs. A group of salary men, who had been out late at a dinner party, came in then.

"*Konbangwa.*"

"Ah ah, sorry for coming back late!"

Their murmurings soon subsided, and all was still again in the building. Mugyŏng locked the door of her apartment and walked to her desk.

2

Even though Apartment 22 was furnished with a table and a wardrobe, Mugyŏng expected that it would take a while for the lecturer to move in since he would have to carry up at least his bedding, some personal items and, presumably, quite a few books. She worried that, despite his caution, he might disturb the sleep of the other residents. Yet everything proceeded quite smoothly, with little noise beyond the sound of busy footsteps. While she was relieved, Mugyŏng also felt a slight sense of disappointment. This feeling did not last long, however, as she figured that he must have brought with him only a few bags for now, planning to gradually move other things in later. She was a bit curious about what his relations were with Ranju. But Mugyŏng had made it a rule not to indulge in the bad habit of poking her nose into the private affairs of residents or their guests. Some time after the new tenant had moved his things in, she heard a pair of high heels walking along the corridor and down the staircase, and then she stopped caring about the issue.

Nothing happened overnight. Morning was the busiest time of the day in the building. With a throng of people moving in and out, exchanging greetings and rushing to get ready for work, it was hard to tell one voice from another. Mugyŏng got up early as usual, washed her face with hot water, and cooked herself a simple breakfast. She read in her room until nine, the hour the office opened. Only after the clock struck nine did she head down. Kang, who worked the night shift, had just finished cleaning the office and had refilled the stove with coal. He retired to his home and would return by ten, as usual carrying a lunch box under his arm. Shortly thereafter the landlord also showed up. For two years now he had left the apartment in Mugyŏng's charge. He dropped by every morning to check the account balance, but he never stayed long. Mugyŏng always had the accounting book ready for his review, during which she gave him a detailed report on what had transpired the day before.

"The salary man in Apartment 22 moved out yesterday. But last night we received a new tenant, a university lecturer named Yi Kwanhyŏng. After subtracting this month's rent from his security deposit, I paid this to the outgoing tenant. . . . " Mugyŏng pointed at the receipt. "I haven't settled the account with the new tenant yet, but I will this morning. I'll count today as his first day. These figures are for this month's rent, and this expenditure is for electricity." Signaling his approval, the landlord stamped his slender seal on the accounting book as well as on each receipt. Without a word, he pocketed most of the money. Then he looked around the corridor and cafeteria, as if inspecting them. "I'm leaving now." His plump body soon disappeared from Mugyŏng's sight into the bustling streets outside.

A while later, Kang came back from his rounds to the furnace room. "Did the new tenant pay his rent yet?"

"No," Mugyŏng replied, "I haven't heard anything from him yet."

Kang started toward the janitor's office but stopped halfway. He turned to Mugyŏng and asked, "What did she say about his occupation?"

"A university lecturer. Why?"

"A university lecturer," repeated Kang in a low voice. He said nothing further for a moment.

"Well, why don't you go and hurry him up a bit?" he said at last, coming closer to Mugyŏng.

"I told her to have him settle the account early in the morning, but he must have forgotten about it. A scholar's neglect of worldly affairs. Why don't you go and ask him yourself?"

Kang stood there with a brooding look on his face. Spring was just around the corner, but the old man still had on his well-worn fur cap. He wore tattered bluish overalls over his pants and an old woolen postman's jacket over his shirt. His misshapen boots, a resident's castoff, were at least made of genuine calf leather.

"All right, I'll go." Kang took off his cap and used his knotty fingers to part his crew-cut hair. He moved slowly to the corridor.

Mugyŏng noticed a sense of disapproval in his attitude. But since he did get things mixed up every now and then for no particular reason, she simply thought that he must have misunderstood something. Kang was old enough not to rashly vent his complaints. Instead, he would simply affect a brooding look. He had the same look when he was staring at Ranju last night.

Although Mugyŏng was not affected much by Kang's behavior, she did think it a bit odd that she hadn't heard anything from the new tenant, despite their morning appointment. It was almost eleven, but there was no sign of him in the cafeteria. She wondered if he were somehow already cooking in his new apartment. It seemed unlikely that Ranju should forget to pass the word onto him, or if she had, that she should not have shown up herself in his stead.

After a long while, Kang came back from upstairs with a deep frown on his face. He didn't tell Mugyŏng right away what the problem was. He just paced in front of the desk, looking quite upset. Finally, he blurted out, as if to himself, "What a rude fellow! And to an old man like me!" Mugyŏng saw trouble coming. Despite her misgivings, she asked, smiling, "What's wrong?"

"Huh, a university professor? Indeed!"

Eventually Kang told Mugyŏng what had happened.

"For the life of me, I can't figure that man out. Look, I knocked on his door, like I always do. I knocked several times, but there was no reply. So I knocked hard again and finally a voice answered, 'Whoever you are, please come in.' The voice sounded refined or arrogant, depending on how you take it. I turned the knob and found that the door was actually open. As I looked in, I could hardly keep my eyes open from all the cigarette smoke in the room. It was like someone was trying to smoke out a bear. Till then, though, I was still thinking, the man must be so deeply engrossed in his writing that he didn't even notice all the smoke. How could I have guessed that he was still lying in bed? And what fine clothes he wore! That hair of his, and that face . . . "

A grimace animated Kang's wrinkled face, as if he could not even begin to describe the horrific sight of the man. After a pause, he continued.

"Last night I knew something looked fishy. After you retired upstairs, I stayed to watch him move in. He got out of the car and walked in, carrying only one bag in his hand. Then that loud woman rushed in ahead of him, and she was also carrying only one small bundle. Our university professor had a hat on. I couldn't tell what kind of suit he was wearing, but he did have a coat on, and it was old and rumpled. . . . Anyhow, things were already getting fishy . . . And now all morning he seems to have been just burning up cigarettes in bed. I told him, 'According to the apartment's regulations, Sir, you have to pay the first month upfront and a security deposit equivalent to three months' rent.' He just answered, 'Leave me alone.' So I said again, politely, 'Sir, if we really went by the rules, we wouldn't have allowed you to move in last night without paying upfront. But we made an exception for you.' Again, he just told me to shut up and wait downstairs. How could I not get upset at that? I warned him, 'Well, if a tenant doesn't comply with the rules, he must vacate his room.' He said, 'Huh, what a hassle! I don't want to talk to you. Send up your boss!' I retorted, 'But we accept payment only at the office.' Then he sprang out of bed and yelled at me, 'Shut up and send up your boss!' I had no desire to mess with him, considering his clothes and how unkempt he looked. So I slammed the door behind my back. A fine university professor, indeed! Last night's woman, she must be a whore. A barmaid or an actress, you know, like the ones who act in movies."

"She said she owns a boutique." Mugyŏng didn't mean to defend the woman but rather to curb Kang's habitual overstatement.

"A *butiku*?"

"Yes, a place where they make ladies' clothes."

This news had an effect on the old man, who seemed to calm down a bit. "I don't care what she owns . . . " Kang's voice trailed off, as he started going back to the janitor's office.

"Thank you for your help. I'll go and see him myself, though I'm not the landlord, either."

Mugyŏng said this lightheartedly, but she was actually quite upset at Kang's report. Facing the door of Apartment 22, she tensed up. Knock knock. Just as Kang said, a voice slowly answered, "Whoever you are, please come in." She felt awkward entering a man's apartment alone. She gingerly turned the knob and put her leg forward first, hoping that the sight of her skirt through the door would alert the man to the fact that she was a woman, and that he should behave appropriately. She waited for a moment, inhaling the smoke that seeped out through the open door. Finally, she pushed her whole body into the room.

The man was in bed, lying on his back with his eyes fixed on the ceiling. He was smoking a cigarette. He did not look her way and remained apparently unaware that his visitor was a woman. Needless to say, he hadn't noticed Mugyŏng's subtle way of announcing herself. The lower half of his body was covered with a thin padded comforter, while the upper half was wrapped in a dazzling bright gown that was unmistakably a woman's garment.

"Oh, my, all this smoke," said Mugyŏng in a low voice as a cue to the man. He lifted his head. Finally recognizing that the caller was a woman, he sprang up from the bed. His hair was uncombed and disheveled, while his face was covered with stubble that had not seen a razor in a while. He had a fair complexion, but he also looked quite pale. A loaf of bread, which it seemed he kept by his arm, rolled down from the bed.

He looked embarrassed, as if ashamed of being caught by a woman in his present state, and especially in such a gown.

"The landlord is not in. I'm his representative."

Upon hearing this, the man's sullen expression returned. Averting his eyes, he said in an accusing tone, "Don't you know any better than to treat a guest like this?"

"Well, there are times when we make mistakes in treating our guests. But tell me, what did the old man do wrong?" Mugyŏng was determined to settle the score with the man without at all humoring him.

After a brief pause, he said, "I'll pay the rent and the security deposit. Can't a guest make a payment without your being rude to him?"

"Yes, of course. But you broke your promise. If the old man behaved rudely, that's probably because things don't quite match up with what we were told last night."

"I broke a promise? Things don't match up? What do you mean? What kind of solemn promise have I ever made to you?"

He was now staring straight at Mugyŏng. She paused for a moment. It all seemed ludicrous to her that she should be having an argument like this, with her standing at the threshold and him still sitting on the bed. But she reminded herself of her responsibilities as the building's representative.

"I just met you now for the first time. So I of course haven't received any promise from you. When I rented this unit last night, I did so by trusting the lady who came by. It's not that I met you in person."

She meant to offend the man's pride. He came down from the bed. He looked comical with a woman's gown draped over his suit.

"What was this promise? Did she say that I won't budge, even if you treat me rudely?" He glared at Mugyŏng.

"She said that you're a lecturer at the Imperial University, and that you needed this apartment for your study. And you were supposed to have cleared your account this morning."

Suddenly the man looked dumbstruck. He was at a loss for words, and he looked as if he was completely drained of energy.

He quietly turned around and walked back to the side of the bed. "A university lecturer." Mugyŏng heard him repeat these words under his breath, as if trying to set them to memory. But soon he turned to face her again.

"If she really told you that I'm a university lecturer looking for a writing studio, then she lied. I take back her words. But what matters in the end is the rent and the security deposit, isn't it? You won't mind whether I write or read, so long as I don't disturb anyone? You certainly don't have any regulation that a tenant should be a university lecturer. . . . "

"True, you could say that."

"In that case," he said, putting his hand into a jacket pocket, "I'll give you the money by today. If you can't trust me, you have me here as a hostage. I'll even leave this golden watch with you. This is the only thing I have on me now."

"Absolutely not! Do you think we're running a pawnshop here?"

"Well, what do you want me to do, then? Are you ordering me to get out right now just because you can't wait a few hours?"

Just as they were about to cause a scene, the sound of footsteps was heard from the staircase. Ranju emerged, carrying a large bundle under her arm. She was followed by a driver who was also carrying what looked like a roll of bedding.

"Hello, good morning. Sorry I'm late."

Ranju greeted Mugyŏng. Noticing the awkward tension in the air, she smiled, saying, "What happened? Is there any problem?" She took the bundle from the driver and with an effort carried it into the room. Then she turned toward the man, who was standing beside her with a sulky look on his face. "Why are you standing there like a wooden pole?" Then she said to Mugyŏng, "I'll come down right away."

Mugyŏng just stood there. She no longer had any reason for arguing, nor did she feel like explaining the situation to Ranju. Yi Kwanhyŏng also seemed to see no point in continuing their argument. He quietly went back to bed. What nonsense! Mugyŏng simply closed the door and returned to the office downstairs. Kang was nowhere to be seen. She found the entire affair ludicrous rather than unpleasant or offensive. She'd taken part in the scene, but she couldn't make heads or tails of it.

What kind of man was Yi Kwanhyŏng? Despite his shabby, bizarre appearance, Kang's portrayal of him did not do him justice. It was obvious that he was no university lecturer. Then why did the woman Ranju settle on this particular profession? He could have been anything, a salary man, a mine developer. . . . Why on earth a university lecturer?

Ranju came down. Seemingly aware of what happened, she gently smiled at Mugyŏng upon entering the office. "I'm sorry I was late." Today, too, she was wearing colorful makeup. A close look at her eyes, lips, and neckline suggested that she was very well versed in the art of cosmetics. She opened her purse and took out her wallet without asking any questions. The red manicure on her nails contrasted with her white, slender fingers, creating a strangely delicate allure.

"The security deposit is one hundred and fifty. And the first month's rent is thirty five. So one hundred and forty wŏn altogether, right?"

Mugyŏng made no reply. She just filled out the tenancy contract form, counted the bills, and deposited them in the safe. As she entered Kwanhyŏng's name into the registry, she paused to ask, "What about his occupation?"

"Well, things are a bit up in the air as far as his occupation is concerned," came Ranju's voice over her shoulder. It seemed that she'd just run into trouble over this issue upstairs. "As a matter of fact, he did teach at the university a while ago, but then he was dismissed. That's why I said yesterday he's a lecturer. To tell you the truth, he's temporarily out of a job now. Since he says he'd prefer to be known as unemployed, why don't we just write 'unemployed'? He is twenty-seven years old, no, twenty-eight. He was twenty-seven last year. . . ."

3

The apartment building had thirty-six one-bedroom units and twenty-five two-bedroom family units. Since the tenants numbered over a hundred, Mugyŏng could not possibly remember all their faces, nor did she have enough leisure or interest to delve into their characters and habits. Once she checked someone in, she hardly had any contact with the person except on special occasions. The tenants were all familiar with Mugyŏng, since she lived in the same building and had her office right next to the entrance. But unless someone violated communal etiquette, she had no intention of communicating with tenants beyond the regular business of collecting rent and utility fees. Even when there was trouble, she did not herself intervene, leaving the job to Kang or the landlord. She exchanged casual greetings with only a few of the older tenants. Yi

Kwanhyŏng could have easily become one of the men whom she failed to notice.

Yet somehow—although she never saw him again, despite his living next door—the thought of him lingered in her mind. Her bizarre exchange with him on the first day and his unusual character were partly responsible for this. Moreover, Ranju's daily visits continued to remind Mugyŏng of this mysterious man. Every evening, on her way back to her apartment, she wondered how he had spent the day in his room. A one-time Imperial University lecturer. A failed man with an unshaven face, who wore a woman's gown and spent all day smoking and nibbling at the bread he kept at his bedside. . . . So odd and scandalous was Kwanhyŏng's image that she kept thinking about him even in her spare time.

One evening Ranju came for a visit, and Kang called attention to her by saying, "The seamstress visits her university professor again." Mugyŏng lifted her eyes from the desk and replied with a smile, "You really don't like her," but he denied it. "I have no reason to dislike her, but don't you think her relationship with that man is a bit strange? It's certain they're not related. My eyes don't deceive me. He boasted of being a university lecturer, but they can't fool me." Without waiting for Mugyŏng's reply, Kang left to check the furnace, mumbling, "Something's fishy! They can't fool my eyes." At Kang's words, Mugyŏng's thoughts again drifted to the couple's mysterious relationship. Although she chided herself for such thoughts and blushed at taking an unwanted interest in the affairs of others, she couldn't prevent her imagination from wandering.

On the morning of the sixth day after Kwanhyŏng moved in, Kang informed Mugyŏng, as she entered the office, "It's strange . . . the seamstress skipped her visit yesterday. I expected her till late at night, but for whatever reason, she never showed up." Mugyŏng simply said, "I see," and did not inquire further. About one o'clock that day, while she was reading one of the magazines at the office, she saw Kwanhyŏng staggering down the staircase for the first time since he had moved in. His face and hair were as messy as before, but he was no longer wearing a gown over his suit jacket. Once downstairs, he took a sweeping look around. He ran his eyes over the signboards for the cafeteria, billiard room, and bathing area on the ground floor. As if intrigued, he walked up to each signboard and inspected the facilities inside before going back upstairs. A while later, he came down again with an envelope in his hand. This time he walked straight into the office.

Upon entering the office, he made a bow to Mugyŏng. She got up from her seat to return the courtesy.

"May I use the phone?"

She moved the phone closer to him. Flipping through the phone book, he asked, "Do you have a delivery service you use?" "Yes, we do." Mugyŏng told him the phone number, which he dialed. He asked for a messenger. After hanging up the phone, he seemed hesitant about whether to go back to his room or to stay at the office while waiting for the messenger to arrive.

"Please take a seat. He'll come in no time. By the way, there's a phone on the third floor, too. You can call from there in the future."

Kwanhyŏng sat down in the chair. Mugyŏng fixed her eyes on the magazines to avoid awkward eye contact. He broke the silence first. "How is it that there's no barber in the building?" As their eyes met, she almost burst out laughing, but managed to check the impulse. He finally wants a hair cut, she thought.

"We had a barber here before, but there's an old barber across the street, so the business wasn't so good. You can't run a barbershop on our residents alone. There are one hundred and twenty-three people living here but many of them are women, and even if the men were to get a haircut twice a month, it still adds up to only fifty or sixty wŏn, hardly enough to pay a barber's salary. So we had to close the shop since there's another so close by."

"Ah, I see," Kwanhyŏng nodded, as if impressed by her explanation.

"In its place there's now a billiard room. You know, the room next to the bathing area."

The messenger arrived. Kwanhyŏng gave him a letter, saying, "If Mr. Yun isn't there, just bring it back, but don't show it to anyone."

Then he went back upstairs. About forty minutes later, the messenger returned. He seemed to have been successful in his delivery. Thirty minutes after that, a rotund, well-dressed, and energetic middle-aged gentleman arrived, asking for Kwanhyŏng. Mugyŏng told him the apartment number, thinking that he must be the recipient of the letter.

Kwanhyŏng seemed to be finally awakening from his hibernation. Comparing him to an animal sloughing off dead skin, Mugyŏng smiled to herself. But when she considered the transformation he must have undergone after the painful end to his academic career, her thoughts took a darker turn. Such reflections on the grim facts of life always reminded her of Sihyŏng. Maybe men are prone to acting out in unusual ways when confronted with serious obstacles. If they reach a wall, do they all become failures and outsiders? In regarding Kwanhyŏng's acts today as part of a struggle to get back on his feet, she no longer felt like laughing at him.

The guest came down and left. When Kwanhyŏng reappeared a while later, Kang happened to be in the office. "Wow, what's going on with him? Now he wants to take a bath."

Mugyŏng caught sight of Kwanhyŏng coming down the staircase with a towel in his hand. He looked into the bathing area and then approached the office.

"I'm sorry to interrupt you again, but since the bank is already closed, I wonder if you could cash a check for me?" It was already half past three.

"Well, how much do you need? I don't have much cash here."

"The check is for one thousand wŏn. But you can give me whatever you have. Even a small portion of it."

"I can give you about two hundred wŏn."

"That should do."

He took out the check from his inside jacket pocket and handed it to her. The name "Yun Kapsu" was written on it. While waiting for Mugyŏng to open the safe, Kwanhyŏng noticed Kang and said, "Are you still upset with me?" He then laughed out loud for the first time. Embarrassed, Kang replied, "Of course not. Do I look like a man who would get upset over nothing?" He answered as if he had forgotten all his rancor, but he still slipped out of the office without saying a word. This made Mugyŏng smile.

"Here's two hundred wŏn. Please count the bills. And I'll cash this check for you tomorrow. The Chosŏn Industrial Bank, right?"

Kwanhyŏng put the money in his pocket. "Thank you." As he turned to go, he caught a reflection of his face in the long mirror hanging under the clock. He looked stunned. Oblivious to Mugyŏng's presence, he stared at his own face for a while and ran his hand over his stubble. Noticing that Mugyŏng was looking at him, he smiled broadly.

"Do you need a razor blade?"

He scratched his head. "It's okay," he said, shaking his head. But he kept gazing at his own reflection with a blank look of surprise.

"My razor should be somewhere here," said Mugyŏng. He turned to look at her. It was odd for a woman to lend her razor to a male stranger. While continuing to search for the razor, she excused herself by saying, "When I was moving in, I had too many things stuffed in my handbag. So I left the razor here somewhere . . . Oh, here it is! I don't know if it's sharp or not. But please take it. I don't need it any more."

Having thus procured a razor, Kwanhyŏng walked toward the bathing area, swinging a case of soap wrapped inside his towel. Mugyŏng watched him through the window until he disappeared.

At about four o'clock, Mugyŏng went to visit her mother, leaving the office in Kang's charge. Her mother and Mr. Chŏng had bought a house in the upscale Aenggujang housing complex, near Changch'ungdan. They always received her warmly and treated her with genuine kindness. But after some lighter conversation, they invariably urged her to quit her job. Her mother thought that it was alright if Mugyŏng preferred to live a simple life in a one-bedroom apartment. But she could not understand why Mugyŏng wanted to keep her job, waiting on others when she had more than enough to live on. There was some sense to her mother's argument, and Mugyŏng even found herself agreeing at times. So every time the topic was brought up, she simply did her best to humor her mother with reassuring words. Today, though, mother and Mr. Chŏng went so far as to suggest that she should go study at a college in Japan, for a change of scenery.

Mugyŏng left early without having dinner, against her mother's wish. She pretended to have urgent business to take care of. Signs of spring were abundant in the outskirts of the city. She spent the sunset hours wandering through the streets, lost in her thoughts.

Mother and Mr. Chŏng apparently took it for granted that things were at an end between her and Sihyŏng. Although they never mentioned it directly, it was implied in their suggestion that she study abroad. "Is it really a known fact that our relationship is over for good? Am I just being silly and stubborn to insist on keeping the apartment and the job, both of which I took on for him?"

Her spirits falling, Mugyŏng hailed a cab and returned to her apartment. Sitting in the middle of her empty apartment, she felt even more depressed.

For sometime now, she had been telling herself that she should no longer trust in his love. But even as she repeated this to herself, a voice in her heart continued to resist acknowledging the end of their relationship.

"This isn't how human affairs are meant to be. Or is it? Is this doubt the only thing that sustains me now?"

Mugyŏng shook her head and turned on the lamp. She busied herself cleaning the room, opening the window, dusting and mopping. . . . After cleaning she felt a bit better. She went to the cafeteria and ordered a full-course dinner, something she hadn't done in a while. When she was almost finished with her meal, Kwanhyŏng entered the cafeteria, looking rejuvenated and almost unrecognizable. At first he didn't notice her in the crowded cafeteria, but as he was looking around for a place to sit, he caught sight of her. His new suit was not all that impressive, but his face, still pale, looked like a marble sculpture. Shaving had made a striking difference. Now, under his soft curly hair, she could clearly see his gentle, intelligent face. It was a good thing she'd lent him a razor. She welcomed him to her table.

"Are you coming for dinner?"

"Yes, it's my first time here. Ah, I tried to return the razor to you, but since you weren't at the office, I left it in my room. Are you working at the office late tonight?" asked Kwanhyŏng.

"I live in the building. My apartment is right next to yours."

He looked surprised. "I never knew, though it's been a week . . . " He turned to the waiter behind him, "I'll have the same as hers." He then looked at her and smiled.

"So your apartment is twenty-three, twenty-four?"

"Twenty-three."

"That's why you had your razor here." He continued smiling. Mugyŏng was also glad that her dinner was ending with such a pleasant conversation.

"I should excuse myself." She left the table before Kwanhyŏng's meal arrived. Back in her room, she washed her teacups and put the kettle on the stove. She was thinking that she should calm down and read a book. As the water began to boil, she made a cup of black tea for herself. At that moment there was a knock at the door. It was Kwanhyŏng.

"I brought you your razor. I was afraid I was knocking on the wrong door . . . "

"You could've just kept it. Anyway, why don't you step in for a second? I was just making tea. Please have a cup. I have some left-over Lipton. Though my room is small and shabby. . . . "

Kwanhyŏng hesitated at the door. "You keep your room so clean. People like me are simply incapable of living on our own in an apartment."

With the bed and kitchen sink hidden behind heavy curtains, Mugyŏng's room offered little in the way of feminine refinements.

"Then may I? It's been a long time since I had tea. . . . Thank you very much." He came in, closing the door behind him. Mugyŏng offered him a seat on the sofa, put on an apron, and began preparing the tea.

"Wow, you're very studious."

Kwanhyŏng looked at the bookshelf behind the sofa as well as the stacks of books next to it. Mugyŏng had quite a collection, as she kept Sihyŏng's book in addition to her own.

"I only pretend to read them."

"Aren't these all philosophy books?" Kwanhyŏng looked genuinely surprised.

She placed the teacup in front of him, yet he kept looking at her in admiration.

"Don't, please. You're embarrassing me." Still, it felt good to be praised for being studious.

"Please drink your tea before it gets cold."

Kwanhyŏng continued to sit with the same expression on his face. Finally he took the cup to his lips. Mugyŏng sat across from him and sipped her tea, too.

"So, what did you teach at the university?"

"Me?" he put down the cup. "Didn't I say that was a lie?" A smile flickered on his lips.

"You're teasing me," replied Mugyŏng, remembering the incident, "though it's true I was rude to you, despite myself."

"I don't know about teaching at the university. I just lectured a bit on English literature."

"Is that your subject?"

"Yes, a shallower discipline than your philosophy."

"Not at all. You're mistaken if you think I'm a serious philosopher. Most of those books aren't mine. Though as it happens, I do read a few pages in the odd book here and there."

Kwanhyŏng turned to browse the books again. "Nietzsche, Kierkegaard, Bergson, Durkheim, Dilthey, Heidegger, Pegis, Ortega, Simmel, Schmitt, Rosenzweig, Troeltsch, Dewey . . . "† He read aloud the names of the authors.

†Translator's note: Beyond readily recognizable names, Sihyŏng's library includes some relatively less known figures. Anton Charles Pegis (1905–?), a Milwaukee native, was a professor of medieval philosophy; José Ortega y Gasset (1883–1955) was a Spanish philosopher who applied German philosophical ideas to the problem of Spanish decadence and, more broadly, to the crisis of Europe; Carl Schmitt (1888–1985) was a conservative critic of liberalism in Weimar Germany who supported Nazism; Franz Rosenzweig (1886–1929), a Jewish philosopher, developed the "philosophy of revelation," which combined religious inspiration with German idealism; and Ernst Peter Wilhelm Troeltsch (1865–1923) was a philosopher of religion and history who tried to reconcile theology with modern scientific culture by grounding his study of religion in historical analysis.

"Wow, all the great names are here, shining like a constellation of stars. All these giants trying to save Europe by upholding its noble, universal spirit. . . . "

He took another sip of tea. "From now on I should read them too . . . " He said this in a reflective tone of voice, as if ashamed of his dissolute life.

Mugyŏng was blushing herself. Although she had shelved the books neatly in order, she could not say that she knew who these stars of Europe were. She felt ashamed in front of the young scholar, who was mistaking her for a mature intellectual. Sihyŏng . . . he told her that these philosophers and thinkers had been his salvation. But those same stars had also taken him away from her.

Mugyŏng lifted her eyes, "Sir, may I ask you a question?"

"What is it? I don't know anything about philosophy." But Kwanhyŏng's modesty did not discourage Mugyŏng.

"Do you have any idea what Oriental Studies is?"

Why did the issue of Oriental Studies plunge Sihyŏng into self-doubt? What was it about Oriental Studies that made Sihyŏng ignore and abuse Mugyŏng despite everything they had shared together? To Mugyŏng, this enigmatic academic subject was closely intertwined with the question of love, and it seemed to hold the key to the leading mystery in her life. Men have their own world. From the day that Sihyŏng left for Pyongyang, Mugyŏng had no longer been sure whether she understood him. For that matter, neither was she sure about Kwanhyŏng. Now he looked like a decent, cultured intellectual. But this same man also maintained a suspicious relationship with an older woman, and he wallowed in a slothful, disorderly life.

Kwanhyŏng at first thought little of Mugyŏng's question, but sensing how serious she was, he grew increasingly reflective in his reply.

"I can answer your question only in a common sense way, since this all lies beyond my expertise. I may well misinterpret something or stumble over some abstraction. . . . But in my opinion, at least, Oriental Studies can be divided into two kinds, the study of the Orient by Westerners and the effort by Orientals to redefine the Orient in their own terms. Either way, it's difficult to approach Oriental Studies as a purely autonomous academic field. If Oriental Studies were just a field where Westerners apply their own methods to the Orient, then 'Oriental' would be nothing more than a geographical label. There wouldn't be any problem in this. But as for establishing Oriental Studies on our own, as Orientals, if you think hard about it, there are many problems. For instance, most of us do our studies by using concepts imported from Europe. Almost everybody with a college education has learned European methods and can't study the Orient without them. If we were to do so, we would need to rely on concepts of our own invention. Maybe because I majored in English literature, I don't think there's much I know that doesn't somehow involve European methods, whether in social science, natural science, philosophy, or psychology. That's why great philosophers like Nishida draw on Western ideas even in striving to create a purely Japanese philosophy. In Korea, too, some people talk about creating a 'pure Korean philosophy.' I have sympathy for them, but this is a name with no real substance. Some people are now trying to study the ideas of Korean philosophers, such as Yulgok. But done like this, Oriental Studies becomes nothing but a confused and irrelevant undertaking."

"But isn't there something significant in Westerners' wanting to study the Orient? Like the decline of the West, or the discovery of Oriental cultural values?"

"I see what you're saying. There are people who would say so, and of course they're not entirely wrong. All these stellar authors whose books you have on your shelf have been talking for a long time about the decline of the European spirit and the crisis of Western civilization. And they have often 'discovered' the East in searching for ways to revitalize Europe. But they have never really believed that the path to salvation lies in the East. On the contrary, they are deeply convinced that the world can be saved only through the European spirit. This way of thinking is rather natural for Europeans and offensive for us, but their so-called discovery of the East is nothing more than that. When a Western scholar visits an Asian country, he doesn't admire any of the modern buildings in its cities. Rather, he sees only ancient landmarks, antiques. An Asian scholar who takes a Westerner on a guided tour soon finds that his guest is merely entertained at what he sees. That is, his being impressed doesn't mean that he finds in our relics the salvation of the West. We need to keep this in mind."

Mugyŏng quietly listened throughout. Then she asked another question, this time paraphrased from what Sihyŏng had written her.

"What do you think, then, about the idea that we should leave behind a single, West-oriented notion of history and replace it with multiple histories of the modern world?" She spoke slowly, fumbling for academic idioms unfamiliar to her.

"You mean the argument that Asia has its own version of world history? That is to say, India has its own history, so does China, and so does Japan . . . We should abandon Western period markers such as the ancient, the medieval, and the modern, and instead look at our history as it is. And we should abandon the West in favor of our own unique culture. Well, these are all worthy ideas for an Asian to think about. But we must remember one thing—that the concept of Asia never had such unity as that of Europe or the West. The crisis of the European spirit, the decline of the West, implies the collapse of a certain common spirit. After all, Europe experienced the middle ages. Don't they say that the decline of Europe is due to the loss of its unifying spirit, which originated in the middle ages? But they must still trust their common spiritual tradition to believe in the possibility of another renaissance. If you compare just spiritual values, Buddhism and Confucianism may well be superior to Christianity. But though they both prospered in Korea, neither can offer a spiritual basis for a unique Korean thought or cultural tradition, since they are from India and China. This, though, is a fault of our ancestors, not of Buddhism or Confucianism per se."

Kwanhyŏng left no room for Mugyŏng to insist otherwise. She felt that she could almost understand why he was living such an unhealthy life. It was a tragedy that an Asian should devalue Asia as much as he did. Mugyŏng briefly thought about Sihyŏng's letter. Did he have this sort of thing in mind when he criticized today's intellectuals for their habit of preoccupying themselves with negative criticism? What is needed today, he had written, is creation, not criticism.

Breaking his silence, Kwanhyŏng took out a cigarette from his pocket, "Excuse me for smoking."

He lit the cigarette with a match and inhaled deeply. "There's a saying I've recently become fond of. It's from a painter named Van Gogh."

He took another puff. "Human life is like barley. If you are not sown in the earth to germinate there, what does it matter? In the end you are milled to become bread. You should instead pity those who are not milled straightaway. What do you think of this saying?"

Then he slowly recited the entire saying again. Mugyŏng also repeated his words in silence. She then asked, "What about it? So you mean it's better to be ground into bread than to be sown in the earth? Or that one may be planted and turn into many ears of barley, but that the ears of barley are destined to become bread all the same?"

Kwanhyŏng smiled. "The interpretation is up to us. A good saying can be interpreted many ways."

"Then, I'll interpret it this way. Since I'll eventually become bread anyway, why not first be sown in the earth and let my flower bloom? Isn't that better than being milled prematurely?"

Still smiling, Kwanhyŏng said, "The saying comes from a nihilistic moment in which Europe is reaching a dead end. What good is it to study philosophy when Europe is in decline—this is how Heidegger would interpret it. I like your interpretation because it's wholesome, optimistic, and forward-looking."

"You failed at the university because you entertain such ideas."

"Or rather, the truth is that I've come to entertain such ideas because I failed at the university."

"You're having these thoughts because you majored in English literature, but now Britain, its home, the origin of liberalism and individualism, is on the brink of ruin."

Kwanhyŏng put out his cigarette. "It's not really like that. I failed at the university because I wasn't liberal enough, and my spiritual home is not Britain at all. We're all Orientals. It'd be truly a wonder if we could acquire an English sensibility after just a few years of college. The problem is rather the opposite, that we've acquired only a smattering of knowledge about European culture. But let me tell you my story. By the way, before we do that, why don't we learn each others' names? I'm Yi Kwanhyŏng."

Mugyŏng also told him her name. They smiled at each other.

"So this is the secret of my life. . . . I told you before that Western travelers to the East do not appreciate our Western-style buildings or culture, but rather frown on them, as if they were poor counterfeits. My family is like a Western-style building. My father is a well-known trading merchant in Seoul. He is a so-called bourgeois. All three of his children received a modern education. I studied English literature, my sister graduated from a music school, and my younger brother is finishing his degree program in German literature this spring. We all studied the best of Western civilization. My family is an advanced, flourishing bourgeois family. In this sense, we're an exemplary family. But then . . . "

He paused, as if for breath, but there was a shadow of gloom in his eyes.

"If we compare my family to Korea in the modern age, we can understand better the class to which families like mine belong. Let's say that it's been seventy years since the advent of the modern age. We started to import the fruits of Europe's Enlightenment at a time when Europeans were already lamenting the decline of the spirit of Enlightenment. What we embraced as new and fresh had already become stale in its homeland. Already, then, Europeans had grown dubious of their own cultural values. They were skeptical of even the very concept of progress. So we embraced an old, outdated foreign culture, mistaking it for something new and fresh. When we realized that Europe was in crisis, it was already too late. We haven't even digested what we imported, but Europe had already reached a dead end over two world wars. I've studied English literature, but the more I try to understand Europeans, the more I bump into the walls of their claustrophobic mental world. My father, a businessman, is cursed to have a son like me. Since he is a trade merchant, he'll lose his business when the government puts a total block on free trade. So far he's been able to use his business sense to capitalize on the current state of affairs. We all dine on Western meals upstairs, then eat *kimchi* downstairs. We've lived long enough like this that we're now all experiencing fatigue and a certain ennui. My family is sure to head downhill in the near future. My sister studied music, but it's been a long time since she devoted much attention to it. My brother has long grown tired of the academy, of study itself. I had a brother-in-law who was a pilot. But this crisp, courageous young man passed away a while ago, when his airplane crashed into a cliff during an emergency landing. He was lost flying home in a fog around Ulsan."

"Was this the accident that was mentioned in the newspaper?"

"Probably. In any event, this is the environment I'm living in. And for about a year now, I've been surrounded with good-for-nothings. That woman Ranju is one of them. When I met her by chance a year ago, I regarded her as a symbol of decadence. She'd be angry if she heard me now, and maybe I have the wrong impression. But whenever I see her, I can't help feeling she's the epitome of decadence and unwholesomeness. So I've been avoiding her as much as I can. And the gentleman who visited today and left the check, he's my uncle. He's still a youthful man, well-built, energetic, and well-off. He has only one ambition, to conquer women. He proudly claims to hold the record in that field. There's also a banker named Paek Inyŏng. He is cunning, but his slyness has driven him into bankruptcy. His concubine is Ranju's friend . . . For some time I kept my distance from these people. But then, one day, I got into trouble with my department at the university.† I got dead drunk that night. When I woke up, I found myself lying in a bedroom in Ranju's house. According to her, she saw me staggering in the street as she left Meiji House, where she'd had a drink herself. I stayed at her house for several days. I had no energy and didn't want to lift a finger. Still, I sent home a postcard, saying that I was going on a trip. I didn't want to go back home. But before long, I grew tired of staying at Ranju's, too. So I came here. And as soon as I arrived, I fought with the old man and you. . . . "

"I see," Mugyŏng nodded to Kwanhyŏng. She got up to turn on the stove.

"It seems that I can't even lose myself in a dissolute life. Perhaps I'm the ear of barley that remains hidden in the earth, rather than being ground into bread. Though it may be more tragic that way."

The water simmered and began to boil.

"To tell you the truth, I have a secret, too, though it's different from yours." She felt like confessing her secret since he'd confessed his.

"Of course you do. Nowadays there're few young people who don't have some kind of secret." Yet Kwanhyŏng seemed uninterested in hearing hers. Mugyŏng made him another cup of black tea. He drank it down at once.

"I'm sorry for having stayed so long. Did I interrupt your work?" He stood up from his seat and said, "Good night now." Before leav-

†Translator's Note: In the first of the trilogy, "Nangbi" (Waste, 1940–1941), which is left incomplete, Kwanhyŏng clashes with Japanese professor Sakizaka, who is on his dissertation committee. The professor questions Kwanhyŏng's ulterior motivation in writing the dissertation on Henry James, "an intellectual with no spiritual home." When Kwanhyŏng defends his choice by relating the writer's influence on James Joyce, the professor becomes even more suspicious, questioning why Kwanhyŏng takes interest in the "[colonial] Irish" writer. Finally, Sakizaka criticizes Kwanhyŏng for taking a "sociological"—read in the context as "materialist" and therefore "Marxist"—interpretive approach in his literary analysis. Kwanhyŏng later complains to his advisor, another Japanese professor, that Sakizaka was trying to trap him by asking such questions.

ing the room, Kwanhyŏng took out a little bottle of pills, which he dangled in front of her.

"I cure my insomnia with this," he laughed cynically. After he left, Mugyŏng opened a book, but she couldn't concentrate. She went to bed, but she couldn't sleep, either.

That night, Mugyŏng fell asleep late. The next morning she woke up early as usual, but she didn't feel like getting up. She thought about Kwanhyŏng's words last night. Human life is like barley! Having learned his story, she could understand him better, regardless of whether or not she agreed with him. Was Sihyŏng also having such thoughts now? Had he also lost himself to such a bleak worldview? His mental life, hardly any simpler than Kwanhyŏng's, might well have been more complicated. More than ever, she wanted to see him. She wanted to listen to all his secrets. Where was he now?

Her wish was soon realized. Sihyŏng came to Seoul.

It was not yet breakfast time. Mugyŏng was wanted on the phone. The caller was Sihyŏng's lawyer. He was asking her where Sihyŏng was staying, since he must be in Seoul by now for his trial. She felt embarrassed. She was ashamed to acknowledge her ignorance, but there was no other way to answer his question.

The lawyer hung up, saying that he had something urgent to discuss with him before the trial that afternoon. "This afternoon? Why didn't Sihyŏng let me know in advance? If he's in Seoul, why hasn't he called me from his hotel? Why hasn't he come to see me?"

Mugyŏng skipped breakfast. She went to the office but then decided to take the day off, claiming a headache as an excuse. She had to go to the courthouse. The trial must have been going on for a while. Regardless, she rushed to the courthouse. She asked a court clerk where the trial was taking place. The proceeding was already well underway. There were some people in the corridors, but she didn't take any notice of them. In front of six seated defendants stood a man in an army-style uniform with a crew cut. It was Sihyŏng. The hearing seemed to be nearing an end.

"Would the defendant please summarize the new thought he has reached in his studies?" asked the judge, a benevolent smile on his face. His hands were resting over documents on his desk, the wide black sleeves of his robe folding gracefully around them. He was looking down at Sihyŏng.

"I think Europeans have a certain view of history. They believe that history is like a ladder or a mountain stream. At the top are the people of Europe. In the middle are all the peoples of Asia, following in their footsteps. Those at the bottom are barbarians. History flows like a stream from the ancient to the medieval to the modern. So even if the European spirit were to lose its unity and collapse, Europeans would still believe that it is they, and they alone, who are able to envision what the modern world will look like. This is the monadic view of history, so to speak. But I believe that we can shatter their illusion by showing that world history has multiple origins. Current events are demonstrating this before our eyes."

"From such a perspective, how does the defendant understand the ongoing war and the orientation of world history?"

Sihyŏng paused, seemingly choosing his words carefully.

"In the course of my developing thoughts, I have moved away from Dilthey's humanism toward Heidegger's philosophy. I'm deeply moved by how Heidegger progressed from an examination of the human condition to his commendation of Hitlerism. It's a current trend among our philosophers to find new subject matter in our present conditions. Scholars like Dr. Watsuji and Dr. Tanabe have proposed many ideas by engaging such issues as nation, race, and people. I have abandoned my past ideas and have become attracted to the construction of the new world order by following this general course of intellectual development."

The judge smiled with satisfaction. Mugyŏng let out a sigh of relief. At that moment, she noticed a young woman beginning to rise from a seat right behind the defense dock. The judge adjourned the court until later in the afternoon. The woman stood up. She was tall and was wearing a white traditional Korean topcoat. Mugyŏng felt her heart sink. Sitting next to the woman was Sihyŏng's father, and next to him was an elderly gentleman. Returning to his seat, Sihyŏng walked up to the woman, his flushed face finally giving way to a smile. Mugyŏng left the courtroom, stepping away from the bustle inside. "It's her! The governor's daughter!" Now it was over. Mugyŏng stopped in the corridor, but unable to stand steady, she started again, dragging her feet along. Soon she was out in the courtyard. The sun shone bright. She felt dizzy.

Somehow she was able to make it back to her apartment. At its entrance she came across Ranju, who was just coming down. Mugyŏng managed to greet her.

"I heard at the office that you were sick . . . " Ranju herself looked pale.

"Yes, I've been to the hospital."

Ranju paused. Then she walked past Mugyŏng, saying, "Take care." Mugyŏng felt an impulse to invite the woman, this symbol of decadence, to have tea with her. But instead of proposing this, she simply climbed to her apartment upstairs.

"What can I do now?" Tears welled up in her eyes as she lay down on her bed. She began to cry, holding back nothing. Then she heard somebody knocking on the door. The sound told her that the visitor was Kwanhyŏng.

"Yes—" Mugyŏng tried to compose herself before opening the door.

"I wanted to apologize for last night. I heard you were sick."

"No, I'm alright."

"Well, I hope you're . . . " he paused for a moment. "I'm going on a trip. I'm going to leave my past behind. I'll keep the room as it is for now and check out later, after I return. I've told my family that I'll be traveling around Kyŏngju with the money I borrowed from my uncle. I think I'll make good on this lie."

"Then are you going to Kyŏngju?"

"I have no plans. I'm just thinking that fresh air might make me feel better. Maybe I'll even sow a grain of barley in the earth."

He laughed out loud. For a moment, Mugyŏng thought of Ranju's sad face.

"It's a good idea. Then let me get you the rest of the cash for your check."

"Thank you."

After sending Kang to the bank with the check, Mugyŏng sat alone in the office.

"Should I also go on a trip?"

"Should I go study in Tokyo, as my mother wants?"

But she couldn't warm up to any of these ideas.

6

YI T'AEJUN

Yi T'ae-jun (1904–?), who is also known by the pseudonym of Sanghŏ, was born to a humble family in Ch'ŏrwŏn in the Kangwŏn province. He became an orphan at age eight and had to work for a living from the age of fourteen onward. In 1926 he entered Chosi University in Japan but had to drop out two years later due to financial difficulties. Despite these challenges, Yi went on to have an exceptionally successful literary career. He was a prolific writer of essays and novels, many of which won him critical respect and commercial fame. In 1931, aged twenty-seven, he became the chief editor of the literary section of the then major Korean newspaper, the *Chosŏn Chungang Ilbo* (1931–1937). From that position he was able to contribute to shaping the cultural scene of colonial Korea for years to come. Yi joined the North upon national division in 1948, and his fate there remains as of today somewhat obscure. In South Korea his works were banned until 1988, but since then his name has been reinstated to the national literary canon.

Throughout his career, Yi was a champion of autonomous literature, which he understood as a literature unconstrained by political agendas or commercial influences. In 1933 he founded and led the *Kuinhoe* (Group of nine), a circle of writers and artists devoted to innovation and experimentation in their disciplines. In promoting modernist writers such as Yi Sang and Pak T'aewŏn, the group brought new vitality to a literary scene that was growing weary of the formulaic productions of socialist literature. In the late 1930s, when the rising militarism dampened the earlier zeal for aesthetic radicalism, Yi launched the literary magazine *Munjang* (Style, 1939–1941) to continue to support writers of artistic integrity. This magazine served as the last stronghold of artistic autonomy amid the surging tides of the war until it was finally shut down in 1941. Afterward Yi retired to the countryside, where he spent the remaining colonial years in isolation.

"Before and after Liberation" (1946, Haebang chŏnhu) is a rare literary account of the situation of writers around the time of the end of the Japanese rule. Written as the memoir of a fictional writer, the piece tells a story of wartime oppression and mobilization, which are followed by the euphoria of liberation as well as the difficulties of rebuilding a Korean nation-state after thirty five years of colonial rule. At the story's core is a personal anecdote of broken friendship, which is emblematic of shifting alliances at a tumultuous time in Korean history. The work notably differs from Yi's earlier stories such as "Kkamagwi" (1936, trans. 1991 Crows) and "Poktŏkpang" (1937, The broker's office), none of which was concerned with politics. At the same time, retained here are many of the writer's distinctive traits, such as a sympathy for marginalized figures, a taste for classical literature, and an elegantly spare style of prose.

Before and After Liberation—A Writer's Memoir

(1946)

Although the word had been changed from "subpoena" to the less offensive "directive," it was always unpleasant to receive a writ of summons, which a policeman would drop off with disdain, as if coming on a petty errand. Hyŏn pretended to accept this summons with the usual indifference he maintained in the presence of his wife, who had turned pale even before he did; but he felt so unusually ill at ease that he wished to leave right away, so as to be done with the matter, instead of waiting until the next morning. Whether they called it a subpoena or a directive, all the same, timid Hyŏn was unable to accomplish a thing afterward, having no appetite that day and bad dreams that night.

Hyŏn was neither a theorist nor an ideologue. Nor was he a convict. His name seemed to have made its way onto their list of the usual suspects ever since they'd called him in under the suspicion for having corrupted the young—perhaps because his books or letters had been found in the houses of some recently arrested young men from the countryside, or because his name had come up during an investigation as one of their contacts in Seoul. Hyŏn supposed that had they wanted to imprison him, they would have done so right away instead of bothering with such things as subpoenas and directives. Still, he was thrown off-guard at each summons and was particularly worried this time. Though a mere novelist, he had been visited by more than a few young men, who were anxiously fumbling for a solution to their complicated situation: as a result of the General Volunteer Law and the Special Student Volunteer Law, they must now not only die against their will but also kill Allied soldiers, such as the Chinese, the British, the Americans, and the Russians—in short, those who offered them their only hope; worse, their lives would be sacrificed for the sake of their enemy, Japan. One of Hyŏn's visitors suffered a nervous breakdown within days of receiving a draft notice, and another young man sent him a suicide note a week after they met. Hyŏn himself had not been drafted, but as a brother of these unfortunate students, he could not simply look out for himself and suppress his indignation in such a grave matter for all Koreans. At times, he wondered whether some strange visitor might not be a detective in disguise, sent to sound out his ideas. He quickly blamed himself for harboring such suspicions, though, and in the end neither modified nor omitted anything of what in his excitement he wanted to tell students. After such visits, Hyŏn sat alone in his quiet library, his face flushed and looking nervous for what he had just done. In his heart he felt inspired to commit himself to a higher, more useful task during this latest crisis for his people. But he had not prepared himself for any task in particular and could not suddenly break out of the hardened crust of his old self.

A life below the current is still not a sheltered life. An old proverb says, "A mulberry field can turn into a blue sea," but you can't change the sea back into a field by throwing a few pebbles into it. Everything is subject to its own destiny.

Thus quoting a passage he himself had recently written at the end of a short story, he smiled wryly at the insignificance of his life.

"You say it's only a matter of days, but what if those tenacious *kamikazes* hold out till the very end? What if they each knock out one ship? America, no matter how rich it is, can't make as many ships as there are Japanese pilots. Waiting for the fall of Japan is like waiting for the skies to fall!"

That day Hyŏn's wife begged her sleepless husband to sell the house and flee to the countryside. She asked him to move to some remote village, far away from the authorities, where they could live in peace and have enough to eat from their own harvest, even if just for a day. Hyŏn had formerly entertained such an idea, too. Since he could not go abroad, he was bound to live under Japanese skies. Where, then, could he find such a remote village, like the one in the Age of Sage Kings, whose inhabitants had never seen an official and never had their peaceful sleep disturbed by even so much as the barking of a dog? All the same, whether or not there existed such a Shangri-la, it was getting more and more difficult for Hyŏn to continue living in Seoul. Since he remained determined to break his pen rather than write propaganda, or start writing in Japanese, he had long suffered a chronic lack of money. If he was going to have to sell the house, which was all that remained of his fortune, he'd rather sell everything at once, not piecemeal, and with that money buy up some land in the countryside. But just as with the crust of his old self, the enclosed shell of his life was not easy to break open.

"Let's wait a bit longer and see what happens." That was Hyŏn's attitude, which had long prompted his family to complain of his incompetence.

Detective Suruda of the Special Higher Division was in charge of Hyŏn's file at the Tongdaemun police station. He was not an intimidating man. In his chief's absence, he would be the first to greet Hyŏn in Korean, apologizing for asking him to come in again for such a trivial affair. But today, he ignored Hyŏn's deep bow and merely directed him to a chair with a sideways glance. The chief was in his office, commanding a formidable presence with his protruding forehead and sunken eyes.

Hyŏn sat down and waited, awkwardly kneading his hat, which was not khaki-colored as theirs were. Only after a while did Suruda stop writing. He asked Hyŏn what he was doing these days. Hyŏn answered that he was not doing anything in particular, so Suruda inquired about what he planned to do. When Hyŏn paused, "Well . . . " smiling in an attempt to be friendly, Suruda glanced back at the chief. The chief was busy stamping his seal onto some document. The detective took out a file and opened it, hiding the file's contents from Hyŏn's sight behind its hard cover.

"Why aren't you doing something to help the current situation?" he asked.

"What power does someone like me have?"

"Don't talk like that. And please, do something. In fact, the provincial police department sent down an urgent directive to bring in a few key figures like you for questioning. They want to know things, like if you've done something to cooperate, or if you're doing something right now, or how you're planning to make a contribution in the future, and also how you make a living."

"Well . . . " Hyŏn, now feeling even more awkward, could do nothing but to simply stare at the detective's face.

"Anyway, it'd be better for you to be on record as doing something. Why don't you change your name? It's a very easy thing to do."

Suruda seemed to think that Hyŏn had not done this yet due to the inconvenience of the procedure. Once again Hyŏn made no reply.

"Low-level officers like me don't know very much, but from now on, nobody will be allowed to remain uninvolved."

"I agree with you."

Hyŏn was relieved by the fact that this summons did not mean imprisonment, as he had feared.

"In fact, I'm about to start something soon," he said, after some hesitation. "Please, file a favorable report for me."

On his way out, Hyŏn headed for a publisher whose chief editor had asked him to translate *A Chronicle of the Greater East Asian War*. The project had not been initiated by the publisher but was rather ordered by the Police Bureau. The editor advised Hyŏn that he had better demonstrate his loyalty if he wanted to exonerate himself in the eyes of the military, which had complained after he spoke Korean at the last meeting on the current situation; he had fulfilled his obligation on that occasion by reading a passage from *The Tale of Chunhyang.*

Back in his study—which his wife, sympathetic toward her agitated husband, had cleaned with scrupulous care—Hyŏn emptied out a heap of Japanese newspaper clippings on the floor. Never before had his study looked so untidy.

Ever since I came of age, I have been living in a state of humiliation. In the forty years of my life, I've never experienced the joy of love, the privilege of youth, or the glory of art. Why should I write a war record in favor of Japan, and not a record of Japan's defeat instead?

Hyŏn really wanted to live. No, it's not that he cared overly for life itself, but that he wanted to make it through these times. Once, a German poet, who had placed all his hope on a socialist overthrow of the Nazi regime (the enemy of his country, humanity, and culture), committed suicide, in his rather simplistic despair, after Molotov shook hands with Hitler during the signing of the Russo-German Non-aggression Pact.

Hyŏn thought that the poet had rushed to judgment. Isn't the Soviet Union now fighting against Germany? The Americans, the British, and the Chinese are all fighting against Japan. Let's believe in an Allied victory! Let's trust in the justice of history! If history betrays mankind, there'll always be time to despair afterward.

Hyŏn did not sell his house. The second front had yet to materialize in Europe, and the Japanese army was announcing that it would defend Rabaul in the Pacific. Still, Hyŏn envisioned two or three more years of war at most. He borrowed what he could on his house and left Seoul. He went to a mountain village in the Kangwŏn province, partly because the local public doctor was an acquaintance of his. The leisurely, backward place, which was about twenty miles away by bus from the railway station, had its old magisterial office replaced with a resident office and a township office. He chose this town in the hope that his friendship with the doctor, who would likely have connections with town officials, would help him evade the draft. Hyŏn was expecting to find enough food in the town, which was known for producing a variety of crops. He was also glad to have the Imjin River nearby so that he could spend his time fishing as he waited for better days ahead.

Yet when he actually arrived, none of these considerations worked out quite as he had anticipated. The head of the township office was no exception to the general contradiction of society at the time: he had as many certificates of merit on the walls of his office as he had earned complaints from the people. The doctor, a man of integrity who always called a spade a spade, had long before fallen out of favor with him. Besides, the doctor soon left for Seoul to complete a six-month-long training course, crushing Hyŏn's hope of being exempted from the draft. Other than the doctor, the only neighbor he knew was Kim, an old-fashioned scholar associated with the local Confucian school. The doctor had introduced them to each other. This old man, who still wore his hair up in a topknot, was remembered by the villagers only twice a year for the memorial rites he performed in the spring and fall. Kim's uncalloused hands, however, were not fit for looking after even his own household, let alone a friend's.

The river, which Hyŏn had thought would be near the village, turned out to be over two miles away. Not only was it too far for regular fishing, but the shortcut to the river also ran past the resident office. To avoid running into the police chief or his subordinates, Hyŏn had no choice but to climb a mountain to reach the river from a different direction. One day, as he turned the corner of the post office, Hyŏn caught sight of the Korean officer Kanemura. Startled, he took a step backward and quickly hid his fishing gear behind his back. Some township clerks were examining the tree bark brought by the villagers, and Kanemura was swaggering around the inspection site in his undershirt and gaiters, a sword at his side and a whip in his hand. Since the inspection seemed like it would take a while, Hyŏn decided to climb the mountain again this time.

He wandered around for a long time up along the slippery slope of the forest. When he finally reached the flat ridge of the mountain, a dark, bearlike figure confronted him. It was the police chief. More startled at the sight of him than he would have been of any animal, Hyŏn dropped his fishing gear.

"Where are you going?"

"Oh, I just came up for some fresh air."

It seemed to Hyŏn that the chief was glaring at him. Hyŏn took off his straw hat and made a belated bow, but by then the chief had already turned around. The head of the township office was also there, and to their south lay a cordoned-off rectangular area, about the size of a tennis court. From the conversation between the two men, Hyŏn inferred that the site had been marked off for a *Shinto* shrine. Hyŏn stood as still as a post, not knowing what move to make next. He did not have the courage to pick up the fishing gear he had just dropped, let alone the nerve to pass through the shrine site, which would have meant crossing the cordon twice. Both men looked back at Hyŏn from time to time and then whispered something to each other. Had there been a flower nearby, Hyŏn could have pretended to pick it up, but there was not one in sight. After a while, as the two were looking in another direction, Hyŏn quickly gathered up his things—all evidence of his wartime idleness—and hurried back home.

"Dad, why'd you come back so soon?"

Hyŏn could not think up a good excuse for his children, but a neighbor's boy, who had followed him into the house, responded for him: "Your dad came back because he got caught by the chief."

On days when he could not go fishing, Hyŏn read books or visited Kim. And Kim often visited Hyŏn as well, should Hyŏn happen to be at home. The more often Hyŏn met, or rather attended on, the old and guileless Kim, the more he came to respect him as the only man of noble character in the town. At times, Hyŏn felt that "a man of rare integrity" must mean someone like Kim. After the demise of the Chosŏn dynasty, Kim had been to Seoul only once, when he was sent to prison during the March First Movement in 1919; other than that, he had never set foot in the capital, where the Governor-

General now reigned. He not only refused to adopt a Japanese name but had also made a point of wearing a topknot and a Korean top hat on the very day of his release from prison. Kim was older than Hyŏn by dozens of years. Hyŏn was unable to read Kim's classic poems, due to his poor knowledge of Chinese, and Kim could not discuss modern literature with Hyŏn out of his indifference to the new literature. But aside from this regrettable lack of communication on literary matters, they were able to talk heart-to-heart after just a couple of meetings. They both felt the fathomless misery of an ill-fated people and shared the same secret hope; their ardent hearts beat to the same rhythm, so much so that they could understand each other even without words.

One evening, Kim visited Hyŏn with traces of tears in his wrinkled yet spirited eyes. Hyŏn welcomed him by lighting a precious candle.

"Today, I whipped my grown-up nephew on the street."

Kim's hands were still trembling. One of his nephews worked at the township office. This nephew's brother-in-law, that is, the husband of Kim's niece, had run away after being drafted by the Japanese. The head of the township office discovered that the runaway had taken refuge at his in-laws and ordered Kim's nephew to arrest him. The draft-dodger realized what was happening and fled to the mountain. The nephew had the mountain surrounded with the support of the Reserve Corps. He captured his brother-in-law, as if the latter were a rabbit, and delivered him to the resident office.

"What a heartless man!" Hyŏn added with regret.

"My nephew was told that if he didn't turn in his brother-in-law, he'd be drafted instead. Still, how could he lead the Reserve Corps to his own brother-in-law, when he knew all too well what would happen to the poor man? Did he really have to join the Corps in throwing stones at him? Today's youths don't have any integrity."

"But then, at a time like this, can even parents really punish such behavior in public?"

"How could I hold back my anger? Who cares if we were on the streets! I caught him coming out of the office. I didn't say a word but just beat him till my bamboo pipestem broke in two. He knew why he was being beaten. And even the onlookers, at least those who'd caught wind of what had happened, must have known. But what does it matter?"

It had been a gloomy day for Hyŏn as well. He had received a telegram from the Patriotic Association of Writers in Seoul, which ordered him to participate in an upcoming rally. The resident office, which had been counting every single postcard sent to Hyŏn, must have noticed the lengthy telegram. Even the Japanese postmaster seemed curious to know whether this man, who spent his days fishing during this state of emergency, would respond to the call of the writers' rally. One evening he asked Hyŏn's daughter if her father was going to Seoul the following day.

At first, Kim told Hyŏn not to go to the rally. But his discouragement only served to aggravate Hyŏn's anxiety about the consequences of not going. Over the next two days, Hyŏn received two more telegrams demanding his urgent reply. Kim found out about the telegrams on the second day and visited Hyŏn early that afternoon.

"Old men like me haven't got much left that needs to get done, even if we do live to see the new world, but a young man like you must survive and do your share of the work later. So don't be too stubborn over little things. Just try to escape the draft."

That day, Kanemura showed up to ask when Hyŏn was leaving for the rally, now only two days away. He wanted to know if Hyŏn needed any travel permits issued before he left; and if he wasn't leaving, why wasn't he attending the rally. On his way out, Kanemura said that he'd like to ask Hyŏn to take his pocket watch to Seoul for repairs.

"I want to survive!" Hyŏn cried once again inside. One day before the rally, he picked up Kanemura's watch and headed for Seoul in the rain to visit the Patriotic Association of Writers (PAW).

There was a reason behind Hyŏn's being telegraphed three times. A few days earlier, the main members of the PAW had invited seven or eight established writers, none of whom had shown much inclination for cooperating with government policies, to a dinner with the chief of the Information Bureau. Since Hyŏn had been absent that evening, it would look good for him, and would help demonstrate the group's sincerity as a whole, if he could be persuaded to be one of the speakers at the rally. Hyŏn was asked to dedicate some sort of memorial as a representative for the novelists. Hyŏn remained uncommitted for a while, but since he had shown up, he could not hold out for long, so he followed them to the rally the next day. The rally at the Civic Center was an extravagant spectacle, with everyone wearing a khaki uniform or a ceremonial costume. The list of guests read as a who's who of the ruling elite: Lord So-and-so from the Governor-General's office, His Excellency Somebody-or-other from the Korean army, all dressed in stately attire or military uniforms; and among the writers in attendance there were many well-known names from Japan as well as from Manchukuo. It was the most glorious rally since the formation of the Korean literary society. Hyŏn wore a mud-stained jacket, which he used for fishing in the countryside, non-khaki-colored flannel pants, and no gaiters. He had no excuse for his inappropriate appearance, which was hardly befitting the wartime situation. But since there was no way he could spruce himself up on the spot, he simply entered the hall in what he was wearing. As he followed the course of all the proceedings, Hyŏn gradually became more engaged in the rally. Having grown accustomed to the simple sight of fish and to the artless sound of backwood orioles, he was jarred by the brutality of what he heard concerning the cultural policy of the Fascist regime. A certain Excellency even went so far as to cite Hitler, claiming that since a culture could be suppressed for a time and then later revived overnight when needed, whatever did not serve the current war effort, whether in art or literature, was better-off if eliminated altogether. Poets, critics, and novelists—the producers of culture—applauded the eloquent speeches of such armed Excellencies and talked themselves hoarse pandering to the vulgar taste of bureaucrats and soldiers, rather than protesting the decline of culture.

Hyŏn felt particularly sympathetic toward a pale, gaunt Manchukuo writer who read a congratulatory address in clumsy Japanese. Speaking in a foreign tongue, he looked so small and sad, and his face assumed such unnatural expressions. Most Korean writers were fluent in Japanese. Yet why does their fluency make them sound rather repulsive than agreeable? Hyŏn thought of the honor a dog or a pig retains since it could only utter sounds unique to itself. It was tantamount to a tragic resignation in the face of destiny for the people of a weak and small country to begin acquiring the language of the people of a bigger and stronger one. And yet it could not be said that the arguments and congratulatory addresses of the Japanese writers sounded any more natural or proper. From Hyŏn's perspective, the Japanese writers were even harder to understand. Yanagi Muneyoshi had once pleaded, "My brothers, abandon militarism. Abusing the weak does no honor to Japan. If we continue to sin against morality, the world will turn against Japan. When that happens, it will be Japan, not Korea, that will be ruined." There had also been cultural figures at one time in Japan who denounced Hitler's expatriation of the Jewish people—who had no nation of their own—and condemned the burning of books of philosophy and literature regarded as being too complicated. Where are they now? Why do they remain silent? Do they not have more freedom and a greater duty than Koreans or Manchurians to voice their candid concerns for the sake of their country and people? If the conscience of cultured men is really still alive in Japan, how could there be these many unsympathetic pseudo-religious figures who only try to paralyze the critical instincts of Koreans and Manchurians? Is it not a disgrace to Japan that its men of culture have become the pawns of a barbarous bureaucracy, the blind supporters of the "national" theater, "national" unity, and the elimination of the Korean language and culture from which their own originates? Of course, those with a conscience among the Japanese cultural elite must have their own troubles to worry about, too. Yet why are they being so complacent now?

Hyŏn was brought back from such reflections by the sound of applause. He realized that it was his turn to execrate even more malodorous words in Japanese than those of the Manchukuo writer earlier. His own facial expression would be even more contorted. When he thought of how he had been heaping blame on Japanese writers, Hyŏn could not help but ask himself: "What about you? Why are you sitting here?" It was as if he were in a nightmare in which he ran and ran only to find himself forever at the same spot. Mustering as much energy as he could to keep up this onerous running, he forced himself to stand. Unlike in a nightmare, however, once up from his seat he could walk away. Hyŏn sneaked out of the hall, where it seemed as if every eye were casting a hook for him. Outside, he remembered he'd left his hat behind.

What's going to happen? Chairman Kayama is going to call on me soon. The staff of the PAW will look for me, calling out my Korean name in front of all those high officials and officers!

Somebody was coming down the steps. Hyŏn slipped into the restroom. He heard the clanking sound of a sword. Its owner might well be the same Korean lieutenant who had earlier, in the hall's restaurant, told the writers that his sword would not forgive their necks should they fail to prove their loyalty as imperial subjects. The clanking sound now seemed to come from within the restroom. Hyŏn ducked into a stall. After a few moments the owner of the sword finished washing and left. But soon another pair of shoes could be heard entering the bathroom. Although no one would ever look into the stall, Hyŏn felt paralyzed, just as he had been when he had stumbled upon the police chief on the mountain ridge on his way to fish. The stall had a flush toilet but still smelled pungent. Hyŏn took out a cigarette and lit it. Even a prison cell wouldn't be this small or smell this bad; he laughed under his breath. Of all the places people go, the toilet is the worst to be stuck in for any other purpose than its intended one. Applause was heard from the third floor. It gradually subsided. Some time after the hall had quieted down, Hyŏn stepped out of the restroom. Saying to himself, devil come what may, he ran, hatless, to his friend's place in Sŏngbuktong, far away from downtown.

Still, Hyŏn's trip to Seoul had not been in vain. Kanemura, who before had been too haughty to return Hyŏn's greeting, became more friendly ever since he received his repaired watch. And the police chief, the head of the township office, and the postmaster, who doubled as the chief air-raid warden, all seemed to think more highly of Hyŏn, whom the Writers' Association had invited to the rally by telegraphing no less than three times. They now greeted him right away when they came across him, so that Hyŏn could even go around carrying a fishing rod in their presence.

Hyŏn found fishing a peculiarly Asian pastime, maybe because his equipment and method were Asian. When the hook remained still, keeping him waiting, he felt like dozing off, leaving his mind under water. And when he occasionally began humming, despite his untrained voice, a *sijo* or a classic poem in Chinese seemed to suit him better than a modern poem.

A small village rests at the mountain's foot
The local office must have hung out a bell
Amid the birds' chirping I read a book
And I listen to a plea as the flowers fall
I'm called a poor official for my purse is thin
Though I'm free as a hermit with my leisure wide
With a fishing group I've newly joined in
I spent half a month on the riverside

This was the classic poem Hyŏn enjoyed reciting whenever he wanted to hum something. One time, as he was talking to Kim about different types of calligraphy, their conversation drifted to old memorial stones; so for a diversion, the two set off to see a row of stones dedicated to past local officers that stood along the village gate. The first in the row was the memorial of Kang Chin, whose pen name was Taesan. Hyŏn saw it for the first time and was greatly surprised at the fact that the famous poet, who was known as the heir to the poetry of four eminent *Sirhak* literati, had once served as this small town's magistrate. On his way back, Hyŏn borrowed Kim's two-volume collection of Taesan's poems. Upon reading them later, he discovered that most of the poems, which the poet had written in his middle age, were composed in their very town. Hyŏn himself had already frequented most of the places that appeared in the literary magistrate's works: he sometimes climbed Mount Man'gyŏng, went fishing at the Nine Dragons' Pond, or passed by Tumundong, where a certain Ho, one of the surviving retainers of the Koryŏ dynasty, led a recluse life. Taesan seemed to have been content to retire to this scenic backwoods, having admired from an early age the leisurely style of Han Tuizhi, who sang, "Away I go to the beautiful countryside, I will read in a forest of pine and cinnamon trees." Taesan wrote his own poem to celebrate his idyllic life in the countryside: he received a modest pay, but he could read amid chirping birds, preside over a trial under falling blossoms, and spend half a month on the riverside with his fishing companions. If only holding an office were as easy as Taesan made it seem, Tao Yuanming would not have abandoned Pengze. Even if one's bound by official duty, as long as one finds pleasure in the wind and the moon, one has literature; and if one returns to the countryside, relinquishing an official post, there's still the same poetry of the wind and the moon to be enjoyed.

Read a book amid birds' chirping, and listen to a plea under falling flowers! Unfortunately, contemporary politicians can't indulge in such a romantic pastime while in office. Will there ever be a time again, Hyŏn wondered, when politics can be so romantic? Contemporary writers are also misfortunate, since they can't spend their time contemplating the wind and the moon. Will the days ever return when poetry can simply extol the pleasures of the wind and the moon? But then, why should such a time come at all? Or rather, could contemporary politicians and artists ever come to admire and honor such a life of leisure?

Although Hyŏn regularly recited Taesan's poem, he considered this habit a hobby, comparable to caressing the antique stationery of a bygone dynasty, and did not necessarily perceive any relevance between this hobby and his own literary life.

What has my own literary career been like? How different is it from the feudal idea of literature as a pastime?

Hyŏn did not develop this self-criticism after reading Kang's poems, nor did it begin with his move to the countryside, where he had more time for reflection away from writing. In fact, it had been a while since he came to look upon his past writings, mostly about personal subjects, with a critical eye. But if he had so limited his subject matters, he did so because he saw no better alternative. Hyŏn was against the proletarian literature of the leftists, for he was more concerned about the sorrow of Koreans in general rather than that of any particular class. At the same time, like any other Korean writer, he was too weak and isolated to directly criticize Japan's policy toward Korea. Sometimes, he felt a resentment seethe within him, as any ordinary man would, but under the brutal censorship he had no other choice but to submit and withdraw to the world of resignation.

So, what should I write? And how? It's all but inevitable that Japan will be ruined. Let's prepare in advance! But if Japan shouldn't lose? Then literature and culture won't even be a question in Korea. Since the Korean language will be lost, it's not just the language, but even the character of the people, that will be destroyed completely. Will history permit Japan to realize the horrors of such an imperialist scheme?

Hyŏn repeatedly assured his wife and Kim that the war would be over no later than a year from now, but he felt unsure and uneasy when he was alone. Yet his fear that the Fascist regimes might still triumph in the end soon disappeared. The reports in Japanese newspapers—such as Mussolini's downfall, the development of a second front, and the fall of Saipan—all made it clear that the outcome of the war had already been decided.

Still, Hyŏn was unable to resume his writing. He did not have enough spare thoughts in his head to read others' writings, let alone to write himself. Although he recited, "Amid the birds' chirping I read a book / And I listen to a plea as the flowers fall," he could hardly concentrate on lengthy Western classics. Even after a year's worth of reading, he hadn't finished the second volume of *War and Peace*. Everyday he came home to face new worries—worries about food, wood, a tear in the papered floor, various inconveniences in the rustic kitchen, lack of shoes, lack of clothes, lack of medicine, and, lastly, the quickly dwindling funds on a loan he had drawn on his house in Seoul. He had expected the money to last for three years. A new law regarding the National Volunteer Corps expanded the age limit for draftees to sixty, but he had yet to secure his exemption. One day, the resident office summoned him. The rural office had not even bothered to send a directive; instead, a servant came to call on him. Yet the unease he felt was as unpleasant as always. One good thing, though, was that he needn't wait around nervously all day, as he would have had to in Seoul, but could go right away to find out what was wrong.

The resident office was packed with townsmen, right up to the door. Hyŏn quietly observed the scene to see whether the crowd had anything to do with his summons. The people had come to plea for food rationing. They were asking about how they were supposed to survive when their harvests of wheat and barley were being confiscated down to the last grain, with no ration given in return under the pretext of their being farmers; how they could increase production and make their quotas of wild vines, pine knots, and oak bark, when they themselves had nothing to eat. The head of the office, who had been smiling became straight-faced at the sight of Hyŏn. He came out to meet him.

"You didn't go fishing today, did you?"

"No, I didn't."

"The reason I didn't have you drafted for the Reserve Corps or the air-raid watch was to give you time to devote yourself to writing for the nation. But you keep going fishing, which makes a bad impression. Yesterday, when I visited the main office, they asked me who it was they always saw going on his way to fishing whenever their bus passed by our town. Now, let's leave off fishing for a while, until our Japanese Empire consolidates its victory."

"Did they question you? I'm sorry," Hyŏn felt obliged to say.

"Also, you never show up when we give farewell parties here for the departing soldiers."

"I'm sorry. I'll come in the future."

Hyŏn was greatly disheartened. The summer's first rainy spell had just passed, and it was a time when nicely fattened fish were beginning to move around in schools. He'd been prohibited from fishing during the best season of the year. He shelved his fishing gear and spent his time talking to Kim, whom he now met more often than before. Whenever they met, they talked about the current state of affairs. In their optimistic reading of the latest events, they naturally dreamed of the day of liberation: Germany was already defeated, and Japan's enemy had landed on Okinawa.

"Did you say the name of the new nation will be Koryŏ?"

"They say the People's Republic of Koryŏ." Hyŏn had told Kim this once before, after he had first heard about it in Seoul.

"Why did they decide on 'Koryŏ'?"

"Because 'Koryŏ' is better known overseas than 'Chosŏn' or 'Taehan.' What would you call it?"

"Whatever the name is, I just hope the day of independence comes soon. But if possible, I would prefer the name Taehan."

"Taehan! Wasn't that the name briefly used at the end of the Chosŏn dynasty?"

"Yes. The Royal Court chose it, just like 'Silla' or 'Koryŏ.'"

"But what would be the point of calling the new nation Taehan, since we won't be returning to the Yi dynasty? Dynasties come and go. They're given different names at the whim of the king or his court, but hasn't the name of our people always been Chosŏn from the very beginning?"

"Well, that's true. *The Records of Three Kingdoms* also has plenty of names made from Chosŏn, like Kochosŏn and Wiman Chosŏn, but I wish . . . " Kim put down his pipe and sat up. "I want to name the nation Taehan, bring back King Yŏngch'in, and have him remarried to a Korean woman, so I can serve the Yi dynasty one more time. . . . "

"You miss the last dynasty that much?"

"Of course. Not that an ordinary man like me abides by the old saying that thou shall not serve two masters, but shouldn't we have our independence restored right before the Japanese eyes and have a good revenge on those villains?"

"So you'd like to go to Japan as a Governor-General?" The two laughed lightheartedly.

"People's Republic of Koryŏ or what have you, does it have an army and the approval of the Allies?"

"I don't know how much it's worth, but it's already declared war on Japan, and its army is said to have over three hundred thousand soldiers, including the troops of Kim Ilsung, Kim Wŏnbong, and Yi Ch'ŏngch'ŏn."

"Over three hundred thousand! What a large army! In the old days, an army of one hundred thousand was considered more than enough! Well, then, when we gain our independence and our government returns home, won't that be quite a sight to behold! Maybe I haven't lived this long in vain after all!"

Kim took up his pipe again. Amid the rising smoke, he pictured the stately image of the resplendent leaders of the Korean government being escorted by a great army of three hundred thousand soldiers. He sighed, as if overwhelmed with emotion, his eyes brimming with tears.

Soon afterward Kim was called in to the resident office. While he was there, the county chief called the town guardhouse to summon Kim to the county office. The next day Kim took the bus to the county office, which was over fifteen miles away. The headman welcomed him with a dinner at his official residence and asked Kim the following question:

"Why didn't you go to the provincial rally of Confucian scholars in Ch'unch'ŏn last month?"

"Is that why you summoned me?"

"No, not just for that."

"Please, go ahead and finish what you have to say."

"Aside from the past rally . . . you know, as well as I do, that the present situation doesn't permit anyone to remain uninvolved. Excuse me for saying this, but you seem too conservative. It's said that even a sage should follow the manners and ways of his time, and the general trend is not on your side."

"So?"

"This time round, before the National Confucian Rally, the county will give a lecture on national language and the imperial spirit. You should come to the lecture, and excuse me, but get a haircut and buy a khaki-colored uniform. You'll need it anyway, for the rally."

"Is that all?"

"Yes."

"Your Honor the Magistrate knows well that I'm a Confucian scholar. How can a Confucian be a Confucian, and what good would a Confucian rally be, if he can't follow the sage's teaching to preserve one's body, hair, and skin, which are all the gifts of his parents? It's not from personal honor that I've kept my position at the local Confucian school. Since there's nobody who can perform the procedures properly, I've taken charge of the memorial rites to fulfill my duty to the sages as a local scholar who strive to follow their steps. Now you're telling me to cut my hair, learn Japanese—even though I'm an old man who's losing his teeth—and change my clothes. It seems obvious that you want me to resign from my position. I get your point."

Then he took his leave. Yet within three days he was called again to the resident office. The order originated in a phone call from downtown like before, but this time he was to go to the police station. Kim went straight to Hyŏn.

"Mr. Hyŏn, they seem to be thinking of using force against me."

"Well, since their rage is on its last leg, try to avoid conflict and just ride things out."

"What if I ignore their call and refuse to go?"

"That won't do. Since they're now making arrests at the slightest provocation, they'll charge you for violation of an official order and cut your hair in prison. Then you won't be able to resist at all, just like in 1919."

"Right, you're right."

The following day Kim went downtown, yet he did not return as usual, not even after three days; the fourth day was August 15.

Hyŏn passed this historical day without noticing a thing, since the town had no radio and got its news only from newspapers, which were always delivered two or three days late. He sensed something only on the following morning, when he received a friend's telegraph, "Come to Seoul quickly." He visited the resident office to have a travel license issued, hoping as well to have a look around, but neither the office head nor the police officer on duty betrayed anything unusual. He obliquely asked Kanemura why Kim had not yet returned.

"Such a stubborn old man should sweat a little over there!"

"Then, is he in prison?"

"I don't really know. Don't go spreading any rumors." He didn't say anything further.

Nothing had changed.

"'Come to Seoul quickly,' what can this mean?" Hyŏn kept wondering about this as he waited for the bus. The bus arrived earlier than usual that day. Kim did not happen to return by this bus, either, and so Hyŏn had to leave without having a chance to see him. There was not one familiar face on the bus. Most of the passengers were wearing khaki uniforms, and no sign of change was visible. About ten miles down the road, Hyŏn's bus came across another bus heading in the opposite direction. The driver of Hyŏn's bus managed to stop the other by thrusting his arm out of the window.

"What's happened?"

"What do you mean?"

"You must have newspapers in Ch'ŏrwŏn."

"The same as yesterday's broadcast."

"I couldn't hear clearly because of all the noise. By the way, didn't it say something about an unconditional surrender?"

When the conversation between the two drivers reached this point, Hyŏn sprang up in the crowded car before anyone else did.

"What are you talking about?"

"The war's over."

"What? Over?"

"It's all over now."

"Over! How?"

"Well, that's what I'm trying to find out."

"At last, Japan's lost the war," the driver of the other bus said. "If you go to Ch'ŏrwŏn, you can read about it in the newspapers." Then he drove away. Hyŏn's bus, too, suddenly started moving again, and Hyŏn sank back into his seat.

"At last! What was fated to happen has finally happened! The long tedious waiting . . . " Hyŏn looked around at the other passengers, blinking his clouded eyes and trying not to get choked up. None of them looked Japanese, and yet they all appeared disinterested.

"Didn't you just hear what the driver said?" The passengers looked at each other but made no response.

"You know what'll become of Korea," Hyŏn asked again, "if Japan really has lost the war, don't you?"

"Whatever happens happens," responded an old man dressed in Korean clothes after a pause. "Who'd open his mouth these days without knowing for certain?"

"True. Just asking about it is frightening enough." Even the driver, who had shown some interest during the previous conversation, adopted the usual tired expression of a bus driver, revealing his wrinkles and sunken eyes.

Hyŏn lowered his head. He was more disconsolate at the stupefied look of his hapless compatriots than joyful over Korea's independence, and it made him want to cry. "Is all this merely a dream?"

After arriving at Ch'ŏrwŏn, Hyŏn was finally able to read the *Seoul Daily* and confirm that it was not a dream. He duly made the appropriate visits to people, shook their hands, and wept aloud together with them. The blue sky with its clouds like white blossoms, the fields with crops growing taller day by day, and the luxuriant trees—Hyŏn wanted to bow to each of them, then jump in the air and shout for joy.

At dawn on August 17, Hyŏn approached Seoul in an open sand truck packed with people, all busily talking about who would be president and who would be defense minister and shouting "Long Live Independence!" at the top of their voices. As each stop passed, and with it a sea of waving Korean national flags, Hyŏn was anxious that he might miss the National Independence Rally. The Rally was scheduled to take place at ten that morning.

He sensed something was wrong as he walked out of Ch'ŏngnyangni Station. Despite his expectations, people in Seoul looked impassive, and only a few flags were to be seen. Downtown, spiteful Japanese soldiers were keeping guard at every corner, ready to respond swiftly to any provocation, and the *Seoul Daily* maintained its normal tone.

Hyŏn went to see the friend who had telegraphed him. As soon as they had shaken hands, Hyŏn asked where the National Independence Rally would take place. The friend answered that he did not know. Hyŏn asked further where the key members of the government were, as they were said to have returned by air. But the friend didn't know that, either. Hyŏn asked if the news of Japan's surrender was true at all. The friend said that it was. Feeling a sense of fatigue all over his body, Hyŏn sank into a chair and relaxed for the first time in many hours. Then his friend told him what had happened in Seoul in the two days since August 15.

Hyŏn was unhappy with what he heard of the situation in Seoul: the Governor-General and the Japanese army were still in command over Koreans, and while rumors circulated about the return of the Provisional Government from abroad, some were hatching their own plans for founding the nation. In the cultural sphere, while Hyŏn himself remained too dazed to tell whether it was all real or only a dream, and while most writers had yet to arrive from their rural refuges, some were already hanging out placards, as if reclaiming their vested rights. Hyŏn found their move rash and suspicious. What disturbed him even more was the fact that those who hung banners and led the hurried assembling of a central cultural organization were mostly former leftists. Since neither the literary world nor the country as a whole was ready for the rampancy of the Left, he feared its possible takeover, which might lead to a catastrophic internecine conflict. Hyŏn thought that if he were to be honest with himself, he should not just be sitting around, so he visited the Central Council for the Construction of Korean Culture. There he found some of his old friends from the Club of Nine or from the magazine *Munjang*, but as he had expected, the core of the organization consisted of leftist writers and critics. They were revising a proclamation that had just been drafted. Hyŏn read it cautiously. He read it a second and third time. He was vigilantly searching for any hint of hypocrisy in their faces or behavior, yet he could not help but wonder, "Have they really prepared this much already for Korea's current situation?"

Once Hyŏn was informed of their positions and arguments, he had no objections to raise: their purpose was "to coordinate various cultural groups and to promote a harmonious dialogue between them, until the future Korean government establishes its cultural policies and creates an agency to implement them"; and their slogan was, "Liberation of Korean Culture, Construction of Korean Culture, and Unification of All Cultural Fronts." Hyŏn had also thought of united action as an important principle in the future path of the Korean people, Left or Right. Fearing that the leftists would diverge from this path, he had at first rashly turned against them. But all his worries were in vain. Their program was already quite concrete, but a class revolution was not in their priorities. This did not seem to be due to any hesitation or reservation on their part but rather to their genuine self-criticism and deep reflection on Korea's place in the current international situation. Otherwise, they could not have been content with such an apparently simple statement. Hyŏn considered this fortunate and gladly added his signature to the proclamation.

Nevertheless, he did not feel at ease. "All power to the people!"—flying banners and resounding songs were delivering this message and others from the meeting hall of the Council to the streets below. While this was a fine thing to say, it would not suit the people who were longing to see their nation, Taehan, emerge like a mirage on the sea. Absorbed in majestic fantasies and emotions, the people remained indifferent to their due rights. Hyŏn thought that the leftists were shouting, "All power to the people" not in advocacy of democracy but out of pure communist habit. In the previous century Hugo had already cried, "Not to the citizens but to the people," and so Hyŏn was well aware that "to the people" was neither a new nor a dangerous phrase in this age or in Korea's present situation; yet he was still wary, and many of his closer friends had indirectly expressed their concerns about Hyŏn's involvement with the group. Moreover, the political situation was growing more complex with each passing day. Members of the Provisional Government were not returning in a timely manner, not even individually, let alone making the grand appearance of which the people had been dreaming. In the north, the Soviet army was said to be routing the Japanese, thoroughly extirpating the enemy in full sympathy for the bone-deep resentments of Koreans. The American army, by contrast, was ignoring popular sentiment and had at first distributed leaflets making generous offers to the Japanese still in Korea. Such a measure consequently fuelled the continued boasting of the Governor-General and the Japanese army before the Korean people: "See, America still deals with Japan. A people like yours doesn't matter." Within Korea there appeared an organization calling itself the People's Republic of Korea, a development that augured future conflict with overseas powers; finally, a cultural activist group exclusively consisting of leftist writers was launched under the name of the Korean Proletarian Art Federation (KPAF), in opposition to the Central Council for the Construction of Korean Culture.

On the surface, the Council members, including Hyŏn, scoffed at the formation of the KPAF; "Neither history nor the present will permit them a separate existence." Yet, as sincere as the Council members were in their commitment to the unification of all cultural fronts, the KPAF's defection was an issue that urgently needed to be resolved. What particularly agitated Hyŏn was that the KPAF had announced a platform that did not differ much from the Council's. This suggested that the former leftists might be rejecting the Center for the Construction of Korean Literature (CCKL) specifically because their past adversary, Hyŏn, was its deputy chairman. At one point, right after the launching of the KPAF, some of Hyŏn's right-wing friends, as if they had been waiting for just that moment, took him out to a quiet place.

"We understand your intentions. But you won't be able to stay there much longer. All your efforts will be thrown away. In the end, So-and-so is more on the side of KPAF than on yours. Since you're likely to end up with nothing, despite all your efforts, let's organize our own group. Why disgrace yourself in the presence of such unbecoming company?"

Hyŏn told his friends that this time he would seriously reconsider his position. Then he parted from them. The very next day, a demonstration march sponsored by a leftist grassroots organization passed through Chongno. Of all the Allied national flags demonstrators carried only red ones and sang only the Red Flag Song. The crowds in the street adopted a reserved attitude toward the demonstration. But those in the Council building greeted the demonstrators with enthusiastic cheers and bursts of applause. To make matters worse, a senior member unwound the Soviet flags from the many prepared bundles of Allies' flags in the office, carried an armful of these red flags to the fourth floor, and scattered them over the procession, covering the street in red. Hyŏn ran up to stop him and prevented him from going back for a second load.

"Let's calm down."

"Why should we be calm?"

The two glared at each other. The young writers standing around the two all gave Hyŏn a contemptuous look. Instead of scattering red flags, they continued cheering the leftist demonstrators by shouting, clapping, and stamping their feet. After the procession passed, no one would come near Hyŏn. Upon leaving the hall, Hyŏn felt very alone. He was confident that if he were to resign, he could found a literary or cultural organization no smaller than the Council.

But . . .

Still . . .

Hyŏn slept on the thought. The following day he didn't go to the Council.

Why should I work only with friends who agree with me? What kind of effect could such a narrow clique have on this immense, new reality? The new freedom and independence of Korea should belong to all its people. Not only do I understand the leftists' ardor for a mass movement, but I, too, in good conscience, want to learn from them and make whatever contribution I can. All I want is to point out that waving red flags doesn't appeal to the public at this point, and that those supportive of the Red Flag don't account for all of the Korean people. If they don't understand me on this point and know no better than to interpret my views as merely reactionary, how can I continue to cooperate with them?

Hyŏn didn't feel like going to the hall the next day, either. As he was sitting idle and alone in his room, the man who had scattered the red flags over the demonstrators came for a visit.

"Hyŏn, you were quite upset the day before yesterday, weren't you?"

"Yes, I was."

"Hyŏn, I'll be honest with you. A Red demonstration, wasn't this the vision we've been dreaming of for so long? When I saw this vision out there, I lost my head and ran wild. To my shame. If it hadn't been for you, our recklessness would have gone farther. A man like you is worth ten of us in our present situation." His voice trembled at the end of his speech. After smoking a cigarette together in silence, the two got up and went back to the hall.

After the Red demonstration, Koreans, whether they were students, ordinary citizens, or intellectuals, seemed to split clearly into two camps, Left and Right. In the evenings, some of Hyŏn's friends would stop by to talk with him. Hyŏn was sincerely advised to make up his mind and withdraw from the Council, but he defended the organization, emphasizing that it was not as biased as it seemed. While at the hall next day, he received a phone call from friends whom he had met the night before.

"Either what you said was a lie, or you're being deceived as we told you. As evidence, take a look at the new slogan in capital letters, which was hung out this morning." They hung up the phone before Hyŏn could reply.

Hyŏn refrained from asking anyone around him about what he had just heard. He ran down to the ground floor and looked up at the four-story building from the street. He couldn't help but be surprised at what he saw. He had not noticed it on his way to the hall, but there was a cotton banner hanging from the rooftop to the second floor, which had "ALL SUPPORT FOR THE PEOPLE'S REPUBLIC OF KOREA" written across it in bigger letters than had been used in any previous slogan. The crowd in front of the Hwasin department store were straining their necks to look up at it. Their faces had doubtful, uneasy expressions. Hyŏn felt disheartened at this repeated betrayal. At the hall, neither the chairman of the Council nor the secretary had shown up yet. But the secretary of the CCKL was just then entering the building, following Hyŏn, and so Hyŏn led him by the hand to the rooftop.

"Who wrote that?"

"What?"

It was drizzling outside, so the secretary had not noticed the banner on his way in, either. It seemed that he had not been present at the meeting where the banner had been discussed.

"You really didn't know about it, either?"

"I honestly had no idea! Who in the world could have done it?"

"If neither of us knows, despite the fact that we've been here all along in the hall, then the absent members must be even more in the dark about this. This is tyranny. If they're going to do things like this, then their talk about the unification of all cultural fronts is a lie. I don't want to trust them any more. I'm leaving, let them know."

Hyŏn turned away, but the bewildered secretary stopped him.

"Let's find out what happened first."

"It doesn't matter."

"*You're jumping to conclusions.*"

"They deserve it. I never thought that they would be so narrow-minded about their mass movement."

"Please, stay. If we part today, it's suicide for all men of culture in Korea."

"Then, why are you committing such a suicidal act?" Hyŏn had raised his voice unintentionally.

"I swear. I didn't know, either. But if we don't condemn this kind of thing and try to correct this misguided orientation, who will?" Tears began to fill the secretary's eyes.

Then he ran to the banner and set out to pull it up like an anchor cable—for every inch he dragged it up, the banner, which was wet and heavy on one side, slipped back half an inch. Soon, Hyŏn's eyes were moist, too.

"That's right!" Hyŏn cried inside, "It doesn't matter whether I'm used, duped, or mocked. The fact that I take offense at such things proves my lack of sincerity!" Hyŏn ran to help the secretary pull up the heavy banner.

Later, he learned that neither the chairman nor the secretary had known about the banner. After the People's Republic of Korea had been announced, a member of the secretariat wrote up the slogan on his own after the propaganda squad of the art department had asked him if there was anything to paint. He had been aware of the general opinion in the Council that whatever name the new nation might take, it should include "people's republic." The squad thought that the slogan was simple but important and thus wrote it across the entire length of the broad cotton cloth. Because hanging dry posters was their responsibility, they came in early before breakfast and suspended it from the rooftop. For three months, the Council had to offer its excuse for this banner, which had been exhibited from just eight to eleven that one morning. The organization suffered quite a blow from this incident.

But this incident also provided an opportunity for all of the Council members to be more reflective in their self-criticism, their judgment of the political situation, and their campaign to bring the KPAF back into the fold.

With the arrival of the American army, the Japanese were no longer pointing their guns at Koreans, but as the leaflets had foreboded, the United States declared a military occupation. As for political parties, since anyone was eligible to found one, scores of them were created overnight. Dr. Syngman Rhee appeared amid the frantic cheers of the people and said that all Koreans should be one and united; meanwhile, traitors and profiteers resumed their activities, taking advantage of certain loopholes they spotted in Dr. Rhee's earnest words, as was the case of the former president of the colonial aviation company, who reemerged as the vice president of the new national airline. Politically, the people began to diverge more than converge, becoming more prone to suspicion rather than trust. The people could do nothing but invest their hope and faith in the Provisional Government, albeit in the form of individuals, as they had so deeply loved it and had fantasized for so long about following its leadership, to the extent of even disregarding their own rights. Yet a habit can be a hard thing to break for a group as well as for an individual. The Provisional Government, which had had no people to govern over during its years abroad, saw no need at all to talk to the people in Seoul now, far from addressing them from the makeshift podium of an oil carton in front of the Hwasin. Conflict with the KPAF was growing more acute, the 38th Parallel was ever tightening the waist of the Korean peninsula, robbery increased, and prices of goods soared—the question of trusteeship exploded at this time, just as the Korean people, after their protracted excitement, were on the brink of having a nervous breakdown.

All lost their calm. Outcries against trusteeship were raised here and there. Hyŏn, too, joined some of his friends at an anti-trusteeship rally, and his speech was published in a newspaper.

But Hyŏn, as well as those friends who participated in the rally with him, harbored misgivings and soon regretted what they had earlier said in their speeches. They gradually came to realize that the issue of trusteeship could not be so simply judged; after all, the Korean Communist Party raised the issue first. The Party's meticulous observations and precise judgments of the current political situation were something to appreciate; yet it was a great misfortune that the Party was the first to offer its support for the Moscow Agreement, since some people misunderstood the issue on account of this fact. Thus it became a subject of political disputes.

"We've been too hasty about trusteeship!"

"We made a big mistake!"

"Mistake? But we can't say that we really made a mistake, given public sentiments right now. It's also a good thing that we were able to articulate the pride of the Korean people as much as we did."

"But I mean there's a methodological difference between expressing our pride while understanding the situation and becoming enraged without knowing anything at all."

"Exactly! Since all this has just revealed how simplistic Koreans are and how lacking in real insight, what pride is there for us to talk about?"

"How can you work without ever making a mistake? Even Lenin said a man can't work without mistakes, and that whoever makes no mistakes is not working. Now that we know more, we should just try to do our best to effectively inform the public of the subtle international policy involved here."

As Hyŏn was discussing this matter with others, an old man, whose top hat made him look out of place, entered the hall.

"Oh my!" Hyŏn ran to greet him. It was Kim, who had often surfaced in Hyŏn's mind since the liberation. Kim had come to visit Seoul.

"Sir!"

"Mr. Hyŏn!"

"How's your health?"

"I'm feeling well enough for some sightseeing in Seoul."

But he looked very tired and weak, perhaps because he had walked a lot. He had had to ride a truck across the 38th Parallel from the north.

"When did you get here?"

"Yesterday."

"Where did you stay?"

"Well, I dropped by Ch'ŏrwŏn on my way here and saw your family. They're all doing well and all want to come here."

Hyŏn's family had not been able to return to Seoul and was still staying at Ch'ŏrwŏn.

"It's enough just knowing they're doing well."

"Since you, too, are far away from home, I first found a place to stay and then came right away to see you. So you all must be working hard?"

"Nothing really worth mentioning. I imagined how much you must be rejoicing. I've really been hoping to meet you. By the way, did you have a hard time when you went to the county police?"

"I almost lost my topknot. Luckily I escaped that."

"I'm so happy to see you."

It was about lunchtime, and since Hyŏn wanted to quietly reminisce about the past, he took Kim to an out-of-the-way restaurant.

"Mr. Hyŏn, I heard you've changed a lot."

"Me?"

"Rumor has it that you've changed much."

"Well . . . "

Hyŏn felt a bit disheartened. This was not the first time he had been told such a thing. Ever since the political scene had come to spilt clearly into conservative and progressive camps, he had seen many of his pre-liberation friends, who had once seemed willing to stand by him in an emergency, turn away from him at the mention of just one or two words, as if he were just a stranger. The political divide was causing rifts between friends.

"Mr. Hyŏn?"

"Yes?"

"How much did our people dream of independence? How much did we long for the return of the Provisional Government?"

"I know."

"Then why did you join the Communist Party?"

"Who said that I joined the Communist Party?"

"It's the talk of town. They say you're being used."

"Do you think so, too?"

"I know that you're not the type of man who can be tricked by anyone, though you might have changed your mind on your own."

"Thank you for saying that. As for having changed, I never had a clear enough standpoint before the liberation, so it's hard to say now whether I've changed or not. Most of my friends at that time were passive men of the world. Now that we're liberated, I don't want to just get by without actually doing some work."

"Does a man's way of life change after the liberation? A wise man doesn't live under suspicion."

"I disagree. At a time like this, if a person sees something's wrong, it's wiser to go against the grain than to worry about what others think of you. Just looking after your own affairs is a selfish attitude. Now is the most critical time for our nation, when we should exert ourselves, regardless of all the dangers, especially to our reputations."

"At any rate, a man should keep his moral obligations. What have we ever done? It's only right that we should absolutely obey those who have spent their lives overseas in a life-or-death struggle for the Korean people."

"I understand your point very well. And I'm no less grateful or deferential than anybody else to them. But the current situation is not that simple, either inside or outside Korea. You mentioned obligations, but think about what happened under the reign of King Kwanghae. After Ming helped Chosŏn during the Imjin War, Ming was attacked by Qing, and didn't Ming ask Chosŏn for reinforcements?"

"That gave a rise to the dispute over loyalty in Chosŏn."

"Chosŏn had no capacity to help Ming in the new war, since the Imjin War had just finished. But the Ming loyalists argued that on principle, they could not stand by, even if this meant the ruin of Chosŏn along with Ming. On the other hand, their critics gave priority to the people over the principle, arguing that the people should not be plunged into more misery so soon after their recent suffering at the hands of the Japanese, even if Chosŏn's refusal disgraced the throne or the whole dynasty. Didn't King Kwanghae support the latter view to the extent of being dethroned himself? I believe that King Kwanghae, who abandoned his throne like an old shoe, saying that the impoverished people should not be made to suffer in a fight between kings or dynasties, was a truly virtuous leader—far better than those who worried only about the interests of the ruling class, regardless of what would become of the people. Besides, why should we feel obliged only to those who came from abroad?"

"But they fought for national independence in foreign lands for twenty-seven or twenty-eight years, and so don't they stand out for their irreproachable integrity?"

"By no means am I trying to cheapen their hardships. Anyone who has faithfully continued to fight for us, either at home or abroad, deserves our respect. You talk about hardships and life-or-death struggles, but as for bleeding under torture or suffering the numbing pain of cold hands and feet, I think those who've fought at home and been dragged to detention cells and prisons had it many times worse. And physical suffering wasn't all of it. They also had to fight against all kinds of repeated threats and enticements to win them over mentally, so I think if a man fought at home without changing his mind, he's the greatest fighter."

"You're advocating only the communists!"

"Was everyone at home a communist? Right now, the Communist Party is wise enough to set its goal not on a proletarian revolution but on a capitalist, democratic one for all of Korea. There's no place, then, on principle, for a polar division between Left and Right, and for the most part they're succeeding in keeping such divisions and disputes among Koreans to a minimum. For the sake of Koreans, I think this is a very good sign."

"I don't understand what you're talking about, but I still think the fault lies with the Communist Party."

"Why don't we drink?"

"What does an old man know . . . " Kim did not hold his alcohol well. His face soon turned red. "But even at my age, a man has dreams. If only the communists remain quiet, we'll soon have our independence, and the key figures of the Provisional Government will take their due positions, which they've earned through their suffering. And won't they make good rulers? Wasn't it the communists who caused the problem of trusteeship with their senseless fighting?

Kim was quite angry. He said that Korean independence was being blocked by the Soviet Union overseas and the Communist Party at home. Hyŏn found it impossible to enlighten someone like Kim, who had no knowledge of history or international affairs but simply believed that liberation came as a result of a war of independence. Such a task required a certain skill, one which Hyŏn did not have. He just smiled and urged Kim to eat more food.

Kim visited Hyŏn again the next day, and Hyŏn returned his visit the day after that.

"Why are you in favor of trusteeship?" Kim asked when Hyŏn visited him.

"I'm not in favor of it."

"Then are you supporting trusteeship, something you don't even like, merely because the Provisional Government's against it and you want to oppose everything it does?"

"You can be quite radical, too."

"Should I just let myself be sold off at the end of my life to the foreign ministers of three countries and be dragged into trusteeship without any protest?"

"That's a bit extreme! Do you think I've got such bright prospects now that I've sold my support for the Moscow Agreement?"

Kim made no reply, but he did not hide his disapproval of Hyŏn's position. Hyŏn tried his best to avoid provoking Kim and to explain his reasoning: since liberation had been achieved not by the power of the Koreans themselves but by an international alliance, it can't exist now outside the sphere of international politics; he supports the Moscow Agreement not because he favors, or is happy with, trusteeship but because Korea is caught between the capitalist United States and the socialist Soviet Union and needs to secure an international guarantee of its national independence and neutrality; otherwise, if the Soviet Union, the United States, and China all start their own underground diplomacy in Korea, where the government and economy are still fragile, Korea will fall into an ultimately ruinous internecine dispute, just like the time when King Kojong had to take refuge in the Russian embassy at the end of Chosŏn; so, Korea has no choice now but to seek an international warrant of its hard-won freedom; since this victory wasn't won through a war of independence led by the Yi dynasty, deluding the public by chanting Taehan, Taehan in some nostalgic call for the imperial period of the feudal dynasty isn't the right way to lead the Korean people to true happiness; and since the United States and the Soviet Union are in every respect the most pragmatic of all nations, Korea won't be able to deal with them, unless it arms itself with a cogent international perspective and makes a thorough preparation, without relying on illusions based on emotions. Hyŏn emphatically tried to explain his position, but Kim, who used to praise Hyŏn as a man of rare integrity before the liberation, obstinately refused to understand him at all. He simply found it disagreeable that Hyŏn, as a Korean, should be criticizing Taehan. He kept insisting on his own explanation that the trusteeship must be the result of some evil communist scheme.

Kim did not return for a while after that. Hyŏn didn't visit him either, partly because he was too busy but also because he no longer cared for Kim.

The trusteeship proved to be an onerous political trial for Koreans. If an opposition demonstration took place one day, the supporters of the Moscow Agreement marched in the streets the next. The masses collided, and there were leaders who exploited this conflict, making their scramble for political power all the more vicious. In the end, students, who had borne the brunt of the national ordeal before liberation again bore the cross during this unfortunate time.

On one of these gloomy days, Kim visited Hyŏn at the hall. He was returning to the countryside that day. Hyŏn invited him out to lunch, but Kim turned down the offer, unlike on previous occasions, and also deterred Hyŏn from coming downstairs to see him off. He seemed to have stopped by just to say a good-bye, for the sake of their old friendship, but did not care for Hyŏn's treating him or paying him any courtesies.

"When will you come to Seoul again?"

"I don't want to come back to this Seoul. When I return, I'll settle in the seclusion of Tumundong." Kim then resolutely walked down the steps without once looking back.

Hyŏn stood there for a while, stupefied, before going up to the rooftop to get some fresh air. Amid the American Jeeps swarming like whirligig beetles, Kim cut a very conspicuous figure in his white overcoat and black top hat. Hyŏn thought of Wang Guowei, a scholar at the end of the Qing dynasty. When Wang went to Japan to give a lecture on Ming's songs, Hyŏn had also gone to see him. Wang was still wearing his hair in Qing-style pigtail. The Japanese students sniggered at him, but Hyŏn, who did not have a nation of his own, became teary-eyed, thinking of the scholar's loyalty to the passing dynasty, and admired his integrity. Later, Hyŏn heard that Wang had gone to Shanghai and then on to Peking only to witness the vanishing shadow of his beloved dynasty wherever he wandered. When he drowned himself in Lake Kunming—after singing, "The blue water and the green mountain have not changed / The rain washes the moss off of a stone beast"—he was still wearing his pigtail. Yet when Hyŏn came to think of it now, what destroyed Qing was not foreign enemies but a revolution for truth and the happiness of the Chinese people. Although Wang's affectionate devotion to his king was admirable, had he devoted his passion and life to the revolution, wouldn't it have made him a greater man and his life even more honorable, a life committed to a larger truth? Hyŏn gazed at Kim's back as it disappeared into the distance. The figure of the old man, who had braved the 38th Parallel to come to the old capital in search of Taehan and who still wore a topknot, which he had managed to preserve despite all the abuse and contempt he received during the colonial period, was now drifting away, like a speck of dust, below the great waves of world history. Hyŏn could not help but recall the pitiful last moments of the Chinese scholar.

The wind was still chilly, but there was already a hint of a soft spring breeze. Hyŏn smoked one more cigarette and went down to the hall. His friends had concluded the union with the KPAF and were busy preparing for the Writers' National Rally.

(March 23, 1946)

Glossary

Central Council for the Construction of Korean Culture (The): *Chosŏn munhwa kŏnsŏl chungang hyŏbŭihoe* was founded under leftist leadership on August 18, 1945. It was the first cultural organization to be established in liberated Korea. Under the Council was the Center for the Construction of Korean Literature (*Chosŏn munhak kŏnsŏl ponbu*), which Im Hwa, the second and last chairman of the Korea Artista Proletaria Federatio (KAPF), organized by gathering together ex-KAPF members as well as other sympathetic writers such as Yi T'aejun. On September 17, however, the Korean Proletarian Art Federation (*Chosŏn p'roletarian yesul tongmaeng*)—named after the KAPF (Korea Artista Proletaria Federatio) of the colonial years—was founded by Han Sŏrya and other leftists who were dissatisfied with the conciliatory standing of the Council. On December 13, 1945, the two rival organizations finally merged into the Korean Writers' Alliance (*Chosŏn munhakka tongmaeng*).

changgo: A traditional Korean drum, which is played on two sides and has a body shaped like an hourglass. Also called *changgu,* this instrument dates back to the Silla period (57 B.C.–A.D. 935) and is used in diverse genres of Korean music ranging from court music to shaman ceremonies.

Chientao: An eastern district of Manchuria that was a traditional destination for Korean emigrants. After the insurrectionary movement of March First, 1919, the district also attracted many political exiles and served as a base for Korean guerilla activities.

chŏn: The *chŏn* and *wŏn* were the basic monetary units of early modern Korea. One hundred chŏn equals one wŏn.

Group of Nine (The): *Kuinhoe,* an intellectual circle comprising nine writers and artists, was organized by Yi T'aejun in 1933 with the purpose of promoting pure literature as opposed to the proletarian literature of the KAPF. Although its members pursued little collective activity, their prominence as individual artists helped boost the cause of politically autonomous literature and arts in Korea. The group included well-known writers such as Yi T'aejun, Pak T'aewŏn, Yi Sang, Chŏng Chiyong, Yu Ch'ijin, and Kim Kirim. *Kuinhoe* is today widely remembered for its members' pioneering experimentations with language and with Western modernist trends, such as surrealism and imagism.

History of Three Kingdoms (The): *Samguksagi* is a historical record of three kingdoms—Koguryŏ, Paekche, Silla—compiled by Kim Pusik (1075–1151) in 1145. It is regarded as the oldest history book of Korea.

Hwasin Department Store: Hwasin was Korea's first contemporary department store. First opened in Seoul in 1931, it reopened after a fire in 1937, in a six-story stone building equipped with such modern facilities as an elevator and an escalator. Throughout the colonial years it remained the only department store in the northern, predominantly Korean part of the city.

Imjin War (1592–1598): A military confrontation also known as Hideyoshi's invasion of Korea and as the Seven Years War. At the start of the war, Japanese general Toyotomi Hideyoshi's troops rapidly overran the Korean peninsula until they were stopped by reinforcements from Ming China and successful campaigns by Korean generals such as Yi Sunshin and Kwŏn Yul. In addition to causing a political and economic crisis within Korea, the war also contributed to the fall of the Ming dynasty in China.

Ishikawa Takuboku (1886–1912): Japanese poet and novelist best known for reviving the traditional *tanka* form of poetry. Ishikawa innovated the genre, characterized by a strict thirty-one syllables schema, by capturing everyday experiences through fresh language and imagery.

Kim Ilsung (1912–1994): The founder of the Democratic People's Republic of Korea. During the colonial period Kim gained a reputation as the leader of a Korean guerrilla group in Manchuria. Upon the end of Japan's rule in 1945, Kim returned to Korea with the Soviet Army and established the communist regime of North Korea in 1948. Kim's one-man rule, fortified by a cult of personality, outlasted his death in 1994.

King Kojong (1852–1919): The twenty-sixth king of Chosŏn, who reigned between 1863 and 1907. After his royal consort, Queen Myŏngsŏng, was murdered in the palace by a party of Japanese assassins in 1895, the king fled to the Russian embassy and remained under foreign protection for about a year. During this period, he changed his title to that of Emperor and the name of the country to *Taehan* (Great Korea) Empire in an attempt to strengthen his compromised sovereignty. He was deposed by Japan in 1907.

King Kwanghae (1575–1641): The fifteenth king of Chosŏn, whose reign lasted from 1608 to 1623. He tried unsuccessfully to suppress a factional struggle between Ming loyalists and their critics over the question of whether Chosŏn should side with the declining Ming dynasty, a longtime ally, or the rising Qing dynasty of the Manchus. The king's policy of attempting to appease both sides led to his eventual dethronement.

King Yŏngch'in (1897–1970): The last crown prince of Chosŏn. After King Kojong's dethronement in 1907, Yŏngch'in was designated at age eleven as the royal heir of Sunjong, the new king, and he was immediately taken away to Japan to be educated there. He was married to a Japanese princess who was known in Korea by her Korean name Yi Pangja. Although he was never to ascend to the throne due to the 1910 annexation by Japan, Yŏngch'in was widely regarded as the legitimate king of Korea in the years to come. After the 1945 liberation, he was prevented from returning to Korea by the new republican government, which was concerned about the possible instability his return might cause. He was allowed to return to Korea only in 1963.

Kochosŏn: An ancient kingdom widely regarded as the first proper nation of the Korean people. It is believed to have been established in the northeastern part of the peninsula by the mythical theocratic monarch Tan'gun and to have lasted from 2333 B.C. to A.D. 108. Later, the founders of the Chosŏn dynasty (1392–1910) adopted its name to reinforce the historical legitimacy of the new dynasty.

Kong Jung (153–208): Confucian scholar and a minister of state under the late Han dynasty of China.

Korean Proletarian Art Federation (The): See **The Central Council for the Construction of Korean Culture**.

Korean People's Republic (The): Upon liberation, Korean nationalists tried to set up an interim government that would prove the self-governing capacity of the Korean people to the Occupation forces. The establishment of *Chosŏn inmin konghwaguk* was announced on September 6, 1945. The leaders of the new political entity included eminent political figures such as Kim Ku and Syngman Rhee. The new government, however, came under suspicion by the U.S. Occupation authority because of its association with communists, and it was finally outlawed on December 12, 1946.

Korean Provisional Government (The): In the aftermath of the March First Movement, Korean exiles organized the Korean Provisional Government in Shanghai in April 1919. Although the organization existed throughout the colonial period, its diplomatic efforts were largely unsuccessful, and it never gained international recognition. Nonetheless, the KPG remained as an important symbol for the Korean independence movement.

Manchukuo: The puppet state Imperial Japan established in Manchuria following its conquest of the Chinese territory in 1931. The occupation lasted for thirteen years.

The March Uprising: Commonly known as the March First Movement, the anti-imperialist uprising began in Seoul in 1919, and it continued for about a year, spreading throughout Korea. The incident had a shaping impact on the development of nationalist activism in Korea and is remembered today as one of the most significant events in the country's modern history.

modernology: A neologism coined by Kon Wajirō (1888–1973), a renowned Japanese professor of architecture and a pioneer of cultural anthropology. Kon formed the term by combining the Chinese characters for "modern" and "archeology," to refer to a new discipline that would scientifically analyze contemporary social phenomena and, particularly, changing trends in modern culture.

Moscow Agreement (The): In December 1945, the foreign ministers of the Soviet Union, the United States and Great Britain met in Moscow to construct a trusteeship plan for Korea. It proposed a four-power trusteeship of Korea involving the three nations and China for a period of no more than five years. A joint Soviet-American commission consisting of members of the two administrations was created to supervise the establishment of a provisional Korean democratic government. The Moscow Agreement stirred up a tempest of protest from disappointed Koreans. Under the influence of the Soviet Union, however, the leftists soon shifted their positions and supported the Agreement.

Munjang: A literary monthly started in 1939 and headed by Yi T'aejun. In reaction to Japan's policy of suppressing Korean culture, the magazine focused on the study of Korean classics and made a point of publishing only works of apolitical, pure literature. *Munjang* was forced to discontinue in 1941, after its twenty-sixth issue.

Nishida Kitarō (1870–1945): A renowned Japanese philosopher whose academic activities exemplified the effort to combine Western philosophical ideas with Japanese spiritual traditions, Zen Buddhism in particular. After becoming a professor of philosophy at Kyoto Imperial University, he helped recruit such philosophers as Watsuji Tetsurō and Tanabe Hajime, and he became known as the founder of the Kyoto School of Philosophy. A nationally respected philosopher, Nishida in the 1940s became an apologist of Japan's war efforts upon the request of the military.

Patriotic Association of Writers (The): *Munin pogukhoe* was organized in April 1943 to mobilize colonial writers for imperialist propaganda. Many prominent writers, including Yi Kwangsu, were enrolled as members.

Public Cemetery Law (The): The Japanese authority enacted the Cemetery, Crematorium, Burial, and Cremation Regulations in July 1912 as part of its land reform policy in the colony. The new law aimed to increase state-owned territory by preventing the occupation of land by graves. Its restrictions on the indigenous burial customs, as well as a subsequent confiscation of over seven acres of private lands formerly reserved for family burials, provoked widespread resentment among Koreans.

Satō Haruo (1892–1964): Japanese poet and novelist. He is best known for the lyrical quality of his novels, as exemplified in the companion works *Den'en no yūutsu* (Pastoral melancholy, 1919) and *Tokai no yūutsu* (Urban melancholy, 1922).

Schipa: Tito Schipa (1888–1965), a famous Italian tenor. "Ahi Ahi Ahi" is an aria Falstaff sings in Verdi's opera *Falstaff.*

shamisen: A three-stringed Japanese lute traditionally associated with the pleasure quarters and urban theaters of Edo Japan (1600–1868).

Shinto: An indigenous Japanese religion commonly associated with the country's imperial tradition. It has its roots in ancient animism and still enjoys broad popularity in today's Japan. *Shinto* became Japan's official state religion from the Meiji Restoration of 1868. In Korea, starting after the late 1930s, the colonial authority built many Shinto shrines throughout the country as part of a wartime campaign to indoctrinate the colonized with imperial spirit.

sijo: A genre of Korean verse, dating to the Koryŏ period, with a conventional three-line structure, each line consisting of four rhythmic groups of multiple-syllable phrases: 3-4-3(4)-4 in first two lines; 3-5-4-3 in the closing one. Originally an oral art, *sijo* was widely popular in the pre-modern period and continues as a living tradition today.

Sirhak: Usually translated as Practical Learning, the term *sirhak* refers to a barely unified variety of modernizing intellectual trends that gained prominence in Korea in the seventeenth and eighteenth centuries. Famous proponents of *sirhak* such as Pak Chiwŏn, Pak Chega, and Chŏng Yagyong were inspired by their knowledge of the Western sciences, then coming from China, and they advocated reforms of the bureaucratic system as well as improvements to commerce and manufacturing. Their recommendations were widely supported by reform-minded scholars as well as laypersons, but on the whole they failed to overcome the opposition of Confucian mainstream culture.

Special Higher Division (The): *Kōdō keisatsu* was a Japanese police organization created in 1911 primarily to control anti-government political activities, particularly those of socialists and anarchists. Also known as "thought police," the organization gained much notoriety among the leftists and colonial nationalists, especially after its expansion as part of the 1925 Peace Preservation Law.

Syngman Rhee (1875–1965): The first president of the Republic of Korea. During the colonial period, Rhee spent forty years in the United States, campaigning for Korean independence. He returned to Korea on October 16, 1945, amid the enthusiastic welcome of all sides, yet his right-wing, staunchly anti-communist stance soon alienated leftists as well as left-leaning nationalists. Rhee was later chosen by the United States as a strong anti-communist leader of the U.S.-occupied South. After becoming president in 1948, he extended his term several times by amending the Constitution until he was finally ousted by the civil revolution of April 19, 1960. He died in exile in Hawaii.

Taehan: See **King Kojong.**

Taesan: Pen name of Kang Chin (1807–1858), a Confucian official and man of letters, whose low birth hindered his promotion in the central government. Yi T'aejun's mention of Kang's office in the village reveals that the setting of "Before and after Liberation" is the city of Anhyŏp in the Kangwŏn province. The quoted poems are from Kang's poetry collection *Taesan sijipch'o,* published posthumously in 1868.

Tanabe Hajime (1885–1962): Japanese philosopher. Tanabe is known for his attempt to synthesize traditional Japanese Buddhist philosophy with Western philosophical ideas owed primarily to Edmund Husserl and Martin Heidegger. In 1927 he joined the Kyoto school of philosophers, which provided the main theoretical underpinnings for the development of the doctrine of pan-Asianism.

Tao Yuanming (317–420): Famous Chinese poet from the Eastern Jin dynasty. He is considered as one of the greatest nature poets. Averse to officialdom, he served only intermittently over a short period and spent most of his life at his farm, leading a life of freedom and frugality. The last office he held was as a magistrate in Pengze, but he resigned from the position after only three months.

Tokkyŏn: Pen name of Ch'oe Sangdŏk (1901–1970), a novelist and journalist. His popular novel *Sŭngbangbigok* (The tragic melody of a Buddhist temple) was serialized in the newspaper *Chosŏn Ilbo* in 1927. The novel tells the story of a sister and a brother who, having married without knowing the secret of their birth, come to learn of it only upon reading their mother's will.

Tzu Lu (542–480 B.C.): Chinese Confucian scholar from the No dynasty. He was a well-known disciple of Confucius.

Wang Guowei (1877–1927): Renowned Chinese scholar. Introducing many Western theories, Wang wrote broadly on history, aesthetics, and literature. Politically a staunch royalist, he attempted suicide when the last emperor of Qing was evicted from the palace in 1924. After failing on this first attempt, he finally drowned himself in Lake Kunming three years later.

Watsuji Tetsurō (1889–1960): Japanese moral philosopher. In the 1920s Watsuji broke from his earlier preoccupation with Western philosophers such as Kierkegaard and Nietzsche in favor of traditional Zen Buddhism. He became a professor of ethics at Kyoto Imperial University in 1934 and was one of the philosophical masterminds of Japan's wartime ideology of pan-Asianism.

Yanagi Muneyoshi (1889–1961): Japanese art historian and leader of the Japanese folk-craft movement. A founding member of *Shirkabaha* (White birch group), he published numerous articles on painting and sculpture. After his first trip to Korea in 1916, he became an outspoken patron of its artistic traditions as well as an advocate of Korean independence. He founded the Museum of Korean Arts in Seoul in 1924.

yobo: The Korean word "yobo" is an abbreviation of "yŏgi boo," which means "look here." While it is a traditional, conventional term for addressing one's spouse, it is also used to attract the attention of someone younger or of lower rank. During the colonial period, the Japanese used the term to address Korean laborers.

Yoshiiya Nobuko (1896–1973): Japanese popular novelist. Part of a growing wave of mass culture in 1930s Japan, her writings on women's friendship and love, such as *Onna no yūjō* (Women's friendship; 1933–1934), were especially popular among female students.

Yulgok: Pen name of Yi I (1536–1584), one of the most eminent scholar-officials of the Chosŏn dynasty. Yi is known for his non-doctrinaire interpretations of Neo-Confucian thought. He advocated many reform proposals and argued unsuccessfully for a military buildup against Japan. The effigy of this renowned philosopher-cum-politician is today reproduced on Korea's one thousand wŏn note.

Yun Paengnam (1888–1954): Korean novelist, playwright, and film director. His novel *Taedojŏn* (The tale of a great robber), which was serialized in the *Tonga Ilbo* between 1930 and 1931, was one of the first modern popular novels of Korea.

CORNELL EAST ASIA SERIES

8 Cornelius C. Kubler, *Vocabulary and Notes to Ba Jin's Jia: An Aid for Reading the Novel*
16 Monica Bethe & Karen Brazell, *Nō as Performance: An Analysis of the Kuse Scene of Yamamba*
18 Royall Tyler, tr., *Granny Mountains: A Second Cycle of Nō Plays*
23 Knight Biggerstaff, *Nanking Letters, 1949*
28 Diane E. Perushek, ed., *The Griffis Collection of Japanese Books: An Annotated Bibliography*
37 J. Victor Koschmann, Ōiwa Keibō & Yamashita Shinji, eds., *International Perspectives on Yanagita Kunio and Japanese Folklore Studies*
38 James O'Brien, tr., *Murō Saisei: Three Works*
40 Kubo Sakae, *Land of Volcanic Ash: A Play in Two Parts*, revised edition, tr. David G. Goodman
44 Susan Orpett Long, *Family Change and the Life Course in Japan*
48 Helen Craig McCullough, *Bungo Manual: Selected Reference Materials for Students of Classical Japanese*
49 Susan Blakeley Klein, *Ankoku Butō: The Premodern and Postmodern Influences on the Dance of Utter Darkness*
50 Karen Brazell, ed., *Twelve Plays of the Noh and Kyōgen Theaters*
51 David G. Goodman, ed., *Five Plays by Kishida Kunio*
52 Shirō Hara, *Ode to Stone*, tr. James Morita
53 Peter J. Katzenstein & Yutaka Tsujinaka, *Defending the Japanese State: Structures, Norms and the Political Responses to Terrorism and Violent Social Protest in the 1970s and 1980s*
54 Su Xiaokang & Wang Luxiang, *Deathsong of the River: A Reader's Guide to the Chinese TV Series* Heshang, trs. Richard Bodman & Pin P. Wan
55 Jingyuan Zhang, *Psychoanalysis in China: Literary Transformations, 1919-1949*
56 Jane Kate Leonard & John R. Watt, eds., *To Achieve Security and Wealth: The Qing Imperial State and the Economy, 1644-1911*
57 Andrew F. Jones, *Like a Knife: Ideology and Genre in Contemporary Chinese Popular Music*
58 Peter J. Katzenstein & Nobuo Okawara, *Japan's National Security: Structures, Norms and Policy Responses in a Changing World*
59 Carsten Holz, *The Role of Central Banking in China's Economic Reforms*
60 Chifumi Shimazaki, *Warrior Ghost Plays from the Japanese Noh Theater: Parallel Translations with Running Commentary*
61 Emily Groszos Ooms, *Women and Millenarian Protest in Meiji Japan: Deguchi Nao and Ōmotokyō*
62 Carolyn Anne Morley, *Transformation, Miracles, and Mischief: The Mountain Priest Plays of Kōygen*
63 David R. McCann & Hyunjae Yee Sallee, tr., *Selected Poems of Kim Namjo*, afterword by Kim Yunsik
64 Hua Qingzhao, *From Yalta to Panmunjom: Truman's Diplomacy and the Four Powers, 1945-1953*
65 Margaret Benton Fukasawa, *Kitahara Hakushū: His Life and Poetry*
66 Kam Louie, ed., *Strange Tales from Strange Lands: Stories by Zheng Wanlong*, with introduction
67 Wang Wen-hsing, *Backed Against the Sea*, tr. Edward Gunn
69 Brian Myers, *Han Sōrya and North Korean Literature: The Failure of Socialist Realism in the DPRK*
70 Thomas P. Lyons & Victor Nee, eds., *The Economic Transformation of South China: Reform and Development in the Post-Mao Era*
71 David G. Goodman, tr., *After Apocalypse: Four Japanese Plays of Hiroshima and Nagasaki*
72 Thomas Lyons, *Poverty and Growth in a South China County: Anxi, Fujian, 1949-1992*
74 Martyn Atkins, *Informal Empire in Crisis: British Diplomacy and the Chinese Customs Succession, 1927-1929*

76 Chifumi Shimazaki, *Restless Spirits from Japanese Noh Plays of the Fourth Group: Parallel Translations with Running Commentary*
77 Brother Anthony of Taizé & Young-Moo Kim, trs., *Back to Heaven: Selected Poems of Ch'ŏn Sang Pyŏng*
78 Kevin O'Rourke, tr., *Singing Like a Cricket, Hooting Like an Owl: Selected Poems by Yi Kyu-bo*
79 Irit Averbuch, *The Gods Come Dancing: A Study of the Japanese Ritual Dance of Yamabushi Kagura*
80 Mark Peterson, *Korean Adoption and Inheritance: Case Studies in the Creation of a Classic Confucian Society*
81 Yenna Wu, tr., *The Lioness Roars: Shrew Stories from Late Imperial China*
82 Thomas Lyons, *The Economic Geography of Fujian: A Sourcebook*, Vol. 1
83 Pak Wan-so, *The Naked Tree*, tr. Yu Young-nan
84 C.T. Hsia, *The Classic Chinese Novel: A Critical Introduction*
85 Cho Chong-Rae, *Playing With Fire*, tr. Chun Kyung-Ja
86 Hayashi Fumiko, *I Saw a Pale Horse and Selections from Diary of a Vagabond*, tr. Janice Brown
87 Motoori Norinaga, *Kojiki-den, Book 1*, tr. Ann Wehmeyer
88 Chang Soo Ko, tr., *Sending the Ship Out to the Stars: Poems of Park Je-chun*
89 Thomas Lyons, *The Economic Geography of Fujian: A Sourcebook*, Vol. 2
90 Brother Anthony of Taizé, tr., Midang: *Early Lyrics of So Chong-Ju*
92 Janice Matsumura, *More Than a Momentary Nightmare: The Yokohama Incident and Wartime Japan*
93 Kim Jong-Gil tr., *The Snow Falling on Chagall's Village: Selected Poems of Kim Ch'un-Su*
94 Wolhee Choe & Peter Fusco, trs., *Day-Shine: Poetry by Hyon-jong Chong*
95 Chifumi Shimazaki, *Troubled Souls from Japanese Noh Plays of the Fourth Group*
96 Hagiwara Sakutarō, *Principles of Poetry (Shi no Genri)*, tr. Chester Wang
97 Mae J. Smethurst, *Dramatic Representations of Filial Piety: Five Noh in Translation*
98 Ross King, ed., *Description and Explanation in Korean Linguistics*
99 William Wilson, *Hōgen Monogatari: Tale of the Disorder in Hōgen*
100 Yasushi Yamanouchi, J. Victor Koschmann and Ryūichi Narita, eds., *Total War and 'Modernization'*
101 Yi Ch'ŏng-jun, *The Prophet and Other Stories*, tr. Julie Pickering
102 S.A. Thornton, *Charisma and Community Formation in Medieval Japan: The Case of the Yugyō-ha (1300-1700)*
103 Sherman Cochran, ed., *Inventing Nanjing Road: Commercial Culture in Shanghai, 1900-1945*
104 Harold M. Tanner, *Strike Hard! Anti-Crime Campaigns and Chinese Criminal Justice, 1979-1985*
105 Brother Anthony of Taizé & Young-Moo Kim, trs., *Farmers' Dance: Poems by Shin Kyŏng-nim*
106 Susan Orpett Long, ed., *Lives in Motion: Composing Circles of Self and Community in Japan*
107 Peter J. Katzenstein, Natasha Hamilton-Hart, Kozo Kato, & Ming Yue, *Asian Regionalism*
108 Kenneth Alan Grossberg, *Japan's Renaissance: The Politics of the Muromachi Bakufu*
109 John W. Hall & Toyoda Takeshi, eds., *Japan in the Muromachi Age*
110 Kim Su-Young, Shin Kyong-Nim & Lee Si-Young: *Variations: Three Korean Poets*; trs. Brother Anthony of Taizé & Young-Moo Kim
111 Samuel Leiter, *Frozen Moments: Writings on* Kabuki, *1966-2001*
112 Pilwun Shih Wang & Sarah Wang, *Early One Spring: A Learning Guide to Accompany the Film Video* February
113 Thomas Conlan, *In Little Need of Divine Intervention: Scrolls of the Mongol Invasions of Japan*
114 Jane Kate Leonard & Robert Antony, eds., *Dragons, Tigers, and Dogs: Qing Crisis Management and the Boundaries of State Power in Late Imperial China*
115 Shu-ning Sciban & Fred Edwards, eds., *Dragonflies: Fiction by Chinese Women in the Twentieth Century*

116 David G. Goodman, ed., *The Return of the Gods: Japanese Drama and Culture in the 1960s*
117 Yang Hi Choe-Wall, *Vision of a Phoenix: The Poems of Hŏ Nansŏrhŏn*
118 Mae J. Smethurst & Christina Laffin, eds., *The Noh* Ominameshi*: A Flower Viewed from Many Directions*
119 Joseph A. Murphy, *Metaphorical Circuit: Negotiations Between Literature and Science in Twentieth-Century Japan*
120 Richard F. Calichman, *Takeuchi Yoshimi: Displacing the West*
121 Fan Pen Li Chen, *Visions for the Masses: Chinese Shadow Plays from Shaanxi and Shanxi*
122 S. Yumiko Hulvey, *Sacred Rites in Moonlight: Ben no Naishi Nikki*
123 Tetsuo Najita & J. Victor Koschmann, *Conflict in Modern Japanese History: The Neglected Tradition*
124 Naoki Sakai, Brett de Bary & Iyotani Toshio, eds., *Deconstructing Nationality*
125 Judith N. Rabinovitch & Timothy R. Bradstock, *Dance of the Butterflies: Chinese Poetry from the Japanese Court Tradition*
126 Yang Gui-ja, *Contradictions,* trs. Stephen Epstein and Kim Mi-Young
127 Ann Sung-hi Lee, *Yi Kwang-su and Modern Korean Literature:* Mujŏng
128 Pang Kie-chung & Michael D. Shin, eds., *Landlords, Peasants, & Intellectuals in Modern Korea*
129 Joan R. Piggott, ed., *Capital and Countryside in Japan, 300-1180: Japanese Historians Interpreted in English*
130 Kyoko Selden & Jolisa Gracewood, eds., *Annotated Japanese Literary Gems: Stories by Tawada Yōko, Nakagami Kenji, and Hayashi Kyōko* (Vol. 1)
131 Michael G. Murdock, *Disarming the Allies of Imperialism: The State, Agitation, and Manipulation during China's Nationalist Revolution, 1922-1929*
132 Noel J. Pinnington, *Traces in the Way: Michi and the Writings of Komparu Zenchiku*
133 Charlotte von Verschuer, *Across the Perilous Sea: Japanese Trade with China and Korea from the Seventh to the Sixteenth Centuries,* Kristen Lee Hunter, tr.
134 John Timothy Wixted, *A Handbook to Classical Japanese*
135 Kyoko Selden & Jolisa Gracewood, with Lili Selden, eds., *Annotated Japanese Literary Gems: Stories by Natsume Sōseki, Tomioka Taeko, and Inoue Yasushi* (Vol. 2)
136 Yi Tae-Jin, *The Dynamics of Confucianism and Modernization in Korean History*
137 Jennifer Rudolph, *Negotiated Power in Late Imperial China: The Zongli Yamen and the Politics of Reform*
138 Thomas D. Loooser, *Visioning Eternity: Aesthetics, Politics, and History in the Early Modern Noh Theater*
139 Gustav Heldt, *The Pursuit of Harmony: Poetry and Power in Late Heian Japan*
140 Joan R. Piggott & Yoshida Sanae, *Teishinkōki: The Year 939 in the Journal of Regent Fujiwara no Tadahira*
141 Robert Bagley, *Max Loehr and the Study of Chinese Bronzes: Style and Classification in the History of Art*
142 Edwin A. Cranston, *The Secret Island and the Enticing Flame: Worlds of Memory, Discovery, and Loss in Japanese Poetry*
143 Hugh de Ferranti, *The Last Biwa Singer: A Blind Musician in History, Imagination and Performance*
144 Roger Des Forges, Gao Minglu, Liu Chiao mei, Haun Saussy, with Thomas Burkman, eds., *Chinese Walls in Time and Space: A Multidisciplinary Perspective*
145 George Sidney & Hye-jin Juhn Sidney, trs., *I Heard Life Calling Me: Poems of Yi Sŏng-bok*
146 Sherman Cochran & Paul G. Pickowicz, eds., *China on the Margins*
147 Wang Lingzhen & Mary Ann O'Donnell, trs., *Years of Sadness: Autobiographical Writings of Wang Anyi*
148 John Holstein, trans. *A Moment's Grace: Stories from Korea in Transition*
149 Sunyoung Park in collaboration with Jefferson J.A. Gatrall, *On the Eve of the Uprising and Other Stories from Colonial Korea*
150 Brother Anthony of Taizé & Lee Hyung-Jin, *Walking on a Washing Line: Poems of Kim Seung-Hee*

151 Matthew Fraleigh, *New Chronicles of Yanagibashi and Diary of A Journey to the West: Narushima Ryūhoku Reports from Home and Abroad*
152 Pei Huang, *Reorienting the Manchus: A Study of Sinicization, 1583–1795*

DVD Monica Bethe & Karen Brazell: "Yamanba: The Old Woman of the Mountains" to accompany CEAS volume no. 16 *Noh As Performance*

Order online at www.einaudi.cornell.edu/eastasia/publications or contact
Cornell University Press Services, P. O. Box 6525, 750 Cascadilla Street,
Ithaca, NY 14851, USA.
Tel: 1-800-666-2211 (USA or Canada), 1-607-277-2211 (International);
Fax: 1-800-688-2877 (USA or Canada), 1-607-277-6292 (International);
E-mail orders: orderbook@cupserv.org

www.ingramcontent.com/pod-product-compliance
Lightning Source LLC
Chambersburg PA
CBHW081327090726
47907CB00010B/2397